In Ho

CHRISTINE WEBBER

All the best

Christine Webber

☎ On Call

I am dedicating this book, with all my love, to my wonderful husband David Delvin, who died in March 2018. During our very happy marriage, he read everything I wrote, taught me so much, and helped me in every conceivable way.

First published in Great Britain in 2018

A CIP catalogue record for this book is available from the
British Library.

Cover design by J D Smith Design

Published by On Call

Printed and bound in Great Britain by Clays Ltd, Elcograf S.p.A.

Typeset by the BORN Group

ISBN 978-0-9954540-5-7

Acknowledgements

I am delighted to be doing a third book with the people I now call 'my team'. They are the amazing Georgina Aldridge at Clays, brilliant editor and proofreader Helen Baggott, Daniel Knight, expert typesetter at the BORN Group, and the wonderfully talented cover designer, Jane Dixon-Smith. I would be absolutely nowhere without these marvellous individuals and their various skills.

Thanks too, as ever, to The Alliance of Independent Authors, Book Connectors, The Creativist Club Café, and Books for Older Readers – and to all the bloggers I know who support so many writers with their social media activity and reviews.

I am also very grateful to BBC presenter Joanne Good, for her generous and thoughtful cover quote.

Finally, I want to express enormous gratitude to my great friend Helen McDermott for her support in all my various endeavours, which has been invaluable.

Foreword

Thirty-four years ago, I was a television news presenter. I loved my life and every day was exciting, but suddenly it wasn't enough.

As a child, I'd written plays, masses of stories and some rather bad poems. Now, I had an overwhelming urge to start writing again.

One day when I was reading *Cosmopolitan*, I noticed that they were planning to host an event for would-be novelists at a London hotel. I booked up immediately.

I can't remember what it cost me, but it was one of the soundest investments I ever made. If I tell you that the panel of experts included Maya Angelou, Margaret Drabble, Clare Boylan, Fay Weldon and Angela Carter, you'll understand why.

I was really inspired by the occasion and began my book that night. Then, soon afterwards, *Cosmopolitan* announced that they were holding a competition – in conjunction with the publishers Hutchinson – to find the best novel from a previously unpublished writer. That was great motivation.

I'd love to tell you that I won the competition, but I didn't. However, the judges got in touch to say that they liked my novel and that they wanted to call it *In Honour Bound* and publish it.

It came out in 1987 and did quite well, and I always intended to write more fiction. But then, I left television news, became an agony aunt, trained as a psychotherapist and was lucky enough to be commissioned fifteen times over the years to pen non-fiction and self-help books. I also worked as a ghostwriter.

By the time I returned to fiction, twenty-nine years later, I had no contacts in that area of the industry and, as a consequence, decided to go the independent publishing route.

In early 2018, having brought out two novels – *Who'd Have Thought It?* and *It's Who We Are* – I was planning another title, but my husband was very ill, and I felt my head wasn't in the right place to write something entirely new.

But one day we found ourselves discussing *In Honour Bound*, which he had always loved, and came to the decision that, as it had gone out of print two decades previously, I could revisit and rewrite it. So, that's what I did. In fact, my husband even did some of the typing for me despite his worsening health.

I've kept the narrative in the mid-eighties – with big hair, shoulder pads and far too much sex, smoking and drinking – but just tried to improve the original text. Working on this book has reminded me what a very different world it was back then, though it all seems quite recent to me! In 1984 most of us had never heard of AIDS, though by 1986 there was a nationwide campaign to alert us to its dangers. And none of us had email or mobile phones, so our behaviour when contacting our friends and lovers was very different from that of today.

My experience of having worked as a psychotherapist for over twenty years – helping heartbroken people as they struggled to save or leave their relationships – has also influenced this rewrite. Romantic passion can generate truly extreme behaviour, and in my practice, I've seen countless individuals become almost insane with torment. Some of that has found its way into this edition.

Finally, though I was a TV presenter in the mid-eighties, this is not my story. I never had a Middle Eastern boyfriend for a start. But the crazy features that I've described in the novel – the lion tamer, the knife-thrower and so on – did happen, and I conducted all those interviews. Happy days!

Here then is the new *In Honour Bound*. I really hope you like it.

Best wishes, Christine Webber

Chapter One

'So, are you primarily interested in surgery or show business?' she demanded.

From somewhere on the floor, Helen heard a sharp intake of breath. There was a long pause which, had the interview not been live, might have been mistaken for a freeze-frame.

'Miss Bartlett,' the guest replied, eventually. 'I do sympathise with your desire to appear probing rather than merely decorative, but surely this trashy, tabloid approach is unnecessary?'

In the 'box' above the studio, Mark – the director – squirmed uneasily in his swivel chair.

'Oh-oh. How long to off-air?'

'Two and a half minutes,' came the reply.

'What the hell's happening down there? I know Aziz is a bit of a playboy, but no one faults him medically, as far as I know. Is Helen onto something, or is she just bitching? And why? Why would she do that?' Mark's questions hung as heavily in the air as the smoke from three lighted cigarettes and one cigar. He depressed the key that would connect him with his presenter's earpiece.

'Helen, you don't need me to tell you that this isn't going well. I suggest you wrap up early and do a longer end link.'

She was off-camera to the viewers, but on one of the monitors

1

above him he saw her incline her head in acknowledgement of his instruction.

'My point is this, Mr Aziz. Heart transplants are glamorous – people up and down the country support your efforts by running football matches, coffee mornings and so on, while less headline-grabbing branches of medicine are grossly underfunded.'

'My dear lady, I have a God-given skill. And I have developed that through research, hard work and simply *doing*. I can give life to really sick people, and I'm not going to apologise because it offends your particular type of social conscience.'

The PA and the vision-mixer in production control were flustered now; they could see that the surgeon was deliberately trying to imply that Helen was a lightweight, and that her approach was superficial.

'What a pig!' Sandy, the PA, was incensed.

The vision-mixer, who was engrossed in cutting between the two protagonists, nodded her agreement. The editor, puffing nervously in the corner, said nothing.

Helen was winding up. Those watching from the box knew that she was rattled, but technique was taking over. She sounded in command as she said they would have to leave many questions unanswered.

'Cut to camera two,' instructed Mark.

'Twenty seconds to captions,' said Sandy.

'And that's it for tonight.' Helen smiled in close-up. 'Tomorrow our consumer feature asks: "Is knicker elastic as elastic as it once was?" We have our cookery spot, viewers' letters and, of course, the summing up of all the stories of the day. Who knows what they may bring?' She grinned. 'Have a good evening.'

The director had spun in the music. The caption was up. 'Five seconds to off-air,' said Sandy. 'Four, three, two, one – off-air!'

'Thanks very much, everybody,' Mark smiled at his colleagues. The editor was already collecting his papers together. A semblance of normality returned.

On the floor, Aziz unclipped the microphone from his tie with a deftness that indicated television was not unfamiliar to him. He gave Helen a withering look.

'I can't say this has been a pleasure, Miss Bartlett,' he snapped, then strode away.

She remained slumped in the position she had adopted the moment the cameras were off her. A good programme left her feeling exhilarated; a bad one was utterly draining.

The sound engineer removed her microphone. Helen could see that he was wondering whether to try to console her.

He risked it. 'Don't worry, love. He's a pompous ass, and that's what your viewers will think.'

Helen looked at the immaculate dark figure disappearing through the heavy double doors. She turned back sadly and shook her head. 'I blew it, Alan. I got it totally wrong.'

'Can I strike this chair?' It was one of the stage crew, unmoved by the recent drama and anxious to leave for home.

'Oh… yes. Sorry.' She gathered up her scripts and slowly walked out of the studio.

Aware that she was going to have to face some company criticism, she made for the hospitality room. But as she reached the corridor that led to it, she could hear that the post-mortem was already in progress.

'He was infuriating,' said the director. 'I've seen him in the gossip columns. Rich bastard. Over confident Egyptian playboy. She was right, in a way…' He tailed off.

Other voices joined in; she could hear that the controller, the head of stills and the company secretary were also in the room.

The controller, the most senior executive present, spoke next.

'She handled the end beautifully, I will say that. She lifted the mood very skilfully, but it was hardly Helen at her best.' He sighed before continuing. 'By the way, did anyone offer Aziz a drink?'

No one knew.

'Is Helen coming up?' asked Bunny, the elderly head of still photography, who had – as everyone knew – a very soft spot for their presenter. 'Paul,' he leant over and lightly touched the controller on his arm, 'why don't you go and find her? Tell her it wasn't that bad.'

'But it *was* that bad, Bunny,' Paul responded. 'However, I'm going to the club in a minute, and I'll talk to her if she turns up there. She'll probably bounce back tomorrow, but my guess is she won't want to face any of us tonight.'

Helen had heard enough and backed away. In the newsroom, Laura, a reporter and close friend, was waiting for her.

'We need a drink,' Laura said.

Helen took her arm. 'We do. But let's go down the road to the hotel. I don't want to see anyone from the company.'

The women had a good relationship and quickly fell into a routine that was almost unconsciously re-enacted every time either of them had a bad day. The wounded party sat in a corner while the other played the combined role of host and agony aunt.

It was a dark and sparsely populated room. Helen was glad of its gloominess. She put her elbows on the table in front of her and allowed her head to drop into her hands.

'Oh God, Laura!' she said at last.

'Do you want to talk about it?'

Helen sighed. 'I don't know what to say. I don't know what happened.' Her left hand pushed back her hair impatiently as her right hand reached for the gin and tonic.

'Look,' said Laura, 'I know we've said it before, and it doesn't help at the time, but the virtue of live television is that once it's over, it's forgotten. You're back on tomorrow. You'll be great; few people will remember today. Certainly, nobody else is agonising over it as you are.'

'I know, I know… Let's talk about you instead.'

So they did.

Laura was younger and taller; she had superb, wavy auburn hair and was involved in a long-term relationship, which Helen was not. Like Helen, though, she took the job very seriously and knew exactly what her friend was going through.

'Helen, why don't you come back and have supper with Ian and me? He's had his own ups and downs in the business – and he'll understand if you want to talk and understand if you don't.'

'No, I can't. Heavens, what time is it?'

'Quarter past seven, why?'

'I'm going to a dinner party and it's the last thing I want to do.'

'Can't you scrub it?'

'Not easily. They're the sort of people who do the table properly. It would upset the numbers. He's a dentist in Harley Street. They've got a son who's a cameraman or something. I met them at a party. They asked me to dinner. I expect they thought I'd be interesting because I'm "that girl off the telly".'

Laura grinned, knowingly.

'Anyway,' Helen continued, 'apparently they always watch the programme and seem to like it, though I expect tonight was the exception.'

Laura jumped up and kissed her friend on the cheek. 'It's probably a good thing you've got something definite to do. What time do you have to be there?'

'Soon – I'll be OK. Go home to Ian and I'll potter over to the studios, do the face and put on the posh frock. You know us – back in the old routine.'

As they parted, Helen noticed that her friend's face was slightly troubled, and realised that it was her own behaviour which had caused Laura's unease.

Once in the make-up room, Helen made good the damage to her face; the veil was perfect, but her eyes betrayed the anxiety beneath it. She looked coldly at her image in the large mirror, which was surrounded by brightly-lit light bulbs.

'Not so clever after all, are you?' she muttered.

But a decision following a whole day of decision-making had yet to be made. She had told Laura she would go to the dinner party. Had she meant it, or had she said it simply to stop her friend worrying, and to prevent any prolonged exchange? She wanted – needed – to dissolve, but she would not do it in company.

Her public-self took over. She would go. The dinner party in itself was of little consequence, but it would serve as a dress rehearsal for tomorrow. She walked to her dressing room and selected her favourite pale-pink Chanel suit. It was appropriately sedate, but feminine, and she felt good in it.

There was a knock at the door, and the duty security man called to her.

'Your taxi's here, Helen.'

'Thanks, George.' She emerged, smiling. 'Have a good evening.'

'I don't suppose it will be as good as yours, love,' he muttered.

If only he knew, she thought, as she climbed into the cab.

'Evening, Miss Bartlett. Good show tonight?'

The driver's tone was jaunty, but then, he would have been working and not watching the programme. The guests at the dinner party, on the other hand, might well have made a point of viewing it prior to meeting her. She checked her face in her compact mirror as the taxi sped through the streets of central London towards the leafier calm of St John's Wood. No amount of lipstick or extra mascara was going to hide how strained she looked, but maybe no one else would notice.

All too soon, the cab drew to a halt. She paid the driver and tipped him more than necessary before running up the steps to the front door. The Harrisons, it seemed, lived on the fourth floor. Betty Harrison answered the intercom, and Helen waited for the click of the lock, then pushed open the heavy door, to find herself in a blue, deeply carpeted hall. She struggled with the lift gates and broke a nail in the process. Calm down, she urged herself. Then, after taking several deep breaths, she pressed the button that would elevate her to the site of an ordeal that, almost certainly, would last a good three hours.

Betty opened the gates at the top and kissed her warmly on both cheeks. 'My dear, how nice of you to come – but before we go in, I must tell you something. It's my fault, and I did think you would have so much in common and it would all be so perfect...'

'Helen!' boomed Reginald from the doorway. 'How's my girl? Looking as luscious as ever, eh? Pity I'm not twenty years younger.'

'Thirty,' murmured his wife drily.

His insistent hand on her shoulder propelled Helen into the assembled gathering. 'Let me introduce you to everyone.' His voice was proprietorial and proud. 'I'm sure this lady is a familiar face... Now, this is my son, Herbert and his wife, Dorothy.' Helen smiled politely. 'My partner, Cyril and his wife, Sally – second wife, actually, lucky dog! Got time off for good behaviour and all that.' He chuckled at the joke, which Cyril and Sally appeared not to find funny any more, if indeed they ever had. 'And this...' Reginald gestured towards a distinguished-looking, dark-haired guest in the corner, who was studying a painting.

The man turned. 'We've met actually.'

It was Aziz.

There was absolute silence. Like the pause in the studio, it seemed to go on for ever. Helen closed her eyes and bit her lip hard. The pain was real but so, unfortunately, was he. For when she reopened her eyes the surgeon was still before her, solid and supercilious.

'Excellent,' said Reginald.

'What is?' asked his wife sharply.

Reginald looked surprised for a moment at her tone. 'That these two young people know each other, of course. Come along, my dear, let's get you a drink. I expect you've had a long day.'

Helen allowed herself to be led to the drinks table, where she was poured the second large gin and tonic of the evening. She smiled at Reginald with new fondness; he had rescued her. He talked at her, pleased to have such an appreciative audience, and she used the one-sided conversation to regain her composure.

After five minutes or so, her resolve, liberally laced with gin, was taking effect, and she chatted away to Reginald about some new dental implanting technique she had researched for an interview. She had previously resolved to act a part, but now that Aziz was here it was to be an Oscar-winning performance. Anger was replacing the hurt and shock. She remembered why she had asked her questions and felt more justified by the minute that she had done so.

Reginald broke away to supervise the seating plan, and Helen allowed herself a glance at the enemy. He was being well taken care of by Dorothy and Sally.

'You're here,' Reginald's voice broke into her thoughts, 'on my left, Helen. We'll put Cyril beside you, Dorothy there, Herbert at the other end, Betty next to him, Sam in the middle, Sally next to me. Am I lucky or am I lucky?' he looked lecherously at the women each side of him.

Aziz was rather close for comfort but not impossibly so, Helen decided. She wondered what his connection was with the Harrisons and why Reginald had referred to him as Sam. It seemed an unlikely name for an Egyptian.

The octagonal plates indicated that the meal was going to conform to the nouvelle cuisine vogue. Betty Harrison was a spry sixty-year-old who clearly belonged to the breed of wives who believe their place is in the home, and in supporting their husbands no matter how chauvinistic they might be.

The salmon mousse was delicious and the perfect dish for someone whose appetite had deserted her. Reginald was proud of his knowledge of wines and, if the array of glasses at every place was anything to go by, there was to be a lot of it. He explained each one as he poured it, and Helen asked what she hoped were intelligent questions. She was no wine buff. 'You're safe with Sancerre,' she always told herself on the rare occasions that she entertained.

Suddenly, she became aware that Cyril, on her left, was talking to her. He gave her an account of how he and Reginald had set up in practice together, and explained that all the men round the table, Aziz included, had consulting rooms, and private beds, in the same clinic in Harley Street.

She asked, quietly, what the surgeon was like.

'Funny sort of fellow,' answered Cyril. 'Quiet, very well-bred, totally absorbed in his career. Some might say publicity-seeking, but I don't know. Doesn't mix much. Occasionally see him with some blonde or other, but he never brings them to anything. Bit surprised to see him here, actually. He tends not to accept invitations that are purely social.'

Helen encouraged Cyril to continue talking and, by giving him her whole attention, she could mostly avoid looking at Aziz. She noticed, though, that he was pleasantly attentive to the women on each side of him and indulgent of Reginald's pleasure in producing bottle after bottle of interesting wine – though imbibed very little of it himself.

Helen had no such inhibitions. She knew she was drinking too much, but it was helping her to relax and to recount various behind-the-scenes stories of what could go wrong in television, which seemed to be going down well – especially with those drinking as much as she was.

The food came and went. A trio of tiny pink lamb cutlets. Next, a salad or cheese and later, zabaglione, which Helen declined, though Aziz did not. They left the table and Helen wondered fleetingly whether the ladies would be encouraged to disappear altogether while the men indulged in men's talk and drank port or brandy. But no.

To her horror, as they adjourned to the sitting room, she found herself next to Aziz. She felt sure he was as uncomfortable as she, but to refuse to sit by him would have spoiled her act of bravado. She broke the ice. 'How long have you been in this country, Mr Aziz?'

He looked surprised. 'I went to school here.'

They fell silent. She imagined that, like her, he was pleased that everyone else was chatting away noisily. He looked at her dispassionately, almost disinterestedly, she thought.

'Why do you dislike me so much, Miss Bartlett?' He spoke softly.

It was Helen's turn to look surprised. 'I don't even know you.'

'What was all that about different branches of medicine and my depriving them?'

Earlier she would have sounded off extravagantly about one of her hobby-horses, but she recognised his attempt to defuse the situation; moreover, she was mellowing with wine and the lateness of the hour. Suddenly, she felt extraordinarily tired and unsure. It was an effort to explain, but she did so, calmly.

'I receive letters all the time from people waiting and hoping for treatment for awful conditions like cystic fibrosis. Pensioners tell me how they're crippled with arthritis and have to endure pain for years before they get near the operating table for a replacement hip. A woman wrote yesterday, who's bleeding continuously. She's distraught, because the earliest available appointment with a consultant gynaecologist is four months away. All I meant was, people fundraise like mad for up-front medicine like open-heart surgery, and there's a scanner appeal in practically every county now because cancer continuously grabs the headlines. I'm not saying that's bad. But I am saying that there's a hell of a lot of suffering in other areas that mostly gets forgotten.'

He looked at her more kindly. 'I see. I don't know much about you, Miss Bartlett. I had no idea you really cared.'

His gentleness caught her off-guard. She looked at him, feeling strangely vulnerable. 'Do you know, I think I ought to go. I'm awfully tired,' she said.

'You're not driving.' It was a statement, rather than a question.

'No, I'll get a taxi.'

'I'll drive you.'

'No!' She surprised herself with her vehemence. Instantly, she regretted it. 'I'm just not very good company.'

'Miss Bartlett, you've probably done enough talking for one evening. I'll drive you – in silence, if you like.'

She disliked him again. He was obviously mocking her.

They said their goodbyes together, much to Betty Harrison's astonishment. It was raining, but his car, a silver Mercedes convertible, was parked right outside. How efficient, and perfectly predictable. He opened the passenger door, helped her in, reached for the seat belt and handed it to her before shutting her inside.

'Where to, madam?'

'Holland Park, please.'

'Ah, that's good. Having made this noble gesture, I wondered if you lived in a completely different direction from me. As it happens, you don't.'

'Where do you live?'

'Near Kew Bridge, so you're on my way.'

'Oh, good! I wouldn't want to be a nuisance.' She was sarcastic now. She was also dejected and exhausted.

Naturally, he drove expertly and, true to his promise, did not talk until he needed to ask for directions. They motored slowly down the quiet avenue and came to rest on a bed of wet, slippery autumn leaves. He leapt out and walked around to help her.

'Thank you,' she said.

'Miss Bartlett, I'm not sure, but I think I may owe you an apology.'

She was almost too weary to reply, but not quite. 'If you're not sure, you don't,' she snapped. 'I'll tell you something, though,' she went on. 'I'm sorry. Sorry about lots of things. And I'm especially sorry today ever happened.' Her voice was rising. She suspected she sounded hysterical which, of course, would confirm his worst suspicions. She made the final effort that day to be reasonable. 'Thank you for driving me home, Mr Aziz.' And she was gone.

Upstairs in her flat, something made her look out of the window. The surgeon was sitting in his car. His interior light was on and she could just make out that he was doing something with the cassette player. For a moment, she wondered what his taste in music might be. Then she saw him start the engine, and flick his hair off his forehead, with a slightly impatient gesture, before driving off at speed.

Helen jumped into bed and began shedding the tears that had been threatening all evening. Uncharacteristically, she had not removed her make-up, and dark, damp streaks of mascara stained the cream pillow as she sobbed noisily into the stillness. What is happening to me? she wondered. I've got a life most people would give their eye teeth for. But the more she tried to count her blessings, the more the tears flowed.

Damn the man, she thought. It's all his fault. She switched off the bedside lamp. The sobs gradually subsided, and she slept.

Chapter Two

A milk float stopped in the street below. Helen heard the ratchet-like sound of a handbrake, the tinkling of bottles on a stone step, and a hum as the vehicle restarted. She listened as the process was repeated several times with a gradual diminuendo. Longing for more sleep, she turned over, thumped the pillow and closed her eyes, but before long was forced to conclude that she was fully awake.

Her head ached. Her eyes were heavy and her mouth dry. She had rarely felt less enthusiastic about a forthcoming day. Quickly, she ran over the events of the previous evening and blushed as she recalled the parting from Aziz. It would be best, she decided, not to dwell on her embarrassment but to concentrate on getting through today.

Her raging thirst needed to be quenched so, reluctantly, she abandoned the warmth of her bed and padded into her all-white kitchen in search of mineral water and orange juice.

Knowing she must look dreadful, she avoided all mirrors till she had downed two glasses of her rescue-mixture. Her feet felt chilled on the white tiled floor, but she endured the discomfort while she swallowed handfuls of pills. A primrose-oil capsule to soak up the alcohol, two vitamin B tablets for nerves and to keep grey hairs at bay, a high-dose vitamin C pill to prevent colds and to counteract the harmful effects of the odd cigarette, two ginseng capsules (though for what she was suddenly unsure), and three vitamin E tablets to halt the ageing process and maintain her sex drive.

'And that's a bloody waste of time,' she said aloud.

A plan, that was what was needed: a plan of action for today. She picked up a ballpoint and twiddled it in her fingers till her priorities became clear.

1. 7.45 Do Jane Fonda workout.
2. 8.15 Switch on heated rollers. Get in bath.
3. 8.30 Put in rollers.
4. 8.35 Make up face.
5. 9.00 Listen to news.
6. 9.10 Skim through papers.
7. 9.20 Ring for taxi. Take rollers out.
8. 9.50 Leave.
9. 10.00 Arrive at work.
10. 10.30 Meeting.
11. Do letters on migraine.
12. Lunch – canteen.
13. Read biog. on Polish pianist, due in next Tuesday.
14. Go to make-up.
15. Do prog.
16. Drink with Laura.
17. Come home – early.

She underlined it twice at the bottom. She could cope with that.

Back in her L-shaped bedroom, she inserted the Jane Fonda cassette into her video machine and positioned herself so that she could view both the television and her own image in the full-length mirror that ran along the side wall. Good thing the great British public can't see you now, she thought, as she took in, for the first time, the ravages of the night before.

She bent and stretched with the class before her. Their contrived and almost brutal jollity was even more irksome than usual. Exercising was not her favourite activity, but as she flexed and reached out, feeling her lungs expand right to their base, she had to admit to feeling better.

As a rule, she went to the studios without bothering about her hair or make-up. The daytime was for preparation, picking up on the news and features of the moment, arranging items and answering letters and phone calls. Glamour had no part in it. Come four-thirty, however, she would spend an hour preparing her face and hair and emerge transformed into the front person the viewers expected to see.

Today was different. She sensed that if she looked good, she would be better equipped to deal with the criticism that must come.

Lying in the bath, she allowed herself a sneaking analysis of her state of mind. It was like levering open a jack-in-the-box in the hope of seeing the surprise without it springing out and taking over. She wondered, as the substance of a recent magazine article popped into her mind, if she might be suffering from 'burn-out', but until yesterday her workload, daunting though it might seem to others, had posed no problems.

Her fair skin was rosy after the bath, and she appraised her body in the mirror as she towelled herself dry. She was in good shape for a woman of thirty-four, though it was hardly a matter for congratulation since no one nowadays saw her undressed. She stared at her image and cupped a breast in each hand, then squeezed, gently. It was comforting. A vague feeling of desire was stirring, desire for good sex and the release it brings rather than for anyone past or present.

She allowed her hands to wander over her body. Her nipples became erect almost immediately and a faint flush began spreading from them into her neck. She shook her head. Sexual relief might help. Or it might not. She chose not to find out.

By the time the taxi arrived, Helen felt she would pass muster. That was the easy part; now she must act as reasonably as she looked.

'Morning. Morning. Morning…' She greeted everyone in her familiarly buoyant style as she wandered through the untidy and smoke-filled newsroom to her office through the double doors at the far end. There was a mound of fresh letters on her already crowded desk; perhaps a coffee injection would spur her on to deal with them.

Purposefully, she walked back through the newsroom to the canteen beyond. Were people looking at her, strangely? She hoped not.

'Shall we start some of the mail before the meeting, Sue?'

Her secretary was standing in the middle of a group of youngsters discussing the weekend ahead. She looked puzzled. Helen rarely tackled her post before eleven. Raising her eyebrows at her companions, she picked up her pen and shorthand pad and followed Helen to her office.

A couple of dozen letters later, which comprised the usual press releases, enquiries about recent features, requests for photographs and invitations to open bazaars, finally Helen called a halt. Sue left to type the replies, evidently delighted to escape.

So far so good, Helen thought, but she knew that it was one thing to act normally with her secretary and quite another to convince her colleagues at the ten-thirty meeting that she had not lost the plot.

She had long maintained that the morning gathering should begin with an assessment of the previous day's performance, and she had campaigned for a rundown of all the dissatisfactions with it – and for questions to be asked and answers to be given. She had lost that battle and, now that the only glaring mistake of yesterday's programme had been hers, she was glad. No one mentioned her interview as they focused on the day ahead. It was to be a typical Friday, with the usual 'end-of-week' items, except

16

for the fact that a women's action group had brought out a paper on sexual harassment at work and Helen was to conduct a live interview with one of the authors of the report.

'She'll be deadly earnest, I expect,' moaned Derek the editor, 'but do what you can, Helen, you know, lift it a bit. It's probably very worthy but it'll bore most of the viewers rigid.'

On any other day Helen would have challenged Derek about his attitude to the difficulties of women in the workplace, but this did not seem a propitious moment.

'News is twelve minutes,' the editor went on. 'That might change; there's not a lot about.'

'Where do you want me?' Helen turned to Mark.

'Stand in front of the desks for the opening,' he said as the PA and the lighting man took note of his directions. 'Go to the upper desk for the rest of part one and all of part two, and we'll have you in the soft set with a sofa and pot plants for all of part three.'

She breathed a sigh of relief after the meeting as she retreated to the sanctuary of her own office. Immediately the phone rang. It was Paul, the controller. She held her breath, waiting for him to mention the previous night's programme. Instead, he said:

'Helen, I hate to bother you, but I've got Kurt from the New York office coming in for lunch, and I wondered if you were free to cheer it up a bit?'

She was grateful, realising that this was Paul's way of reassuring her that one bad mistake did not wipe out her value to the company.

But, just as she began to relax, Derek's secretary called on her internal phone to say that the editor wanted to see her.

'Tell him that's fine,' Helen said, with a calmness she did not feel.

Derek was her immediate boss. He was in a difficult position, which Helen recognised. He had to weigh up all the stories of the day, five days a week, fifty-two weeks of the year. He had to try and please everyone, which was an impossible task. He got his backside kicked if the programme failed to make the top ten; he had to keep a horde of temperamental egocentrics within bounds; and he had to answer to the monitoring of the watchdog committee. If they wanted to know how often Birmingham, Brighton or Buckingham had been mentioned in the past six months, he must supply the figures. Each day, he had to obtain a balance between a good geographical spread of coverage and the production of the best news and features on offer. It was the worst job in the company.

Helen renewed her lipstick before walking along the short corridor to his office.

'Sit down, will you?' He was busy writing something and did not look up.

His secretary arrived with coffee. There was silence till she left them.

'I'd like you to look at the recording of last night's programme,' he said finally.

'Derek, I know why, but I promise you, I remember everything I said. It's not necessary.'

'OK. Well, what happened?'

'I pitched it wrong. Mind you, I still think I was right in a way – Aziz regularly appears in the gossip columns. One can't help feeling he cares at least as much about his image as he does his patients. And heart surgery does get a good press...'

'Off the record, I agree. But it seemed like a private row. Frankly, it was embarrassing.'

To her horror, Helen felt her eyes fill with tears. 'I'm sorry.'

Derek looked uncomfortable. She had never broken down in front of him before and she could see that he was surprised.

'I didn't mean to upset you, Helen. We do overload you, I know, but it's your fault. You positively welcome it, and you've seemed, up till now anyway, absolutely impregnable.'

Through her tears, she attempted to smile. 'Derek, please forget about yesterday, and me being upset today. It won't happen again.'

'I don't think it will, but I've been wondering if it wouldn't be a good idea for you to take a break. I checked the diary – you haven't had any leave for over a year.'

'I'll think about it,' she responded defensively. 'But first I have to lay the ghost of our last programme.'

He nodded. She sensed that he would like to continue but would not waylay her if she interpreted his silence as meaning that the conversation was at an end, so she left.

It was with a degree of relief that Helen tackled yet another cup of coffee in the quiet of her own room. She was shaking, though whether from her unusually high intake of caffeine or her state of mind, she could not be sure. She felt humiliated that she had cried, but Derek had let her off more gently than she believed she deserved.

In light of yesterday's fiasco, the prospect of today's programme frightened her much more than usual, so the fact that she was required as the lunchtime cabaret was a diversion rather than a chore.

'Ah, Helen,' Paul welcomed her as she arrived in the boardroom, 'you know Kurt, don't you?'

Helen flashed the smile that daily warmed the hearts of viewers. 'Yes, of course. Kurt, how are you? I haven't seen you since I was in New York.'

'I don't think you realise, Paul,' Kurt said expansively, 'how nearly you lost this lady in the States. Everywhere I took her, they fell at her feet. I really think if she'd pushed for it, she could have landed herself a lucrative contract.'

I can put up with plenty of this, she thought, though she answered modestly, 'Oh, I couldn't leave here. They've taught me everything I know.'

The game was afoot, and each of them understood the rules. Kurt flattered her, which was affirming. She indulged in a spot of arch-grovelling, which the company appreciated. And Paul glowed with the suggested compliment that not only was he a wise man for having picked Helen in the first place, but also an astute one for managing to retain her services. Still, there was no harm in it, for the basic sentiments were honest, if a trifle exaggerated.

'Derek should have given that sexual harassment interview far more time,' Laura said as soon as she had taken a large mouthful of the Riesling which was the social club's wine of the month.

The girls were holding a much happier inquest on the show than they had the previous night.

'I don't think any of the blokes believed we should be tackling the subject at all. If the nationals hadn't picked up on the recent research, we wouldn't have touched it.'

'It made me think, actually,' Laura mused. 'You know how we get our bottoms patted all the time, especially by that slimy letch in promotions, and how that old bastard in the props department seems to think it's OK to pin us against his desk when we have to order stuff for the programme – well, maybe this isn't right. Maybe it's not just horseplay. Maybe it's just plain wrong.'

'That's bold talk. You know if you ever complain they always say you're frigid or gagging for it really. I always laugh it off. Feel sorry for them actually.'

'I dunno. I reckon your interviewee had a point, though, of course, because she was a bit earnest and make-up free, all the guys in the newsroom were having a go at her while you were on air and saying stuff like: "Her cherry's safe from me".'

'God, that's so awful.'

'I know.'

'Probably won't ever change though. Not in this industry anyway…'

'More Riesling?'

Helen wrinkled her nose. 'Not up to much is it? I think I'll have a glass of red. I'll get them. It's my turn. What's yours?'

'Same as you.'

Helen fought her way to the bar and returned with wine and crisps.

'You know,' Laura said, giving Helen a quick glance and then focusing on her own drink, 'lots of us have been thinking, and saying, for ages that your galloping lifestyle is going to catch up with you one day. Not sure if you're aware of that. Anyway, I can't help feeling that maybe yesterday was the day. I'm only saying this because we're friends, and it's not in any way a criticism, but don't you think it's time you went away for a bit? OK, when you and Barry split up, it was probably therapeutic to throw yourself into the job, but that's a long time ago now.'

'Derek said much the same thing this morning,' Helen admitted, 'but I'm not mad about going away on my own – I'd sooner be working.'

'What about the devoted David?' Laura was referring to the most recent of Helen's escorts.

'I'm not seeing him any more. I know he's wealthy, well-connected and unattached, but he's also terminally boring. Last time we went out I found it was infectious! If I said, "This trout is really lovely, David" once, I must have said it ten times. He didn't even notice. Oh, and talking of men – you'll never guess what happened last night.'

'Tell me.'

'Aziz was at the dinner party.'

Laura's mouth dropped open. 'What! Did you speak to him?'

'Not much – till the end. I suddenly got ever so tired. You know me – one minute I'm tap-dancing on the tables, and the next I'm in a heap in the corner. He offered to take me home.'

'I hope you refused.'

'I did, but he said he wouldn't bother me and wouldn't even speak, so it seemed less trouble to accept.'

'Well, that was stylish anyway.'

'Hmmn, he's that all right. Silver convertible Merc – well, you'd expect that. But also, I don't know… courteous, I think. Yes, very courteous.'

'Are you seeing him again?'

'Certainly not! Especially after his closing statement: "Miss Bartlett, I'm not sure, but I think I may owe you an apology".' It was a wickedly accurate impersonation.

'How insufferable.'

Yes, he was insufferable, thought Helen in the taxi heading for her home. Still, the crisis had passed, and the weekend was to be busy with two charity functions and many miles of driving between them. It was how her life was. Mercifully, there would be no time to think.

Chapter Three

'Who are they from?' It was Sharon on the newsroom switchboard. She had taken the message from reception that there was a large bouquet for Helen and was eager to know more.

'Oh, a past interviewee,' Helen responded. 'Where's Laura?'

'I think she's in the cutting rooms,' Sharon replied. 'Shall I try and find her for you?'

'If you don't mind. I'll be in my office.'

Helen had taken delivery of the flowers – a massive arrangement – and had left them in the wash basin in her dressing room. She had removed the accompanying card however, swiftly, almost guiltily, though why she should feel that way she was unsure. Now, safely back in the office, she reread it.

It was Monday. The weekend had been tiring but rewarding. She had been on safe ground till this moment. The phone rang. It was Laura.

'Hi. Anything wrong?'

'Not exactly, but you'll never guess what's happened... oh, damn, there's the other phone. Hang on, will you?'

She lifted the other receiver. 'Hello.'

'Helen, I've got a Mr Aziz on the phone. Will you speak to him?'

She returned to Laura. 'The plot thickens by the minute. I guess you're busy?'

'That's an understatement. I'm just recording a commentary and then I've got to go out again. A baby's been found dead in its cot, and they think it died a whole month ago. I wish Derek could send someone else. I don't think I've got the stomach for it.'

'Oh, that's an awful thing to have to deal with,' she sympathised. 'Take it easy.'

She replaced the phone and picked up the other one. 'Sharon, yes, fine, you'd better put him through.' There was a brief pause.

'Miss Bartlett, good morning.'

'Hello.' Helen realised she sounded apprehensive.

'Did you get my flowers?'

'They've just arrived – a lovely but quite unnecessary gesture.'

'You're wrong. It *was* necessary. I've thought about Thursday a great deal, and I wanted to apologise properly.'

'Well, Mr Aziz, I accept your apology but, to be quite honest, I think we should agree to share the blame for what happened.'

'Now *you're* making an extravagant gesture.'

Helen smiled. 'I would have telephoned to thank you, you know.'

'I know you would, but you'd have thought about it for a while, wondering if I was making a play for you, or if I was being rather too flashy… You might even have considered I was being ever so slightly condescending.'

How irritatingly accurate, thought Helen, as she remembered her initial reaction, not ten minutes before. 'Well, you could have given me a little time, and the benefit of the doubt,' she retorted, quite sharply.

'Yes, I could. But I didn't, Miss Bartlett.'

'For God's sake, no one calls me that, apart from the occasional taxi driver.'

'Well, maybe I should continue since it's quite apt in my case!'

She laughed. 'I'm not sure if I like you or find you stunningly annoying.'

'My thoughts about you exactly! Shall we start again and give ourselves time to find out?'

24

There was silence.

'Miss Bar... Helen, will you have dinner with me?'

'Not dinner – lunch.'

It was his turn to laugh. 'Quite right. Lunch. How proper. When? Today?'

'I can't today,' she replied, which was true because she did not feel prepared, but untrue because there was nothing in the diary.

'Tomorrow then.'

'You're very persistent.'

'That's right, I am.'

They discussed where to go, and he named a seafood restaurant in Soho. It was a favourite haunt of hers.

'Shall I pick you up?' he asked.

'No, parking round there is a nightmare. I'll get a taxi.'

'You're infuriatingly practical.'

'That's right, I am.'

They both laughed.

'Can you make twelve forty-five?'

'I'll be there,' said Helen.

'I'm looking forward to it,' he said.

'Are you?' Her question belied her confident manner and instantly she regretted it.

He did not appear to notice and answered quietly, 'Very much.'

Helen hung up. How confident he was, and how smooth. She was strangely excited, yet frightened and agitated at the same time. Well, lunch doesn't mean anything, she told herself and, with a toss of her head, she began an assault on today's pile of post.

She opened a couple of letters and read them both without absorbing their contents. Her brain was racing on to tomorrow, much as she tried to engage it with today. Defiantly she pulled the little card out of her handbag and read it again: 'I've thought about it. I'm sure now that I owe you an apology.'

It occurred to her suddenly that her hair needed cutting and could do with fresh highlights. She glanced at the day's running order. There were no interviews that afternoon, so she could go out. It was important for the viewers that she kept up appearances, after all.

The next day, she made light work of the Jane Fonda routine and reached the office early. She and Sue tackled the letters and then she went to the ten-thirty meeting where she made various animated comments before shutting herself away and researching that afternoon's interview which she was due to do at three-thirty. With half an hour to spare before leaving for lunch, she made her way to the make-up department, where she encountered Laura.

'I tried to find you after the programme yesterday,' Helen said. 'You must have shot off.'

'I did,' replied Laura. 'That baby story really got to me.'

'I'm sorry. Are you OK now?'

Laura nodded. 'Shall we have lunch?'

'No, I can't, actually. I'm going out.'

Helen could see that Laura was taking in her coiffed and coloured hair, but she did not explain her appearance or her lunch plans.

'See you later, then,' Laura said, clearly curious.

Helen took special care with her face. Quite apart from any other consideration, once she returned this afternoon, there would be hardly any time before the interviewee, a Polish pianist who had recently defected to the West, turned up. She sprayed herself with a perfume she had bought on the way back from the hair-dresser yesterday, then made for her dressing room and, without realising it, began humming to herself as she walked along the corridor.

'Someone's happy,' remarked Joe, one of the stage crew, as he passed her.

'Hi! Yes, I suppose I am. Are you OK?'

'Mustn't grumble.'

In the quiet of the little room, which was filled with far more clothes than she kept at home, as well as an equal amount of

Laura's outfits, she finally plumped for an old favourite, a translucent dress in navy by Parigi. It was really a summer frock, but the restaurant was bound to be warm. She added pearl earrings and surveyed the effect in the mirror. She would have to do.

Her taxi drew up at the restaurant at ten to one. For a moment, she was sure she must have arrived first. She almost asked the driver to make another tour of the block, like a bride anxious not to arrive too early at the church, but suddenly she saw Aziz, sitting at a table by the window and raising his hand in welcome.

He rose as she reached him and shook her hand. 'You look wonderful,' he said. 'What will you have to drink?'

'Perrier, please.'

'You too? The wine waiter's in for a thin time of it.'

She smiled as she sat down. There was a moment's silence.

'I'm sorry.' They spoke in unison, and then laughed.

It was a very easy and pleasant lunch, and despite some anxieties on her part that they might not have much to say to each other, the reverse was true and they chattered away without pause. She noticed – and she supposed he did too – that other diners recognised them, and she could sense interested glances being trained on them. Still, she was used to the feeling and probably so was he.

Independently, they selected the same items from the menu: avocado with apricot yoghurt and prawns, followed by turbot grilled in herb butter. Then as they continued to talk, each learned a little of the other's background.

He was certainly a very interesting man, she thought.

An hour and a half flashed by; she would have to leave soon. Much to her surprise, she found herself clinging to the last few minutes she could allow herself. She felt quite extraordinary – not ill, just light-headed. The mirrors round the walls seemed to sparkle more than they had on her previous visits, and the clientele reflected within them seemed extra colourful and dynamic.

She sneaked a last look at Aziz. He was terribly attractive, of course, but perhaps quite unmoved by her presence. However, suddenly as she watched him press his full lips to the snowy-white napkin, she caught him playing the same game as herself. He looked up at her from under his dark eyelashes. Their wandering glances met. She fancied that her face flushed as she watched him. He seemed pensive now and began to finger the rim of his glass with his perfectly manicured hands. She tried to imagine them, clad in surgical gloves, saving somebody's life with breathtaking skill. Yes, 'breathtaking' was the word – literally – for she found herself short of breath, but in an excited sort of way.

With a monumental effort, she gathered up her bag from the floor and said, 'I have to go.'

'Yes, I have a busy afternoon too,' he responded quickly.

'I'm sure you do.' She looked him straight in the eye and smiled broadly. He relaxed then, and she could tell that he had worried, just for a moment, that she had been dismissing him from her life.

'I've enjoyed this tremendously,' he murmured. 'We should do it again.'

'I'd like that,' she whispered. 'Now, we must get the bill. Will you let me pay?'

'Certainly not.'

'Share it then. After all, the flowers must have cost you a fortune.'

He laughed. 'Helen, modern though I may be in some ways, certain things I cannot cope with. One of them is women picking up the tab.'

'That's ridiculous, when both people earn good money.'

'We're not going to argue, are we?' he asked, raising an eyebrow.

'We'll discuss it next time.' She put out her hand. Why was this so difficult? She was generally somewhat theatrical in her greetings and farewells and thought nothing of throwing her arms round comparative strangers. He grasped her hand and suddenly inclined towards her, pulling her gently as he did so and touching his cheek to hers, then, rotating slightly, he brushed her face with his lips. She felt herself blush, before she turned and walked away.

'Well, what was he like?'

Helen had invited Laura for a drink in the social club after the programme.

The afternoon had gone well. She had recorded the interview with the Polish pianist, who had proved to be a charming inter-viewee; he had also performed a Chopin Polonaise with staggering verve and virtuosity. The recording had been dropped into the live programme after the news, and the rest of the schedule had gone smoothly and according to plan. If only all days were as successful.

'What was who like? The pianist?'

'Don't be deliberately dense! Aziz of course.'

'He's nice. Very nice, actually,' she replied softly.

'That's not what you were saying last Thursday.'

Helen smiled and mischief glinted in her eyes as she shrugged her shoulders and said, 'I changed my mind.'

Laura laughed. 'Life's never dull when you're around. Is he going to be The One?'

'Oh no,' she replied quickly. 'It's just friendly – not at all romantic. I'm sure he doesn't even fancy me.'

'Do you fancy *him*?'

'Absolutely not.'

'Well you look as if you're sitting in a golden aura, so I don't believe you. Are you seeing him again?'

'Yes.'

'When?'

Helen looked anxious for a second. 'I don't know. He didn't say.'

He rang the next morning – and a pattern of lunches became established. They met frequently, delighting in their new-found friendship and the pleasure with which they anticipated each rendezvous. Privately, Helen wondered about other consorts. She suspected he did too. Lunch was innocuous; it was public; it had

29

a time limit. Theirs was a pleasant routine but one that, with courage, was bound to be altered. An innocent question sparked the transition.

'What star sign are you, Sam?'

'Scorpio.'

'You must have a birthday soon then?'

He looked embarrassed. 'It's next Tuesday, in actual fact.'

'Well, that gives me the perfect chance to buy you lunch for a change.'

'I can't make it – not Tuesday. I'm sorry.'

Helen was cast down by her blunder. Birthdays are spent with wives, girlfriends or families, not with an occasional luncheon date.

He looked in his diary. 'I'm going to Birmingham to speak at a seminar, but you can buy me dinner if you like. I'll be back by the time you finish the programme.'

How absurd that she should feel such a rush of relief. How amazing that he should want to spend the evening of his birthday, a special occasion, with her. How surprising that no one else had a greater claim.

It was the first time he had picked her up at the studios, and his first visit since he had marched out in high dudgeon after their interview.

As she ran down the stairs to meet him, she heard him say to the security man: 'I've come for Miss Bartlett.' And she felt a wave of pleasure that that was the case.

'Goodnight, boys,' she cried as they made for the door.

She heard another security guard ask of the man Sam had spoken to: 'Is that Helen's new bloke?'

'Dunno, Bob. He didn't say. Looks like he wants to give 'er one though!' Helen giggled and hoped that Sam's hearing was not as acute as hers.

*

In his car, they sat without speaking for a moment. Meeting at a different hour made it seem like a first date. She was surprisingly nervous. Was he? It was hard to tell. She searched in her bag and brought out a small, gift-wrapped box. 'Happy birthday.'

She had agonised over the choice, seeking a stylish memento but deciding against any item which suggested intimacy, and had, in the end, settled for a little silver bookmark in the shape of a hand.

He coloured slightly. 'You shouldn't have.'

'Of course I should. It's your birthday. How old are you anyway?'

'A little more than ten years your senior – forty-five.'

'How did you know my age?'

'I've done my research.'

She grinned. 'You can open it. It's nothing much.'

He ripped the paper away, switched on the interior light to get a better view, then lifted the lid to find the little hand nestling in cotton wool. 'It's lovely.'

'Do you know what it is?'

'Certainly. It's a bookmark.'

'Oh good. I wouldn't have known if it hadn't been labelled in the shop.'

He laughed. 'Well, you probably turn the corners of the pages down. You're far too impatient to go in search of a marker.'

'That'll do – you're getting jolly personal. Take me to Richmond!'

He leant over and gently kissed her on the cheek before turning off the light and starting the engine.

The choice of restaurant – which was Helen's since it was her treat – had caused her much thought. It was too important an occasion to settle for chicken-in-the-basket in a pub, but on the other hand, she had wanted to resist picking anywhere that was overly expensive or romantic. Indeed, she had changed her mind about the venue several times, and might have gone on doing so, had she not started worrying that if she left it too late everywhere might be booked.

'Where are we going?' he asked as they drove off.

'It's a little place on the river called, rather unoriginally, "The Bistro".'

He looked at her by the light of the passing street lamps and grinned again. She felt naked, and suspected he had guessed all the processes of thought that had gone into making her choice.

After a while, his left hand crossed the great divide between their two seats and came to rest, palm upwards, on her thigh. Instinctively, her right hand clasped his, and, in the twilight, they looked deep into each other's eyes.

When they arrived at the restaurant, he helped her out of the car and, for the first time, put his arm around her as he steered her into the building.

Throughout the meal, she savoured the change and promise between them. They talked much less than usual, touched more, and ate hardly at all. The candlelight enhanced the luminous quality of his eyes, which kept looking intently into hers. She felt like a willing participant in a spell that was being woven around her.

As he had in the car, he reached for her hand; the feel of him made her glad. He was soft and sensitive, yet strong too. His mind fascinated her, but his body was making its impact in a less cerebral way. Those eyes looked through her into places she did not generally care to expose. Suddenly, still clasping her hand, he lifted it to his lips and kissed each finger caressingly, one by one.

After they had eaten, he drove her back to her flat in Holland Park, remembering, without being told, exactly where it was. They parked in the discreetly-lit avenue, and he switched off the car headlights. He let his seat recline, then adjusted hers to the same level and they lay in the darkness emotionally entwined but without further contact.

She wanted very badly to invite him in, but at the same time did not wish to disturb the moment. She suspected he was hoping for the invitation but was hesitant about suggesting it. They talked instead. He told her how he had been sent to Harrow at the tender age of thirteen, and what a shock to his system the coldness of the climate and his welcome had been.

'Can I ask you something?'

'Of course,' he responded.

'What's your real name? It can't be Sam.'

He laughed. 'Ahmed Sami Aziz. But, you see, being a foreigner, I had to have a nickname at school – we all did, come to that. No one could pronounce Ahmed, and they couldn't capitalise on Aziz, so they shortened Sami to Sam. It amused them. I wasn't exactly coloured, but I did come from the African continent, so they figured Sam, short for Sambo, d'you see?'

'That's terrible,' said Helen. 'God, kids can be so cruel.'

'They can, but I survived. In fact, I got to like it, though you can call me Ahmed if you like.'

She laughed. 'No, you're Sam to me, if that's all right.'

They fell silent. She was as sure as she could be that he was as reluctant to part as she was. The tension was tangible. At any moment, one of them might take a step too far and invite the other to spend the night – but what if it were too soon, or a wrong move?

Helen forced herself to say, 'I must go to bed, Sam.' She was relieved to have said it, but disappointed with herself.

He sighed. She sensed he felt the same way. 'Of course,' he responded. 'Have a good night.' He kissed her gently on the cheek, but then, sought her mouth and locked onto her lips leaving her in no doubt that spending the night with him at some point was no longer a question of 'if' but 'when'.

The phone call woke her.

'Did you sleep all right?' His question confirmed the new status of their relationship.

'Very well. Did you get home OK? You hadn't had too much to drink?'

'Everything's fine. That's why I'm ringing, I think. Everything's really fine. Thanks for the best birthday I've ever had.'

'I don't know what to say.'

'Neither do I, which is strange, since neither of us pauses for breath as a rule.' He laughed. 'What I want to say is... I'm tingling after last night – I want to see you soon. I want to hold you... intimately.' He sounded surprisingly old-fashioned.

'What about lunch tomorrow?'

'No,' he said. 'Dinner tonight. I want to speak to you.'

'Oh God, that sounds ominous.'

'Helen, stop it.'

'Stop what?'

'You don't need to be flippant, or frightened. That's part of what I have to tell you.'

She paused to think of a suitable reply.

'Have I offended you?'

'No,' she answered in a small voice. 'No, you haven't. I'm just a bit taken aback.'

'Why?'

'Because I've finally admitted to myself that you seem to know me quite well.'

'I don't, but I'd like to.'

'OK. Thank you. I'll see you after the programme.'

The same two security men as the previous night were on duty, and they nodded knowingly at each other when Helen swept past, calling goodnight to both of them, as she launched herself through the revolving doors to the waiting car beyond.

This time, there was no birthday, no excuse for her to hold the reins, make the choices, give the directions or proffer the credit card. Sam drove, without saying much, to a pub at the Strand-on-the-Green which, she suspected, was near his home.

She sat down in an alcove without her usual struggle to be first at the bar to prove that she was one of the boys, and certainly not mean. He joined her, carrying a bottle of champagne and two rather ordinary-looking wine glasses.

He smiled, reading her thoughts. 'Well, I was amazed they had the bubbly – I think we can forgive the lack of crystal.'

He poured out a little, but even that frothed over the top of each glass and pooled onto the table. 'It's a bit frisky,' he said, before adding. 'And I'm nervous.'

After topping up the glasses, slowly to prevent any more spillages, he handed one of the drinks to her and picked up the other, murmuring, 'To us.' They sipped in silence.

'Can I ask you something?'

He looked at her indulgently, and she realised he had noted that she too felt diffident.

'Yes,' he replied. 'Anything you like.'

'Are you married?'

'Good God, no. Do you think I'd be pursuing you like this if I were?'

'Is that what you're doing?'

'Hadn't you noticed?'

She smiled. 'Anyway, you still might be – you might have a wife tucked away in Egypt.'

'I haven't.'

'Have you never been married?'

'No. Why?'

'I don't know. I just can't imagine someone like you getting to forty-five and not being. Anyway, I once interviewed a psychiatrist who said that no one remains unmarried past forty unless they have a problem.'

'Well,' he said mock seriously, 'far be it from me to quarrel with a fellow-victim but I don't think I have a problem.'

'You've had hundreds of girlfriends?'

'Lots,' he agreed. His candour was both pleasing and unsettling.

'I'm not surprised. You're an attractive and successful man.'

35

'I don't see it like that. I'm not successful with women. Well, let's say I sometimes am initially, but women don't generally understand my schedule or ambition, and, so far, whenever anyone has said, "It's the job or me," there's been no contest.'

'That's a bit harsh.'

'Maybe no one's mattered enough to me before.'

She looked at him but ignored the last word. She did not want to feel that she was being sweet-talked. She could see quite plainly how easily he could break a heart – and why should hers be an exception?

'*You're* attractive and successful,' he said.

She shook her head.

'Of course you are. And you know it. I'm sure you're propositioned a great deal.'

'I suppose I know quite a few men who I can go to things with.'

'There you are then,' he responded sharply. Then, modifying his tone, he asked her about her marriage.

She found it difficult to talk, at first, being more used to covering up the hurt and despair she had felt when it had ended. She reached in her bag for a cigarette and lit it, not noticing the surprise that flitted across his face. Looking around the old pub, with its panelling, beams and tapestry upholstery, she thought that she would remember this moment for the rest of her life.

He put his hand on hers and leant over to kiss her cheek. 'Don't tell me if you don't want to.'

'I do. It's just hard.'

'Were you badly hurt?'

'In a way, yes.'

Suddenly the floodgates opened. She told him how she had originally wanted to train as a musician as she was quite a reasonable pianist, but that in the end, she had applied for a place at drama school rather than music college. After graduating, she told him, she had worked in several plays that had toured the country. 'Nothing grand, you know. And I was a very also-ran actress!

36

Anyway, I got a job in a production of Agatha Christie's play *The Hollow*, and one week, in Cardiff, I met Barry, who was the editor of a local paper.'

She described their meeting and their marriage, and how subsequently she had given up the theatre and set up a public relations firm. She told him of its success, which had led to her being offered a spot on a regional television programme, giving advice to people on how to improve the profile of their businesses.

'I didn't mean for it all to take off – it just did. At the same time, I made sure that I was always there for my husband when it was important. He worked crazy hours too. But when he needed me to join him for dinner with advertisers and so on, I always went. And I walked the dog before I went to work. I baked bread and froze the beans we grew in the garden. I did honestly try to be a good wife.'

'What happened?'

'I was offered the TV job in London. You won't remember, but there was a nationwide search for the right girl and, unbelievably, I got it. Barry and I discussed the move. He said we'd always be together at weekends and that he'd come to me if I couldn't get to Wales, and I thought everything was all right. But one day, a friend told me he'd been having an affair with his secretary for two years. Obviously, that pre-dated, by quite a while, the start of my new job. I couldn't believe it. I expect it was my fault…'

'And maybe it wasn't,' said Sam.

'Well, there we are. If I'm honest, I think my pride was hurt more than anything else. I was so desperately trying to be the perfect wife.'

'Did you love him?'

'I'm not sure now, but I think so. However, it wasn't a wild, passionate thing – not at all – but we were good friends, and I suppose I assumed we'd always be together.'

'Helen, you're the sort of woman who should have passion too.'

'Maybe... After the divorce, I went a bit mad and did dreadful things. I had a lot of men, and my fair share of passion then, but no love. That wasn't right either...' She sighed. 'I don't know why I'm telling you all this. It doesn't go with my image.'

'I don't care a damn about the image. I care about you.'

He bent forward and lovingly kissed her on the lips. 'Let me take you somewhere nice to eat.'

'No, don't,' she said. 'It's fine here. It's cosy and quiet.'

'Well, I'll order sandwiches,' he said and disappeared.

Helen felt near to tears after her revelations. Sam had unlocked thoughts about her past that surprised her. On top of that, her growing interest in him was bewildering. She was excessively aware of his presence, and of being vulnerable to him, yet at the same time she had a sense she might depend on him too.

Suddenly, she realised that she had been recognised. A young man hovered.

'It is, isn't it?'

She smiled.

'I couldn't believe it. You – here. I've never met anybody famous before.'

She laughed. 'I'm not famous.'

'You are!' He was indignant. Clearly, he did not want her to downplay the importance of his moment. He picked up a beer mat as Sam returned with the sandwiches. She could tell that Sam was anxious not to intrude, but that he was protective and would intervene if the fan outstayed his welcome.

'Could you sign this for me?'

'What's your name?'

'Henry.'

To Henry, she wrote. *Nice to see you. Love, Helen Bartlett.*

'Gosh, thanks,' he said and was gone.

'I'm sorry,' she said to Sam.

'Why? I guess I'll just have to get used to the fact that my lady is loved by most of the population.'

38

The words 'my lady' hung in the air between them.

They began to eat the brown-bread sandwiches filled with rare beef and salad. Suddenly, she asked, 'Why do you think we hated each other on sight the day we met?'

'I'm not sure,' he replied. 'I hadn't seen you much on television myself, but when some of my colleagues knew that I was going to be interviewed by you, they went on and on about how marvellous you were, and it sort of put my back up. It was like being told you must read a particular book or see the latest film. You can never believe it can be that great.'

'I know,' she said. 'Maybe we were just too sensitive of each other's media image. Sorry, terrible phrase, but you know what I mean. I'd only seen you in gossip columns, with a succession of women.'

'I think that's the point, Helen, isn't it?' he reflected. 'A different one for every day of the week. It made you suspect my commitment to my career, and now you're suspicious that I don't really mean what I'm saying to you.'

Helen pushed her plate away.

'Had enough?' he asked.

'I have actually. The food's fine, but I seem not to be very hungry.'

'OK. Let's go.'

In tacit agreement, they drove the short distance to his house, which overlooked the river. He led the way and, as if in a dream, she followed him into a cream room which was sparsely furnished, but dominated by the sculpture of a ballet dancer, which she recognised instantly as the work of Tom Merrifield – whom she had interviewed not long previously.

She kicked off her shoes in order to feel the warmth and luxury of the deep-piled carpet, and then he drew her into a passionate embrace, pulling her hips towards his as, urgently, they sought complete contact for the first time. She felt his hardness pressing into her and then heard him sigh and pull back from her, breathing heavily, as if the sensations were too intense to handle. He led her upstairs and into his bedroom, which was painted pale blue and was subtly lit, and proceeded to undress her slowly, kissing each part of her as he uncovered it, and complimenting her on her skin, and her figure.

She had never thought of herself as frail, and tended to believe that men found her too capable to want to cherish her. Yet he was muttering something about looking after her. It was her last coherent thought as she relinquished her usual stance of performing and controlling. A sense of almost unbearable delight flooded through her body as he laid her on the bed, while continuing to kiss and caress her and explore her whole body. At last his mouth settled where she longed for it to be and she was overwhelmed with an unaccustomed and almost violent longing. He nuzzled her with increasing pressure and she moaned with happiness, moving slightly up and down, and around and around, beneath his flickering tongue. Then, suddenly and miraculously, she was on fire with wave after wave of intense passionate pleasure. Her whole body stiffened. It was happening, and it was all so easy and so right.

She lay, panting, as he moved himself up to kiss her lips. How wonderful he was. Usually, in bed she concentrated on her partner's satisfaction. It made her feel important and worthwhile, but her determined unselfishness generally left her unfulfilled. This was so different.

He put his hands under her buttocks, lifted them slightly, then plunged deep inside her. She grasped him to her, thinking he might need urgent relief, and wanting to make it good. But he raised himself up and refused to be hurried. He thrust slowly in and out of her. Her breasts hardened against him.

'There's no hurry, sweetheart,' he whispered in her ear. 'Love me, relax, ride with me.'

Then he was saying other things that no one had said before. 'Helen, one day I'm going to come into you like this, higher and higher, slowly and deeply. I'm going to explode in you, my angel, and together we're going to make a baby.'

It had never been a consideration before. It could not be tonight – she was a product of the Pill age – but the distant possibility and the sense of belonging, mixed with such potent physical intensity, drove her beyond any frontier of feeling she had reached before. She felt the spasm of his orgasm begin, and as she rose to meet it, the tension and the shuddering and the frenzy engulfed her. She came, noisily, warmly and endlessly.

Chapter Four

'Wake up, sleeping beauty. I'm not much of a handsome prince, but I'll have to do.'

Helen shrugged off her slumber with a start. 'What time is it?'

'Seven o'clock.'

'Oh God, I knew we must be incompatible in one way or another. Why are we up so early?'

'*We're* not, it's just me. But I didn't want to leave without speaking to you. I'm operating at eight-thirty.'

'Sam, I'm sorry. I never even thought about your schedule. How awful!'

He jumped. 'Awful!' he said. 'Awful's not a word I would have chosen in association with last night. In any case, you couldn't possibly be expected to know my movements.'

'Don't get cross.'

'I'm not cross. I just want you to feel the same way about what's happening as I do. Maybe we should have chosen an occasion when we might have dallied through the whole of the next day, but one can't always plan sensibly with emotions. It's not like organising a timetable.'

'You make me sound aggressively practical,' she sighed. 'Why is everything so tense this morning when it was so perfect a few hours ago?'

'I expect we're nervous. All I'm trying to say was that last night was the best, the best ever, and I don't mind being up. I'm quite happy, but I do suggest you go back to sleep. I'll re-set the alarm.'

'Do I look terrible then?'

'Helen!'

'Sorry, sorry. You're right, I'm nervous.'

Sam sat down on the bed beside her. He raised her right hand to his lips and kissed each finger before pulling her to him and enveloping her in a bear hug. 'It was selfish of me to wake you, but I wanted to tell you: I love you, Helen. I love your mind and your body and your spirit.'

'That's most of me.' She grinned. He kissed her passionately, and she responded for all the world as though they had been lovers for months, instead of just a night. 'I love you too. I don't know what's happening. I don't know what we're going to do, but I'm very happy.' They kissed again. 'I read somewhere,' she went on, 'that surgeons aren't supposed to drink or indulge in any sort of hanky-panky before intensive surgery. It makes their hands shake.'

'My darling, I'm trembling all over, but I promise you the patients won't suffer.'

She smiled. 'I should ignore me. I know an awful little about a lot of things.'

'But you store it so well in your marvellously clever head. I hope I finish in time to watch you tonight. I shall think, "That's my lady". And then… I'll have to rush off and take a cold shower!'

She punched him on the shoulder. 'Don't be ridiculous.'

'I'm not. Can we meet later?'

'I'm doing a phone-in after the programme till eight-thirty. Maybe we ought to sleep tonight.'

'We will sleep – as well. You go home, and I'll come over to you. I'll bring a bottle and a takeaway.'

'Ah, how wise. Don't trust my cooking, I see.'

'I don't view you in a domestic light, it's true, but, more than that, you'll have a long day and so will I. Let's just relax.'

'That sounds great. You'd better go, hadn't you?'

'I had,' he said, then he added quietly, 'Helen, I hope we always feel like this.'

'Me too. It's probably not possible, but...'

Putting a finger to her lips, he murmured, 'Don't think about it. Go back to sleep. We'll talk tonight.'

He kissed her again, walked to the bedroom door and turned. 'You're very special,' he said, seriously. Then, as though drawn by a magnet, he moved swiftly back to the bed to sweep her into his arms. He clung to her for several seconds, as if afraid that the next few hours would forge an impossible distance between them. 'See you tonight,' he said unsteadily, as he tore himself from her and ran down the stairs and out of the house.

Helen looked around the blue bedroom, taking in the mirrored wardrobes, the bookshelves and the small television set. It was a room where somebody came to sleep, she decided, not one that the occupant had personalised to any significant degree.

They had made love through the night, until finally they had fallen asleep exhausted, around four. Yet, for all that parts of her had enjoyed more exercise and attention than they had for ages, she was far from replete. Deep inside her was a longing for more and more and more. It seemed that having been unleashed, her sexuality was taking over and dictating the message loud and clear that it had lain dormant long enough.

She picked up Sam's pillow; it smelt of him. She crushed it to her and curled round it, as he had curled round her through the night. She tried to sleep, but her mind and body would not be still. 'I'm in love,' she said aloud. 'Yesterday I wasn't – at least, I don't think so – but today I am.' She remembered his mention of children and wondered if he had meant it. Everything was going at such a pace she was slightly panic-stricken; yet at the same time, it all felt so right.

On his bedside table, she found the remote-control panel for the television set, so she switched on the breakfast show. The presenter, a comfortably familiar figure, bridged the enormous gap between this extraordinary morning and all the days that had gone before. She watched the news, then the features that followed on fashion, cooking and what the papers said, but was not in the mood to concentrate.

She decided to run a bath. As she waited for it to fill, she found herself scanning the shelves for signs of a previous female presence. There were none: no cosmetics, no cleansing cream, no bath essence, no cotton wool.

She had meant to soak in the bath but could not relax, so she jumped out and towelled herself quickly before touring the house.

The sitting room, where he had pressed himself so hard against her the night before, was a large room but without much character. The walls and ceiling were cream, there was an expensive-looking light-coloured carpet and beautifully-made brown velvet curtains. The sculpture of the dancer was the sole notable point. It was the first time – outside the Festival Hall, where Merrifield often exhibited – that she had seen one of his pieces close-up. What was it about the little figure that had moved Sam to purchase it? she wondered.

The wall behind her was covered in bookshelves which she had not noticed the night before. But there was no light-reading here, just great tomes like *A Short Practice of Surgery*, which looked extremely long and not short at all.

Apart from the books, the room might have belonged to anyone. It was, she supposed, more masculine than feminine, but it gave little away. Indeed, the only hint that the householder might not be English lay in two drawings of Egyptian scenes by David Roberts.

Next, she wandered into the kitchen and smiled suddenly at how similar it was to her own. It was white, with gadgets that looked pristine through lack of use. Curiosity got the better of her, so she opened the door of the refrigerator. Her smiles turned to laughter as she viewed the contents that could so easily have been hers: four bottles of wine, a mouldering pack of butter and a vacuum-sealed portion of cheese, long past its sell-by date.

What sort of a man did all this add up to? Not a home-maker, almost certainly a workaholic, and definitely an enigma. She had learned all she could, so she called a taxi and went home to change.

Once at the studios, Helen made for the dressing room to check on her outfit for that evening's programme, before applying kohl pencil around her eyes and a little blusher to her cheeks. When she entered the newsroom, it was still not quite nine.

'You're early.' Laura looked very surprised.

'I know – I didn't sleep very well.'

'Well, you don't look tired. You look fantastic.'

'I feel fantastic. Come and have coffee in my office. I'll just go to the canteen and get some.'

'What happened?' asked Laura when they were safely alone.

'What do you mean, what happened?'

'You can't fool me. You look like a cat who's been at the cream.'

'You'll have to keep this to yourself; I've just spent the night with Sam.'

'How was it, as if I need to ask?'

'Laura – it was sensational. The best thing that has ever happened to me in my whole life.'

'I knew it. When are you seeing him again?'

'Tonight.'

'This is serious.'

'I think it may be.'

Helen had believed – somehow it had seemed necessary to do so – that her celibacy was responsible for her boundless energy. It was strange then, she thought, that having made love all night, she was possessed by greater verve and enthusiasm than ever before for the working day ahead.

Just as well, she thought with a chuckle. It was a day that she had to get right.

47

Eighteen months ago, after a couple of meetings with a very innovative social worker, she had pioneered an adoption-by-television spot.

'We're not talking about little white babies for infertile couples any more, Derek,' she had explained to her boss, 'but about the best possible families for kids who're in care and shouldn't be. The families might be old, or have no religion, be in second marriages... even single people could be considered.'

Derek had listened carefully. She had realised that he was slightly amused by her enthusiasm for this new project, but he had given her the go-ahead. Some dozen children later, today they were featuring two more. She had worked for over four months with the youngsters in question, and now they were judged ready for the public exposure it would entail.

Patrick and Philip were orphans. Their mother had been unmarried, and nothing was known of either father. The family had been watched by Social Services for years as the children, plagued by a succession of traumas in the house, had exhibited symptoms of unsociable and neurotic behaviour. The mother had died, unexpectedly, thus freeing them for adoption.

Helen, as always, longed to tell the complete story so that the kids would gain all the sympathy they deserved, but she was forbidden to do so. Instead, as she always did, she worked out a way to build the whole experience into a treat, so that the children would remember the adoption process as having been fun even though it was so serious.

Philip's great ambition, she had discovered, was to fly in an aeroplane, so she had decided to arrange a flight, and film the children in the process. The cutting editor knocked on her door before putting his head round it. 'It's ready for you to see. If you're happy with it, we can go to the dubbing theatre at two.'

She leapt up and followed his retreating figure into the darkened room and sat with him at the Steenbeck machine, viewing what they had: the plane taking off, a chat with Patrick and Philip in the air, an interview in the rear of the plane with their social worker – over which they had dropped in several shots of the excited faces of the two brothers – and then a more probing talk with them about the sort of family they would like to find. The sequence ended in a lighter vein with the pilot helping them down from the plane and presenting each of them with a flying-club badge.

'I think that's fine,' she said to the editor. 'I suppose the only thing is that we could have tightened that bit where Philip is so hesitant.'

'I will if you like, but it's very genuine.'

'Yes, you're right. It speaks volumes. I mean, the fact that he can't conjure up the perfect Identikit of a mum should suggest to the viewers that he doesn't have much to go on – which is perfectly true, of course, poor little soul.'

'So, see you at two o'clock?'

'Sure. I'll write a couple of commentary sections – it doesn't need much – and I'll record it to picture upstairs. Then you're going to pop some music over the exteriors at the beginning, aren't you?'

'Yes, no problem.'

For the rest of the day, she answered phone calls and letters, and set up future stories. As the hours ticked by, she thought about the children a great deal. She knew the programme would go well, but she was anxious all the same. Knowing that Sam would be watching, she wanted it to be exceptional.

Since Patrick and Philip were coming in, she dressed more casually than she might have otherwise, in a lavender mohair sweater and pale grey leather trousers, before walking through to the reception area to greet them.

'You go up to the boardroom now with Jackie,' she said, indicating the duty receptionist, 'and you can watch the beginning of the programme there and have some Coke, or something. We'll get you brought in to the studio later on. You'll be there while I

49

introduce the film of you to the viewers. Then we'll see it go out, just as if we were watching it at home, but then the viewers will be able to see the two of you in the studio and I'll ask you a couple of questions each. And then, I'll invite people to phone me to talk about you. And if there's time you can say goodnight to the viewers. OK?'

'I'd like that!' There was a touch of bravado in Philip's tone.

'Can I go to the toilet again?' asked the elder boy.

Helen laughed. 'Of course, but you're not getting nervous, Patrick, are you?'

'I'm not, but my tummy is.'

'Shall I tell you something? My tummy is too, but it'll be all right as soon as we get started. Now, off you go.'

The siblings raced upstairs with the receptionist, while Helen made her way into the studio. She settled herself at her desk and marked up the scripts.

'Pick up the phone to the box, will you, Helen?' said the floor manager.

'Sweetheart!' It was Mark, the director. 'Have you done something different with your make-up?'

'No. Why? Do I look dreadful?'

'Not at all. You look absolutely ravishing.'

'Are you trying to tell me that I usually look like rubbish?'

'Yes, you old bag! No, of course not, but you look specially good today.'

'Thanks, Mark.'

'You're welcome. Are the children here?'

'Yes, they seem fine.'

'Excellent. Enjoy it.'

The programme went without a hitch. The children were thrilled to see themselves on film, and quite at ease on camera.

'If you had a family, Patrick,' asked Helen after their film was finished, 'what would you most enjoy doing with your new mum?'

'I'd like to make cakes,' he giggled.

'What sort of food do you like best, Philip?'

'Chips,' he answered quickly, 'and I'd like a mummy who made them for us every day!' The cameramen laughed as the picture cut to a close-up of Helen.

'Well, that's all we've got time for. I'll be taking calls about the children till eight-thirty – so I hope to hear from some of you. And otherwise, please join me at six tomorrow.'

The shot broadened to include one child on each side of her.

'Would you like to say goodnight?' she asked them.

'Goodnight,' said Philip obediently.

But Patrick was enjoying it. 'Yes, goodnight from *Reporting At Six*, especially to everyone at Woodlands Children's Home and Grove Road Middle School.'

'Hey, a presenter in the making!' Helen laughed. 'That's it. Goodnight.'

They crashed out of the programme meaning that the end captions were up for a second only, but Helen knew that Patrick's impromptu speech would reap a reward that far outweighed a slightly messy end to the proceedings.

The two youngsters left for the children's home, and Helen grabbed a drink in Hospitality before making for the newsroom, which was already buzzing. Three girls were talking on the telephone and scribbling furiously.

'Lots of calls,' said Sharon, who was on the switchboard. 'I've taken some and so have the others, but one or two people really want to speak to you.'

'OK. When the rush is over, we'll call them back.' The phone rang. 'I'll take it,' said Helen.

The next hour and a half passed quickly, and Helen was so engrossed in what she was doing, and so enjoying the response from some potentially viable candidates, that thoughts of her own late-evening encounter could not have been further from her mind.

'I'd like to adopt *you* actually,' announced the next caller. This was the only hazard. Helen sighed. There was always some 'nutter' who got through. She was about to put the phone down when she recognised Sam's voice, and laughed.

'Where are you?'

'I've just got home.'

'Have you been operating all day?'

'Most of it.'

'You must be exhausted.'

'So must you.'

'Well, my day hasn't been quite the matter of life and death that yours has.'

'I don't know. The adoption will change the children's lives.'

'Oh, you must have missed it.'

'No, I watched it at the hospital, in the common room. It was strange having to share you with my colleagues. It went very well. Does it sound chauvinistic to say I was proud of you?'

'Not at all. Look, I'd better go. Do you mind? I just want to gather all the messages together, so I can pass them to the adoption agency. The whole thing with this is that it's not just about these two brothers – some of the people who phone in might be good for others also looking for families. So, I have to get the details down properly. Still, I won't be too long. Then I'll come home.'

'Good. I'll join you about nine-thirty.'

Helen noticed that Sharon was looking at her with interest. '*Not* a possible adopter,' she explained.

'No, I thought not. New man?'

Helen felt herself blushing as she nodded.

She was aware that, as Sharon was the usual switchboard operator in the newsroom, the younger woman knew more about her than most people. Since her divorce, some of her discarded 'dates' had tried to contact her at work and she had had to ask Sharon to lie and say that she was out of the office. 'Just say you can't find me,' she would tell her, aware that she was giving away more about her private life than she cared to.

'You go, Sharon. I'll just tie up the loose ends and I'll be off as well. Tell the others that they can finish too.'

'If you're sure?'

'Absolutely. I expect you've got some gorgeous man lined up for tonight.'

Sharon laughed.

Helen picked up the phone to ring Guy, the children's social worker who, she knew, would be at the children's home with Philip and Patrick. She told him the good news about the telephone response. 'About ninety-five calls, actually. And of those, about a third are marked as sounding suitable. So, let's hope you find the perfect family for our two, and maybe a few other kids will get homes as a result of the programme too.'

She had learned through experience that the drop-out rate for families was enormous. The vetting of candidates was lengthy and intrusive, and many previously well-intentioned people came to the conclusion that they could not cope with it.

'Got my fingers crossed, anyway,' Guy replied. 'Thanks for everything. Oh, and Philip wants to say "goodnight".'

The little boy sounded pensive. 'I wonder if my real dad saw it,' he murmured.

Helen was taken aback and searched her mind for an appropriate response.

'Sweetheart, your dad hasn't been in touch since you were a baby, has he? I don't think he'd recognise you now. And, to be honest, he wasn't very good at being a father, was he?'

There was silence.

She went on, 'We'll just have to hope that someone else *will* be.'

'OK,' he said, jauntily. 'G'night.'

'You heard that, I suppose,' she said as Guy came back on the phone.

'Yup. I thought he was quiet about something. Don't worry. I'll have a session with him tomorrow and iron a few things out. I'll let you know what happens.'

Inside her Saab, Helen switched on Radio Three. The familiar frenzied theme to the finale of Brahms' *First Symphony* blasted from the quadriphonic system. She turned down the volume slightly, then sat soaking in the music. With a jolt she realised that it was nine o'clock, and that Sam would be at her home in half an hour.

Twenty minutes later, she surveyed her flat and wondered how to make it as inviting as possible. She turned up the central heating, lit a few candles, selected a record by jazz guitarist Martin Taylor and played with various light switches till she achieved the effect she wanted. Next, she checked the bedroom. Imagining how Sam would view the chaos before her, she grimaced before thrusting various pieces of clothing into drawers and then deciding she just had time to change the sheets.

'You're out of breath,' he said when she opened the door to him.

'I was making the bed. I'm not very organised.'

He laughed, and she leant forward to kiss him, noticing that he had champagne in one hand and a carrier bag packed with little foil parcels in the other.

'Come on, give me those. Let me get you a drink,' she said as she closed the front door and led him into the lounge.

'You relax after your long day. I'll pop the food in the oven.' He kissed her again and went in search of the kitchen. 'That's funny,' she heard him say, 'it's just like mine.'

She smiled, remembering her impressions that morning on seeing his kitchen for the first time.

Sitting waiting for him, their situation seemed surprisingly comfortable and familiar – as if they had known each other for ages. But then, as he returned to her side, the mood became more charged and emotional and they fell into the first passionate embrace of the evening. His hands were stroking and seeking while his mouth pressed itself to hers. She felt that her breasts must explode as she pressed against him, anticipating the glorious surrender that must come.

54

Sighing, he pulled away. 'Doctor says you must eat.'

'Oh, Sam!'

'I mean it. You hardly ate a thing last night and, come to think of it, on the evening of my birthday neither of us managed much. Was that really only two nights ago?'

She smiled at yet another example of how closely his thoughts mirrored her own. 'Yes – you're forty-five and two days. Let's celebrate!'

'We are. I'll get the food,' he said, and disappeared to the kitchen.

Before long, he returned and set two piled plates before them and opened the champagne.

'You think of everything,' she said.

He grinned, and she thought how boyish he looked – and how pleased. 'I like looking after you,' he said. 'I think that's what I want to do.'

Helen's eyes filled with tears.

'Darling, I'm sorry.' He looked anxious. 'What did I say?'

'I'm probably just tired. I'm certainly overwhelmed. I simply find some things you say almost unbearably touching.'

'If that's the reason you're weeping. I'm pleased,' he said.

Their need for each other could not be put off indefinitely and, despite his earlier insistence that they must eat a good meal, it was not long before they gave up on it. Sam removed their leftovers, while she blew out the candles and wandered to the bathroom.

She scrutinised her image in one of the many mirrors. In spite of her tiredness, a glow shone from her eyes, lighting up the thirty-four-year-old face that, until now, had often depressed her for its rather too accurate reflection of her age and experience. She stepped out of her leather trousers before tearing off the rest of her clothes. As a gesture towards Sam's presence, she dropped all her garments into the laundry basket instead of leaving them littering the bathroom floor. She grinned to herself, wondering if she should be even more tidy and throw her shoes in there too, before deciding that she was being ridiculous.

As she came, naked, into the bedroom, Sam was sitting on the edge of the bed and he looked at her, almost as if he were seeing her for the first time. He reached for her hand and pulled her down beside him and then hugged her. His clothing was rough against her bare skin. She was totally vulnerable in her nudity as he, pressed against her, remained reliable, business-like and dressed for action. He moaned slightly. They fell back onto the bed and with a swift movement, he turned her around, held her close with his left arm, and with his right unzipped his trousers. She gasped as he pushed inside her. The thrill of his passion as he thrust into her and then quickly climaxed overwhelmed her, and she heard herself cry out in a voice she barely recognised as her own.

'Helen, my darling,' he was murmuring as he kissed the back of her neck, 'you must be squashed. Let's get into bed properly. That was selfish of me, I'm sorry.'

'Not at all. My God, Sam, I hardly know what's happening to me.'

'That's exactly how I feel. I want to take you in love, not lust, for I do love you, but the lust blows my mind.'

He undressed swiftly then lay down beside her. They cuddled in silence. She kissed the beads of perspiration from his brow and hairline as he enfolded her to him. Gradually his caresses became firmer, his kisses more demanding and just when she thought she would die of her need to be owned again, he was ready, and gently entered her once more. This time he was more careful; more leisurely. He reached down and fondled her with his right hand, and his lips and tongue performed a magic act in her left ear. Together they rode for their goal and she relinquished her mind and body to the waves which were tumbling over and around and above them, culminating in a cascade that took her breath from her, and finally ebbed gently away.

How long they lay together, bound by shared passion and melting cohesion, she had no idea. Perhaps she slept a little.

His voice interrupted her thoughts. 'I never believed,' he said, 'I would ever, could ever, be as in love as I am at the moment. I don't want to die, believe me, but were I to – right now – I couldn't die happier.'

She held him, awash with love and gratitude, and experiencing uniquely simple and unashamed pleasure which she wished she could bottle and revisit whenever she wanted. And in that moment, she knew that she would always remember this split-second of her life, but would have no need to say, 'I was happy then but I didn't realise it,' because she *did* realise it and knew that no amount of romantic retrospection could heighten the joy she felt.

I am so utterly happy, she said to herself, and the word 'happy' reverberated around her brain so loudly that she felt he must hear it. Perhaps, in fact, she had spoken it aloud.

'Helen,' he murmured, 'all anyone can ever hope for is that they might find the person they care for most, and complete that person's circle with authentic love. I'd like to believe it's starting.'

She squeezed his arm, and they slept.

Chapter Five

It was quite impossible for a relationship between two such public figures to remain a secret. Both had to attend their fair share of functions and, quite naturally, they began to invite each other to fulfil the role of 'partner'. In this way, Helen was introduced to the elite of the medical profession, and Sam learned just how long journalistic award ceremonies can last. He also, if he was free, accompanied her when she kicked off charity football matches or opened bazaars.

In the gossip columns, they were referred to as 'constant companions', and snapped occasionally at 'in-places', though since neither of them had recently divorced or discarded another partner, and had no scandal attached to them to make them more interesting, they were not bothered too much.

Very few people at the studios commented either; perhaps they were too busy with their own intrigues to realise that Helen's man was lasting the course longer than any former love-interest. Derek, for example, alluded to it only once, and that was because he could not avoid doing so. During one morning meeting, word reached them that a heart-and-lung transplant had been carried out on the youngest patient ever. Helen was already privy to this information, since Sam had performed the operation late the night before and had telephoned her to say that he would not be joining her as planned.

'I think we should speak to the parents, and also to the surgeon,' Derek said. 'It's your sort of thing, Helen, but we can't really have you interviewing your own bloke, so I'll send Laura.'

After the meeting, Laura came to find her. 'So, I'm to meet this miracle of perfection at last,' she said.

Helen smiled. 'Haven't you met yet?'

'You know damn well we haven't. You've been keeping him well hidden.'

'You saw him last Tuesday, after you and I'd had a drink and he came to pick me up.'

'Well yes, a shadowy figure waiting in the car.'

'I'm sorry, I never thought – perhaps you and Ian could have dinner with us one night?'

'That would be great, but by the time we find a day when he's not performing a transplant, you're not in Bristol, I'm not in John O'Groats, and Ian isn't filming in the Philippines, we'll probably be drawing our old age pensions! Anyway, to come back to today, I'm a trifle anxious since you had such a rough ride interviewing him when he came here.'

'Oh God, don't remind me,' Helen pulled a mournful face. 'Still,' – and a smile spread from her mouth to her eyes – 'it's been worth it. You'll probably fancy him.'

'Yes, and he won't be able to keep his hands off me.'

'What!'

Laura burst out laughing at Helen's shocked face, until Helen suddenly saw her friend was joking and laughed too. 'You really have got it bad when you think your own man is so desperately sexy that every woman under ninety-five wants to take him to bed.'

'What's with the age limit?' Helen grinned. 'Anyway, be nice to him. He's been up all night.'

'That's not unusual, is it? It's just a pity he no longer gets any sleep when he's not at the hospital or clinic.'

'You beast. Do you think it's beginning to show?'

'Well, I don't know about him, but it's not on you. It's sickening, really. You've lost weight, though there's nothing haggard about you. You're swinging from the chandeliers twice nightly. And you look absolutely marvellous. There's no justice.'

'I do feel good,' Helen agreed.

'I know you do, and I'm glad. You deserve it.' Impulsively, Laura kissed Helen's cheek. 'I'd better go. I just hope he's gentle with me.'

'Oh, I think he's revised his opinion about television people – and our ratings must have gone up! Before we met, he hardly watched the programme, but now he never misses it. In fact, if he knows he's going to be out, he videos it.'

'My goodness, he's as bad as you. Do you think he'll recognise me, then?'

'Definitely. Anyway, I talk about you a lot. He knows who you are.'

With Laura gone, Helen felt deflated. She would have liked to have seen Sam herself. She had missed him the previous night.

They had fallen into an undiscussed schedule, staying alternate nights at each other's homes. Apart from one occasion when she had been at a function on the south coast which he could not attend, and another when he was giving a paper in Manchester, they had not slept apart since the night of his birthday, some six weeks earlier.

Soon it would be Christmas, and she had not yet broached the subject of what they should do. Sam was not a religious man, so she guessed that apart from the rampant commercialism all round, the season would make little impact on him. But he loathed bad weather and said that he would never get used to it, while Helen loved cold crisp days, so long as they were dry. However, he did enjoy some aspects of the winter, particularly pubs in the country with open log fires who served mulled wine and comforting home-made soups and steak and kidney pies. Sometimes Helen found herself forgetting that he was Egyptian; but, as he never tired of pointing out, he had lived far longer in the United Kingdom than he had in his homeland.

The phone rang. 'It's your mother on the line,' said Sharon.

'Really! Oh, OK. D'you mind putting her through?'

'Helen, how are you? We haven't heard from you in ages.'

'I'm fine, Mum. I'm sorry – it probably has been weeks.'

'Your father and I were wondering about Christmas. Will you be coming down?'

'That's funny. I was thinking about Christmas not two minutes ago.'

'Well?'

'Um… well, of course, I'll be there – for some of it, anyway. I haven't got around to making any arrangements.'

'You can bring your new fellow if you want. What's he like, anyway?'

Helen grinned as the purpose of the call manifested itself. 'How did you know I had a new man?'

'Well, we saw something in one of the papers, as a matter of fact.'

'Mum! Fancy you reading all that old rubbish.'

'Isn't it true, then?'

'Articles in those sorts of papers often aren't.'

'Ahmed Aziz, isn't it?' Her mother pronounced the first syllable like 'arm'.

'Actually, it's pronounced "Achmed" – "ch" as in the Scottish "loch", with "med" on the end – although the "d" is a sort of cross between a "d" and a "t".'

'How complicated,' sighed her mother.

'It doesn't matter. Everyone calls him Sam.'

'Is he kind to you? What's he look like? Seems a bit serious in the newspapers.'

'He's very kind to me. But how shall I describe him? Think of Omar Sharif – well, Sam is a younger version of him. He's got black, crinkly hair, greying at the temples. He's a little under six feet tall. He's quite slim, apart from a slight roundness in the tummy and he's got a darkish complexion, brilliant white teeth, and slightly fleshy lips. I'm not making a very good job of this. But he's really wonderful. Come to think of it, Laura's out interviewing him now. If you watch the programme tonight, you'll see him.'

'I'll do that. He sounds quite handsome.'

Helen felt herself grimace at the old-fashioned word. No one of her generation, she thought, would say 'handsome'. Still. Her mother probably meant well. 'Yes, I think he is,' she said before adding, 'oh, and he's got the deepest, biggest, liquid-brown eyes in the world.'

'Yes, well I can see that you're quite taken. Are you getting married?' Her mother always came straight to the point.

'It's early days, Mum. But maybe – one day.'

'Ooh, how marvellous! Well, you must bring him down for Christmas.'

'Hang on, I don't know that I will. I haven't asked him yet and he might feel a little out of place.'

'I do think he should make an effort, especially if he's to be our next son-in-law.'

'Mum, please don't get carried away. I'll talk to him and I'll call you in a couple of days. I'd better go now. I'm supposed to be working. Love to Dad.'

'All right, dear. Take care of yourself.'

Helen felt guilty that she had been deliberately out of communication with her parents, yet the phone call had borne out her reasons. It was natural that they might worry about her and hope that she might settle again, but she was not yet ready to be cross-examined about this precious relationship.

The conversation had unsettled her, so she determinedly threw herself into the papers and the mail until – eventually – her friend returned.

'That man thinks the world of you.'

'How do you know?'

'Well, when I introduced myself, he said he was delighted to meet me at last, then immediately asked how *you* were!'

Helen smiled and looked at her watch. 'That's understandable. We have been apart for twenty-eight hours.'

Laura laughed. 'Anyway, I must say that I was impressed. He's like a god to his staff, and as for the parents of the child, well, he showed me pictures of the baby before the operation... so tiny, so ill-looking. But already he's turning a pretty, pink colour. The man's a genius and, better than that, he really cares. I thought he'd be anxious for all the publicity he could get, but once we'd finished he kept all the other crews waiting while he took me off for coffee. Mind you, he only wanted to talk about you, so I jolly well told him off.'

'What about?'

'I just said to him that apart from a quick drink after work, I never see you now.'

'What did he say to that?'

'He said that he supposed he did commandeer your time, but that he had years to catch up on.'

'How sweet – did he really?'

'Yes, so I asked him if you and he would like to spend Boxing Day with us. He said you hadn't discussed what was happening at Christmas.'

'That's right. We haven't.'

'Why on earth not?'

'I don't know exactly. I suppose I didn't want to presume too much, if you know what I mean. Still, now you've brought up the subject, I might well mention it tonight.'

Sam brought flowers when he arrived at Helen's flat that evening. As she opened the door, she thought he looked terribly tired, but as soon as he saw her, a smile spread over his entire face, lighting up his eyes. They kissed in the doorway.

'I can't bear to have you out of my sight for so long, Helen,' he murmured. 'I've had the most wonderful day, really exciting. But

I kept counting the hours till I could tell you about it. Of course, to be honest, I was anticipating getting you into bed! But at the same time, I was really looking forward to just talking with you.'

They had never seemed closer than they were that night, Helen thought. And as he made love to her passionately and possessively, it seemed as if he wanted to own every fragment of her.

'What was your husband like in bed?' Sam's question came right out of the blue, but she realised that he had the same joy mixed with fear and uncertainty that she was experiencing.

'It was never great.'

'You don't have to say that.'

'I know I don't. To begin with, it was very loving, but... Look, I've never told another soul this, but, the thing is, I didn't have orgasms with him.'

'What? You're joking. You're not faking with me, are you?'

Helen was stunned. She knew he was struggling with his own powerful feelings, yet there was no excuse for questioning, even momentarily, the extraordinary quality of their love-making.

'I'm sorry,' he said quickly. 'That was a lousy thing to ask.'

'It was,' she agreed. 'When you couldn't possibly doubt what we have.'

'Do you miss him, though?'

Helen was annoyed, but at the same time she understood that he could not help himself. 'I'll make a pot of tea. I think we should talk this out.'

He nodded, then leapt out of bed to light a cigarette. She watched as he returned and puffed away moodily. She had never seen him smoke before.

Helen took longer in the kitchen than was necessary. She was preparing what she might say, as well as giving Sam time to collect his thoughts. When she returned to the bedroom, he took the mugs of tea from her, put them on the bedside table and kissed her.

'I'm sorry, Helen. Really. I've never been possessive before. Part of me is excited by my need for you, but part of me is terrified.'

Snuggling up to him, she gently kissed the ends of his eyelashes, before telling him of her early days with Barry – of how she had cared for him and also how she had been determined to be content with their relationship despite their sex life failing to improve.

'Especially when I got into television,' she continued, 'I was so aware that it was difficult for him to have a wife in the public eye that I certainly couldn't have told him then that he didn't arouse me in bed. He did to begin with, you see, but when it never goes on long enough to allow you to climax, and when someone never touches you where you're desperate to be touched, well, in the end you shut yourself off. You stop even hoping… The sorry truth is that by the time we split up – and let's face it, by then he was doing it with someone else anyway – I had a permanent crick in my neck through hanging over my side of the bed, so that nothing made contact, not even our feet. Then, when we decided to get a divorce, he told me that he hadn't really fancied me since before we got married. His actual words were: "You were so fucking capable I found it totally emasculating".'

With her confession came tears; tears that should have been wept a long time ago. Sam held and rocked her like a baby until the crying stopped, then kissed her tears away.

'I understand, sweetheart. I truly do. And I'm glad you've told me. I'm sorry it's been so upsetting.'

'Thank you, I'm better now.'

They sipped their tea in silence.

'Do you remember,' he asked suddenly, 'that the first night we made love, I told you that I wanted you to have my child?'

She nodded.

'Well,' he went on, 'you never commented on it.'

'You never said it again. I wondered if you'd regretted it.'

'No. I want you to marry me, Helen. I daren't hope that you will, but I have to ask.'

They fell into each other's arms.

'Sam, I love you so much. Please marry me. Please give me your child. And please always voice your thoughts and your fears.'

'I promise,' he said.

Then, more gently now, they made love again.

Later, lying in the dimly lit room, she mentioned her mother's phone call. 'She wants to invite you for Christmas.'

'Oh no,' he said quickly. 'I don't think I could cope with that.'

'I'm sorry. Can you explain why?'

He sat up, looking serious, and recounted details of some of the Christmases he had experienced in the past, and how he had felt out of place.

'You wouldn't feel left out with me there!'

'No, probably not, but your mother and father will be looking forward to seeing you, and you should give them your full attention. I'd like to meet them soon, but Christmas is too emotive a time for you all. Let's leave it for now.'

She agreed, but despite his earlier promise, she was not at all sure he was sharing everything in his mind.

'Anyway,' he said, 'among the consultants I'm the only bachelor, and the only one with no family in the UK. So, I usually volunteer to be on duty for Christmas; it's only fair. We don't have many patients in the hospital, but I carve the turkey at lunch for those who can manage it. And I often have private patents in the clinic, so I pop over there too.'

'I thought you couldn't bear to be away from me.'

He beamed at her. 'That's true, which is why I was hoping you'd come back on the morning of Boxing Day. As long as one of the other consultants is prepared to work, I could have the day off, and we could do what Laura suggested and join her and her man.'

It had been a long day and an emotional evening. It seemed to Helen that there was some niggling disquiet at the back of her mind that was struggling to emerge as an identifiable idea.

'Do you never feel that perhaps you owe it to your own country to go back and practise there?' she asked. 'And don't your family ever say that they'd like you to come home?'

'I'm very tired, Helen,' he answered. 'Can we have this conversation another time? I'm practically English, as I've told you before and now I'm going to have an English wife. I love you, and I want to be here with you.'

He curled round her, and the warmth and strength of him soothed her body and mind. It was natural in two such independent characters that there should be some ups and downs, and whatever her abstract anxiety was, it must be possible to resolve it. She relaxed and slept.

Helen was astonished at her reaction to this festive season, compared with the last few. Life was hectic. Her days were crammed with personal appearances, recordings and programmes, her nights spent in passionate exchanges – but for all that, she was full of invigorating energy. Somehow, she found time to go out and shop properly for thoughtful presents for everyone. This contrasted with the previous two years when she had bought gifts from Fortnum's food hall – via their catalogue. They had been real luxury treats, she acknowledged, but totally impersonal. This year, nothing was too much trouble. She was full of goodwill to all men and women, and even found herself, in quiet moments, offering up a prayer of thanksgiving for her good fortune and her wonderful life.

On Christmas Eve, the programme took the form of an old-fashioned music hall, and she and the other presenters and reporters donned Victorian costumes and performed for the viewers. Sam was off duty that night and, for the first time since their meeting, came to the studios to watch the programme go out live.

The social club was buzzing when all the participants arrived there shortly after seven.

'Best Christmas programme ever,' announced Derek, as he always did and – as *they* always did – everyone agreed. Was not Christmas, after all, a time for tradition and ritual?

After a while, Helen's friends and acquaintances drifted away, either to drive to ageing parents or to play Father Christmas to their offspring. When only a handful of revellers remained, Sam took charge and devoted himself to giving them a party. He took them to a little Indian restaurant, where he ordered for all of them and entertained them with medical stories. It was obvious to Helen that they had fallen under his spell.

At the end of the evening, he persuaded them to join him in a bottle of champagne. When the cork popped, he said, 'As the only foreigner in our party, may I wish you every joy this Christmas.' They drank to that, but Sam had not finished. 'May I also propose a toast,' he turned towards Helen, 'to this lovely lady, who is shortly to become my wife.'

There was a moment's silence, and then the congratulations flowed, not only from their table but also from the other diners – who had not been oblivious to the celebrity in their midst. Sam and Helen kissed, and it seemed to Helen that the lights in the restaurant were spinning all around her. She had consumed a certain amount of wine, but whether she was high on alcohol or on sheer bliss, she was unsure.

Back in her flat, she kicked off her shoes and made two cups of decaffeinated coffee. In a few hours, she must leave for Bournemouth and the family Christmas, but this was the real celebration. She presented Sam with a Christmas stocking which she had bought and filled with ridiculously inconsequential items: a pair of clockwork feet, a tiny jack-in-the-box, a tin shaped like a vintage Bentley and filled with old English confectionery, and a packet of seeds which claimed to contain the necessary ingredients to grow a tweed jacket. Clearly, Sam had never received such gifts before, and Helen felt it was like watching a child at the first Christmas he is able to appreciate. She felt her heart would burst as he unwrapped each nonsensical present with gasps of merriment.

Next, she gave him his proper present, a pair of platinum cufflinks set with cornelian stones, which had been engraved on the underside with his initials. He took her hand, then kissed her, and she noticed that he was close to tears. They sat for a while, holding and touching and loving. He then excitedly made his presentation, which was a finely-woven red wool evening skirt with pointing detail finished in gold thread, a gossamer-fine top with the same gold detail and a huge fire-red cape with a spider's web embroidered on it in gold, and two diamond pieces worked into it to represent flies caught in the tangle. It was breathtakingly beautiful, and she could not even begin to guess at the cost of it.

'Sam, it's too expensive.'

'Don't you like it?'

'I love it. I've never had anything so lovely. It's just – it's too much.'

'Nothing is too much for you, my angel. I want to give you the world, and I'm only just beginning.'

Somewhere she knew she had a recording of carols sung by the choir of King's College, Cambridge. She found it and put it on the sound system. At twelve he wished her happy Christmas, before picking her up bodily and carrying her to bed.

Next day, her parents' pleasure at seeing her tempered her happiness with guilt as she consciously tried to slip back into the role of dutiful daughter. Both her mother and father ate too much at lunch and then slept, so Helen washed up before waking them for the Queen's speech – which customarily signalled the moment when they might exchange gifts.

It was all as it had ever been, but not quite because phone calls punctuated the day. She had rung the hospital, and Sam had phoned later, after serving lunch to his patients. He rang again around six, just before Helen's family settled in front of the television set, for the usual fare of films and variety shows.

Later in the evening, when Helen was washing up again, her mother joined her in the kitchen. The inevitable questions followed, about Sam and their relationship, and his reason for declining the Christmas invitation. Helen explained as best she could. It was obvious that her mother was hurt, and also that she felt excluded from their arrangements. Helen wondered if this was the lot of all parents and, for a second, considered whether the children she was hoping for with Sam would be as careless of her concern as she knew she was being of her mother's.

'It's not that we mind him being from the Middle East, dear,' her mother was saying. Helen was angered by the implied prejudice, but at least it provided a focal point for her unrest. She felt torn between her past and her future, yet she believed they could co-exist.

'Why would you?' she replied.

'Well, they're from a very different culture. I'm sure you can understand our point of view – it would have been easier if you'd picked a nice young British boy.'

'I did that once, remember? It was hardly a success. And "young" is difficult too – there aren't many young, unattached guys around when you're almost thirty-five. And there aren't too many men either who can cope with an up-front, financially secure workaholic. It does narrow one's choice. And don't forget,' she continued, 'your grandchildren will be Anglo-Egyptian.'

Her mother dropped the china plate she was drying and burst into tears.

'I'm sorry, Mummy. Don't let's quarrel. It's Christmas.'

'I don't want to quarrel. I just don't know what's going on.'

The phone rang.

'That'll be him again, I suppose. He might as well have come here since he can't seem to leave you in peace for five minutes.'

Helen kissed her mother on the forehead. She wanted to gather her to her, for was she not regarded as a tactile person? But somehow, she could not act in this way with her parents.

She picked up the phone. It was Sam.

'Darling, I'm missing you. How are you?'

Helen, standing at the antique table in the hall beside the drawing room door that remained resolutely open, felt stilted and awkward. 'I'm fine.'

'You're not. What's wrong? Did I ring at a bad moment?'

'Um – sort of.'

'Helen, I can't bear this. Have you gone off me?'

'No, no, no, no, no. It's just a bit… difficult.'

'Ah, you can't talk there.'

'Not really.'

'Isn't there an extension?'

'I'm afraid not.'

'Can you ring me back later, any time?'

'I don't think I'd better. I'll explain tomorrow. I'll get back early. I could be at your house by eleven. We're not going to Ian and Laura's till one, are we?'

'No. Helen, you do love me, don't you?'

'I absolutely do.'

'You see, I never want you to go to bed anywhere in the world where they have a phone, without ringing you before you sleep, to tell you how much I care for you.'

'You have a knack of saying the nicest things,' she murmured, then, with a look at the open drawing room door, she drew a defiant, grown-up breath. 'Sam, I do love you. I adore you, in fact, and I'm counting the hours till I can be with you.'

He sounded satisfied. 'Sleep well, darling.'

Helen put the phone down and took another deep breath before joining her parents to ask if they would like a drink. They opted for small medium-dry sherries, which she was happy to pour and distribute, before getting herself a brandy. She saw her mother's eyebrows rise in response to her choice. Probably, she disapproved of Helen drinking spirits.

'Let's play Trivial Pursuit,' she suggested, freshly determined to pay full attention to her family for the final few hours. As they played, she reproached herself. Surely, she chided herself, you can enjoy this and put Sam out of your mind for a little while. She persevered – and experienced a sensation of watching herself behaving normally and lovingly, while inside she was in torment, going over and over the misunderstanding on the telephone and hating herself for her treatment of her parents in this quiet suburb of Bournemouth. She was alarmed too at her dependence on Sam, and his on her. Yet, secure in the belief that they were to spend their lives together, she persuaded herself that their focus on each other was justified.

By the end of the evening, she judged that she had remedied the situation somewhat. In the kitchen, when she and her mother were making hot chocolate, she asked, 'Would you like to meet Sam soon, Mum?'

'Of course. Isn't that what I've been saying to you?'

'Sort of. Why don't you and Daddy come up one Saturday when neither of us is working, and have lunch and go to a matinee?'

'That would be very nice,' said her mother. And on that note, Helen felt entitled to take herself off to bed.

Very early the next morning, she set off and as she wound up her speed on the M3, her spirits rose, and she started singing along to the radio. The night-time hours had seen the first snowflakes of the winter. Did that count as a White Christmas? Whether or not it did, it was as if the Almighty had sprinkled the countryside with a dusting of icing sugar from a giant sieve in the sky.

Surprisingly quickly, she was back at Strand-on-the-Green. Though she had a key, she rang the doorbell. Then, as she heard Sam's movements, she sang 'Once in Royal David's City' through the letter box.

He opened the door and they embraced before he reached into his pocket for a pound coin, which he pressed into her hand. 'A reward for the carol singer,' he laughed.

'Gosh, thanks. That was easy money. What else can I do for a reward?'

'I'll show you,' he answered, taking her hand and leading her upstairs.

'We can't, Sam. We're supposed to be going out for lunch.'

'We can and we will, and we'll still go out to lunch!'

Afterwards, as they lay together in his bed, he held the underside of his arm to hers. 'Look,' he pointed out. 'Different colour, different texture, different cultures, different countries – yet you are the other side of me. All my life, I've waited for the right lady. I grew impatient. I didn't think there could be such a person. But at last I found you.' He leant over and kissed the inside of her wrist.

'And I'm very pleased to have been found!'

'Yesterday,' he said, 'my latest transplant patient had a visit from his wife, who was very pregnant. It was lunchtime, and I thought, this time next year, we'll have Christmas Day together and I'll have to pull back your chair further than usual, and then push it in ever so gently – because you'll be enormous with my child.'

Later, as he helped her to her chair at Laura's dining table, Helen smiled up at him, remembering his words. He beamed at her in return.

Laura had gone to enormous trouble over the lunch. She had cooked a boned goose, stuffed with turkey breasts, and the blend of light and dark meats was exquisite.

It was a while since Helen had been in her friend's flat; it struck her that it had become much more of a real home than it had once seemed. It was obvious that Laura and Ian were very comfortable together and that, though they were both active in – and enthused by – their careers, they were consciously, or unconsciously, building a nest for their future. Helen wondered if they ever sneaked off to bed in the middle of the day. She could not imagine it because they seemed more grown-up somehow, more settled… maybe less passionate? Of course, they had known each other longer.

The two women grew more animated as time and the wine flowed. They giggled at the foibles of various colleagues and moaned about their bosses. The men observed them indulgently.

At last Ian pointed out, 'This isn't meant to be a company conference.'

Helen, caught in full flood, laughed and took Sam's hand. 'I'm sorry. We'll stop.'

'No, don't,' replied Sam. 'I like career women. I like what makes you tick.'

'I like what makes *you* tick,' Laura joined in. 'I was terribly impressed...' She laughed. 'I can probably only say this 'cos I'm a bit pissed, but I was terribly impressed the day I did the TV piece on you. In fact – I don't know if you'd agree – I'd like to do an extended feature, a sort of "Week in the Life Of".'

'Oh, I don't think so,' Sam said quickly.

'It's a good idea,' Helen's voice was encouraging. 'Come on, Sam, great publicity. You know your cardiac programme needs more money. It could only benefit from this.'

'What about all the less headline-grabbing branches of medicine that are just as deserving?' he asked wickedly.

'You so-and-so!' She laughed. 'Is this where I came in or what?'

'Well, that's settled,' said Laura. 'I've sounded Derek out already, actually.'

'Saints preserve us from organising women,' sighed Ian. 'We might as well give in – we're surrounded. Have another drink, old boy. Better still, why don't we have a game of backgammon, while we leave the girls to sort out our future and theirs?'

Sam threw a look in Helen's direction. She was not sure what it meant. Did he want to be rescued? Perhaps he was not enjoying himself. Maybe he was not keen on the other couple? But surely they should be sociable sometimes? After all, the friends she had made since her divorce were important to her; they had seen her through the bad times. Had she not always maintained that anyone new in her life must be able to embrace not only her lifestyle, but also the other people who mattered?

She watched as the two men began to play. Before long, it seemed to her that Sam looked more settled and, from the determined set of his jaw, she surmised that he had every intention of winning. She continued talking and giggling with Laura but, unlike her friend, she had an acute awareness of the scene in the corner – only relaxing once she heard Sam laugh. What a complex person he was. How efficient at work, how romantic with her, and yet how uneasy he could seem.

'Am I an organising woman?' Helen asked him later. They were in bed, as Boxing Day drew to a close.

'Yes,' he answered, 'but in a perfectly adorable way. It's one of the things I like most about you. You're capable but you're loving, efficient but sweet, and I'm very lucky. You leave me space, and I need that. The one thing I can't cope with is a clinging female who expects me to provide her reason for living.'

'I'm suitably warned,' said Helen.

'What? Oh, I wasn't talking about you.'

Helen was puzzled. 'Well,' she said quietly, 'I thought we had a terrific day.'

He smiled. 'We did,' he agreed, wrapping her in his arms, 'as every day is with you.'

Secure again, she kissed him and promptly fell asleep.

Chapter Six

It was nearly as difficult to fill a daily programme between Christmas and New Year as it was in August – news-wise, the least interesting month of the year. Naturally, no one hoped for treacherous weather and a resultant crop of traffic accidents, or a political crisis here or elsewhere, but without them the serious element of the programme was bound to be a bit thin. It was no surprise then when Colin, who was Derek's deputy and at the helm during the editor's seasonal holiday, announced that they would do fifteen minutes of the next day's programme from a circus on the edge of town. Helen would record it from the Big Top in the morning.

'Who's setting this feature up?' asked Colin.

'Gary,' someone said.

'Well, where the hell is he?'

'I'll get him,' said Helen. She returned within seconds, accompanied by the reluctant researcher.

'What do you have for us, Gary?' asked Colin.

'Well,' sighed Gary, 'they've got dancing fountains that use God knows how many gallons of water per show. There's a trapeze artist happy to be on the box. Then there's a good talker in the lion tamer. And we've got a clown lined up who's worked in forty countries.'

'OK, we'll gather there at ten o'clock tomorrow morning. We'll record an interview with Helen and the lion chappie and see what happens from there. Sort out a few more possibles though, Gary. Put your back into it.' Colin sounded impatient.

Back in her office, Helen was at a loss as to what to do. There was no post to speak of, and the next day's visit to the circus hardly needed any in-depth preparation. She went in search of Laura, who had just returned from shooting a piece about babies born in London and the Home Counties over Christmas.

'Poor little buggers,' laughed her friend. 'Two Noels, one Rudolph and one Carol.'

'Oh God!' Helen giggled. 'Has Rudolph got a red nose?'

'He's red all over, actually. I can't say babies of that age do much for me. Have you got time for coffee?'

'I thought you'd never ask.'

They chatted for a while about the day they had spent together with their respective men.

'They seemed to get on quite well,' Laura ventured.

'Yes – I think so. Sam's funny though. I sometimes think he's got no urge to socialise. I've met a few of his colleagues, of course, but no close friends. Perhaps he doesn't have any. It's a miracle he was at the dinner party where we met – and we've only seen those people once since then, at some do at the clinic they all work at. Still, when he does get out and make an effort, he's terrific.'

'Someone told me that he announced your engagement in the Taj Mahal on Christmas Eve.'

'I think "engagement" is a rather formal word for us but, yes, he did. Changing the subject, did you mean what you said about small babies not doing anything for you?'

'Yes... No... I don't know. Perhaps it's because they belong to other people. Why, do you feel differently?'

'I think so. I'm becoming broody, I suppose. Do you and Ian ever talk about getting married?'

'Sometimes. But neither of us is keen. I don't really do much with my freedom, but I like to know it's there.'

'I know what you mean. Of course, you're only twenty-nine. When I was your age, I wasn't aware of the pressing passage of time.'

'Poor old soul! You were married, though.'

'Yes, that's true. But, do you know, I never considered having children with Barry. Funny, isn't it?'

'Do you and Sam discuss it?'

'Yes, and he's keener than I am.'

'Well, when are you getting married?'

'I don't know. This'll probably sound odd, but he refers to our getting married, being married, my being pregnant, and our lives with our children, but he never suggests a date. Still, it's early days.'

'Well, it is, and also maybe he's waiting for *you*. You're an assertive woman, after all.'

'I don't think I am with him. But then, I don't need to be, because he treats me exactly the way I want. Even if he didn't though, I always feel that our relationship couldn't possibly work if I were running it. I know that's not a very modern statement to make, but it's how it is.'

'You're sure he's quite genuine? I don't mean it unkindly, but you don't think he's just in love with the idea?'

'I don't think so. You see, I'm quite happy as it is. He's the one who keeps mentioning marriage and children. Do you know, even the first night we slept together, he talked about it? I promise you, I'm not pressurising him.'

'I didn't think you were for a second. I just wonder if he can make the commitment. He is forty-five – why hasn't he done it before?'

'He says that he's been too busy, and that no one disturbed him sufficiently to make an impact before. It's nice to hear... Oh dear, you've got me worried now. To be quite honest, to begin with I felt swept along, and just felt happy, actually, that he seemed even more in love with me than I was with him. But, I think I'd die if anything went wrong now.'

Laura looked at her friend anxiously. 'Why should anything go wrong? It's wonderful. It's obviously far more intense than my thing with Ian. Why be pessimistic? He worships the ground you walk on.'

'Maybe it's because it's too wonderful. Maybe I can't quite believe it can last. Maybe I don't believe I deserve it.'

'Well, you do. Forget what I said. You could just get pregnant.'

'No, I told you. I'm not that desperate. And I would always wonder if he felt trapped and had only married me for that. Anyway, I'm so beastly independent that if I ever conceived without it being planned by us both, I'd probably walk out of his life, just to prove I wasn't holding a shotgun to his head. I'm still on the Pill, anyway.'

'Well, why don't you tell Sam that you're coming off it just to see if you're still ovulating properly, and see how he takes it?'

'Hmmn, I might – it's a good idea.'

The door burst open suddenly. It was Gary, the researcher.

'Is this women's talk, or can anyone join in?'

'Oh dear, you found us out,' said Helen. 'We were just discussing how fanciable you are.'

Laura edged past Gary's not inconsiderable bulk and mouthed 'May you be forgiven' as she winked and departed.

The following morning, when she arrived at the circus, the unmistakeable stench of animal excrement filled her nostrils. Helen's stomach was never at its best early in the day, and for a moment she had to fight the urge to vomit. But she had done stories in circuses and zoos before, and she knew that she would grow accustomed to the smell after a while.

Nothing much seemed to be happening, so she found her way to a tatty café at the back of the Big Top. Most of the crew, who had finished rigging, were there before her, wolfing down fried egg sandwiches and drinking builders-strength tea.

'Have a sandwich, Helen. Do you a power of good,' suggested one of the electricians.

She grimaced. 'No I don't think I could cope with that. Is there a tab, or are we paying for our own?'

'Certainly not! Eddie'll settle up at the end of the day.'

She ordered a milky coffee, which looked like sludge, but when she sat down, she realised it was not as hot as she would have liked. Steve, the outside broadcast director, spotted her and strode over to join her.

'Gary and I had this great idea,' he said enthusiastically as he sat astride a chair beside her.

'What's that, then?'

'You interview the lion-tamer—'

'I know, we discussed it yesterday.'

'—in the cage, with the lions.'

'Fine. Then I'll walk on water,' she joshed.

'I'm serious.'

'Come on, Steve, it's too early to wind me up. I'm not awake yet.'

'I mean it, Helen.'

She realised he did. 'The company wouldn't let me do it. They'd never get insurance – well, not within our budget anyway.'

'That's where you're wrong. The company secretary's got it sorted.'

'I don't think Derek would have let me do it, if he'd not been on holiday. What does Colin say?'

'He says he hopes you don't get too badly injured, because he hasn't got a spare presenter for six o'clock.'

'Oh great! I feel truly cherished now. You seem to have thought of everything. Has the lion-tamer ever had anyone in the cage before?'

'I dunno. But listen, sweet, I wouldn't ask you if I thought it was dangerous. It'll make terrific television.'

Of that she had no doubt. 'One take, then. If you screw up on cameras or anything – tough. I'll do it, but only once.'

'Are you serious?'

'Yes, Colin.'

'You're not.'

She sighed. 'Were you serious when you asked me?'

'Yeah, sort of.'

'Well, I'm serious. I'll do it. Bring the bloke over and I'll talk to him.'

Alfonso the trainer dismissed her fears. He would do his act first, he told her, and then come to the edge of the cage and bring her inside it. 'Just keep your left hand on my right shoulder, that's all. I make them very angry in the act, but it's just for show. I've had them all since they were cubs and they adore me.'

'What confidence!' she retorted.

'What are you going to ask me in the interview?'

'Heavens, I haven't even got round to thinking about that. Let's just hope something occurs to me.'

As she walked back to the Big Top, she passed several of the crew. The word had obviously got around, for their expressions, as they looked at her, were a mixture of admiration and incredulity.

'Can I have a cigarette?' she asked of no one in particular. She was embarrassed by the profusion of brands suddenly made available. 'One'll do.' She laughed.

'Are you sure about this, Helen?' It was one of the cameramen.

'Ask me another.'

'Look, love, you don't have to do it. Steve wouldn't.'

'I know. He told me. But now I've said I will.' She looked around. 'Has anyone got a sheet of paper?' The PA obliged. 'I'm just going to write a note to someone, and then I'll be ready.'

She sat down in a seat just outside the ring, and realised that she could see the lions waiting in the tunnel. They looked bored and sleepy. She told herself that was a good sign before quickly scribbling her message.

Dear Sam. You'll only get this if I die or am seriously injured.
I'm sorry – it was a stupid thing to do. I got seduced by the
glamour of being a 'have a go' girl. I love you. Thanks for
everything. Love, Helen.

She folded the paper, and gave it to the PA. 'That's in case anything happens to me,' she murmured.

'Helen, nothing's going to happen.'

Helen rounded on her. 'Listen, sweetheart,' she snapped, 'you're not the one who's going to face eight man-eating creatures. Just allow me to be a little bit twitchy, OK?'

The PA exchanged glances with the soundman. Helen thought she heard him say something about her not usually being temperamental.

I should have said 'no', she mused. Still, it was too late now. She felt the PA and various other personnel watching as she walked around in circles for a couple of minutes, puffing nervously. Then, she took a deep breath, found somewhere safe to stub out her cigarette and forced a smile.

'I'm sorry. Give me the hand-mike and let's go.'

It was fortunate that she had not seen the act before she agreed to go in the cage. As he had promised, Alfonso made the animals appear ferocious. The performance lasted eight minutes. Even in the midst of her panic, Helen realised that it would have to be cut down for tonight's programme and wondered if anyone had booked editing time.

The lions all returned to their podiums, then stood on their hind legs and pawed the air. Alfonso cracked his whip and they returned to all fours. This was it. He opened the cage door and, suddenly, she was inside, clutching her microphone.

She heard her voice speaking normally while she clung to his shoulder for dear life. 'How long does it take to train animals to this state of, um, excellence?'

He was talking back to her – so far, so good.

'Alfonso, what do you say to people who think it's cruel to keep animals in captivity, and to make them perform for their keep?'

'They don't know what they're talking about. The animals love it, and they're much better cared for here than they would be in the wild.' He answered somewhat robotically. Presumably, he had given this answer on previous – and probably numerous – occasions.

One of the lions, a hairy male, snarled as Helen looked at him. He raised his paw and sliced through the air as if he would have liked to bisect her from top to toe. This was not the time to argue with Alfonso. A lioness came down off her perch and walked towards them.

'Lions are essentially lazy,' he was saying. 'This way, they're fed and watered, and they don't have to do much about it.' He cracked his whip and, miraculously, the lioness returned to her place.

'What do they eat in a normal day?'

The lion tamer answered with a list that sounded like a luxury menu. Clearly, he was warming to his subject.

'Have they been fed today?' She did not register the answer, while thinking up the next question – but she fervently hoped that they had been.

Somewhere outside the ring, she could see the floor manager, looking much as usual, bearded, uninterested, wearing suede shoes and corduroy trousers. She observed his hand countdown, and she finished neatly as he reached zero, by saying, 'Thank you, lions – for not eating me.'

She walked backwards to the ring's edge, and out of the cage. As she did so, she could hear the director shouting instructions to his crew through her earpiece.

'Where's Camera Three? Go for the close-up! God, look at her, she's gone to pieces! Go in tighter.'

The camera caught Helen in a quite untypical pose. Her head was in her hands, and she was trembling all over. 'Great television!' she heard Steve say. 'Good girl – I love you.'

84

Helen tried to think of something cutting to say – along the lines of that nothing had changed much in entertainment terms since the Christians and the lions in the Coliseum but her voice would not connect to her mind.

Suddenly, Steve was in front of her. 'Wonderful, Helen.' He put his arm around her shaking shoulders. 'The interview was fine, and you're still alive.'

'That's true. Was it really all right? I can't remember what I asked.'

'It was stupendous.'

'Sorry – I'm better now. I didn't feel terribly frightened in there. I just felt very strange when I came out.'

'Let's buy you a brandy.'

'Good idea – if we can find a pub that's already open.'

'Sussed that. Come on.'

Later, back at the studios when she was watching the playback, she had to admit that it did, as the director had promised, make terrific television. She smiled at her apparent composure in the circus ring and felt again the engulfing reaction as she watched herself emerge from the cage.

In the live programme, she signed off by saying, 'Well, all in a day's work, I suppose. But I think I'd rather not do it again. That's it from us for tonight. I'm going to have a relaxing evening and weekend, and I hope you have the same. See you on Monday. A very goodnight to you.'

The music came in; the captions were up. It was the end of another routine day in the mad world of television.

Back in the newsroom, Helen gathered up her diary and papers and was just leaving when the temp on the switchboard stopped her. 'Do you want to speak to someone called Sam?'

'Yes, sure. I'll take it over here – extension 228… Hi, Sam.'

'Why did you do it?'

'It was great television.'

'I suppose you could say that, but why on earth didn't you tell me what you were going to do? You said you were going to do some recording at the circus. You didn't say you were going in a cage with eight lions.'

'I didn't know then.'

'My God, Helen, you're mad!'

'You're right.'

'Are you coming home?'

'On my way.'

'Helen, I don't like you doing this kind of thing.'

The tension of the day erupted. 'For God's sake, Sam,' she cried, 'you don't own me! I was doing "this sort of thing" before you ever came on the scene. I'm the best judge of what I can cope with and what I can't. It turned a very mediocre show into compulsive viewing. I'm OK. It was worth the risk.'

'I'm sorry,' he said coldly. 'You're quite right. I obviously have no say in the matter.'

'Oh, Sam, forgive me. I didn't mean to shout. Don't let's argue. You're probably right – it was absolutely crazy, and I certainly wouldn't do it again. Do you still love me?'

He sighed. 'Of course. That's why I got so upset, you idiot. Shall I come and get you? I don't think you should drive now. Let's eat out.'

'Good idea. Thank you. I'll be next door, in the social club.'

All eyes swivelled to the door as she arrived. One or two people raised their glasses in her direction.

'You look all in,' said the controller of programmes. 'Have a drink.'

'Thanks, Paul. It has been quite a day. Bloody stupid thing to do, really.'

'Terrific television, though. You're a good girl – and you get better and better.'

Helen beamed at him and began to relax. This was her world. She was among the people who mattered and who understood why she did what she did. By the time Sam arrived, she had recovered her equilibrium. She offered a chaste cheek as greeting. He declined Paul's offer of a drink.

They drove off in silence. 'Where do you want to go?' he asked.

'I don't know, Sam. I'm sorry I was so awful on the phone.'

'It's OK – you were quite correct anyway, I don't own you.'

'Maybe that's the trouble.'

They drove on. Parking was difficult, but eventually they found a space in Long Acre. He slipped an arm round her shoulders, and she snuggled up against him.

Once inside the restaurant, he took charge – asking for a table near enough to the piano player to be able to enjoy him, but far away enough for them to be able to talk. He ordered two glasses of the trendy Kir royale, then looked into her eyes.

'Why was today like this when two days ago, everything was so marvellous?' he asked.

She sipped her drink and decided to tell him the truth. 'Well, today frightened me. I wasn't sure if I was doing the right thing or not, and also, well, to be honest, some things that Laura said yesterday have been playing on my mind.'

'Do you want to tell me about them?'

'Yes and no... Sam, you know you talk about us being married and having children?'

'Yes.'

'Well, it's not that I'm desperate about it.'

'I know that.'

'It's just that you never say *when*. It's real and yet not quite.'

'Ah,' he said, and he studied his drink intently before continuing. 'Let me guess. Laura said that maybe I wasn't as keen as I made out. Maybe she wondered why, at forty-five, I'd never been married? Was she worried that I was just impressed with your body and your status?'

'That's pretty near the mark.'

He sighed loudly. 'Helen, do you love me?'

'More and more each day.'

'I wonder if your love is strong enough to cope with what I ought to tell you.'

'You're not married after all, are you?'

'No – no, I'm not, but I do have a sort of tie. I come from a very different culture from yours. Marriages are sometimes arranged; particularly in wealthy families. Sometimes there's an "understanding" from childhood.'

He stopped.

She peered at him, willing him to go on, but not at all sure she would be able to deal with it if when he did. After a moment he cleared his throat.

'When I was about twenty, and on holiday at home from medical school, my father – whom I adored – told me it was his dearest wish that I should marry the daughter of a great friend of the family.'

'But Sam,' she retorted in a frightened and shrill voice, 'that's antiquated. You're practically English. You're always saying so yourself.'

'Sweetheart...' He took her hand and pulled her towards him and kissed the top of her head. 'Please listen. I'll make it as easy as I can – for both of us.'

She nodded but did not look up into his eyes.

'Please believe me when I tell you that I never cared for her. I did, as you say, think of myself as English, but to keep peace in the family, I found it easier to agree; so we were, I suppose you might say, betrothed. It didn't mean anything to me. I was interested only in my career. In any case, she was just a child. Eight years old at the time. But, she grew up into a modest, pleasant but rather dull young woman who, much to my horror, took our arrangement seriously.

Helen nodded again, then sipped from her drink, still avoiding his gaze.

A movement at her elbow alerted her to the waitress's presence. She was carrying their first courses – tiny slices of calves' liver on a bed of shredded lettuce mixed with mayonnaise and yoghurt and decorated with strips of smoked ham. Sam ordered a bottle of wine from the young woman once she had placed their plates in front of them. Everything was normal, except that it was not, and she was having to make a real effort to absorb what Sam was saying. Surely an ancient custom could not possibly have any relevance to their modern life and future?

He sampled his meal and then began to speak again. 'I had girlfriends, and sex, of course. To be honest, I never honestly considered honouring the arrangement. Then, when I was thirty-two, my father died. I went home, obviously. And I can't begin to explain the impact his death made on me; I was devastated. It removed a layer of emotional skin, no doubt about it. For the very first time, I had an acute sense of my history and heritage. I felt it was up to me to carry things on. So, in an attempt to glorify his memory, I tried to take an interest in Hamaida. We spent some time together – but always in the company of other people, of course. I really tried to like her.

'What happened?'

'Well, one day, she somehow engineered it that when I called, all her family were out. There were only servants in the house. She begged me to make love to her – saying that she wanted to know what sex was like. It was not a natural thing for her to do, not with her background. She didn't like it much, I'm afraid. She was very tense and I found it difficult to penetrate her. I remember she closed her eyes tightly. I felt she must want me, somehow, if she was prepared to put herself through what was obviously pain, but I was confused because she made me feel so undesirable that I almost hated her. It was awful, especially because she bled all over the place. There was absolutely no passion and I felt no real pleasure. Just guilt. Loads and loads of guilt.'

'She didn't get pregnant did she?'

'No, she didn't. It would have been difficult for that to happen as I was so put off by the whole thing that I never ejaculated. Of course, as you probably know, men can sometimes have lively sperm in their pre-come secretions, so a pregnancy wasn't out of the question. I was playing with fire. My only excuse is that I was grief-stricken over my father and wasn't thinking straight. So, I was lucky in that she did not conceive, but I felt I had rendered her unmarriageable. In terms of our culture, the fact is that she was damaged goods.'

'But she begged you to do it. It's not your fault. She's hardly an innocent victim. My God, you're not making all this up, are you?'

'I'm afraid not, Helen. It's all true.'

She sighed loudly with exasperation and disbelief.

'So,' he went on, 'I offered to marry her. It was all arranged. Her house and mine were filled with expensive gifts – gifts that have remained unopened to this day. You see, on the night before the wedding, one of her brothers came to see me and he told me that the whole thing was off because – and these were her words "I don't want to see you tomorrow, or ever, ever again".'

Helen breathed a sigh of relief. 'Well, that's all right then.'

Sam continued. 'I came back to England. I absorbed myself in work. I was free. But I was troubled. You see, I realised that although I had asked her to marry me, I hadn't done it joyfully or with kindness. And I felt sure that's why she had called it off. Basically, I offered her no love and no promise of a happy future.'

'That's life, Sam. So why are you telling me this – does it affect us?'

'Darling, it does. Hamaida and I have never discussed the past. Every time I've been home, I've seen her, always in her family's presence. She's never said much, just nodded and smiled rather sadly.'

'What a wimp.'

'Helen, it's not like you to be so harsh about someone. You must understand that I didn't know you then, so I never had to face up to this before. Maybe at some level I always assumed that I would go back one day and do the decent thing and marry her, but now it's different. You're the first woman in my life I've wanted to marry, but I somehow feel that before we can I have to seek permission from my past.'

'You still feel guilty?'

'Yes.'

'Do you ever feel that you might have to end up marrying her, just to assuage your guilt, and honour your father's memory?'

It was a shot in the dark. She had no idea why she was using such formal language. Was it to jolt him out of this ridiculous notion? Surely he would see sense and suddenly say: 'No of course I don't. That would be like something from the Dark Ages.'

But there was silence. He was serious. And she could see that he was struggling to breathe and – suddenly – so was she.

'Yes,' he replied at last. 'Yes, I do.'

The room dissolved before her eyes. But through the confusion, she felt him grasp her hands strongly – indeed, painfully. After a moment, he relaxed the grip in one hand and picked up her wine glass, holding it to her lips while she drank, like a baby. The room steadied.

'Let's get out of here,' she whispered.

Both of them were silent until they were in bed in Sam's house. He held her to him and she sobbed, wearily, into his hairy chest.

'Helen,' he ventured at last, 'I will sort this. I can't let you go, and I won't. You're right, it is antiquated. Nothing, and nobody, will prevent me from spending the rest of my life with you. They can't expect it. I can find happiness only with you. I have to be with you.'

She was so tired that his voice was reaching her – vaguely – through a funnel of fatigue.

'That…' he was saying, 'is why I've invited my mother here.'

She was suddenly wide awake. 'What!'

'I've been meaning to tell you but just not really found the right moment. She'll be here in two days. You'll like her. She's a very cultured and intelligent woman. Half Egyptian and half French. Of course, being partly European makes her rather more dominant than perhaps she might have been otherwise. But I want her to meet you. We can go to shows together, and lovely restaurants. She'll enjoy it here. She always does. She'll adore you. And she'll understand that my life is here, and that you're part of it. Everything will be all right.'

Helen blinked in the dimly lit room. 'Where will she stay?'

He sighed. 'Well, she'll be here.'

'But what about me?'

He sighed again. 'She's seventy... I can't expect her to, you know, be faced with our normal living arrangements. I want to see you at least as much as usual, but we can't sleep together. Not while she's here. But it won't be for long.'

Helen knew she was being illogical, but for a moment, she felt utterly degraded. It's as if I'm a 'fuck below stairs', she thought. What a horrible expression that was. She was unclear why it had come to her, but it seemed apt. Her reasonable side could see what distress any obvious manifestation of their sex life might cause a morally upright older woman – indeed, she would have found it difficult to sleep with Sam if her parents were under the same roof. Nonetheless, she felt bereft and devastated.

For the first time since they had slept together she was too tired to make love; too overcome by what he had told her, too disappointed, too isolated.

The following morning, the atmosphere felt strained. Sam insisted on her eating breakfast. He had bought croissants, Normandy butter, strawberry preserve and honey. She peered at him across the gleaming white kitchen table, and her heart filled with gladness. He must love her to go to all this trouble. She knew he would never have shopped for such items had they been for him alone.

It was as if he had read her thoughts because he said suddenly, 'You could never doubt how much I love you, Helen, could you?'

She shook her head. 'No. I'm sorry I got so upset last night. Thanks for telling me everything – it must have been awfully difficult for you. Maybe now everything's in the open, I can help in some way.'

'I don't think there's anything you need to do,' he reflected quietly. 'You are you. You are perfect. You are the woman I love and intend to marry. I have to sort it, that's all. And I'm absolutely determined to walk away from the past and firmly into the present.'

Helen breathed a sigh of relief; she believed him, she trusted him, and surely fate could not be so cruel as to deny them each other.

'What about the other lady?'

'I don't know. I've hoped over the years that, despite our arrangement, she would marry someone else. But she hasn't. And now she's thirty-two.'

'Younger than me,' observed Helen. 'Plenty young enough to find someone else.'

'Pretty old in my culture, though,' he responded, hopelessly.

Because Sam had patients to see at the clinic, Helen was left alone in his house. She skimmed *The Guardian* and *The Times*, poured more coffee and washed up the breakfast dishes. Sam had not, she realised, asked her to clear away all evidence of her presence in the house for his mother's arrival. Probably, though, she ought to. That would be a courteous way to behave, even though it angered her that she should have to. Their relationship to date had not been constrained or clandestine, and she was offended that now, somehow, it was being forced into that mode.

She ran upstairs to the bedroom, opened the wardrobe and found a pair of leather trousers, two sweaters and her boots. She shrugged her shoulders then proceeded to pull them out and bundle them up. In the bathroom, she was taking up a whole shelf with her skin care and cosmetics. They would certainly have to be cleared. She searched around for a bag to put them in. There was a Harrods carrier in one of Sam's drawers. At least this was to be an upmarket removal. She crammed all her items into it, trying to suppress a fear that this removal of her presence might end up by being permanent.

The phone rang. It would be Sam. She sprinted back to the bedroom to pick up the extension by his side of the bed.

93

'Darling,' he sounded breathless. 'All the way over here, I kept thinking that either I should have told you everything before now, or that perhaps I should have just struggled with it on my own and sorted it. I don't know about anything any more…'

'Sam,' she interrupted him. 'Can I ask you something?'

'Of course.'

'You don't think that I should feel that you're as good as married and bow out honourably, do you?'

As the words spilled out of her, she was surprised by them. Until that moment, she had not realised she was thinking along those lines.

'No! Categorically, no. I'm going to make this right, Helen. I want to come home and be with you, but I'll need to hang on a while longer. I, uh, I lost a patient this morning.'

She was silent for a moment before speaking. 'I'm so, so sorry. And here I am bleating on and…'

'I know. It was a routine bypass. I did it yesterday. He was quite poorly, but I didn't expect him to die. Shortly after I got here this morning, he just went. No reason, really. Except, I wonder what he had to live for. Apart from his elderly sister – and I'm going to have to go and talk to her in a moment – it sounds as if there was nobody in his life.'

'Maybe he didn't have sufficient reason to fight.'

'I'll probably dismiss it as that because it'll help me feel better, but it's too simplistic. I'll see his sister in a moment, then I'll write up my report and come home. I wondered if you'd like to go to the National Portrait Gallery to that exhibition of thirties photography?'

'I'd love it. Shall I come into town to save you driving back out here?'

'No, don't. I want to come home and get out of this suit, but also, to be quite honest, I need to hold you. I'll be there as soon as I can. Helen… I've told you before that I've never been in love with anyone as I am with you. Never forget I adore you.'

'I won't. In any case, I intend having you around every day of my life, so you can keep telling me.'

He laughed. 'That's my girl. Stay happy.'

Helen felt reassured and yet restless in his house without him. She opted to listen to some music. She almost picked out Britten's *War Requiem*, but then rejected it. Perhaps she should have played it for Sam's patient, but she was too afraid for herself. The only end she feared was the possible untimely death of their love affair. She chose Elkie Brooks instead.

Breathing deeply, she wandered around the house until she came to a halt in front of the Tom Merrifield sculpture she had noticed on her first visit. It was remarkably fine – and lyrical. The young dancer was poised in preparation for what Helen thought was probably called a 'posé turn'. It was like one frame of a film, with all the suggestion of a joyous, spinning movement to follow. Gazing at it and marvelling at its creation, while indulging her ears with the glorious sounds of her favourite singer, she found tranquillity. It was almost a religious moment, and she clung to it, in the hope it might sustain her.

When Sam returned, she walked calmly to greet him. He kissed her deeply and lovingly, and they stood together, swaying slightly, almost merging one into the other.

Suddenly, he saw her clothes hanging on the hat stand and the large Harrods carrier bag on the floor beneath them. 'What's this?'

'I'm moving out, aren't I?'

'What are you trying to tell me?'

'Nothing. I just thought I was doing the right thing. There's not much point in my not sleeping here if there are signs around the place that I do so as a rule.'

'Oh, Helen.' He brushed his hair back off his forehead. 'What a mess. Is it too early to have a drink?'

She smiled, mistily. 'Maybe not.'

He made them both a large gin and tonic and led her to the sofa. As he sat next to her, he put the drinks on the table beside him and then leant into her and kissed her, lightly and tenderly. Suddenly, his lips hardened on hers. He was all over her, as if he were trying to possess every fragment of her body and mind. He tore the bottom half of her clothing away and quickly unzipped his trousers and, kneeling before her, he entered her with an urgency that she had never known before. He began to sob, and with each thrust he cried out her name. She was squashed. Her neck was bent backwards awkwardly and she was pinned down by his full weight upon her.

Suddenly, she felt the full flood of his climax flowing into her. He shuddered and moaned as if he were in pain, then collapsed.

She had to move eventually. Sam was totally disoriented – breathless, sweating and rambling. For a second, she feared he was going to have a heart attack. She persuaded him to lie down, full length, on the sofa, and she sat, still half-naked beside him, stroking his brow and encouraging the Sam she knew, understood and depended upon to reappear. At length his gasps for breath subsided into little sighs, which turned into deep breathing and he fell asleep.

She gazed at him, this weary man, and realised that no matter what her anxiety was, it could only be a fraction of his. She lay down beside him, uncomfortably, on the edge of the sofa, and held him in the hope that her warmth and support might somehow lighten his troubled dreams. Then she too, exhausted by the pull and influence of a vastly different culture, just a short flight away, closed her eyes and sought oblivion.

Chapter Seven

Oblivion lasts only if you're dead, of course, she thought, as she had to accept that she was, most unfortunately, wide awake.

She had woken up several times during the night and then in the morning had turned over, abandoning herself to the unaccustomed expanse of the whole bed. But there was little enjoyment to be had now that she had squeezed out every last drop of slumber.

Before Sam, she had had a ritual for Saturdays going into Sundays and had regarded it as her special time for relaxing and recharging her batteries. Routinely, she had unplugged the phone, shut her alarm clock away in a drawer and slept till she could sleep no more. Then, she had spent several hours, in bed, reading all the newspapers, which she had delivered.

It was curiously ironic that only last week, she had cancelled her newspaper order because, since she and Sam had been together, she had spent most weekends at his place.

She sighed. With no paper delivery, she was going to have to go and face the outside world.

Back home again, with her pint of milk and bundle of publications, she rejected the idea of returning to bed and instead made tea and toast, sat at the kitchen table and tried to focus on catching up with the world news. It was half past eleven and Sam would be making his house ready for his mother's visit and, later, driving to the airport to meet her.

Her mind kept wandering and she found herself going over and over everything that Sam had told her the previous day.

After their strange sexual encounter, they had both slept for a couple of hours but had then spent what was left of Saturday in Camden Town.

'I used to have a flat here,' he had said.

She wondered why he had never told her that before.

'When I was a registrar,' he had continued, 'I tried to live on my salary. It didn't last long, I'd been too spoiled!'

It was as if, now that he had told her his deepest, darkest secret, he was prepared to share lesser ones. 'In truth, my family are so wealthy I need never work again if I didn't want to.'

Helen was surprised. She had assumed that his house, his car and every other acquisition had been financed by a more than adequate salary. She felt awkward. What else did she not know about him? Was he, at all, the person she had believed in, and thought him to be? There were no answers, only questions – endless questions.

He had wanted to drive her back to Holland Park and to sleep with her. She had refused both offers. So, she had left him and made her own way home.

Why, she asked herself on this lonely Sunday morning, had she stopped him coming here? She wished he was with her now. But she had told him that they both needed time to think. She suspected that she had been trying to punish him – or was it herself?

The papers palled. She took a bath, put a treatment on her hair, and a pack on her face, then she shaved her legs and painted her toenails – and it was still only twelve forty-five. She grinned wryly, remembering the vintage *Hancock's Half Hour* on the subject of boring Sundays. She plugged in the phone and, after looking up the number, called Deirdre.

'Hi.'

'Who's that?'

'Helen.'

'Didn't I use to know you?'

'Don't be like that! Do you want to play tennis?'

'It's the end of December, Helen.'

'It's sunny, though.'

She walked down the street to where she had parked her Saab a few days previously. What an age ago that seemed now.

She loved her car: it represented the life she had achieved for herself, but she rarely drove it nowadays. Quite apart from considerations about drinking and driving, Sam had driven them much of the time since she had met him. But as she drove away and the vehicle gathered speed, she rediscovered a sense of satisfaction at the feel of the steering wheel in her hands, and the power under the bonnet. Being alone wasn't so bad.

Deirdre was waiting at the hospital tennis court. She was a friend from Helen's schooldays, and was now a consultant paediatrician.

Helen began the game shakily, but soon had her old chum running around the court. She felt her full weight guiding every hit and focused on the ball as though her life depended on it. Usually, she was content to play ground strokes from the back of the court, but today she jumped on every short ball and volleyed it away.

After half an hour, Deirdre gasped, 'That's enough. Quite enough. I don't know what's got into you. Let's go to the canteen.'

They walked from the tennis court into the hospital, slipping back into easy companionship. Months passed – sometimes years – between meetings but their relationship, always uncomplicated, never altered.

'Are you still seeing the ever-aloof Sam Aziz?'

'Is that what you think of him?'

'Doesn't everybody? If you've found what makes him tick, you're a rare beast. How long have you been together?'

99

'About a couple of months, I think.' Helen decided not to be too accurate.

'Well, I tell you, I'm surprised. I always thought he was a completely cold fish.'

'He isn't at all.' Helen's voice was defensive. 'How do you know him anyway?'

'I don't, really. But you can't be in medicine in London and be unaware of him. I always thought he was only interested in the job. Still, you're not much different.'

'What do you mean?'

'Oh, come on, Helen. Remember the old crowd? No, you probably don't. We all get together from time to time. Your name comes up – no one's ever seen you, except on the box. It's just how it is, I suppose. But why do some people sink themselves in their work to the exclusion of everything else? I don't know. It probably makes for success, but does the job do that to people, or do people do that to the job?'

Helen smiled sweetly, changing the subject. 'I'm going to go mad and have the shepherd's pie.'

Later, as Sunday evening spread uninvitingly before her, she reminded herself that this wasn't Hancock's East Cheam, this was Holland Park and there was lots going on. She had options. It was just a question of choosing one.

Suddenly, she remembered that the TV company's ski club was holding a meeting at the social club that evening, to discuss their forthcoming trip – and though she was not a member, she decided to join them.

A short Tube ride later, she was greeted with smiles and not a little surprise. 'Coming skiing then, Helen?' someone asked.

'Probably not. But I could murder a drink.'

'You old lush!' It was Ian, Laura's partner.

'Hey, good to see you.' She leant over and kissed his cheek. 'I'd forgotten you'd be here. Thanks for Wednesday, by the way. It was great.'

'Yes, it was,' he agreed. 'Where's wonder boy?'

'Um, a bit tied up with family stuff. His mother is visiting.'

Laura came up. 'What? I didn't know she was expected.'

'Neither did I till Friday night.'

'Is everything OK?' Laura asked.

'It's fine,' lied Helen. 'I'd forgotten what it was to have a day and an evening to myself. I'm enjoying it.'

'Well, before Sam you rarely had one; you were always out doing personal appearances! Are you sure you're all right though? You look tired and frightfully skinny.'

'The Duchess of Windsor said: "You can't be too thin or too rich!".'

'Lot of good it did her in the end!'

'Laura, can I ask you something?'

'Of course.'

'I saw Deirdre today. You remember her – we went to school together.'

'Yeah. I met her at a couple of your parties.'

'Well, would you say I'm aloof? Do I give the impression of being self-sufficient and wrapped up in the job?'

'Yes, you do!'

'I don't.'

'You do – and you did ask.'

'I don't see myself like that at all,' Helen mused.

'Don't you?'

'No! Well, I don't think so.' She sighed. 'I'm not sure I know myself at all… To be honest, things are *not* quite right, and I don't think I can bear it. I love Sam so much, Laura. Frankly, it isn't easy for me to admit that to you, but I do. I'm lost without him, and I don't like it.'

'What's going wrong?'

'I can't really tell you but, you see, he's everything to me. It's the first time it's all come together – love, friendship, passion. I can't do without it.'

'Well, I don't think you have to. Surely you're not nervous just because his mother's coming?'

Helen shrugged her shoulders.

'Listen, it'll all be fine. Won't she be delighted to see her self-contained son ready to settle? Of course she will – and even if she isn't, wait till you present her with a grandchild! Look, Helen, you've got it bad, but so has he. Don't lose your sense of proportion.'

An hour later, walking from Holland Park station to her home, she looked around her to check if anyone was watching, and then kicked a small stone and ran after it kicking it again and again till it rolled down a grating.

Upstairs, in the emptiness of her own flat, she called her mother. She was not sure why, for she had nothing to say, but she was *not* feeling aloof and self-sufficient and was hungry for human contact.

Later, just as she climbed into bed, the phone rang. She had forgotten to unplug it after the call.

'Where have you been all day?' Sam demanded.

'Out, mostly. How's your mother?'

'She's fine. She's in bed now. She was tired.'

The conversation continued, with neither of them discussing what was really on their minds. At last he said, 'I've missed you.'

'Have you?'

'Massively. Obviously, it's great to have my mother here. I do love her, though we find it difficult to get close, but I've thought about you so much. I've told her about you, by the way.'

'Oh!'

'Look – I'm not working tomorrow. What are you doing?'

'There's a New Year's Eve programme but I'm free after that.'

'Good. I'll get my mother to watch you, and then maybe, if I can get some tickets to something good, we could go to the theatre.'

'That's a great idea. And it might make the initial meeting rather more relaxed.'

'Hmmn.'

'Look, Sam. Let me get tickets for something. I've got a few contacts who sometimes let me have the house seats if they haven't allocated them to the backers or whatever.'

'Helen.' His voice was quiet and anxious. 'You do care for me, don't you?'

'Of course. Absolutely. You know that.'

'Good. It's just that you suddenly sounded so efficient.'

'Oh God, not you too.'

'What?'

'It doesn't matter. I do – anyway. I care for you hugely.'

'Good. Helen, please always remember that I love you.'

'You often put things that way. And it always feels sad when you do. Why don't you just say, "I love you"?'

'I don't think I know. It means the same, doesn't it?'

'I'm not sure.'

He appeared to ignore the uncertainty in her voice.

'Helen,' he whispered. 'Are you in bed?'

'Yes.'

'Will you turn onto your side now and imagine that I'm curled up behind you. Can you imagine the feel of me behind you, becoming more and more aroused as I hold you?'

She closed her eyes. 'I can,' she murmured.

'I love you. Go to sleep now. Remembering those feelings.'

The next evening, Helen was nervous, and it was no help that she had decided – despite it being New Year's Eve and a time for merriment as a rule – to drink sparingly and remain sober. She could not predict how the encounter with Sam's mother would go. This was, after all, a meeting that might hold the key to her future happiness. But at least she could keep her wits about her and remain in control of her behaviour.

'You look fabulous,' Laura told her as she entered their shared dressing room just as Helen was putting the finishing touches to her appearance. 'New outfit?'

'Yes.' Helen beamed. 'Sam's Christmas present to me. He had it designed specially. Wonderful, isn't it?'

'Amazing. When are you going to meet his mother?'

'Rather too soon! I've managed to get us into *Forty-Second Street*. Do you remember, I interviewed some of the cast and producer just before it opened? I called in the favour, as it were! Lucky, eh?'

'About time you accepted the odd perk. You never do as a rule. Let's hope the mother loves it. Everyone else seems to. I'm sure she'll fall under your spell too. Go and sock it to her. Think of it as another performance.'

In spite of her anxiety, Helen felt a little thrill of excitement as she walked into the Theatre Royal, Drury Lane. Because of her background, she had an insider's knowledge into the build-up of tension backstage and of how much the audience could contribute to making an evening great. Luckily everyone waiting in the foyer seemed to be buzzing with expectation, and the energy as they mingled together was palpable. Soon, they would be in the auditorium, and the orchestra would start drifting into the pit, tuning up and laughing among themselves. Meanwhile, the artists would be behind the tabs, humming to warm up their voices or loosening up at the barre at the side of the stage then, reluctantly, removing the leg warmers that were keeping them cosy till curtain up.

'There you are, Helen.'

Her heart leapt, and her eyes sparkled as they met his. God, he was so magnificent. So, everything. He kissed her and somehow contrived to stroke her breast as he steered her to meet his mother. She leant against him for reassurance as they threaded their way through all the people queuing to buy programmes.

Having told her that his parent favoured a French title to an English one, Helen spoke quickly as soon as she spied the lady.

'Madame Aziz, how lovely you look. Welcome. I'm delighted to meet you.'

Sam's mother was dressed entirely in black apart from a silver-mink jacket. Helen was slightly taken aback – but perhaps the anti-fur campaigns had not reached Egypt.

The older lady's jewellery was exquisite though and her legs were in such good shape that it was hard to believe that she was seventy. She was much shorter than Helen had imagined – even though she was wearing three-inch heels – but nonetheless, she was, obviously, a formidable presence; a force to be reckoned with.

Taking the older woman's hands in hers, Helen kissed her first on one cheek and then the other, hoping that this would be seen as a suitable greeting.

Sam disappeared to order drinks for the interval, leaving Helen feeling apprehensive about what best to say.

'How was your journey?' she began.

She wished Sam would return but began to relax when his mother answered her in perfect English with just a hint of a French accent. Her journey had been fine, she said, and she added that she had enjoyed watching Helen's programme. She then fingered Helen's outfit and remarked how fine it was. Helen was thrilled and quickly explained that it had been a Christmas present from Sam, but as she did so, she found herself wondering if she was being too frank, too soon. Was she implying a level of intimacy between her and Sam that his mother might find unacceptable? She sighed inwardly. How difficult it was to know what to do or say.

The conversation continued with Madame Aziz graciously thanking Helen for arranging the tickets. She said how much she loved West End theatre and how excited she was to be back at Drury Lane.

Helen began to unwind as she realised that she was looking into eyes that were very like Sam's. Not identical; definitely not as warm in their expression but not hostile either.

As Sam returned, Helen beamed at him and watched as the anxious look he had been wearing began to disappear at finding the two women deep in conversation.

In the stalls, he directed his mother into the row first, then put Helen in the middle and sat himself on the aisle. She would have preferred him to sit between his mother and her, but she recognised that he was making a statement that she was part of the family scenario.

As the lights dimmed, his hand reached for hers and squeezed it gently. Helen responded gratefully, then glanced at his mother. As the first notes boomed out of the orchestra pit, the older woman's expression was one of happy anticipation and when the dancing began, with the curtain rising slowly on a stage full of talented, tapping feet, she applauded heartily. Helen breathed out and smiled at Sam in the half light and he raised her right hand to his lips and kissed it.

'It went much better than I dared to hope,' he said – not for the first time – when later they sat outside her flat, in his car.

The three of them had enjoyed dinner together in a little restaurant in Covent Garden and at midnight had joined hands with the other diners to sing 'Auld Lang Syne'. Helen had longed to throw herself into Sam's arms and feel the urgent pressure of his lips against her own. But in his mother's presence, she had contented herself with a kiss on the cheek and a quick hug.

'Next year!' he had whispered. And she had felt her spirits soar.

'Yes,' Helen agreed. 'I think your mother had a pleasant evening.'

Sam pulled her close. 'Darling, I love you so, so much. And it's really important that my mother likes you.'

'Is it?'

'Yes. I love her – but, to be honest, I hate her too. However, her hold over me is absolute. I can never escape it. She's impossible, yet wonderful. Do you know, when she writes me a letter, which she does once a week – I always look at how she's signed off before I read the rest of it, just to see if I am in favour or not. I've lived away from her for most of my life and yet I crave her love and approval. Most of the time, I feel I don't have it.'

'I'm sure she loves you. I'm amazed you feel so insecure about her.'

'It's complicated.' His voice broke slightly. 'But what I know now is that you show me more love than I've ever had, or even believed possible. I need you, Helen. Please don't give up on me.'

As if I could, she thought, in the quietness of her own flat as she went over and over the happenings of the evening they had just spent as a trio – and mulled over their significance.

As the days passed, Helen became fond of Sam's mother and could not help but be impressed by the way she masterminded the family business – though technically, she discovered, it was run by Sam's two younger brothers.

This was a source of great surprise to her. Sam had never thought to mention his siblings and she had assumed that, like her, he was an only child.

When she had asked him about them, he had shrugged and said that he hardly knew them – and they were very different people from him.

She learned more from Madame Aziz, as she chatted about her family one day over tea.

'I'm a mixture of Arab and European. I love Egypt. It's my home. But I have always been too independent to be a good wife in the Middle Eastern sense. Fortunately, Ahmed – my husband Ahmed, that is – loved me for what I was. He was the most brilliant and remarkable man. None of his sons measure up to him.'

Helen glanced at Sam and saw that he was hurt by his mother's words. She jumped to his defence.

'But Sam's a famous surgeon. He gives life to people who otherwise would have no hope. That's a wonderful thing to do. Surely you applaud that?'

Madame Aziz laughed, though without much humour. 'Ah, this Ahmed,' she countered, 'was born to be different. He's always gone his own way. It was my husband's idea that he came to school here. But when I saw how that changed him – maybe he was always the strange one – I decided not to risk it with the other two. I put my foot down. They did go to English schools but in Alexandria, not here.'

Sam remained quiet all evening until he drove Helen back to her flat.

'Well, it hasn't taken long, has it?' His voice had a bitter tone that was unfamiliar to her. 'She's been here less than a fortnight, but the criticisms are beginning as well as the disapproval and the comparisons with my father. I'm sorry I'm not the son she wanted, but I can't really help that.'

Helen could not understand the paradox. Sam's mother was half-European herself and yet she seemed determined to suppress this cultural heritage in her offspring.

What could she say to help? It was hard. And what was harder still was that all their meaningful conversations these days seemed to take place in the dark interior of his car or hers.

'You know, Sam,' she ventured, 'maybe this isn't such a bad time, or won't be when you look back on it. Maybe you'll use it to sort out exactly what you feel about your mother, your family and your country and… the lady back home. And maybe, although it's difficult, we should be glad to have this opportunity of taking our relationship back a step.'

'What are you trying to say?' He sounded upset and angry. 'Is there someone else? Don't you want me any more?'

'Oh my God, Sam…' she sighed and then pulled him to her and kissed him. 'Of course I do. More and more. I'm trying to say and do the right thing. And to be honourable and grown up, I suppose. Please understand.'

'This is terrible,' he murmured.

'I know. But what I'm trying to say – badly – is that maybe it needn't be, and perhaps it isn't.'

Had he understood, she wondered, as she let herself into her empty flat. She felt truly alone now – like she had before she had known him. And that feeling compounded the anxiety she had felt in Sam's company. She had tasted paradise in the weeks she and Sam had been together before his mother had arrived, and the growing sense that she was losing it made her not just anguished, but panic-stricken.

There was no point in trying to sleep so she scanned her shelves for something to read that might absorb her mind. There were books she had reviewed, books she ought to read, books she had read and might read again. But what would fit the bill now?

Eventually, she selected a slim volume by Anita Brookner. In bed, she read the first page, and then the next; it was like licking a cream cake slowly. She was some way through chapter four when the phone rang.

'Helen…'

'Sam, you should be asleep.'

'So should you.'

'I know.'

'Listen, Helen. I've just had a call to say that a young man's dying after a road accident in Holland and his parents are willing to donate his organs. You know that Laura's been doing this piece on me? Well, they've been waiting for something like this to happen, so we're all flying to Amsterdam. Then I'll come back and go straight into theatre and tackle the transplant. But this means I have to change our plans for tomorrow.'

'Of course, Sam. This is important. Who's going to have the operation?'

'A very sick man from Dublin. They're contacting him now.'

She felt so proud of him and what he was able to achieve. 'Well, go carefully. This couldn't have happened at a better time. Your mother will *have* to understand how important your life is here now. This will bring it home to her, I love you, my darling. More than you will ever know.'

'And I love you. Desperately. And if I don't have you to myself soon, my balls are going to explode!'

109

She laughed. 'I'll go and be with your mother tomorrow evening while you're working.'

'You don't have to do that.'

'I want to, though.'

The next day was one where there was little news about, so at the morning meeting, Helen learned that she was to interview the author of a book called *Food for the Taking*.

'Are we just talking,' she asked the researcher who was setting up the feature, 'or is he planning to do anything practical?'

'He's asked for a country-kitchen set because he wants to demonstrate some of the dishes. It's all stuff you can get from hedgerows, he says. You can discuss the menu when he arrives – which should be about two-thirty.'

'Has he got any television experience?' Derek the editor asked with a slightly weary air.

The researcher shook his head.

'Oh God. Let's record it then,' Derek suggested. 'I don't think we should risk it live – not with all those food things and props. He won't have a clue how to angle them to camera. We'll record at three-thirty.'

The author was much as Helen had expected – bearded, wearing a huge sweater and thong sandals. He was, she thought, a bit of a caricature, but for all that, she found herself quite won over by him once they began to chat. He was articulate, and a real enthusiast.

'So,' he said, 'I thought I could run through how to make woodlice and slug dip, squirrel casserole and worm and apple pie.'

'Are you joking?'

'Absolutely not.'

'Oh my God. Is this the sort of meal you actually eat yourself?'

'Not all the time,' he admitted. 'But it's all excellent protein.'

'Well, there's no doubt it'll make good television,' she laughed. 'But I can't promise I'm going to sample any of it myself!'

They discussed whether or not they should record the squirrel being prepared, but it was going to take too long, so that idea was jettisoned. But they did decide to show some raw slugs and wood-lice in a glass jar before they cooked them.

Really, she thought, this item is getting more bizarre by the minute.

After a quick rehearsal with the three cameramen, and the director making rude comments about the guest in her ear, Helen began the interview by asking the author about preparing the squirrel.

'Oh, it's easy, you just skin and gut it like you would a rabbit.'

'Mmmn,' she remarked. 'I can't say I've ever eaten rabbit myself, let alone skinned one. And to be honest, I think I prefer to see squirrels running around rather than in a casserole.'

'They are vermin though,' countered the author, which made Helen less inclined than ever to taste the finished product. But when it came to it, she took a deep breath and swallowed a mouthful – after all, it was much less frightening than being in the lions' cage.

The crawling woodlice and slugs, on the other hand, did not tempt her – even though she was assured that, once fried, they were crunchy and delightful and really delicious when mixed with sour cream and chives.

She noticed that the floor manager was looking distinctly squeamish. Poor man.

'So,' she turned to camera and grinned, 'I'm sure this interview has gone far too quickly for many of you to take it all in, so don't forget the title of the book which will tell you much, much more about the delights of nature's free food. It's called *Food for the Taking* and it's written by my guest today, Robert Ashenhurst.'

The recording ended with a long freeze in close-up of the cooked food. This would make it easier to cut to Helen in the studio later in the live programme.

'Helen!' the floor manager called across to her. 'How many people are going to be throwing up all over their high tea this evening then? God that was revolting. As if anyone in their right mind would want to feast on that. Blimey, I've seen it all now... No disrespect, sir,' he added as an afterthought in the direction of the departing author.

Sam's mother was not expecting her when she turned up. But the older woman quickly recovered her poise and asked what the squirrel casserole had been like.

'Oh, please don't remind me,' Helen laughed. 'I still have the taste in my mouth. Shall we have a drink? Here or, I could take you somewhere nice.'

'Here is fine,' Madame Aziz seemed slightly ill at ease at having Helen to herself, but she went to Sam's kitchen to find a bottle of chilled Chablis, a corkscrew and two glasses and indicated to Helen that she should open it.

Sam's mother rarely drank alcohol, so Helen was surprised that soon she had to refill the older woman's glass. They chatted about nothing in particular, but Helen sensed that they both had Sam on their mind. Should she, she wondered, in his absence, broach the subject of their relationship? Would it help? Might it hinder? While she was considering how best to start, Madame Aziz jumped in with her own question.

'Are you going to marry Ahmed?'

Helen almost answered 'Who?' before remembering that his mother never referred to her son as Sam. 'Why do you ask?' she managed.

'Because he's never acted like this before and he's never come close to marriage either.'

Helen knew that the second statement was untrue. Had his mother wanted the arranged marriage as much as Sam's father had? Was it a painful memory? Had she simply obliterated the past from her mind? She tried to keep her voice calm as she responded with the words, 'Perhaps you ought to ask him?'

'I couldn't do that.' His mother's voice was terse and uncompromising. 'We don't have conversations of that type.'

'Well, I don't think I should answer on his behalf,' Helen murmured.

'I was nearly twenty-five when he was born,' recalled his mother. 'I didn't marry till I was twenty-three which was quite old then in my country. My husband was considerably older than that. I admired him so very much. I loved him too, but once we had the number of children we wanted, I never slept with him again. I didn't need that. It was enough to love him as a brother. Maybe there's something wrong with me. I am not very close to any of my children. It's probably because I find it hard to be tactile. I could never behave with anyone like he does with you. He gazes at you, he touches you, you embrace… It's really rather disgusting.' She spat out the last word.

Helen was taken aback. She had a fleeting image of Sam as a small boy and wondered if his mother had ever held or hugged him. His hunger for love was making more sense by the second.

'Sometimes,' his mother continued, 'I almost feel I've missed out. But when I see how other people mess up their lives with passion and drama, well, I'm glad I'm like me.'

Mercifully, the two women heard Sam's key in the lock at that moment. He came into the sitting room, smiling but looked ashen with tiredness. 'What are you two talking about?' he asked.

'Just girl-talk,' Helen answered and she saw a look of something akin to gratitude spreading over his mother's face.

Sam's exhausted appearance made Helen long to take him into her arms. But the word 'disgusting' had wrought its damage. As a result, she contented herself with a peck on the cheek and a quick squeeze of his arm before she disappeared to the kitchen where she rustled up omelettes and salad.

The conversation between the three of them was stilted and uneasy and Helen was aware of looking at her watch and wondering how soon she might escape to her own flat and her own company so that she could think.

'I'll just phone for a taxi,' she announced when she felt sufficient time had elapsed for her departure not to seem rude.

'No!' His voice was full of urgency. 'I'll drive you.'

'It's not necessary, Sam. You're tired. Stay here and talk to your mother. I'll be fine. You've had an extremely long day. You need to rest and sleep.'

'No,' he said again, quietly but firmly. 'I'll take you.' Turning to his parent, he said, 'I'm sure you'll be all right, Mother. I won't be long.'

'Of course, Ahmed,' she replied. 'There's a film I want to watch on TV. Your television is so much better than ours. Do you know,' she turned to Helen, 'they even stopped showing *Dallas* in Egypt because it was thought that it might adversely affect the morals of the peasants? Mind you, I think the powers-that-be had a point.'

'Oh, that's um, quite uh, a decision, isn't it? Well, enjoy your movie. I hope it's... entertaining,' Helen said, weakly. 'I'll see you soon.'

'Will you be here tomorrow?'

'Unfortunately, no. I have to drive to Northampton after my programme. I'm compering the second half of a charity concert there. I'll be back awfully late.'

'Drive carefully, Helen.' Madame Aziz was nothing if not proper.

Helen was expecting them to walk through the kitchen to the garage, but Sam steered her out of the front door and along the icy pavement by the river. It was bitterly cold and every surface was covered with a film of frost. Treading warily, they walked on to the pub where he bought them both a brandy.

She watched as he gulped at his drink. He should not be considering driving now – especially as he was so tired. Not in these conditions.

'Sam, please do something for me. It's an awful night, there's no way anyone should be driving if they don't need to. Let me get a taxi. It would be better for us both.'

'Helen,' he snapped, 'after a long, long day, I'm enjoying having you to myself. I don't want to hear your reasoning. I'm driving you and that's that.'

114

'You don't have to tell me off,' she said in a small, quiet voice. 'I was only trying to be considerate.'

He smiled. 'Sweetheart, I know. I do know. You've been marvellous since my mother came. You've come out with her and made her welcome and been bright and lively and made her feel special. You didn't have to do all that.'

'It hasn't been a chore. I like and admire her – though she frightens me a bit.'

'What were the two of you talking about when I came home?'

'I'm not sure I should disclose that. It was surprisingly intimate. But she did ask if we were going to marry.'

'Old busybody.'

'Don't be like that, Sam. A few weeks ago, you told me you wanted to resolve the past so that you could move into the present. She's taking an interest. That's what you wanted.'

He sighed. 'I'm sorry. My mother always did have the ability to make me feel as though I were a schoolboy caught cheating in an exam.'

'In her own way, I'm sure she loves you a lot. It may be no bad thing that the two of you will spend the evening tomorrow without me.'

He shrugged then drained his glass and got to his feet. She almost asked him again if he was sure about driving but managed to restrain herself.

They walked through the pub to the road. His car was parked outside his garage. Inside the vehicle, he switched on the engine and the heater, then he held her as they warmed up, and kissed her, hungrily, before moving off in the direction of Holland Park.

As the temperature rose, he let his left hand drop from the steering wheel and stretched over and stroked her thigh. Her breathing became more audible as he found his way inside her clothes. He drew to a halt by the kerb and caressed her with increasing speed till an overwhelming sense of pleasure and relief swept through her body.

'Good,' she could feel his smile though could not see it. 'That's to keep you going till I get you home.'

Once in her flat, they made straight for the bedroom. They wasted no time on stroking or romantic endearments or tender love-play but tore their clothes off in a frenzy. In bed, he lay full length on her and they clung together wordlessly. She kneaded his buttocks and felt his hardness almost immediately. They made love ferociously. She climaxed and felt him abandon himself to the intensity of their passion as his cries joined hers. They lay, breathless and entwined, knowing they must not sleep.

'I hate this, don't you?' she said at last. 'Having to be so furtive, it makes me feel cheap somehow. That's not what I want to feel.'

'I know, angel. But you're not cheap. And neither am I. This state of affairs won't go on, I promise. We're going to get married. I can't live without you, and I *won't*.'

With that assurance, he leapt off the bed and was dressed in seconds.

'Sam, calm down,' she cautioned him. 'Please. And when you get out in those frosty conditions, please drive carefully.'

He smiled, and his expression grew calmer. Then, he blew her a kiss from the doorway and was gone.

The next day passed without incident in the office. Certainly, there was nothing to compare with the slug and woodlice dip on the previous programme. She was amused, though, by the number of telephone complaints they had received about that item.

Her major concern as the hours passed was the dreadful weather. For all that Northampton was a straight run up the motorway, the evening forecast was full of dire warnings of hazardous conditions with long stretches of freezing fog. The Met Office presenter on the programme urged anyone who had no need to travel to stay home. She wished she could comply, but her engagement was a longstanding one, and she was not about to disappoint the organisers of the concert.

The public relations department who had arranged for her to compere the concert rang to suggest that they should book her into a hotel in Northampton so that she had no need to travel back to London late at night when the conditions would probably be even worse.

'Can you get me into anywhere?' Helen asked.

'No problem,' said the girl. 'Apparently the nearest hotel to the concert hall has had loads of cancellations today because of the conditions.'

'OK, well in that case, don't bother booking. I'll see how it goes. Obviously, I'd sooner get home if I can, but if it's too terrible, I'll book myself into the hotel and come back first thing in the morning.'

The road was as bad as she feared. She was a good driver, and an experienced one, but she found the journey more and more frightening. Normally, she loathed being stuck behind large lorries, but on this occasion, she tucked herself up fairly close to the back of one, and let him guide her through the fog.

Eventually, she left the motorway and negotiated her way to the concert hall and into the parking place reserved for her. The stage door keeper was hovering, and as it was almost nine o'clock and the second half was due to start in ten minutes, she allowed herself to be hurried into a dressing room and quickly changed into her favourite evening dress, a cream lace creation by Christina Stambolian. It was a fairy-tale frock and she always felt good in it.

There was a knock on her door and she opened it to find the family who were running the concert jumping up and down in excitement at her arrival. She had met them before at another charity event.

'How's my girl,' she asked as she lifted Samantha, the child whose health had sparked off years of fundraising. 'Gosh, you're heavy now,' she laughed.

'Well I am ten!'

Helen put her down gently. 'Goodness, so you are.' She turned to the child's parents whose eyes were misty with emotion. They were remarkable people. And, as they had often told her, every day that this little girl survived, felt like a bonus.

Samantha had been born with a hole in her heart and, because of that, her lungs were severely damaged. Faced with a hopeless prognosis, this very ordinary couple had thrown all their energy into raising funds which not only paid for an intensive nocturnal oxygen programme for their daughter but helped other similar children to be cared for too. Against all the odds, Samantha was surviving. She would always be tinier than most girls of her age, but she was alive. And she was as engaging and spirited as a normal child, as Helen was quickly reminded when she turned around and found Samantha playing with her make-up and smearing a bright red lipstick onto her little lips.

The parents rounded on her.

'You can't be cross with her, honestly. She's such a pet,' said Helen.

However, they were angry and made Samantha apologise and remarked that though their child might be a walking miracle, that did not entitle her to be a spoiled brat.

Helen ran through the details of the acts in the second half just to check that they had all managed to get through the bad weather to perform. She was amazed at the number of big names on the bill and surprised too to be told that the theatre was almost full. It never ceased to amaze her how charitable so many people were. Or how many individuals were born with problems that impacted on their own lives and those of their families. She always felt that this kind of event gave her real perspective on her own life. It might be stressful – and indeed now her private life seemed to be chaos too – but that was nothing compared with the pain and suffering of so many other people.

It was a delightful and uplifting concert and Helen was able to forget the inclement weather outside and her own current troubles.

There was a party afterwards but as soon as she had swallowed a glass of tonic water and a ham sandwich she excused herself saying that she must drive back to London.

In truth, she had not decided as yet whether or not to brave the conditions, but she felt a real need to speak to Sam and went in search of the concert hall's manager to ask if she could call home.

'Where are you, Helen?' Sam answered his phone after one ring.

'Still in Northampton.'

'Are you OK? The weather's not too bad is it?'

'Not entirely sure. I haven't been outside since I arrived two hours ago.'

'Are you coming back? I, I... what I mean is, *could* you come back?'

'I haven't decided yet. I think I might have to check into a hotel.'

'I understand. But do come if you can.'

'Is something wrong?'

'Yes. My mother and I have had a blazing row.'

Her heart froze though she tried to keep her voice calm as she said, 'Well, we all row with our parents sometimes.'

'Not like this. I shouted and ranted and raved. It was terrible. She's stopped speaking to me and is upstairs packing and says that she's flying back to Egypt tomorrow.'

'That's awful. Really. For both of you. I'm on my way.'

'Helen! Listen. Don't drive fast. I should really be telling you to stay where you are. And perhaps you should. It's just I need you so much. But go steadily. It doesn't matter how late you are. I'll be waiting.'

The decision was made. She did not even stop to change her clothes but simply wrapped her big coat around her flimsy evening dress.

The cold air stung her face and her lungs, and she found herself breathing heavily as she stumbled in her high heels over the car park's uneven, frosty ground.

119

Still, there was one advantage to being mad enough to risk the M1 on such a night, which was that she had it almost entirely to herself. And she consoled herself with the thought that if she did, accidentally, drive off the road onto the hard shoulder, or go into a skid, at least she would not involve another vehicle or driver. At that moment, she felt the back wheels lose their traction and she slid out of control for a moment. The road surface was like an ice rink and despite Sam's warnings, she was not driving slowly, even though for much of the time the ghostly fog encased her in a cloudy bubble that would have been quite tranquil had it not been so terrifying.

It was a nightmare of a journey and she needed so much concentration that she did not dare even to put the radio on.

It was almost one o'clock by the time she rang Sam's doorbell. He said nothing as he let her in, simply took her in his arms as soon as he had shut the door against the cold. After a moment, he led her into the sitting room where he had lit a fire and handed her a generous measure of brandy which he had obviously poured in anticipation of her arrival.

'What happened?' Helen whispered.

He also kept his voice low. 'She was a bit off with me this morning. She had gone to bed last night before I returned from your flat. I suspect she resented being left alone for so long. Anyway, once I got home this evening, I was exposed to the full force of her displeasure. Apparently, I'm not half the man my father was, nor will I ever be. I've betrayed my country by not using my skills there. I've ruined Hamaida's life. And I'm denying my heritage by having a relationship with an English woman. There was more… I kept quiet as long as I could, then I got angry too. In fact, I completely lost it. I suppose it's been building up for years.'

Helen, trying hard to absorb everything he was telling her, murmured, 'I thought she was actually beginning to like me.'

'Helen, darling, it isn't personal.'

'It feels personal. Absolutely and overwhelmingly.'

She wept then as her pent up anxiety about tonight's drive and all the difficulties of the last few weeks finally exploded. He used his crisp white handkerchief to dab at her tears and then he cuddled her, swaying backwards and forwards in an attempt to soothe her pain.

'You adore your mother, don't you?' she asked when the sobbing subsided.

He sighed. 'I do. And yet I've never been able to please her. Do you know that even as a child I was never hugged by her. The problem is, as I've told you before, I feel European. I always have. That's to say, I have until recently. But now something is happening to me, and for the first time I feel more Egyptian and I do feel some anxiety about the fact that I work to save lives here and not there. I suppose it's partly that there's a growing sense at home that the country doesn't want to continue being as western as it has been. Maybe it was all the upheaval and fundamentalism that took hold in Iran six or seven years ago. I just don't know. But I feel things are changing and that there could be a lot of upheaval. Or course people who are devout Muslims have their own agenda and they're entitled to feel the way they do. But they do pose a threat to individuals who live like my family, and my mother is terrified of them. I mean, she's not someone who would ever go about with her head covered, let alone her face, but there could be a day when her sort of attitude may not be tolerated. It's hard to predict – but it's worrying.'

Helen's heart was thumping in her chest. 'So, is that one reason why you sometimes feel you should go home and be with Hamaida?'

To her horror, he nodded. 'Yes, yes it is.'

But perhaps, she wondered suddenly, there was another way. She savoured the new thoughts that were surprising her brain. She wanted to marry him. Perhaps she could only do so if she went back with him to Egypt and lived with him there. But could he ask that of her? Would he? She had always assumed that their married life would go on much like their single ones had. She would have her television career, even if it was compromised to a degree by having a family, and he would continue as a surgeon, in London. But what if their married life could only be in his country? Did she love him enough to follow him and make her home there? Her heart cried out that so long as she had him, she would do anything, but her head advised caution.

'Would it help,' she asked at last, 'supposing you could resolve the thing about Hamaida, if I gave up everything here and we settled in Egypt?'

Now his eyes filled with tears. 'My darling,' he replied, 'you can't comprehend the reality of what you're suggesting. Egypt is a very civilised country. It's a fine country. But it's nothing like you're used to. There'd be no job for you, at least not in television.'

Wordlessly, they sat, contemplating a life in which she kept house and waited for her lord and master to return to her at the end of each working day. She could sense that he was no more convinced that they could live like that than she was.

Their love, their fear, their frustration and their anxiety mounted. He pulled her down onto the carpeted floor and made love to her, gently covering her mouth with his hand when she moaned aloud in relief fused with dreadful despair.

Chapter Eight

The lights in her mirror were annoyingly, and dangerously, close. They were distracting her attention from the icy road and making it even less clear just where the kerb was on this freezing, foggy night.

She pulled in to allow the pursuer to pass and saw, too late, that he was a policeman.

God, that's all I need, she thought, as the car pulled in, blocking her own vehicle. How large a measure of brandy had she drunk? she wondered. It was stupid to have had a drink at all, particularly since she had eaten nothing but a tiny sandwich since lunchtime. Quickly, she stepped out of her car.

'Bit late to be out and about, madam.' The routine remark bristled with smugness.

Helen's heart was thumping as she replied, 'Yes, absolutely. You're so right, officer.'

'Oh! It's Helen Bartlett,' he said, stepping back.

'Is anything wrong?' Sometimes there were advantages in being recognised; though of course not everyone was a fan, so it did not always play well.

'I was just thinking you'd be safer if your fog light was on.'

'Heavens, wasn't it? Sorry.'

Dare she hope he was going to let her go?

'I suppose you've been out at some function or other?' He indicated her evening dress.

'Yes. In Northampton. A charity event, actually. Not the best night for it.'

'No. You've probably had a hell of a drive. Tell me where you live, and I'll escort you back.'

Awash with relief, she gave the address and jumped back into the warmth of her car to follow him. His guidance made the journey much easier. She wondered if she should invite him in for coffee; probably she should, though it was the last thing she wanted to do.

'Thanks very much,' she said when, having parked outside her flat, she walked over to him. 'Could I offer you some coffee?'

'No thanks. Got to get back to the station. But would you just sign this autograph?'

She would have signed away her life at that moment.

'You've been very kind,' she said and shook his hand.

And, she thought, I've been extremely lucky. God knows if I'd have passed a breathalyser test. I mustn't take this kind of risk ever again.

Upstairs she slumped on to the chair in front of her dressing table mirror. What a mess she was. Her eye make-up had run; her hair was tousled, and her dress, crumpled.

Suddenly a wave of fury swept over her at the thought of what Sam's mother was doing to the two of them. By rights, having driven back from Northampton, she should have been tucked up in his bed – not forced to travel back to her own place in these awful conditions and at such an ungodly hour. How dare the old woman pick a fight with her son, causing him such torment. How devious of her to wait till the night when the unsuitable, unfavoured girlfriend was risking life and limb on the motorway.

It was so unfair, and she felt hurt and despondent at the realisation that all her attempts at friendliness towards Madame Aziz had counted for nothing.

As for Sam, how could his mother have failed to see what a huge effort he had made during her visit? And why could she not be pleased that he had finally found someone he adored, someone who would support him, share his life and give him the love that, plainly, he had never had?

Exhausted though she was, it was hours before she could sleep, and then finally, when it did come, it was fitful, fragmented and not at all restorative.

Somehow, she bustled through the following day and summoned up the necessary energy for the programme, but it was a struggle.

Laura was waiting for her in the club. 'I'm sure you won't thank me for saying this, but that was one hell of an act tonight – considering that anyone who knows you can see a mile off that you're on your knees with exhaustion. What's going on?'

'Sam's mother's gone back to Egypt.'

'Good!'

'Well, yes and no. Last night, there was the most terrible row. She doesn't approve of me at all.'

'So what? She doesn't live here. She won't be involved in your life. Forget the old bag.'

Helen wondered whether to divulge more but decided against it. She was aware, though, that her friend was concerned as she took both her hands in hers.

'Helen, this must have been awful for you, but you hold all the cards. He loves you. You'll see – it'll be all right now you have him to yourself again.'

It was certainly better. They made love ferociously; it was as if he was unable to absorb enough of her. And, as the next weeks wore on, it seemed sometimes as if his mother had never been there, and Hamaida did not exist. But there was an undercurrent of anxiety. She knew that he felt it too, but that she should not mention it. Would it go away? Or were they simply becalmed – temporarily – with the remainder of a difficult course yet to be negotiated.

Occasionally, when she felt brave, she tried to engage Sam in a conversation about the obstacles to their happiness, but he refused to discuss them, except to say that the solutions lay within himself. Then he would kiss her, almost dispelling her disquiet, as he promised that he would 'sort it'.

But could he sort it? He was the most capable man she had ever known. And in him, she had believed she had found a partner who was stoical, utterly reliable and supportive. Was that true, though? Or did she simply wish it were so? The questions hammered at her brain.

Then one day, as he raised the subject of her forthcoming birthday, he said, 'Helen, I can't bear this any more. Let's both book leave, go to a Greek island, and come back married.'

There was a wild look in his eyes, like that of an ensnared animal, flailing about helplessly in search of escape. Her impulsive, romantic and gambling nature longed to agree to his suggestion. But she said nothing for a few moments.

'Suppose,' she said eventually, striving to sound casual and reflective, 'we did do that, or something similar, but then returned to find that your mother had been so incensed at our news she'd died of a heart attack without forgiving you?'

'Don't be so melodramatic!'

'Sorry,' she responded, quietly.

'No, I'm sorry. That was unforgiveable. You're right to challenge me. And I know it's your way of reminding me that I can't duck the issue in this way and that our future can never be happy unless I properly resolve the past. And I will do it. I must. For you, for me and for our children. I love only you; your mind and your fantastic body, and your spirit. I won't let you down.'

She gazed at him, too choked to speak. All her life she had waited to be adored in this all-consuming way. She was not at all sure that she deserved it, but she knew she had never had it before – not from her mother, her father or her ex-husband. Somehow, unbelievably, she had it now, and life without it would be intolerable.

'Don't even think about it.' His voice interrupted her train of thought.

'You don't know what I was thinking.'

'Not exactly, perhaps. But please trust me.'

On her birthday, a bright, March Saturday morning with more than a hint of spring in the air that floated in through her open window, Sam woke her with a kiss and a glass of Buck's Fizz.

His gift to her was a gold wristwatch.

'It's delicate, and special, like you. But it also carries a message from me to you, which is that I want you to learn to take life easier, and I hope that whenever you look at this little watch you'll remember my words "Take your time. Take your time".'

Was he asking for time, or speaking more generally? She was unsure, and she did not ask, because she had a feeling he would not know the answer himself.

They spent the morning in bed, then at midday Sam prepared a lunch of smoked salmon, granary bread and strawberries.

She watched, grinning, as he organised everything – clearly enjoying his role. For Helen, it felt strange to have a whole day unravel slowly with no control over its elements or outcome, but she forced herself not to interfere as she would not have spoiled Sam's happiness in his arrangements for anything.

He left her for a while, to go to the clinic, but promised to return mid-afternoon. He also advised her to put on a dress rather than the trousers she might have chosen normally.

In his absence, she took a long bath and then phoned her parents.

'We haven't met Sam yet.' Her mother's voice was pained.

'I know, I'm sorry. And I'm sorry I'm not really keeping you in the picture. But it's hard to talk when he's here. It's just that some things have to be sorted before we can be together properly, and I don't want to tempt fate by having him meet you and Dad first.'

'What sort of things?' her mother demanded.

Helen knew she could not tell the story of Hamaida, so she confined herself to the difference in their backgrounds and his loyalty to his own mother and country.

'What do you mean? Are you saying his mother doesn't approve of you? That takes the biscuit I must say.'

'Well, look at it this way, Mum, I mean you weren't very keen that he was an Arab, were you? And she's not keen that I'm English.'

'Good heavens. It's not the same thing at all!'

'I think,' Helen murmured, 'you'll find that it is. Why shouldn't it be?'

'Well…' Her mother was clearly searching for an answer. 'Well, you're a very good catch and, well, those people, well, they have no background.'

Helen threw back her head and laughed, 'Oh, Mum. Have you never heard of the pyramids? For goodness' sake, don't be so British and colonial. They had a background before we were living in clay huts or whatever it was we did. Perhaps I shouldn't have told you anything about our situation. I certainly don't want to get into an argument – particularly today. Anyway, I'd better go, we're off out somewhere later but it's a surprise so I don't know where.'

Sam turned up shortly afterwards, dressed in a dark suit, and shepherded her into his car. Their destination turned out to be the Waldorf Hotel on the Aldwych, where there was a tea dance. It was absolutely charming with its potted palms, a quartet that specialised in music from the thirties and solicitous waiters. They sat at a small table and watched the brave people who had already elected to take to the dance floor. There were Americans, who were easy to identify because they tended to smooch and shuffle. Then there were couples of her parents' age – mostly somewhat overweight, and yet skilled dancers who were surprisingly light on their feet.

Normally, she would not have eaten more than a couple of sandwiches, let alone the toasted teacakes, scones with jam and rich, thick Devon cream. As for the cakes that followed, they would as a rule have been taboo. But today felt different. Both she and Sam ate heartily, and she smiled as she watched him and decided to live each moment for what it was, and to enjoy it.

After a while, Sam invited her to dance muttering something about working off the calories. She accepted shyly. They had bopped together occasionally at nightclubs, but it was ages since she had had any reason to try out the ballroom training of her youth. Also, she had no idea at all if he could dance. She also suspected that they would be recognised. He was so dark, and she was so fair, and they were younger than many of the participants, so they were bound to attract some attention.

Sam danced superbly, and Helen, who never considered that she did, found the effortless unity of their movements as sensuous as the sex act itself.

The band suddenly switched from its thirties repertoire and launched into a Viennese waltz. Sam insisted they stay on the floor and try it. 'Keep your head up,' he advised her. 'That way you won't get too giddy.'

She beamed, replete with love for this utterly amazing and wonderful man, and as she did, he gazed back at her with the broadest smile. He held her closer and more tightly. The room was spinning but she knew he would not stumble. In his arms, she was secure, and the dizziness was delightful.

Eventually the music stopped and they sat down, flushed and giggling and ordered more tea. Then the band struck up 'Happy Birthday'.

'Oh my God,' she groaned. 'Everyone's looking at us now.'

'My darling,' he soothed her. 'Of course they are. Everyone loves to see an attractive, vibrant woman and you were born to be noticed even if you hadn't followed the career you chose.'

A waiter appeared at her elbow bearing a huge basket of spring flowers, whereupon everyone in the room applauded. Blushing, she stood up and acknowledged them by bowing and smiling, then quickly sat down.

'How embarrassing, Sam,' she said, though she was pleased all the same. She could not help but love the attention her job brought her. Could she live without it, in another country, where she had no role, and no one knew what she used to do? She tried to suppress the swift answer that told her it would be impossible.

She looked again at the flowers and reached for the little card that was attached to a large fern. 'This is a very special day,' it read. 'Thank you for making it so. Like the day and the year, you are more than special. All my love, Sam.'

Tears blurred her eyes. Surely this potent and overwhelming love could not be denied.

After the dance, they went to the theatre next door to a Tom Stoppard play which they both enjoyed. Then, despite a table booked at a nearby restaurant, they agreed that they were not hungry enough to eat dinner and made for the car which was parked nearby.

On the way back, the passion they had for each other, which was always simmering just below the surface, flared into intense desire. And Sam began to describe what he planned for her as soon as they reached her apartment.

'I'm going to fill you with such intense and exquisite feelings that you'll beg for me to stop, but I won't. I'll go on and on and I'll take you to places you've never experienced. You'll cry out – over and over again – like a cat. And you will be mine. Mine to own. Mine to love. Mine to hold.'

And so it was.

In the nature of things, anti-climax often follows climax. She knew that well. It was just a pity, she thought sadly, that the joy they had had the day and night before was cut so short.

They had spent the night at Helen's flat and then driven out to Chiswick to have lunch before making their way to Sam's house for a relaxing afternoon. But, almost as soon as they had sat down with the newspapers, the phone rang. They exchanged a slightly anxious glance and Helen could see Sam flicking through the file in his mind of his current patients and wondering whether any might be in danger.

'It would be serious if they called me,' he told her. Several senior colleagues are on duty this weekend...'

With a worried look in his eyes, he reached for the phone.

'Oh,' he said, 'hello, Mother.'

Helen mouthed a suggestion to him that she should leave the room, but he shook his head vigorously.

'No, I haven't been here much. It was Helen's birthday yesterday.'

There was a pause while he listened.

'Yes, I'll tell her. Thanks. Yes, she's fine. Very well in fact.'

Helen felt uncomfortable about being there. So, avoiding his gaze, she left the room. She ran upstairs and sat in his bedroom with the door closed. A presentiment of something dire taking place engulfed her. She had no idea what was being said, but she knew real terror in those minutes. Flinging herself onto the bed where they had known so much laughter and pleasure, she tried to breathe deeply and to reassure herself that she had nothing to worry about.

As soon as he came looking for her, she knew that her instincts for the worst had been accurate. He looked stricken.

'Hamaida's been very ill. Apparently, she almost died. She's had a total hysterectomy.'

With some years of fertility still ahead of her, Helen felt real sorrow for a woman who now had no possibility of motherhood. In the next moment, she recognised that her own chance of being a parent was diminishing with Sam's news. She crossed her arms and hugged herself for comfort.

Sam stood, watching her, before saying, 'Nobody wanted to marry her before...'

131

Helen reached out for his hands. She wanted to give him strength and feel support from him flooding back into her body, but she could not resist finishing his sentence, '…and no one will want her now.'

Over the next few weeks, they clung together, endlessly discussing all the problems and possible permutations. Helen wished that she could unburden herself to a third party but felt that their situation was too private to share. She was not sure either how she could find the appropriate words to describe what she was learning about loving someone from an entirely different culture. She did contemplate telling Laura but could almost hear her friend saying – simplistically – 'If he loves you enough, he'll stay.'

Loving her enough was not in question; she knew that. But how could she begin to explain to anyone how the power of his inner struggle was tearing him apart. Though she had loved him for months, her love deepened now. She believed him to be totally honourable and unselfish. If it were otherwise, he would not have to suffer this torment.

But even though she thought she knew him so well, she was taken aback when he told her of a new plan as they were driving from the studios to a little taverna in Camden Town, which had become a favourite haunt of theirs.

'Helen, I'm going to have to go back to Egypt to see Hamaida and her family and mine. There's no other option. I'm also going to visit a number of hospitals and see for myself how things are and whether, if I went home, I could make a difference.'

Despite the panic in her chest at the seriousness of his tone and message, Helen was amazed at how calm she sounded as she responded, 'I think that's a good idea. There's only so much wondering and agonising you can do here. When will you go?'

'May the thirtieth.'

'You can't! That's the day of the Celebrity Gala.'

Helen had agreed to appear in a concert in aid of Sam's transplant department.

'No, it's the day after.'

'Oh. OK. By the way, I've now been asked to narrate *Tubby the Tuba* with the Royal Marines Band as well as compering the concert.'

'And I'm sure you'll do it very well,' he said, before adding, 'though I have no idea what that is!'

'Oh, it's a fun piece for the band, aimed at children, with a story about an instrument that never gets the main tune. It was always on the radio when I was little.'

He took his hand off the driving wheel and stroked her arm. 'I shall enjoy it. I love everything you do.'

She sighed loudly. 'Well, let's make the concert great, because God alone knows what will happen once you're out of my sight. But can I suggest one thing, which is that you don't contact me at all while you're in Egypt. I know you'll want to. And heaven knows I'll be desperate to hear from you, but I think you need to concentrate on the situation there.'

He was quick to agree, which both surprised and hurt her.

'You're right. I'd already come to that conclusion myself. You see, in a way, my love for you mustn't determine the outcome. If I am honour bound to go back to Egypt, then I must, irrespective of you and us.'

Helen began to cry as her whole world seemed to cave in around her.

'And for that reason,' he continued, 'I don't even think we should make love before I go. I don't want to feel that I'm using you, and I need my mind to be free.'

Suddenly all her distress exploded. 'How can it be free?' she demanded. 'Bloody hell, Sam. You can't just eradicate months of loving. You can't just switch it off because it's no longer conven- ient. Or if you can, then I have misjudged your feelings. And what about me? Let's forget your sense of honour for the moment. It looks like I may have to live my life without you and that prospect is more than I can cope with. In fact, I can't see how I will carry

133

on living if you make that decision. But for pity's sake, please let us be together, properly, for the time we have left. Please. I won't be able to bear it otherwise.'

They were almost in Camden Town. He turned down a side street lined with grimy flats and switched off the engine and the headlights and gathered her to him. Covering her face with kisses, he did everything he could to soothe and pacify her, but she was inconsolable.

'If you free me,' he explained, 'don't you understand that I probably won't be able to free myself? But we'll both know that I came to you because I had resolved my situation honourably and because it was right that we should be together.'

It was far too philosophical for Helen. Her head was pounding and she felt as though her heart was breaking into a million pieces. Surely, he must need her as much as she needed him. She grasped his hand and placed it on her right breast, holding it there till his fingers relaxed and cupped and squeezed the soft fullness. Any moment now, he would caress her, overpower her, drive her back to his place or hers and take her. He always had before.

His face remained touching hers and she could feel his tears running down his cheeks and mingling with her own. Time passed but neither of them moved. Neither of them *wanted* to move.

At last he suggested that they go and eat. 'I know that neither of us is probably hungry but we should try.'

Helen drew her compact out of her handbag and squinted at herself in the mirror. She looked terrible. Taking a brush from her make-up bag she tried to flick away the flecks of eyeliner and mascara that were smudged under her eyes and down her cheeks. Then she applied some face powder, but still looked as if she had been weeping and she knew that other people would be quick to spot that she had. She turned to Sam. His appearance was as strained and tearful as hers.

Inside the taverna, the proprietor – who knew them well – guided them to a table in a dark corner and gave them menus but, unusually, did not stop to chat. Instead, he rushed off to find a bottle of the Demestica that they always ordered, and brought them Perrier too.

Alone in their quiet area, they held hands, and in the dim light, Helen saw that her knuckles were white.

When the food came, they each ate with one hand only, so that their other hands remained joined.

Helen could feel that the staff's eyes were glued to them, aware that something was badly wrong with this couple who, generally, were laughing and happy. Her eyes pooled with tears again which spilled down her freshly powdered cheeks. She did not attempt to hide or wipe them away. Just sat, miserably contemplating the end of everything she had come to love and rely upon.

Her look froze as her eye took in the scenario being acted out in the nearby aquarium. A large, aggressive fish was cornering a smaller one who appeared to be cowering in fright. His tail was serrated in a manner that nature had not intended, which made Helen suspect that the big fish attacked the little one on a regular basis.

'How cruel,' she cried. 'And how terrible it must be to be trapped in a situation that is unbearable for you.'

As she spoke, she thought suddenly about Sam, and how, frequently, he had said that he felt trapped by his obligation to Hamaida. But surely if that is what he felt, he would walk away from her? Unlike the small fish, he could – and he should. Laura had told her that she held all the winning cards. Maybe she did. And maybe, if she could be mature about this nightmare and stop making a scene, and take it calmly, he would see even more clearly that he needed her and must have her love and calm support.

She smiled at him. 'I'm sorry I was so upset earlier. Whatever I'm feeling, I know it's worse for you. Could you take me home, do you think?'

He looked puzzled at the change in her, but nodded, quickly paid the bill and walked with her to the car.

Much of the way, he drove with one hand so that he could hold hers, but neither of them spoke. As he drew up outside Helen's flat, her resolve to be calm and adult weakened. She wanted to beg him to come in and to make love with her. Looking at him, she knew that he was on the verge of doing so. His hand crossed the divide between them and grasped her right thigh, sending an intense signal to her secret places, which opened automatically at his touch.

She took a deep breath. 'Goodnight, Sam.' Her voice was brisk and business-like.

His face registered bewilderment then something like anger, and he pulled her back as she tried to get out of the car, turning her face till their lips met and she could feel his passion and hunger.

'Darling,' she pushed him away, gently and sighed unhappily. 'Let's try it your way. I'm going. Goodnight.'

Inside her flat, she realised she was trembling. She went into the bedroom and switched on her electric blanket, then she walked into the kitchen and boiled a kettle and proceeded to fill a hot water bottle. Next, she removed her make-up in record time. 'What the fuck does all this matter?' she demanded angrily of herself. Skin care. Hygiene. Hair brushing. Did any of it help when she felt dead inside? Not at all.

She slid into bed and curled round the hot water bottle, but she needed to hug something more bulky, so she grasped a pillow to her and rocked against it, whimpering.

The phone on her bedside table rang. It could only be him.

'Helen, darling. If I can sort this out, I'll never let you out of my sight and I'll make love to you every day. If only you were here now, I'd...'

She dropped the phone to the floor. She could hear his voice going on and on as she lay sobbing until finally sleep overcame her.

For the next fortnight, they adhered to the arrangement that neither of them wanted. It was absurd, they agreed, as they cradled each other and wept before separating each night. Helen's only consolation was that Sam could not stay away from her. He may not have been penetrating her body, but he was laying claim to every other aspect of her existence. And in no sense did his energy appear to be going in the direction of his obligations in Egypt.

Alone each night, Helen tossed and turned. She waded through vast piles of newspapers and magazines and not a few novels. She had never been so well-informed, so tired, or so thin.

Helen was in the green room, playing the piano when Sam arrived. He kissed her and looked around the large space. 'Where's everyone else?' he asked.

'The artists and band were given a supper break – they're probably in the coffee shop in the foyer.'

'I knew you had played the piano when you were younger, but I didn't know you were that good,' he smiled at her.

'I'm not really – and I'm terribly out of practice. I often think of buying a piano but never quite get round to it. Silly, really. I mean, there's room for it in the flat.'

'You never cease to amaze me,' he said quietly. Then he cleared his throat. 'How was the rehearsal?'

'In time-honoured tradition, it was diabolical. I missed umpteen cues in *Tubby the Tuba* and I didn't feel very fluent in my introductions of various performers. I hope it'll come together later. Well, it'll have to.'

He grinned at her. 'You'll be great. Have you got time for a coffee?'

She looked at the little gold watch he had given her. 'Just about.'

It was a strange evening, for it involved them both in different ways. Focusing on everything she had to do in the concert, Helen was able to forget, albeit temporarily, their imminent separation. They smiled at each other as they sat down in the bar; it was almost like the early days of the relationship.

She was nervous, and told him so.

'How can you be? You're used to appearing before millions! There'll only be a couple of thousand folk here.'

'Maybe it's something to do with me being able to see them, I don't know. I guess it *doesn't* make sense.'

He smiled at her in that personal, twinkly way he had, and suddenly she felt as though someone had punched her in the stomach. She was missing him already and he was sitting opposite. Get used to it, she told herself. It's going to get much worse than this.

As they ate smoked-salmon sandwiches and drank their coffee, she felt they must look an odd couple, he already attired for the evening, and she in jeans and a big sweater. He looked so distinguished, she thought, in his black tuxedo and brilliantly white pin-tucked evening shirt.

'I'd better get ready, Sam,' she murmured after a while. 'And I need to get my brain in gear.' She pressed his hand. 'Do you mind?'

'Of course not. I'll go and mingle. But I'll see you before it starts.'

In the dressing room, the routine of preparation – making-up, teasing out her hair with an electric brush and sticking on false eyelashes – calmed her mind. It was just another performance, in one sense anyway. At the same time, she had high hopes for the success of the evening and for Sam's programme of work and the patients whose lives would be improved by a department with as much state of the art equipment as possible. The NHS could never fund it all. She practised a wide, untroubled smile in the mirror. This was her public face and she would wear it all night. Tomorrow at this time Sam would be in Egypt and it was imperative that he carry with him the memory of her at her best.

At that moment, he put his head round her door. 'You look wonderful.' His voice warbled slightly.

She stood and viewed herself in the full-length mirror at the end of the room. The sunshine-yellow lace top was a good colour for her, and the long, layered taffeta cream skirt was very flattering.

'My golden girl,' he whispered.

There was a knock on the door and a man in an over-sized maroon dinner jacket stood in the entrance almost hidden by a huge basket of flowers. Helen turned back to smile at Sam – for of course they came from him – then took the arrangement and put it on her dressing table.

As she stepped back to view the colourful blooms, he strode to her side and turned her to him; they stood, hugging each other till they were interrupted by a tannoy announcement asking for all performers to assemble in the green room.

'I'll see you in the interval,' she said as she gave him a gentle push towards the door. 'At least I get to do *Tubby* in the first half – and I'll be able to relax a bit more after that. Enjoy it, Sam. I'll do my best for you, and the unit.'

As she walked onto the platform, the applause was gratifyingly enthusiastic. And, instinctively, she did that 'old-pro' thing – ingrained in her since her first week of drama school – of looking up to the highest level of the audience. 'Play to the gallery, darling!' Mr Holgate, her wonderfully theatrical tutor, had always said. She grinned at the memory and launched into her introduction of the Royal Marines Band.

Back in the wings, she sighed with relief. She wished she could have a drink but knew it would be unwise. It was important for her to have a clear mind.

The Marines were performing for the whole of the first half, so she had nothing left to do except her own star-turn which was in the band's final item before the interval.

Her smile as she walked on was genuine and warm. Now that it was time to deliver, she was relaxed. Better than that, she was confident and determined.

Unlike the rehearsal, she picked up all her cues from the band and delivered her narration without any mistakes. It was a heady experience. Then it came to the passages she had been dreading where she had to sing – but her voice took flight in the air and she could feel it pinging to the back of the hall. With an expansive gesture which encompassed the whole band, she delivered the final line. A tremendous crescendo surged around her, almost lifting her off her feet. It was wonderfully exhilarating.

The applause was loud and prolonged. She took three curtain calls.

'Gosh,' she said to the stage manager.

He smiled at her, with a look of understanding in his eyes. 'Nothing like a live concert, is there? Well done, Miss Bartlett.'

Back in her dressing room she was not surprised to find a bottle of champagne nestling in a silver pail packed with ice. Neither was she surprised to see that it came from Sam.

He appeared in the doorway. 'I know you so well,' he murmured, 'and yet I'm constantly surprised by you. What a wonderful woman you are.' He hugged her tightly.

The remainder of the evening went like a dream. She was composed now and enjoying herself. One by one she announced the galaxy of stars who had agreed to appear – Peter Skellern, Cleo Laine and Johnny Dankworth, John Williams and the irrepressible George Melly.

As she walked to the dressing room afterwards, she felt proud to have been included in such talented company. It was an evening to remember.

Sam must have run at the speed of a four-minute mile, she thought as he burst into her dressing room almost as soon as she arrived there herself.

'You're so good at what you do,' he said.

'I haven't been doing what I do,' she laughed.

'Maybe not... I suppose I've always known how many viewers you have at six but seeing just a fraction of those actually watching you in person, I realised more than ever how greatly you're loved.'

'Am I?'

He looked her in the eye and answered very seriously. 'Oh yes. Yes, you certainly are.'

The Royal Marines' musical director put his head round the door.

'Coming for a drink, Helen?'

'Absolutely,' she answered. 'I'll follow you in a moment.'

The green room was heaving with artists and their friends, and Sam and Helen had to push their way into the jostling crush as they tried to get somewhere near the people they had agreed to meet.

Everybody was in high spirits.

'We've exceeded the target,' someone said in passing.

Suddenly, Laura emerged through the crowd. She looked sensational, Helen thought, with her shiny auburn hair swept to one side and some dramatic Monty Don jewellery adorning her purple evening gown.

'You were terrific,' she said. 'I don't know how you did that. I certainly couldn't have. It was brilliant.' Then she turned Helen around away from Sam. 'The good doctor, by the way, couldn't take his eyes off you. You have absolutely nothing to worry about there. He is totally besotted.'

Helen felt her heart leap with delight, but it was temporary. The harsh fact was that within hours he was going to be snatched away.

After Laura left her, she took Sam's arm. 'We need a drink.'

They stood with their glasses in a little island of their own as the rest of the partygoers chatted and laughed all around them. He slipped his arm around her waist and squeezed her tightly. They talked, but not about anything that mattered. She realised that she was trying to hold onto his presence and absorb every bit of him so that she would have these memories to fill her brain in the days to come.

He slipped away for a moment to recharge their glasses.

'Miss Bartlett.' A voice boomed in her ear and she turned to see an elderly, straight-backed woman surveying her. She was reminded immediately of a teacher in her infants' school who had made her stand at the front of the class because she was unable to remember what eight times three was. It had been a humiliation that had never left her. 'I'm Mildred Smorthwaite, secretary to Mr Aziz.' She extended her white-gloved hand in Helen's direction. 'We've spoken on the phone. Congratulations. You did a remarkable job tonight.'

'Thanks very much. It's lovely to meet you at last.'

'I'm very pleased to meet you, especially here with my boss. He isn't an easy man, you know,' she lowered her voice, her eyes checking that Sam was still in the corner waiting for a new bottle of wine to be opened. 'Quite tetchy on occasions, but then gifted people are always difficult. Still, it slots into place now that I see you together. You make him very happy.'

Helen sighed. 'I'm not sure that I do.'

'Oh, there's no doubt about it at all. He's never behaved like this in the fifteen years I've been with him. He's been a bit quieter and more stressed in the last fortnight, it's true, but other than that, he's been like a dog with two tails. Don't let him down, that's all. He's so in love with you, I think it would kill him.'

So, the dragon had a heart after all, and Helen longed to take her to one side and confide that it was Sam who might have to let *her* down – and indeed that it might come sooner rather than later. Instead, she smiled and the urge to tell receded with the passing moments and the assistance of some deep-breathing.

Several of Sam's colleagues, some of whom she had met before, edged towards her in his absence. In different ways, they all broadcast the same message. Sam was hers. He was a changed man since meeting her. Their optimism contrasted so sharply with what she knew of the reality of his situation that suddenly she had to get away. She excused herself and ran back along the corridor to her dressing room where she sat, gazing at her image in the mirror, lost in thought and fighting the urge to break down and sob.

There was a knock on the door and without waiting for an answer, Laura entered. They looked at each other for a moment, then Laura held out her arms and Helen stood up and walked into them.

'What's wrong with you two?'

'Nothing,' retorted Helen, brightly as she moved away and sat down again in front of the mirror. 'I've just been told by at least five people that we're made for each other.'

Laura slid into the chair beside her. 'You are. So, what's up?'

'He's going back to Egypt tomorrow.'

'I know. For a holiday. He told me earlier. Why don't you go too?'

'I can't.'

'Of course you can. Just tell Derek and go. You haven't had any leave for ages. They'll just have to cope.'

'I can't, Laura. Sam doesn't want me there.' Helen breathed deeply.

'It's time you opened up, you old tart,' Laura said quietly. 'I'm probably the closest friend you have other than Sam. I don't want to force myself on you, believe me, but friends share things, don't you know? I want to help, and to be honest, I'm hurt that you're excluding me. I told Ian as much last night. You're in at eight every morning. That's never happened before – not even when you were getting over Barry. You're taking on more and more. You say you're fine, but you don't look it – except on the box where somehow you manage to magic yourself into performing normally every evening. You're cracking jokes in the office but when you don't think anyone's watching, you look, well frankly, as if you're in pain. At first, I thought you were ill, then I saw Sam one evening when he was picking you up, and he had the same haunted expression as you do. I don't understand it. You're still so obviously in love, still seeing each other, but you look absolutely wretched. As for him, I know he's ten years your senior, but he looks all of that. When his guard is down, I can see all too clearly the old man he'll one day become. I popped in on him yesterday because I've almost finished editing the piece I've done with him, and I couldn't believe the difference in the face of the man sitting opposite me compared with the one I've been working with on the screen. In short, you're both a bloody mess. So don't tell me nothing's wrong. I know different.'

'That's quite a speech, Laura,' Helen remarked, softly.

'Don't do that. That thing. Don't distract me. I won't have it.'

'I'm sorry. Actually, deep down, I'm very touched...' tears welled up in her eyes, '...very touched that you care,' she sniffed. Laura handed her a tissue. Helen sniffed again. 'Look, I'll tell you part of it, but you have to promise me that you'll never tell another soul. Not even Ian. It's too private.'

Laura nodded quickly.

'A long time ago, Sam was promised in marriage to a girl back home. Her father and Sam's were close friends.'

'Come off it, Helen, surely such things don't still happen these days?'

'I don't know if they still do. But they certainly did then – I guess it was back in the early sixties. I know Sam wasn't very old.'

'For God's sake, this is 1985! And he loves you.'

'I think he does.'

'*Think!* Listen, Helen, I've deliberately spent tonight watching both of you. Now, you love him, that's quite apparent. I can see it in your eyes when you look at or talk about him. But he, well, he's fanatical. He may be a bit more hot-headed, coming from the Middle East and everything, but it's more than that. He can't take his eyes off you. He tenses the moment any other man so much as talks to you, and he has to excuse himself from any other conversation he's having so he can quickly get to your side. He's really possessive. I mean, I don't even know if that's a good thing, really, but it's like an electric current running between you. The rest of us are having to stand well back in case we get burnt.'

Helen leant over and kissed her friend's cheek. 'You are good to me. And if only half of what you say is true, then it makes me feel better. But, and this is the big but, it's almost like dating someone who's married. He's got to resolve it before we can be together.'

'It's ridiculous,' Laura screeched.

'It is, and it isn't. I can't actually tell you the whole story, which might make more sense. Anyway, my situation's not terrible – not compared with kids dying all over the place in Ethiopia, but it is the worst thing that's ever happened to me.'

Laura reached for Helen's hand and held it tightly. 'I don't fully understand, but I can see it's important, and I suppose that's why he's making this trip home. Did his mother's visit bring all this to a head?'

'In a way. And a subsequent phone call had an impact too. It isn't just the girl – though that's serious enough – it's also that he's developed real guilt about depriving his countrymen of his talent.'

'Oh, Lordy. But he'd never get the facilities back there to do what he's doing here. He's a pioneer. He has to carry on. That's what my film's about. The western medical world depends on him – not just a bunch of peasants in a land faraway.'

'Laura!' Helen was shocked.

'Sorry. That was an awful thing to say. It's just I feel so incensed that you're going through all of this and getting so very badly hurt. He shouldn't have started getting close to you if he couldn't follow it through.'

'I don't think that either of us knew what we were getting into. Unfortunately, having lit the blue touch paper, no one told us to stand well back.'

'I'm so sorry about it all. Would you like to come and stay with Ian and me while Sam's away?'

Helen welled up with Laura's kindness. 'You're the best friend anyone could have,' she said. 'Can I think about it?'

'Of course. We better get back to the green room. You're one of tonight's stars and you'll be missed.'

*

'What have I done to you, Helen?' Sam asked when at last they were alone and driving through a raging thunderstorm to her home. She failed to answer, just watched the hypnotic sweep of the windscreen wipers as they struggled to cope with the conditions.

Eventually, they drew to a halt outside her building. The perpetual question of whether or not they might comfort and console each other hung in the air but remained unsaid.

'I do care, Helen, so very, very much. Do you know that?'

Drained by the excitement and emotion of the evening she could only nod. Suddenly, his face was staring into hers with those terrifyingly piercing and dangerous eyes. Roughly he pulled her to him and kissed her so violently that her lips went numb and she could not breathe.

She fought to free herself. 'You're hurting me, Sam,' she cried.

He sat back. 'Darling, I'm sorry, I'm sorry. But my love for you is altitudinous.'

She smiled wearily. 'That's not a word.'

'It is now. Please will you invite me in for coffee?'

With one gesture, just the slightest inclination of her head, she could have him. He would love her, and hold her through this last, precious night. Her nipples hardened against her flimsy chemise. Yet, she made herself resist.

'No,' she whispered. 'No, I don't think that's a good idea.'

She jumped out of the car and took a step towards her front door. There was a slamming sound behind her a second before he pulled her back to face him. They stood together in their fine evening clothes, which – almost immediately – became so sodden that they clung to their bodies. Rain and tears were streaming down her face; there was a salty taste in her mouth; her hair was plastered to her head; and her eyes stung with running mascara.

'Go home, Sam,' she shouted as a crack of thunder threatened to drown her words. 'Please go, and don't ring me, not tonight, not tomorrow and at no time while you're away.' She blinked

146

furiously in an attempt to clear her blurred vision. 'But every moment from now till we meet again, remember that I'm yours. I was never loved like this before.' She tried to force her mouth into a smile. 'And my love for you is altitudinous too.'

With that, she turned and, without a backward glance, stumbled up the stairs to the big front door, and disappeared.

Chapter Nine

'You look awful,' Laura said.

'Thanks a lot.'

'What happened after you left?'

'It was extremely dramatic. A bit like a third-rate movie with a stage hand heaving buckets of water from a great height while the two of us wept and declared undying passion to the accompaniment of thunder and lightning. He wanted to sleep with me. I wish I'd let him now. He's probably gone away feeling rejected.'

'I don't understand. Why would you turn him away?'

'We hadn't been staying together overnight, or having sex, for a fortnight – so that he could focus on Egypt and what he has to sort out there.'

'Whose idea was that?'

'His.'

'So, you were doing what he wanted.'

'I know. But it made him very sad. He dropped a note in for me overnight, so I know he wasn't sleeping. For some reason he wanted me to have his address in Egypt. What am I going to do with that? Anyway, he'll be at the airport by now. And I might never see him again.'

'Helen, for goodness' sake. His eyes never left you yesterday evening. Just remember that. He'll be back. In fact, it wouldn't surprise me if he didn't manage to stay away for the whole ten days.'

'He will. By tonight he'll be there. They'll manoeuvre him into a corner, and he'll probably find it easier to dismiss me as a pleasant but unreal interlude. You know you said once that you're not desperately in love with Ian but that you can't imagine life without him? Perhaps you're better off than having what we have, which sometimes seems to border on insanity.'

'Who knows? But I'm a different sort of animal from you. You're an extreme individual. You feel things more deeply than I do and can be very, very down in a way I never am. But at the other end of the scale, when you're elated you're so buoyant, it makes me exhausted just to watch! I sometimes envy you that. But at times like now, I don't. What are you going to do with yourself while he's away?'

'Well, if I can just get through today and tomorrow, my plan is to collapse at the weekend and stay in bed and try and sleep. That's all I can think of doing.'

The phone rang. Helen snatched at it. 'Sharon,' she said, 'I'm thinking of going out to get some fresh air. So, whoever it is, can you take a message and I'll... Oh, oh, well, you better put him through then.' She shrugged her shoulders and looked at Laura in bewilderment.

Her friend blew her a kiss and left the room.

'Darling,' Sam said. 'Darling, I'm in the lounge at Heathrow. Hang on, please while I put more money in...'

Helen listened as he fed coins into the pay phone.

'Darling,' he said again, 'I know you said not to phone, but I've been awake all night. I have to know before I go – do you love me?'

'Oh Sam,' she sighed. 'Don't you know?'

'I suppose I do, but please say it.'

'I love you, Sam – massively and with my whole heart.'

'Did you get my note?'

'Yes, I did. Were you driving around all night?'

'Quite a lot of it.'

'Well, thank you for your address and phone number. But I'm not sure what the point of it is. I mean, I'm hardly going to turn up, or ring for a chat. Anyway, we agreed we'd have no contact while you're away.'

'I know that's what we said, but I wanted you to have it in case anything awful happens.'

'Something awful *is* happening. But I won't phone you.'

'OK. Keep it for an emergency.' There was a pause before he continued, his voice trembling with tiredness and emotion. 'Helen, I don't think I can go. I absolutely cannot bear to leave you.'

She said nothing but silently willed him to say that England was home and that she was a part of it and that he would turn his back on his homeland, but she remembered what Laura had said, and recalled the thoughts that had come to her in the taverna in Camden Town. He needed her more than she needed him; she had to be courageous and let him go.

'Sam, listen. It wouldn't solve anything if you ducked out of your trip today. It would still have to be faced at some point. And it would only delay our being together. I can't have you if you don't go and sort this. You know that. I'm not pushing you away, believe me. In fact, and this isn't meant as pressure, I feel that life will be pointless if I can't be with you – and that I might not be able to go on...'

'That's not pressure. It's what I need to hear.'

'No, it isn't. Already, I wish I hadn't said it. You can't be torn in two forever. You must go back to Egypt and I must get on with my own life while you're away. Sam, I love you so much, but you're a man of honour and I'm trying to be honourable too.'

There was a pause. Maybe, even at this late stage, he would insist upon staying. She could do no more.

'All right,' he agreed at last.

Tears flooded down her cheeks. She could have stopped him. What sort of fool was she?

'But Helen, will you promise me something?'

'What?'

'Even if you're very lonely, please don't go to bed with anyone else. Is that too much to ask?'

Helen was shocked. 'I've no intention of going to bed with anyone else. What an idea.'

'Look… oh hell, hang on, I've got to put more money in.'

She waited.

'Helen, I'm sorry. I shouldn't have asked that of you. It's just that if I knew someone else was having you, I think I'd kill him.'

'There won't be anybody else, Sam, but it's more than fair of me to promise that when you're probably going to sleep with Hamaida.'

'*I am not!*'

'OK, sorry. Don't shout. You might. I think we should face up to that possibility. You might. Just to see if you could settle for that.'

'Helen, I'm telling you that I won't.'

There was silence.

'This is terrible,' he said suddenly. 'I've never had such a private conversation in such a public place in my life. Helen, I'll do what you say. I won't phone you, but I will think about you every single second of every day.'

'Sam, that won't solve anything. Just go and do your best to find a solution. I love you.'

She sank into a chair and crossed her arms over her chest and hugged herself to try to stem the bereft feelings that must surely claim her. She pictured him in the lounge at Heathrow. Perhaps he would turn back. Decide he need not go. Be here at the end of the programme as though nothing had happened.

He was not there that evening. Neither were there any calls to her flat once she arrived home despite her shooting angry glances at the phone every time she passed it. She was tired but convinced that she would not sleep. However, the cumulative effect of huge

152

effort to appear normal at work and on the programme, three stiff drinks but no food, plus a series of sleepless nights finally caught up with her.

Defiantly, she unplugged her phone, hoping that perhaps he might call, and then start worrying because he could not reach her. But he was not going to contact her, was he? And now that he was home, he would find it easier not to, and also to forget her.

By the time Saturday morning arrived, some thirty-six hours later, she was in a state of panic. For something to do, she decided to go out to the local shops. She pulled on a tracksuit, pushed her feet into ancient moccasins and, as a solitary gesture to vanity, put on a pair of sunglasses. She ran down the stairs and around the corner to Holland Park Avenue where she suddenly caught sight of herself in a shop window, looking weird and dishevelled. Offering up a silent prayer that no one would recognise her, she bought a few provisions and a newspaper and returned to the safety of her apartment.

Inside, she made herself a pot of tea and wondered how she was going to get through the day. It was half past one in Cairo. Perhaps he was lunching with his mother. Worse still, perhaps he was seeing Hamaida.

The phone rang. She started, then steadied herself before rushing towards it. By the time she answered, she was shaking.

'Helen, it's me.'

'Hi, Laura.' She hoped that her friend did not detect her disappointment.

'Look, at the risk of sounding bossy, I don't think you should spend the rest of the day alone.'

'You're right. I think I'll go away.' As she said the words, she was surprised by them. But suddenly, getting out of this flat, to an entirely different location with no reference points in it to Sam, seemed the only solution.

'When?'

'Oooh, not sure. Soon. I don't know.'

'Don't do anything rash.'

'My whole life is falling apart. Maybe it's time to be rash.'

'Where will you go?'

'What about a health farm?'

'Good idea! I've half a mind to come with you. I never got round to telling you but I booked leave for the whole of next week. I was just going to potter around here but a change of scene would be nice.'

'I'd love you to join me.'

'Tell you what, I'll spend the weekend with Ian, and then we'll see. Do you want to come here for the evening?'

'No, you two have so little time alone. I'll ring Derek and see if I can have a week off. I had a memo the other day from personnel saying if I didn't take the days owing to me within the next month, I'd lose them. Not sure they can do that, can they? But anyway, given that situation, Derek can hardly refuse me.'

'He might try because it's such short notice, but I expect he knows – as anyone would looking at you – that you need a break. You are all right, aren't you?'

'Not sure to be honest. No, I am OK. Just… look I'll be fine. I'll call you when I've decided what to do.'

Next, she rang Derek, apologising for interrupting him on a Saturday.

'Don't worry. I'm trying to persuade myself to do some gardening, but it's all such a mess out there after all that rain, I hardly know where to start!'

Derek lived in Berkshire with his wife, three children and two dogs. He was a rare breed in their business – a faithful husband and a happy family man.

She took a deep breath. 'Derek, I know this is a lot to ask, but you have said to me several times that I ought to take leave. And I had a memo the other day…'

'Yes, I'm aware of that. When do you want to go?'

'What?'

'Helen, listen…' His voice was kindly. Concerned perhaps. 'I'm speaking as your boss, but in a friendly way, if you understand me. I'm very grateful you're so keen on the job, but you work too hard and I'll be very pleased if you take a holiday.'

His sympathy caught her off balance and made her feel tearful. She swallowed hard.

'In an ideal world, I'd like to go now. But it may be difficult, because Laura's away too. I'd be back a week on Monday.'

'It's OK. I'll bring in a different reporter every day to present the programme. What about your features though? Are they ready to go?'

'Yes. The last in the "High Street" fashion series is due to go out on Tuesday, and it's ready. Thursday's "Medical Matters" is in the can too. Dr Murdoch and I knocked off two editions last time he was in.'

'Fine. Well off you go. What are you going to do?'

'I think I'll go to a health farm.'

'Sounds grim. Why don't you go and get some sun? And what about your surgeon chap?'

Helen tried to sound matter-of-fact. 'He's gone home to see his family in Cairo.'

'Ah,' said Derek. 'Well, enjoy yourself. Now, I'd better get into the garden.'

'Thanks for being so reasonable.'

'That's all right. I'd sooner you were off now than, well, you know…'

'Have a breakdown, you mean?'

He coughed. 'Well, yes, I suppose that's what I did mean. You'd be off much longer then, which would be bloody inconvenient!'

'Don't worry,' she said with a confidence she did not feel. 'I'm tougher than that.'

It was the oppressive silence of the flat that urged her on and the huge chasm created by the lack of any possibility that Sam might be part of her day, her weekend, or the following week.

And all it took was a phone call to Leicestershire, and fifteen minutes to pack a small bag.

Outside, the noise of London contrasted dramatically with the silence of her flat and she was glad to get into the safety of her car. She put on a tape of Tchaikovsky's *Rococo Variations* – mostly because she could not recall having ever having listened to the piece with Sam – and headed down to the big Shepherd's Bush roundabout and out of town.

She wondered what he was doing. Since they had met, it seemed that she had known more or less where he would be at any one time. She had not realised that was the case, not consciously, but now that she had nowhere familiar to picture him, the world felt a bleaker place.

It took an hour or so, and much more music, to carry her from London to the Midlands and finally to the winding lanes that led to the health farm. She had been there once before, but she had forgotten how tucked away it was. Rattled suddenly, she castigated herself for not bringing a map. Surely she was near it? It looked familiar. Rounding a bend, she almost collided with a large tractor which was taking up more than its fair share of the road. She stopped the car and took a deep breath and yelled at herself to 'get a grip'.

'That's who I am now,' she continued, out loud, though her voice was calmer. 'A batty, distracted woman who's lost and talks to herself!'

At last, Home Farm came into view and she recovered her public face and demeanour.

'Could you park my car and bring my stuff in?' she asked the very young man in long white gloves as she pressed a pound coin into his hand.

He beamed at her and nodded.

'Good God. Helen Bartlett.' The voice emanated from a plump, reddish face on top of an unflattering powder-blue bath robe.

'Terry? Good heavens. Long-time-no-see.'

'Yeah, darling. And you're so famous now. I've followed your career, you know. Avidly. You're looking wonderful.'

Same old Terry, she thought. How could she look wonderful when her whole life was a shambles?

After being shown to her room, she opted to have a Jacuzzi, where – before long – she encountered her first inquisitive viewer. It was a hazard she had anticipated. But her presence here would be a nine-minute wonder. Also, there was a 'house rule' that urged all residents to respect the privacy of the celebrities who might be staying. Probably there would be inmates here who were much more famous than she was.

She moved slightly to allow the powerful jet to pummel one thigh, then the other. She let it rise higher. Her spine was in knots; it hurt. The water must be doing her some good.

With no requirement to dress for dinner, most people turned up in the towelling robes issued to all the residents by Home Farm. Helen, who thought the garments drab and shapeless, donned a pale-turquoise tracksuit but – apart from mascara – did not bother with make-up, and tied her hair back in a ponytail. There was, after all, no one here she wanted to impress.

Terry motioned for her to join him. 'It's been ages since we had dinner together, my sweet,' he whispered.

Had he always been this egregious, she asked herself as she sat down to melon, herby roast chicken accompanied by a huge green salad, and a pudding of stewed fruit. She was quite surprised at the size of the portions which seemed more than adequate. Terry, on the other hand, complained that 'all this rabbit food' was getting him down.

'Still,' he said, his expression brightening, 'my new series starts soon, so I must lose some weight.'

His voice was loud. Unlike her, clearly he wanted to be recognised as he outlined his future plans and how his agent was convinced that an American contract was in the offing. Or a major film.

Helen wondered if he had looked in the mirror recently. Success of that kind – never having come his way before – was surely out of the question now.

Various other diners left the room and his voice became more conspiratorial.

'Darling, I'm so pleased to have you to myself now. Let's have a drink in the lounge.'

She found herself propelled there without any say in the matter. Still, it was early. Too early to sleep.

There was a choice of Bovril, coffee, Slimline drinks or dry white wine.

'I'll have a Diet Coke please,' she said.

'You will not. They've got a bottle of champagne for me behind the counter, we'll have some of that. Someone said there's only fifteen calories per glass in it. Suits me!'

As they sat, he tried to grab her knee, but she moved away just in time. Unabashed, he leant towards her.

'It's the most terrific stroke of luck you turning up here. It's been deathly dull. Cheers!' He clinked his glass to hers.

'Terry,' she cautioned him, 'I've come here to have a rest. I'm not a bundle of laughs right now.'

'But darling,' he said, gazing into her eyes, which was a well-practised technique. 'You don't look as if you need recuperation. You're gorgeous. I often watch you. You're vastly more attractive than the little girl I deprived of her virtue, all those years ago.'

She smiled, ruefully. 'Oh, you knew I was a virgin, did you?'

'Of course. You were terribly sweet. You were trying so hard to be sophisticated. But it was obvious you'd never gone the whole way before.'

She had met Terry during her first acting job after leaving drama school. It had been a twenty-six-week tour of a play that had proved to be dire. They had begun in 'number one dates' like the Newcastle Theatre Royal and the Liverpool Empire, but as news of their theatre reviews preceded them, they had played out the remainder of the run in less prestigious venues.

Terry had been the star – he was, after all, not just a stage actor but a regular in a long-running TV serial. He had seemed so suave, and she had been flattered by his attention. Probably, he had bedded most of the other women in the company before he got around to her, but still, she had been thrilled to be taken to expensive restaurants where he always made an ostentatious fuss about the temperature of the wine. How utterly pathetic that seemed to her now, but at the time she had thought him immensely sophisticated. How naïve she had been.

Eventually, she had had sex with him in a chintzy bedroom in Weston-super-Mare. He had known what he was doing, so it was not a miserable experience, but not exactly memorable either. In any event, she had realised very swiftly that she was, for him, a mere and temporary diversion.

On the last night of the run, in Swindon, he had sent her flowers, and she had stood on the stage with tears streaming down her face, knowing it was his farewell gesture. Yes, she had been hurt, for she had given him all she had at the time, and it had not been enough. But she had recovered.

Seeing him now, fourteen years later, he no longer seemed glamorous, just seedy. And she felt a surge of relief that she had not become Mrs Terry Summerfield the third. She had a feeling he was on his fourth wife now and she found herself grinning at the thought.

'You've very quiet,' he said as he picked up the bottle of champagne and tried to recharge her glass.

She shook her head, covering her glass with her hand. 'I told you I wasn't very good company.'

'What are you thinking about?'

'Well, to tell you the truth I was remembering how you ditched me at the end of the run.'

'Yeah, sorry about that. Must have been mad. Wouldn't do it now.'

Helen raised an eyebrow and pursed her lips but said nothing. And as soon as she had finished her drink, she jumped up, thanked him and left.

Sunday morning dawned bright, which was cheering, even though a new day brought with it a surge of longing for Sam. Breakfast, served in her room, came in the shape of tea and skimmed milk, with a bran biscuit. She had ordered all the Sunday papers, and did not leave the shelter of her bed till most of them were read and her fingers were blackened with newsprint.

She rang Laura. 'Derek was fine about me having leave, so I booked at the health farm, and I'm here.'

'Gosh, that was quick work. Is it all right if I join you?'

'Terrific. They're full at the moment, but they'll have vacancies tomorrow. Shall I get the girl in reservations to ring you with directions? It's in the middle of Leicestershire and I got hopelessly lost!'

'That would be great. I really need to get away. You see,' she paused as if she could not quite believe what she was saying, 'the thing is, Ian's asked me to marry him.'

'How wonderful!'

'Yes, I suppose so.'

'Mmmn. Can you talk?'

'Not easily.'

'OK. Well, I'll see you tomorrow.'

Helen went to an aerobics class. She swam. She had a G5 massage, which made her feel she was being hoovered all over. She walked in the gardens. She avoided Terry, and when, finally, she went to bed, she was exhausted and expected to sleep immediately. Instead, every time she turned over, Sam's face appeared before her. His penetrating eyes seemed to pierce the gloom, his expression one of stark anguish.

'Sam, my dearest boy, do you still love me?'

His image declined to nod its head.

160

'Dear God,' she said into the stillness, 'please don't take him from me. I'm not strong enough. I'll give up the job, go anywhere, do anything, but please...'

Tears, more tears, another sodden pillow, another restless night without the deep sleep that was supposed to 'knit up the ravell'd sleeve of care'.

On Monday, Laura was not the only newcomer. The Marvellous Merinda Merridew also turned up, she of the TV chat shows, she with the string of notable lovers, she who was the black jewel of the gossip columns.

'What does she actually *do*?' asked Laura, when the two of them were sitting cosily in the Jacuzzi.

'I don't know exactly. I think she's an actress, but she's really known for just being famous. She is fabulous, isn't she?'

'I suppose so. Anyway, your pal Terry's obviously smitten.'

Later, sipping her tea on her balcony which overlooked the outdoor swimming pool, she remembered Laura's words.

The Marvellous Merinda, in the minutest of bikinis, was sitting on the edge, kicking her long legs in the water. Terry was diving – some might have said that was a generous description for his antics – in a bid to gain her attention. He reminded her of a *Survival Special* programme she had seen on the courtship display of a walrus.

The gravel crunched beneath her window. Helen's eyes followed the sound and she found herself looking at Laura, pacing up and down. Her friend was unaware that she was being watched and was kicking the ground with each step, making tiny dents in the path as a flurry of small stones took to the air. With her guard down, she looked oddly vulnerable and Helen's heart went out to her.

Laura had seemed so settled with Ian so why – when he wanted to legalise their relationship – did she feel so out of sorts?

'There you are!' Helen shouted as though she had just walked from her room onto the balcony. 'I was hoping we could have some tea together.'

Laura turned her face upwards, squinting against the sun. 'Good idea. Thanks. Then I was thinking of having a cycle ride. Do you want to come?'

'Only if you want company.'

'I do.'

It was good to have Laura here, Helen thought as she woke to another day. Quite apart from anything else, feeling concerned about her friend was a diversion from her anxiety about Sam.

Laura had not discussed her feelings on yesterday's bike ride, but Helen had a feeling they would get onto it today.

After a calisthenics class that they both giggled through, albeit surreptitiously so as not to offend the instructor, they elected to sit by the side of the pool and to order Diet Cokes.

'How long till lunch?' Laura asked. 'I could really do with eating something. What about you?'

'I'm OK, actually.'

'I think it's because I like a big breakfast and we don't get anything here, do we?'

'Well there is the bran biscuit, even if it's so hard it's practically inedible.'

'Oh! That's a biscuit! I thought it was a cork mat! I put my tea cup on it.' Laura began to giggle, and once started she could not seem to stop. 'Don't mind me,' she gasped at last. 'Obviously, I'm going completely crazy through hunger.' And with that she went off into another peal of laughter.

'This is a pretty mad experience all round, isn't it?' Helen said suddenly. 'Still, I suppose it's a rest. And I'm sure we both need that.'

'Mmmn, you more than me.'

'Another drink?' Helen suggested.

'No. I'm OK. Actually, I've been thinking that I'd like to tell you something. It's worried me for ages and I want to get it off my chest. Just, please, don't hate me.'

162

'I couldn't ever hate you. What an idea.'

'You don't know. Wait till I've told you.'

'Go on, then.'

'Well, I'm really glad we're friends now. In fact, I've rarely been more grateful for anything in my life.'

'You'll make me blush in a minute.' Helen grinned.

'There's more. I need to admit to you that when you first joined the company, I targeted you and decided we had to be friends because, well basically, I was so jealous of you I could hardly see straight.'

'What! That's ridiculous. I don't believe it.'

'It's true. You see, I trained as a journalist. I'd been doing it a while. I had a track record. I, well, I did wonder if Derek might consider me for the programme's presenting job when your predecessor left. And then you turned up and everyone thought you were fabulous and fawned all over you.'

'They didn't!'

'Oh, they did. And I was ready to hate you for it. So, I kind of made a beeline for you and I think that was partly to find out what made you tick, but also, maybe – a tiny bit – to see if I could find out anything about stuff you weren't good at, which I might use against you. I'm appalled at myself now. And if you never want to talk to me again, I'll understand. But I just had to tell you. I've been wanting to for almost two years. Anyway, the thing is that I found I really liked you even though, sickeningly, you turned out to be really good at the job!'

Helen laughed. 'That's quite a confession! But I was very grateful you took me under your wing because I didn't know anyone and no one else was very friendly. Not at the beginning anyway. And now, well, what with Sam and everything, I couldn't cope without you.'

'Good. Because I'm certainly not jealous of you any longer. In fact, I've come to realise that it's much harder for someone in your position to have the right relationship because you're so much in the public eye. I know that your problems with Sam aren't really because of your profile. But it certainly doesn't help, does it?'

'Probably not. Though two o'clock in the morning, when you're wide awake and fearful about the future, is frightening for anyone in that situation, successful, or otherwise. To be honest with you, I'd given up hope of finding someone who might want to share my life. Then Sam appeared. And he persuaded me to love him. And, my God, I really do. But ever since that happened, I feel he's been beckoning me with one hand and holding me off with the other. And now, I actually cannot bear the idea that we won't be together. I still really hope it's going to be OK but deep down I have this desperate sense that I'll lose him. And that's going to be so, so much worse than never having experienced all this. Do you understand?'

'Yes, I think I do.'

'Anyway, enough of me. Do you feel ready yet to tell me why you're upset about Ian? I mean, you two were always going to stay together long-term. I thought you were happy with that?'

'I thought so too, but I'm suddenly worried about my freedom. I'm worried that my ambition will get in the way. What if a phone call came out of the blue offering me the job of a lifetime? And suppose it was somewhere else in the country? Or even in *another* country? I know it's not that likely. But it could happen.'

'Well, Ian's flexible. If you got that kind of offer, he could go too. He probably would. Good lighting cameramen can make a living anywhere – and it's not as if he's shown any tendency to insist you stay home and spend your life in the kitchen bottling fruit!'

Laura's shoulders dropped and she seemed to relax for the first time since her arrival.

'You're right. I hadn't thought of it like that.'

'I watched you and Ian at Christmas, and it certainly is different from Sam and me. But maybe your love is gentler, more realistic, more lasting. Ours is so dramatic, but is that better? It doesn't feel like it at the moment. More than that, I believe that if I lose Sam, all my capacity for love will go with him. I'll have had the best and I'll have to settle for the memory of that. Nothing else will come close. Now is that sane? I doubt it. Perhaps your love is a better version. More authentic. Am I making sense?'

'I think so.'

'Is Ian saying that if you don't marry him, he'll finish with you?'

'Oh no, nothing like that.'

'Well, you could just let it drift for a bit.'

'No, I don't think I can. Now that's he's asked me, I feel he's offering the whole of himself and I can't ignore that. Relationships don't actually mark time, do they? Not if they're working.'

'No,' Helen agreed. 'They don't.'

The days, without work or deadlines, became something of a blur, but passed pleasantly enough. The two women rose early and started their schedule with an aerobics class. They had treatments to their faces and bodies; they took saunas, swam, and ate healthy meals. They were amused by a couple who were clearly having a clandestine affair. Good place for it, thought Helen. The lovers rarely joined in the activities, but when they appeared at mealtimes the man invariably ordered a giant steak.

They played tennis, too. Laura was a better player than Helen's friend Deirdre, so the sessions were quite competitive. Afterwards, they would grin and comment on how strange it was that they could channel all their energies into an activity that mattered so little.

Then, after dinner one evening – a dinner at which the two of them had enjoyed the cabaret of Terry trying to ingratiate himself with the Marvellous Merinda – Laura said, 'I brought a video cassette of the rough cut of my feature on Sam. I'd like to show it to you, if you can bear it.'

'Wouldn't you sooner watch it alone?' Helen asked.

'Not really. I've spent so much time editing it that I'm a bit boggled by it now. I'd like your eye on it. I think it's the best thing I've ever done, but I need to know.'

So, the health farm was not to be without Sam's presence after all.

On the screen, he loomed large both in his office, with the resolutely proper Miss Smorthwaite, and in the wards. He cradled a tiny blue baby in his arms, coaxing the child's wan little face into a grin, and was also seen talking to anxious relatives.

And then there was footage of him looking tired and drawn after the flight to Holland, followed by shots of him in the operating theatre – his own domain. A nurse wiped his brow, sending a stab of unreasonable jealousy through Helen's heart.

'I'm deliberately not doing a *Your Life In Their Hands*,' Laura explained. 'I haven't included much blood and gore. I thought it was better to concentrate on Sam as the force behind the whole project.'

Helen tried to make constructive comments. For her taste, there were more than enough bloody images in the operation scene. The patient's skin, painfully pale, was suddenly stained an angry yellow with iodine; hemmed green drapes were placed around it; then something looking suspiciously like cling-film was applied. There was a flash of steel, and then a swift knife incised the skin, introducing vivid red to the already technicoloured scene. The picture became a florid, unidentifiable conglomeration to her, but to Sam, obviously, every bit of it had meaning. A thin, sizzling poker cut through layers of tissue; it seemed to sever and seal, for it appeared to staunch the blood flow somewhat. Next, a huge mechanical saw came into view, neatly slicing through the breast-bone. The operation was a curious mixture of brute strength and finesse. Sam's capable hands, the hands that had explored every part of her, were never still. The camera zoomed into a close-up of his eyes above the mask. They were alert and concerned.

'It's fantastic, Laura,' Helen congratulated her as the tape finally faded to black. 'It's really great. Marvellous. I'm biased, of course, but it's terrific.'

'He can't go home to stay, you know,' Laura murmured, solemnly. 'It would be like the Pope leaving Rome to work as a missionary in a shanty town. Plenty of people can do that. Some have to accept the responsibility of being leaders.'

Helen was relieved to have her own feelings about Sam's future confirmed by her friend but was too emotional to say so.

During next day's aerobics class, she tried to forget Sam – despite the video images that continued to fill her brain – by working her body harder than was necessary. She allowed herself a glance at the rest of the class. There was Terry, sweating profusely, probably more from the power of his lascivious thoughts than any physical effort, as he leered at Merinda's rear end. Then her attention was taken by the clandestine couple, who exercised so close to each other that their activity looked like foreplay. Merinda herself seemed to be in her own world as she bobbed up and down energetically, but her grace and fitness were in marked contrast to two plump ladies behind her, panting and growing ever more red in the face.

Helen caught Laura's eye and grinned as they heard the instructor yelling: 'Push through. Push through. Come on, harder! Go for the burn!'

After the class, the two women headed for the relative calm of the Slendertone room where two slightly bored looking beauticians gave them a well-rehearsed speech about the benefits they were about to enjoy. Lying beside Laura, strapped into the bands that were supposed to disperse all unwanted flab, Helen would have liked to have had a nap, but the electric pulses that tightened on her thigh and elsewhere were too obtrusive to ignore. Laura's eyes were closed though, so she shut her own and tried to visualise a waterfall which someone had told her was good for inducing tranquillity.

Suddenly, Laura spoke. 'Are you asleep?'

'Unfortunately, no.'

'I saw you being cornered by the awful Terry earlier.'

'Well, you're aware of that sorry part of my history!'

'Mmmn. He really is ghastly, isn't he? D'you know, I am so, so glad I came here.'

Helen looked across and smiled at her friend. 'And *I'm* glad you came, but what specifically has made you so pleased?'

'Well, being away has helped me see what I want. I can either be single, with all its possibilities, but with the downside being that I might very well just become less glamorous, more tired and played out. Or I can marry Ian – and hope to still do the sort of career things I want. And that's what I'm going to do. I've decided.'

'Wonderful. Let's get out of here, and you can ring him and tell him.' She waved at the girl who had attached them to their machines. 'I think we've had enough. Can you release us from these contraptions?'

Laura looked quite pinkly excited as Helen, freed from her torture, gave her an enthusiastic hug.

'I'll be waiting for you in the bar. I'm going to order champagne. And I'll mention to reception that you're checking out.'

'Hang on, am I?'

'You want to, don't you? Now you've made your decision.'

Laura's eyes sparkled. 'Is it the right thing?'

'Yes! It absolutely is. You've got it all in your grasp. Take it. You can still have your career, as well as marriage, babies and someone to go home to. Seize it for goodness' sake. You're miserable here, anyway. And you think of Ian all the time.'

'How do you know?'

Helen said nothing but simply raised an eyebrow.

'Thanks, Helen. Will you be OK if I go?'

'I'll be fine. At least one of us is getting her life straight.'

Despite her bravado in Laura's presence, Helen felt quite bereft once her friend had left. And she taunted herself with the thought that, by the law of averages, her situation was unlikely to turn out as well as Laura's. And without her friend to distract her, Sam now commanded centre stage in her mind. She took his letter from her bag. Was this an emergency? She sat on her hands to prevent herself from lifting the telephone receiver. Had he phoned home? Was he worried about where she was? Should she call to reassure him?

'Stop that!' she said aloud. She had come here to escape the telephone. If she allowed this lapse in her determination, there would be no peace.

Saunas are supposed to be hot, she thought, as she licked the perspiration from her upper lip. Inevitably her mind began to question whether or not the weather in Egypt was making Sam as uncomfortable as she was now.

Suddenly, Merinda walked in, disturbing Helen's reverie about her lover's homeland. No wonder everyone always referred to her as the Marvellous Merinda, reflected Helen, as the black girl slipped out of the towel she had been wrapped in. She was glistening with droplets from the shower. Her legs were endless, and her breasts high and proud.

'Ah, the little television lady,' drawled Merinda. 'It's nice to get a chance to speak to you properly, at last.'

'And you.' Helen could feel herself reddening under the other woman's scrutiny. Perhaps it would go unnoticed; she must be the colour of a mottled beetroot already.

With no embarrassment, Merinda began to stroke her own breasts and then she tweaked her already erect nipples. Helen watched in fascination as they grew bigger; she felt a flush in her own chest and a desire to touch herself.

'God, I feel horny,' growled Merinda. 'Four days here and no sex – it's more than flesh and blood can stand.' She laughed, revealing her perfectly even white teeth.

'Well, there are men around who'd be happy to oblige.'

'None of the men takes my eye,' said Merinda, and she shot a lascivious smile in Helen's direction.

Helen had no idea how to respond, so she sprang up, wrenched open the door and jumped into the plunge pool outside.

When she felt calmer, she returned. In any event, she had to go back through the cabinet to reach the changing rooms on the other side. Merinda, she noticed, was now stretched languorously on a bench, and Helen was forced to climb over her to get to a seat herself.

'You're very pretty,' purred the actress. 'Great tits, terrific bush.'

Helen's heart was pounding. She was both appalled and excited. Perhaps she had misheard?

'Have you ever had sex with a woman?'

'No – no, I haven't,' replied Helen. 'I, um, I didn't know that you... well, that you, er...'

'Are gay?'

'Well, yes.'

'I don't know that I am, honey. I like all kindsa activities. But you're definitely the most attractive person here. I'd love to lick those little pink nipples of yours. I could really show you a good time.'

'I have a boyfriend, whom I love,' announced Helen, hating herself for the sound of her puritanical, schoolgirlish voice.

'So? He's not here is he? Relax.'

Helen shook her head.

'Oh well,' the other woman shrugged, 'you've gotta try, haven't you? If you change your mind...'

Helen shook her head again, grabbed her towel, and edged past the actress.

'Sweet child, you sure don't know what you're missing.'

It seemed to Helen that grown-up, sardonic laughter followed her all the way to her room. It was ridiculous to be so upset, but her blushes would not subside. She rang down and ordered room-service dinner, but when it came she could only pick at it. She tried to read. She watched the news. She walked around the room, and everywhere she turned she saw Merinda's pouting lips, her raised eyebrows, her sculptured torso.

What would it like to kiss her? Helen lay on the bed and stroked her own nipples. And what would it feel like, she wondered, to lie hard on another woman, with two sets of breasts mashed between them? To press the button that would trigger delight in another female? To thrust fingers into that secret opening, and feel another's excitement and silky warmth extending and vibrating with mounting passion?

What would happen if she succumbed to Merinda's kisses from that soft, ripe mouth, and allowed her taut and neglected body to tingle and tighten still more? To join her explosive cries with those of a similar pitch?

Her shriek of surrender shattered the silence. She lay, panting, on the bed; she was on fire, her breasts were bursting. Once was not enough. She leapt up to turn the television sound higher, and then lay stroking and loving her own body. Disturbed by her fantasy of the black actress, she conjured up Sam's image instead, rerunning the close-ups in her mind of their most erotic moments. Her cries of release were, to her relief, just as loud, her orgasm just as shattering, her beating heart even harder to quiet.

Sleep overtook her – and her dreams were full of Sam and Merinda. But unlike in her daytime imaginings, both of them spurned her. She was running, hoping for a kindly word from Sam, but he ran faster than her, refusing to turn.

She woke frantic, to an empty day and the bleakest of futures.

'I'm losing my mind, and it's all your fault, Sam. I hate you. No, I don't. I love you, I love you, I love you. And much good may it do me.'

Her distress felt so overwhelming that she contemplated going home. And yet she was not ready to be there alone. On the other hand, the health farm which had been her bolthole, now felt less safe and secure. Where on earth could she find a refuge?

Swimming up and down the pool, she forced herself to focus on her movements. After last night, her legs felt as if she had run a marathon. She concentrated on her strokes, pushing herself on and on in the hope that she could obliterate the desperate ache in her heart and mind. Did Sam care? Had he called? Was he worried? Did it matter? Would he come back married? Each length brought with it fresh torment. Where would it end?

'Have another drink.'

'I shouldn't, Terry. We've hardly eaten anything for days and we've had a hell of a lot of booze already.'

They were in a pub not far from the health farm.

'Who's counting, baby? You're going home tomorrow anyway.'

'Well, that's true.'

He staggered, rather unsteadily she noticed, to the bar. They were an object of interest to the locals and Terry was enjoying it. It was strange that he was quite so inebriated. Perhaps he was drinking doubles to her singles. He was certainly loud. A blue joke he was telling to the landlord was audible throughout the room. How odd that he had once seemed attractive. She should go. The only problem was that she was terrified of the pain when she was alone.

He sat closer. His leg touched hers. His drink was disappearing fast. She sipped at hers. There were beads of sweat oozing from his brow and in between the strands of his carefully arranged hair. Very roughly, he grasped her knee and pulled her to him and suddenly his lips were on hers. But it was the wrong mouth and very definitely the wrong man.

'What do you think you're doing?' she screamed at him as Sam's words came back to her about not going to bed with anyone else. 'Oh my God. What was I thinking coming here with you? You're an absolute bastard. I'm going back, right now.'

'Christ what a prick tease you've become now you're so high and mighty. Time was when you were desperate for what I could give you.'

'I didn't have anything to compare it with,' she snapped and she swept up her bag and, walking as steadily and straight as she could, she left the bar.

She half ran and half walked to the health farm, along the dark country lane which had not seemed anything like as spooky, or long, from the interior of Terry's car.

'I'm losing my mind,' she said aloud to the empty night air. 'I must get my act together. What's happened tonight was dangerous. And undignified. I'm a total mess.'

Was this all she could look forward to now? Back on the single scene where for a woman of her age the dating game was strewn with pitfalls, like other women's husbands having mid-life crises, fading stars and drunks in bars. Was that all she was worth? She had thought she was done with it. And if Sam would come back to her, then he would keep her from harm. But he was not here. And perhaps he never would be.

They gave her a packed lunch when she left the health farm the following day – in case she felt faint on the motorway. It was a kind thought. The day was bright and sunny, and her spirits rose as though she were a child going on a picnic.

She had to face going home, but perhaps she could leave it a while longer, so she drove to her favourite cinema in Curzon Street where they were having an Alfred Hitchcock retrospective, and bought a ticket for *Notorious* which she had seen before, and loved. If only her own romance could have a happy ending.

Afterwards, in the summer streets of London, with their dappled sunlight, she felt a sense of peace. Life was still good. She was rested; she was calm; she was capable. Sam's energy was hers. He could not walk away from the most meaningful experience of his life.

A gentleman-of-the-road lurched up to her, disturbing her reverie. He was smelly and unkempt, but not dangerous. 'Got the price of a cuppa, love.'

Why was there always pain in pleasure? Why must her happiness be at the expense of Hamaida's? Why was there homelessness in the midst of affluence? And ugliness in the face of loveliness? She sighed, then smiled at the tramp, who had short brown stumps in place of teeth, and gave him twelve pounds, which was all the cash she had with her, and he hopped away.

Perhaps the man had been a test of her moral character – sent by God or the universe. The tramp had needed something she could afford to give, so it was right that she should have given it. Sam needed all that she was, and when he had sorted his life out, she would be able to bestow it on him. That would be right too. Tomorrow, he would return and tell her all was well. How could she have doubted the outcome? It was time to go home.

Chapter Ten

'How was it after I left?'

It was Monday morning and Laura had just come into the office and made straight for Helen's room.

'Pretty uneventful, except for the fact that I was propositioned both by Terry and Merinda.'

Laura giggled. 'Did you accept?'

'Of course not.' She did not divulge the fact that she had entertained some surprisingly titillating thoughts about Merinda since that evening. 'How's life at home?' she asked.

'Wonderful. I don't know why I got in such a state. Any word from Sam?'

'He's not due till later today – that's if he comes back.'

The optimism of the previous night had been replaced by pessimism the moment Helen had awakened to a new week. Now, as she left her office to go to the ten-thirty meeting, she did her best to dispel all the negative feelings that were threatening to swamp her. And, as she sat, in a smoky fug, surrounded by colleagues arguing that their piece deserved more airtime, it seemed as if she had never been away.

Derek caught her as the meeting broke up. 'How are you now, Helen?'

'I'm fine,' she answered, brightly.

'Did you have a good rest?'

She laughed. 'Well, it was different!' And she scooped up the day's running order and left.

Her secretary, Sue, turned up in her office shortly afterwards bearing a large black dustbin bag. 'Here's your post from last week!'

'I love your filing system,' Helen said, drily.

'Yeah, well...'

'OK. I'll sort it and prioritise what we need to answer first. I'll get you back in here later.'

Alone in her office, she spent a couple of hours sifting through the piles of mail. She felt more settled now she was back where she belonged, and though she was anxious about the phone call that would announce Sam's return, she kept herself busy so that she did not dwell on it.

By lunchtime though, when there was still no word from him, she began to panic about the evening. She had not thought as far as that until now, but if he did not return, or contact her, she had no idea how she would get through the empty hours after her working day was done.

Filling the week in the health farm had been easy by comparison because Sam was never going to feature in that. But now she felt rootless at the prospect of a yawning gap which Sam should have occupied.

In the afternoon, she was diverted by a pre-record with a former monk who had left his order so that he could set up a farming project for homeless boys in India. She became genuinely absorbed and inspired by the man and his mission and after the interview, she enjoyed talking to him over a pot of tea in the green room.

The phone made her jump. It was one of the operators from the main switchboard.

'Helen, sorry to bother you but the girls in the newsroom didn't seem to know where you were. I have Mr Aziz for you.'

She glanced at her interviewee and tried to think where she could go that would give her more privacy. At the same time, she was so worried that Sam might ring off that she asked for the call to be put through to the green room.

'Helen?'

'Yes. Hello, Sam.' She tried to sound casual.

'Are you all right?'

'Yes.'

'I'm back in London. Can we meet?'

'Of course.'

'Can you talk?'

'Not really.'

'OK. I've got tickets for *Cats*. I know you saw it when it first came out, but I never have. Will that be all right for you? Can you meet me at the New London Theatre after the programme?'

Her heart was racing. 'That would be lovely.'

'It starts at seven-forty-five.'

'I'll be there by seven-thirty.'

The programme went well, and Helen was relieved to find that she was functioning as normal, despite the turmoil of her private life. She met Laura for a quick drink in hospitality afterwards.

'You were great. No one does it better,' her friend said.

'Thanks, Laura. I'm sure that's not true. But it's wonderful to hear it!'

She downed her gin and tonic and went off to her dressing room where she selected the navy blue Parigi dress she had worn on her first lunch date with Sam.

As her taxi drew up outside the theatre, she saw him before he saw her. But by the time she had paid her driver, he was by her side. He stood back for a moment, then swept her into his arms and kissed her. His enthusiastic embrace reassured her that everything in their world must be all right and oblivious to the crowds of tourists waiting to get into the show, she returned it passionately. There was a ripple of applause from the onlookers.

Sam acknowledged them with an embarrassed wave before rushing her inside. Seated in the unusual and circular auditorium, she whispered, 'What happened?'

'I'll tell you later,' he murmured in her ear.

Suddenly, all around them lights, like cats' eyes, became illuminated throughout the theatre. The music began. It was loud. There was no more time for questions. She leant back in her seat, breathing deeply. He reached for her hand and squeezed it tightly. It was hot in the auditorium. She was finding it difficult to breathe.

'Are you feeling faint?' he asked when there was a break in the music. She shook her head.

'There's something wrong. Tell me.'

'It's nothing.'

The music began again. His hand stiffened over hers. She realised that he felt she was keeping something from him. But she hardly knew herself what it was. He was acting normally. Yet, she had no idea of what had transpired in Egypt. Her whole life was in the balance. Perhaps it was no wonder that she was feeling so strange but could not explain it.

As the music quietened again, she turned to him and whispered, 'Did you ask her to marry you?'

He said nothing for a moment. She willed him to answer. Then he nodded.

'Did she say "yes"?'

He nodded again.

The theatre swam before her eyes as the drama in their own lives took over her heart and mind. She was sitting next to the great love of her life. Their legs and their bodies were pressed together. He adored her, she knew that, yet he had asked another woman to be his wife.

The interval came eventually.

'We can't talk here, Helen,' he said quietly as he swept up their pre-ordered drinks. 'But have some of this before we decide what

178

to do.' He pushed a wine glass into her hand and she sipped from it, blinking back the prickly tears in her eyes.

She must not weep here. Not surrounded by the glances of all the people who recognised her. For a second, she felt a tremendous impulse to run amok, grabbing everyone's glasses out of their hands, smashing them, and racing out of the theatre. Instead, she breathed deeply, leant across and kissed Sam on the cheek, almost platonically, and made for the Ladies room.

In the privacy of a cubicle, she allowed herself a minute or two of silent sobbing. Then she emerged, faced herself in the mirror, grimaced at her appearance and began to repair her make-up. Any minute now she would return to Sam and behave as though everything were entirely normal. An anxious-looking woman raced into the room just as the bells announcing the second half began to sound. She turned a searching stare on Helen before eyeing up her own face and renewing her lipstick. As she turned to go, she spoke, 'You're not in the best of shape, are you?' she asked gently. 'I've just come through a divorce. You look like I used to feel. Do you need a cigarette?'

'I don't smoke – well, not much.'

'OK, but would you like one?'

Helen nodded.

The other woman rummaged in her bag for a crumpled pack of Peter Stuyvesants, shook out one, thrust it at Helen, quickly lit it for her and departed.

As she puffed away, two pensioners came in to use the lavatories in the dying moments of the interval. She could feel them eying her, but she refused to meet their gaze.

Suddenly, she felt very sick. Breathing deeply, she tried to calm herself till they had left, then she rushed into the cubicle she had used earlier and retched noisily. She was shaking as she washed her hands and swilled some water around her mouth. Catching sight of herself in the mirror above the basin, a strange weary figure stared back at her. She brushed her hair, sighing at her own image.

As she came back into the bar, she could hear that the second half had begun. Sam was leaning on a table but rushed to her side as soon as he saw her.

He hugged her to him and murmured, 'I think we better catch the second half another day, don't you?'

She bit her lip.

'Or do you want to go back in?' His voice was gentle.

She shook her head.

'Let's go then,' he guided her down the long escalator and out of the building.

It was much easier finding a taxi than it would have been after the show. Sam gave the driver his address and cuddled her to stop her shivering. Neither of them spoke.

Inside his house, he poured two brandies and sat down on the sofa beside her.

She sipped from her glass, then looked at him sadly. 'Tell me what happened, Sam.'

'Nothing at first. Where were you by the way?'

'You rang then?'

'In the end, I felt I had to. I really needed to hear your voice, but you were never there.'

'I went to a health farm.'

'Oh.' He gulped at his drink. 'Did you have a good time?'

'Sam...'

'OK, I'm sorry. It's just that I was frantic with worry about you. I even rang Laura, but Ian answered.'

'Did he tell you where I was?'

'I didn't speak to him. I felt idiotic. I put the phone down.'

'Laura was with me.'

'Oh. Good.'

'Sam, please, tell me everything. Delaying it is only making things worse.'

He took a deep breath. 'At first I met with my family. I also visited several hospitals.'

'And?'

'They need people like me.'

Helen nodded. 'What about Hamaida?'

'We met a few times. In the company of her brothers.'

'Did she say anything?'

'Not much. She never does. She's very quiet. Boring, really. She certainly doesn't know the person I've become.'

'But you went back to talk and to straighten things out. To see what had to be done.'

'That's correct. So, two nights ago, we went out, just the two of us.'

'How did that go?'

'She told me that she doesn't want to spend the rest of her life alone. And I said, which is true, that neither did I.'

'What happened then?'

'She asked if I intended coming home. I said I'd thought about it, and she said she had always loved me.'

'She doesn't even know you.' Helen's voice rose in anger.

'Helen, sweetheart, I'm trying to tell you what happened. It's agony going over it and watching the impact it's having on you. But let me finish.'

She dropped her head into her hands.

'Hamaida cried and accused me of being obsessed with medicine and my own career and advancement. She also said that I was oblivious to the needs of my own people.'

'Sounds like moral blackmail to me.'

He winced and did not meet her gaze, simply continued. 'Anyway, after talking about my work she talked to me about the fact that she isn't marriageable, which she cares about. She isn't like you – someone with a fulfilling career. She told me quite categorically that she doesn't want to die a spinster.'

'She turned you down before. Why was that then?'

'I suppose that I wasn't kind enough. Anyway, it doesn't matter now.'

'But she's trapping you. She laid the trap all those years ago. And all the years since you've struggled to escape it and now, now that you love me, and you've finally found someone you care for, you're punishing yourself by walking back into the very situation you've tried so hard to escape.'

'That's right. Exactly. But I took away her virginity.'

'You told me that she begged you to do that. You said that you gave in and that you didn't even enjoy it.'

'That's all true. I didn't.'

'Was it so fantastic for her then?'

'Not in the way you mean. But it was significant. It meant, in her eyes, that we belonged to each other.'

Helen nodded as tears rolled down her cheeks. 'God above, I think I could give you up if I felt Hamaida really wanted you and would support and love you properly – but where the hell is she? I know she's been ill, but she's never been here, at your side. Surely if she really loved you, she wouldn't have been able to stay away. She'd be looking after you, appreciating you, being proud of what you do.'

He stood up and pulled her into a standing position too. Then he folded her to him and stood, swaying, pressing against her. It was utterly hopeless and yet she did not want the moment to end. She wanted to stay, glued to him tonight and for life.

At length, she pulled away and looked at his anguished face. 'You must sleep. I'm calling a taxi to go home.'

'No!'

She looked at him uncomprehendingly. 'Why not?'

'Because I love you. Because I can't let you go like this. Please, Helen. Please come to bed with me.'

Then, not waiting for an answer, he took her hand and took her upstairs and laid her on his bed and carefully and lovingly undressed her. She lay motionless, too wearily unhappy to engage in the act with him or to stop it. He touched, and kissed her everywhere and when they were ready, he owned her – and for a few blissful moments, she knew comfort and contentment.

He did not invite her to stay the night. And she was aware that she could not. He called a taxi for her and, with great reluctance, she extricated herself from the warmth of his bed, picked up her abandoned clothes and dressed. By the time the cab arrived, Sam was asleep, his face troubled even in slumber. She felt the same expression of hopeless turmoil etched in her own features as she let herself out and travelled back to the emptiness of her flat.

She was disturbed by the persistent buzzing of her doorbell. It was very early for the postman; if he had a registered package for her, he could come back another day. She punched her pillow and then put it over her head to blot out the noise. But it went on and on and eventually she staggered to her intercom, wishing that she had not medicated her misery the night before with almost a whole bottle of wine, which certainly she had not needed after the large brandy earlier.

She picked up the entry phone.

'Helen!' It was Sam.

She pressed the button that would allow him to enter, and seconds later he was at her front door, looking pale and tired, and carrying a pint of milk.

They looked at each other mutely. Stepping back, she invited him in. He closed the door gently behind him, then put the milk on a nearby ledge and launched himself into her arms.

'What are we going to do?' he whispered.

'I don't know, Sam. I don't know anything.'

'Your eyes are swollen, darling. You can't go to work looking like this.'

'I have to.'

'Is your head aching?'

'Yes.'

'Go back to bed, sweetheart. I'll make you some tea.'

Like a child, she did what she was told. She sat in bed with her knees drawn up and the bedclothes pulled right up to her chin. Almost immediately, he appeared with a white napkin wrapped round a clump of ice cubes. He sat on the edge of her bed and put the pack on her head. Then, he went back to the kitchen and returned with two wrung-out teabags, which he placed on her eyes. She lay down, so as not to dislodge them, meekly grateful for his care.

'You have a great bedside manner,' she said.

He stroked her hand and then disappeared again. A few minutes later, she heard the clinking of china as he returned with a tray of tea. She heard him pouring the beverage into two cups, then felt him remove the teabags from her eyes. She blinked him into focus as he cradled her to him and brought a cup to her lips. The gesture generated fresh tears, just when she thought she had none left to shed.

'Helen,' he sighed. 'I can cure people who have been left for dead, but now I feel I'm destroying the only person I've ever loved. I have to go – I'm operating. Let's talk tonight. Are you sure you're going into work?'

She nodded before adding, 'I have to. I'm covering a royal visit.'

He kissed her and made to leave but paused in the doorway. 'Please believe one thing – I do care for you, I care desperately. And I love you more than I can say.'

'Helen, you look terrible,' Derek said when he bumped into her in the canteen queue. He lowered his voice and continued, 'Frankly, I haven't a clue what this is about, but I'm guessing your private life isn't going too well. But whatever it is, a week off was obviously not enough. You need to get away again soon. I'm a bit of a hypocrite I suppose because I should send you home now, but I really need you to do today's job. I can't get clearance from the palace to use someone else at this late stage. But please book some leave. As soon as possible. This can't go on.'

'OK, I'm going off to make-up, now.'

'Do you think you can deal with this Regent Street thing?'

'Of course.'

He raised his eyebrows. 'Jesus, I hope you're right. Pop into my office for the security passes for you and the crew. You're to meet them at the venue in an hour.'

Laura appeared in the make-up department not long afterwards. Probably, thought Helen, Derek had sent her.

'Are you OK?'

'Definitely,' Helen replied.

'From where I'm standing, I wouldn't say so. Do you want to talk about it?'

'No thanks. I appreciate your concern, but I need to get on now; I'm due to leave in twenty minutes.'

Peering at herself in the mirror, Helen wondered where to begin. Her eyes, for all Sam's ministrations, were still swollen. She squirted eye-drops into them and winced as the liquid stung her. Looking at the little bottle she almost laughed as she saw that they had a royal crest on them. 'Must be good then,' she muttered.

Carefully, she applied a smudge of grey eyeshadow and added eyeliner and a dash of mascara. Next, she used a damp sponge to cover her blotchy face with foundation. It would have to do. She would make sure she stayed out of the pictures as much as possible – after all, the public would have eyes only for the princess.

The streets were bustling and the atmosphere electric. It was a novel idea to have the princess meet underprivileged children from round the globe in the world's biggest toyshop.

The crew were waiting for her when she arrived and if they noticed that she was not looking her best, they kept their thoughts to themselves.

'Get the princess arriving, Jamie,' Helen shouted over the hubbub, 'and we'll follow her into the building. If you can get close enough, we'll catch her chatting with some of the invited children. If not, we'll vox-pop the kids later. I'd better do some sort of run-down of what she's wearing but it'll be in the press hand-out and I can always record that bit back at base if we don't get time to do it out here. Right, let's go!'

From her vantage point, Helen could see the royal limousine gliding into view. She was surrounded by hordes of excited children, all waving Union Jacks and jumping up and down. The car stopped. Two detectives leapt out. One opened the door and the princess leant towards him and raised herself from her seat as her female companion straightened her skirt.

The power of the blast knocked Helen to the ground. The players in this disrupted pageant froze like stilled particles of dust in a beam of light. There was uproar, smoke, screaming, shouting. Bits of building and people flew through the air. The royal car sped away and Helen saw its two occupants fall backwards, hitting their heads on the seat behind them.

In the ensuing confusion, Helen noticed that the detectives, so lively two minutes before, were lying on the ground in a contorted mess of bloody limbs and tissue. She suspected they were dead. In her attempt to get back to her feet, Helen reached out for something or somebody to help her. She touched a leg, then recoiled in disbelief as she realised that it was not attached to anyone. A police horse lay writhing and dying as its guts spewed out onto the road. For a moment, her attention was taken by a little girl disfigured by broken limbs and a face that had lost its nose and skin. Cradling the fragments of this child to her, she rocked her gently and sensed the precise moment when her struggle to survive was ended.

A policeman took her arm. 'Leave me alone,' she screamed. 'I've got a job to do.'

She looked around wildly for her crew.

Jamie was lurching towards her, still carrying his camera and running his free, blood-stained hand through his sticky hair. 'I got it all. All of it. I never saw pictures like it.'

He was obviously in shock.

'Are the others OK?'

'Dunno. I think Charlie may have bought it. He caught the full— God, and where's Cyril?'

They turned and saw the soundman crumpled in the gutter and vomiting.

'I must get back to the studios,' Helen shouted. 'I think we were the only crew here. It'll make the lunchtime bulletin. Everyone will want the pictures. To think that this was a day about kids and fashion. That's why I was here instead of any of the heavyweights. My God.'

She surveyed the carnage about her, and the world suddenly went quiet and dark.

Inside the swaying ambulance, the sound of sirens brought her back from nothingness to the nightmare of reality.

'Let me out of here,' she cried.

'Orders is orders, miss,' said a voice which came from a man bent over a mangled body beside her. We're going to St Thomas's. Nearly there.'

Helen tried to stem her impatience. She would get a taxi from the hospital.

But she was hurried into the building despite her pleas to be allowed to go.

Submitting to the attention of a nurse, she made the point that others needed care far more than she did.

'You ought to be properly checked over, though.' The casualty nurse was quietly spoken but firm.

'Later, I promise,' she shouted and she jumped up and made her escape. A taxi was drawing up outside. She ran for it.

It's always like this, Helen thought, as she made her way through the newsroom. The atmosphere crackles when there's a big story. And I partly hate it and partly love it. Tragedy for some is the lifeblood of others.

Various people viewed her curiously as she made her way to the editing suite. They knew better than to interrupt her. Everyone had their eye on the time and the countdown to the one o'clock bulletin.

Helen cut the film and recorded a commentary. Unusually, she sat in the main body of the newsroom and watched it go out. But no one spoke. No one said: 'Great piece.' She knew they could see that her heart had been ripped to shreds by what she had seen. More than that, she had a bigger version of the story to pull together for *Reporting At Six*.

The film editor she had worked with earlier was already sifting shots. She watched a woman cuddling and weeping over a dead schoolgirl. It was like a television drama. Not like real life at all.

The rest of the day was a blur. The Chairman of the company, whom she barely knew, turned up to congratulate her. She said something appropriate, she hoped, but then turned back to her task. Together with the editor, she looked at all the footage, seeking out the most graphic close-ups and then eliminating them as being too gory to be set before the great British public at its tea.

Gradually, it came together. They inserted a clip that someone else had gone out and shot of the Home Secretary saying how he took the nation's security very seriously. She checked whether they could name any of the victims, but there was no clearance because next of kin had not been informed. So, she recorded a new and longer commentary than her one for the earlier bulletin and finished with a run-down of the estimated figures of dead and injured.

She sat then, suddenly frail and shaking, in the surprising calm of the late afternoon.

Derek appeared by her elbow. 'I'm sending you to hospital now,' he told her.

'You can't do that, Derek. I'm fine. Who would present the programme?'

'Well not you. You're not fit.'

'I *am* fit. Have I let you down, in any way? I'm OK.'

'Of course you haven't let us down. Nothing could be further from the truth,' he said calmly as though pacifying an overwrought child. 'You weren't engaged here as a hard news reporter, but no one could have done a better job than you have today. However, enough is enough. Laura will present the programme. You must go for a check-up. But first you might want to think about changing your clothes.'

Helen followed his gaze as he looked at her and took in for the first time the spectacle of her business suit spattered with blood. A vision of Jacqueline Kennedy came to her mind. Weariness soaked her body and now, suddenly, there was a ringing in her ears.

'All right, Derek,' she agreed.

Gary, the producer, was behind his boss. 'Have to hand it to you, Helen,' he said with some relish, 'you're in a different league now, poppet. If you don't win an award, there'll be no justice.'

A tasteless vision of herself in an off-the-shoulder blue taffeta gown, smiling and acknowledging the applause at next year's Royal Television Society awards filled her mind.

Disgusted with herself and the way they all needed the fix of 'a good story' she rose from her seat and walked out of the editing suite and on through the newsroom. The staff working there eyed her progress. Those standing melted away from her path. She had a sensation of Moses parting the Red Sea. Red. Everything was red. Oceans of it...

In the hospital, they examined her, gave her an injection of something sedative and admitted her for the night to a darkened, peaceful room.

At some point, Laura appeared, all eyes in a white face.

'How many dead now?' Helen asked. She had been dreaming of mutilated bodies.

'About thirty – and dozens and dozens injured. Lots of them children. Many have got life-changing disabilities, that's if they live...'

'Who could have done it?'

'Some group of Arab fundamentalists I've never heard of have claimed responsibility. But there's always the IRA…'

'No, surely not.' Helen's favourite grandfather had been Irish, and she had always found it hard to equate the tragedies of the Troubles with the gentle, funny man she had loved so much.

'Well, you can't rule anything out. It'll become clearer, probably, in a few days.'

She must have drifted off because when she reopened her eyes, Laura had gone, and Sam was beside her, stroking her hand.

'Helen,' he said, when he realised she was awake. 'I'm so, so sorry. I should have been here. But I didn't know anything about the bomb. I was in surgery all day and didn't come out till gone seven. Then people started saying that I must be proud of you, but I hadn't a clue what they were talking about. And so, I fail you, yet again. I'm already plagued with the awfulness of what I'm doing to you. And now people of my own kind have nearly killed you.'

She saw that tears were trickling down his face.

For the first time, Helen was struck by a sense of her own mortality and realised the truth that she could so easily now be dead.

After a while, she spoke.

'Sam, what happened today was nothing to do with you. You can't load that guilt onto yourself as well as everything else.'

'I could have lost you, Helen. Forever.'

'Forget it, Sam.'

His mouth met hers and she tried to pull him even closer to her, but one of her arms was hurting and she was too weak.

'Sam, don't ever leave me. Make love to me.'

He straightened up. 'What, here?'

'Yes, Sam. Here. Now. I want you and I need you. I want you to show me that bitterness and hatred won't take over the world and that love counts for so much more. Lie down with me. Please.'

'I can't. It wouldn't be right. Anyway, you're far too poorly.'

Inside her head, she was screaming. It was deafening her. Someone wrenched Sam's grasp away from her own. Where had all these people come from? Something sharp jabbed into her, and shortly afterwards, the noise stopped.

She left the hospital the next morning, against the advice of the doctor looking after her, but agreeing that she would go straight home and not work for a few days.

Back in the studios, she made for the make-up department and washed her hair. She was lucky that she had only a few cuts on her legs, and no real injuries to worry about, but her body ached. She supposed it was the tension of the incident and the fact that she had been knocked to the ground. She used the jet attached to the wash basin to remove all the shampoo suds but kept the stream to a minimum as the water hurt her head. She looked into the mirror and felt as if the face looking out at her was no longer hers, but she applied skin cream to it nonetheless and then added the usual cosmetics.

Derek started as she came into his office. 'I didn't expect you here today, Helen.'

'Why ever not?' She sounded brusque. Rude, perhaps. It was not what she meant. But she had no wish to be banished from the building. 'Look, Derek,' she tried again, 'it was just another job. I was caught up in a… a major tragedy, but I'm OK. I'm tough. I can handle this business. I need to work, anyway.'

'What did the doctors say about that?'

'They said I was fine,' she lied, and she left him for her own office.

Before long, Laura appeared. 'You shouldn't be here, Helen.'

'Well, I disagree, and I am here. And that's that.'

Laura looked as if she was about to argue, but thought better of it, and disappeared.

The phone rang. 'Helen! What are you doing there? I'm coming to get you right away.'

'No, you're not, Sam. You're busy working. And I'm busy working. I have lots to do. Please don't interfere.'

'I'm entitled to interfere, for God's sake. I love you.'

'When you go back to Egypt to get married, I'll need this job. So, leave me alone.'

She put down the phone as the pain of her situation washed over her, and she allowed herself to review the tragic events of yesterday, and to feel the excoriating hurt of losing Sam.

There were some surprised faces when she turned up for the ten-thirty meeting.

Ron, one of the producers laid out his plans for the programme. 'Today,' he announced, 'we're beginning our series on specialty acts working in clubs and theatres round the country this summer. And we've got a knife-thrower coming in. He's the sort of bloke who'll never hit the big time, but never stops working. We'll pre-record this afternoon. I wouldn't risk it live.'

'Why not?' Helen asked, recalling all too clearly the 'live' events of the day before.

'Well, if you're actually planning to do the programme...'

'I am,' she said quickly.

Ron looked anxiously towards Derek, but went on, 'Well, my plan, which would make great television – but is a lot to ask after everything you went through yesterday – is that you should inter-view him while he throws knives at you.'

'OK,' she agreed.

Someone gasped, and several people exchanged anxious glances, which she ignored.

'You don't have to,' Ron said.

'I said I'll do it,' she snapped.

Back in her own office, Helen went through the day's post. She did not send for Sue; it was easier to work alone and to draft her replies in longhand than face any more human contact than was necessary.

At lunchtime, she wandered into the canteen, selected a tuna salad and a cold drink, paid, and returned to her own office. She ate without tasting it, skimming the newspapers at the same time. Her distressed figure, holding the dead child, stared at her from the front page of several of them.

Pushing the papers away, she tried to gather together in her mind all the strands of the last two unreal days. Why had she been so unkind to Sam? She supposed because he had spurned her twice. Once by getting engaged to the dull woman back home and secondly by refusing to make love to her in the hospital when it was the only thing that would have helped her feel better. She should walk away from him right now. Refuse to be put through any more of this torture. He was bad news. Mixed up. Big trouble. But the fact was, she wanted only him. He was her life and she felt she would die without him. There had to be a solution. And if he would not find it, then she must.

She reached for the phone and rang the television company's regular travel agent. They were used to all her work trips, but she explained that this was personal, and that the bill must come to her. The price they quoted was much more than she had anticipated, but this was not a moment for penny-pinching. Her future hung in the balance. And so did his.

'I need to think about it. I'll call you back soon,' she said.

The Great Jackerello and his assistant Gloria were waiting for her in the green room. He was about forty-five, blond, and in very good shape. His partner looked older. Perhaps the years had treated her less kindly. She was glamorous, though, with extravagant false eyelashes that would have looked entirely at home on a Disney character in a cartoon. And they were both wearing thick tan pancake make-up on their faces that probably looked better in a circus tent or a theatre than it was going to do in close-up on television.

Lucia, one of the regular make-up artists, popped her head round the door to take a look at them.

'We've got the slap on already, dear,' Gloria announced with a laugh.

Helen stifled a giggle at the expression on Lucia's face as she suggested toning down their colour a bit with her lighter powder and brush. Next, she took them to a dressing room so they could change.

When, having changed herself, she collected the couple, she felt very sedate in comparison. Jackerello was now naked to the waist, except for a scarf tied nonchalantly round his neck and was poured into a pair of fringed leather trousers which emphasised his very neat rear end. Gloria wore a sleeveless fringed mini-dress with a daringly plunging neckline. It had been bought probably when its owner had been just a bit smaller, and there were a few bulgy areas here and there, but she was a well-preserved woman with legs, encased in black fishnet tights, that would doubtless give some of the elderly male viewers quite a thrill.

The floor manager asked Helen if she was nervous. To please him, she said she was, but in truth she was numb. She stood watching as the Great Jackerello asked for a moment to practise. Helen supposed it was important for him to rehearse since she was not only new to him as an assistant, but a complete novice. He threw his first knife. She was amazed at its speed as it swiftly embedded its point in the board beside her and continued quivering for a full ten seconds. Suddenly, she felt very frightened indeed, but it was too late to duck out now. She had wanted to impress her colleagues with her ability to carry on, no matter what. This seemed the definitive way to do it.

'If you're ready,' said the floor manager, 'we'll go. Start the clock. Forty-five seconds.'

'We're just identifying the tape,' she told the Great Jackerello, 'so that they can pull the right reel off the shelf when the show goes out later.'

'Oh,' he said, and then as he looked around the crowded studio floor with its monitors, lights and cables, he continued, 'Clever, innit? And complicated, all this.'

'Not as clever as you're about to be, I hope.'

'Quiet, please,' warned the floor manager. He waved his arm at her, and Helen began.

'How do you become a knife-thrower?' she asked.

'It's in my blood,' he said.

'I hope that's an inappropriate choice of word,' she replied. 'Have you ever injured anybody?'

'Oh yes,' he answered with a grin. 'My wife Gloria's been to hospital several times. Just little grazes, mind, nothing serious.'

'That's good then,' Helen tried to laugh. 'Well, I'd rather Gloria did the act than me, but just to get the feel of it, I'll start it off for her. Where do I stand, and what do I do?'

He put her up against the board and told her not to move.

'I wouldn't dream of it,' she said.

'You will, though. Everybody does. You'll flinch, but you won't realise it. Doesn't matter. I know what you'll do, and I'll throw in a way that compensates for it.'

'I just hope I react predictably, then.' Her voice was little more than a whisper.

The knife whizzed past her right ear at tremendous speed and lodged itself into the board. She gasped and tried to think of the next question. Then the second knife found its place by her left ear. She felt hemmed in, and unable to speak.

He threw one more knife, and then she found her voice. 'Stop!' she said. 'I've been a guinea pig long enough. I've found out what it feels like, and it's terrifying! Let's bring in Gloria to take over.'

In her earpiece, she heard the director's instructions. 'Cut to Camera Two, and go in tight on Helen... She's gone a very funny colour.'

Back on the studio floor, Helen watched as Gloria smiled while knives outlined her body. She managed to ask some reasonably intelligent questions and Jackerello answered all of them as casually as if he was sipping a cup of tea rather than aiming lethal weapons at tremendous velocity in the direction of his wife.

195

Time was up; she asked the artist to throw one more knife, and the director cut to a close-up of it as it stuck into the board, only an inch from his worthy assistant.

The studio froze; the floor manager put his finger to his lips. After ten seconds, as the cameras faded, he said, 'OK, everyone relax. We'll just wait for a clear.'

'What's a clear?' asked Jackerello.

'A clear is when we've checked everything and decided the recording's OK. But there can be reasons why we might need to do another take. For example, the editor might think I haven't asked the right questions. Or we might have a problem if the cameras haven't picked up all the good shots of your knives. And then there's always the possibility that there might be a sound problem or some technical difficulty with the tape. But let's hope the gods are with us, because I certainly don't want to do it again!'

'Good-oh, all clear,' announced the floor manager, and the sound men moved in swiftly to un-mike Helen and the two guests. 'Back at five-thirty, everyone.'

Helen had tea with her interviewees, and explained that in this evening's programme, after the recorded close-up of the last knife going in, she would come back into vision, live, and would mention where they were performing for the summer.

'Good! Get a few more bums on seats, eh?' Jackerello winked. 'But I wouldn't want to have to do this every day. Bloody nerve-racking this television business.'

'It's nothing compared with what you and Gloria do!' Helen said.

'You get used to it.' Gloria shrugged. 'Bit monotonous some-times. While he's doing it, I find meself working out what I'm cooking for supper.'

'You don't!' Jackerello sounded indignant and looked surpris-ingly hurt.

'I do,' she replied, in a bored voice.

*

196

Sam was in reception after the show. Without a word, he shepherded her out of the building and into his car, before demanding, 'Have you got some sort of fucking death wish?'

She examined her nails thoughtfully. Perhaps she had, she thought.

'Helen, for God's sake,' he breathed deeply, and she could see that he was trying to calm his anger. 'Yesterday, you were nearly killed by accident. Today, you could have been killed by design.'

'It's a funny old business I'm in, isn't it?' She knew her flippant response was inappropriate but did not apologise for it.

He made no comment, simply started up the engine.

Driving along the Embankment, she sneaked a look at him. She saw that he had noticed; the stern set of his jaw relaxed. He was so very beautiful. So vital to her. She reached over and stroked his left thigh. Turning towards her, his eyes transmitted feelings of such intense love that she tingled all over. Surely, they would never be separated? Various forces might try to keep them apart, but in the end, they must be together. She would not allow anything else.

The Italian restaurant was crowded, and they were swallowed up into its Mediterranean smell and noise and enthusiastic atmosphere.

After a dinner of mozzarella, avocado and tomato salad followed by calves' liver, grilled with sage, he suggested that they talk, and offered her a choice of doing it over coffee in the trattoria or going to one of their homes.

'Let's try here.' She took his hand and squeezed it. 'Maybe if we're in a public place, I'll have a better perspective on it all and, rather more importantly, keep my emotions in check. In fact, let's both try to keep level-headed, even though it's so difficult. As I see it, Sam, the only problem I have is that I am absolutely loopy for the love of you. You, on the other hand, have loads of problems. And I think it might help if you write them down. Why don't we make a list and then see what we've got?'

He nodded.

Still holding his hand, she loosened her grasp slightly and stroked the backs of his fingers one by one. She leant over and kissed his cheek, then sat looking at his face which was pinched and pale in the candlelight.

'OK, so do you want to put down a list of, um, maybe six points? Perhaps, Egypt, Hamaida, Mother, Father. Career and Honour?'

He drew out his diary from his inside breast pocket and quickly found a blank page near the end, for making notes. She watched as he scribbled down the headings.

'OK – how strong is the pull of your own country?'

'I never thought about it till recently, but now it is definitely growing. And I do feel a sense of guilt that I never use my skills there, but only in the western world as it were.'

'How important is Hamaida to you?'

'Not important, but I feel sorry for her.'

'Do you love her?'

'No, but let me explain something. People of my class and culture in Egypt tend to marry for convenience or status. We don't, and I somewhat regret this, put women on a pedestal. We give them children, we provide them with financial security and servants and expect them to be there for us, and to run our household and to support us. I'm over-simplifying it, but maybe it will give you some insight.'

'Do you love me as an Englishman, then?'

He sighed. 'It's certainly the person who's lived in England since a boy who fell in love with you. I adore you, like a man possessed. God only knowns where nationality comes into it.'

'If we married, would that marriage be in any way like the ones in Egypt you've described?'

'Never!'

'Let me ask you this then: would honour be served if you went back, married Hamaida, set her up financially and gave her the status she wants, but left again to work here and to live with me? I don't need to be married to you. Would that be enough for her and give her the position in society that she wants? And would it also respect your father's wishes and memory and keep your mother happy?'

'I don't know, Helen. Not my mother, I don't think. The rest, possibly. But it would not solve my dilemma about working there.'

'No, I suppose not.'

'Except,' he said, 'it has occurred to me that perhaps if I could stay here, I could also negotiate a way I could go to Egypt for three months a year and work, and also help train other doctors. I could set up a foundation to treat people who were sick and had no money.'

Her spirits rose at this suggestion. Perhaps there was compromise? Perhaps they could find their way around the various difficulties and dilemmas?

She looked around the restaurant and noticed a couple sitting down at the table next to them. The woman was in the last stages of pregnancy. She bore her huge stomach proudly, and her male companion was evidently devoted to her. The sense of belonging between them was tangible. If only that could be us, she thought.

Sam had seen the couple too. She knew he had and knew too how much it affected him. He leant across the table and reached for both her hands and held them in his grasp.

'Do you mind if we continue talking at home,' he asked breathily. 'I want you to myself.'

'Good idea,' she replied quietly. Then, more boldly, she added, 'Let me get the bill for once?'

'No, that's not my way. I've told you before.'

'OK, you Tarzan, me give in.'

They both laughed. Some things were still normal.

He did not query which home they should go to but headed in the direction of his own. Inside his dimly lit sitting room, she stood for a moment, gazing at the little sculpture of the ballet dancer.

199

'Did you see that woman?' Sam's voice cracked.

'What woman?' she asked, pretending not to know.

'The pregnant one. That is what I want so much for you.' He reached for her and she felt for a moment that all might be well. He did love her. He could not let her go.

They stood, joined by their shared passion and Helen moved her hand lower till she found the growing evidence of his desire. She stroked him gently, then more firmly. He closed his eyes and his breathing quickened. Then, taking her arms with both hands, he put her firmly away from him and pushed her gently into the sofa.

'Helen,' he whispered. 'I was wrong to take you the other night. I went back to Egypt to sort my life out. Clearly, I am nowhere near doing that. I had you because I could not help myself. And I needed you so much. But I shouldn't have done it. Then, yesterday, you might have been killed. Can you see that I can't allow this to go on? I must make some decisions, and in the meantime, I mustn't make love to you.'

She was as stunned as if he had slapped her round the face. 'All right.' Her voice was ugly. 'I'll just need to buy a vibrator.'

'Helen, that is so crude.'

'Sam, I really don't have to apologise for my sexuality or for the fact that you have awakened an appetite in me that I have to satisfy. I've never known feelings like these. I can't just lock them all away again.'

She jumped up and strode to the other side of the room where he kept a wooden case with a few cigarettes in it. She took one and lit it, and stood, facing away from him and trying to stem her hurt and fury.

When she turned around, he looked so utterly forlorn that tears pricked at her eyes. 'Sam, I'm sorry. I don't mean to be unkind. Would you, I mean could you, consider talking to someone about our situation? I'm too close to you. I'm too emotional. I'm not helping, though I'd like to.'

'I don't really have any close friends,' he admitted, sadly. 'Well, there is one. He's a surgeon, but he's in Paris.'

'I was thinking more of a professional.'

'A psychiatrist? Helen, angel, what are you thinking? I'm not *mad.*'

'I'm not suggesting that you are. But you are under intolerable strain. It would be a responsible thing to do – for yourself.'

'The answer lies within me.'

She tried a different tack. 'You have divorce in your country. Could you go back and marry Hamaida, but then divorce her in a couple of years? And then we could be together. I am willing to come and live with you there. I'd do anything...'

'Darling, you've never been there. How do you know you could settle? What would you do? I might not be enough for you if you had no career, and no outlet for your brilliance.'

'Sam, I'm not brilliant. I have a certain facility. I learn quickly. But, I'm an ordinary girl. And this ordinary girl just wants one thing in life, to be with you.'

'Darling angel,' he whispered. 'I love you so much.' He walked towards her, his face full of wonder. 'You desperately want to make the whole world better. But don't make any more suggestions. I don't want you to demean yourself on my account. A woman like you should not settle for the crumbs from the rich man's table. You should have pride of place there.'

He held her then and in that moment, she knew that she must activate her plan, for her, for him and their future. She had to see his country for herself. She had to go to Egypt.

Chapter Eleven

Winging her way to Sam's homeland, Helen reran that last meeting. She had refused to see him since.

For most of every day, she had told herself that there was no point in believing that she and Sam had a future, yet she could not accept it. That was why she was visiting Egypt. To try to change things.

During their two weeks or so apart, her moods had fluctuated wildly from cautious hope to anger and on to the worst despair of her life. On one such night, as she had gone to take her contraceptive pill as usual, she had asked herself what on earth she was doing filling her body with unnecessary hormones for no purpose, and had flushed the whole packet down the lavatory.

Laura had been her great support. 'He'll never let you go,' she had said, several times each day. And on the night before Helen's departure, she had hugged her, wished her good luck and said gently, 'You can't believe there's no hope – you wouldn't be going to Egypt if you did.'

Helen had hugged her in return and sighed, and then asked a question that was a constant niggle at the back of her brain.

'Laura, be honest with me. Do you think I'm behaving oddly? I mean, is it possible that I am so grief-stricken with all of this that I'm losing my mind?'

'Of course not. You're a bit up and down. Always have been. But I would stake my life on your sanity.'

Helen had remained unconvinced.

A dagger seemed to have inserted itself into her rib cage. She gasped and tried to breathe the pain away. What was Sam doing now? He had not wanted her to go.

Every day, since they had last met, he had phoned her, many times.

'You can't go there, Helen.'

'I can and I am.'

'But when you go to Egypt, I want to take you.'

'Come with me, then.'

'I can't. You know that. Not now.'

'That's that then. I need a holiday. Everybody says so. It'll be warm and I'll feel better.'

'You won't. Don't do this. It won't help.'

The calls had gone on and on. For all that they argued, her heart was always lifted by his protestations that he loved her, had never loved this way before and would never stop loving her. His voice and affirmation were like a drug to her and infinitely more essential than food or water. For all that, he was no nearer to finding a way out of their situation. And that's why she had had no choice but to fly away.

At Cairo airport, she looked for the guide she had been told would meet her. She spotted him holding up the name of Kuoni, her tour company and, for the first time, was able to isolate the plane passengers she would never meet again from those gathering with her.

They smiled nervously at each other, and the oldest woman in the party nudged her husband and jerked her head in Helen's direction. She wondered what they would say to each other later. Probably, they would be mystified that she was travelling alone, and would query why someone like her would have to go on holiday by herself. Would they think it was bold and adventurous? Not likely. Almost certainly, they would feel sorry for her. Unconsciously, Helen shook her shoulders in a bid to rid herself of that thought. She had not come here to feel pathetic. It was important to be strong.

On the coach ride into Cairo, Helen began to weigh up her companions. The older woman's husband was an irascible Scottish former army officer who talked loudly and announced to everyone that he had been here in the war.

'Got the measure of these chappies,' he said, before trying out his Arabic on the driver who either did not understand him or decided not to.

Helen winced and decided she would keep her distance from the couple as much as possible. There was a family of four from Brazil who sat at the back of the vehicle and talked to each other. But there were three other single people of around her age, or slightly older, as well as a young couple, from Leeds, who promised to be fun. Though she was here on a mission, she was glad that she might have some congenial company.

The guide announced that his name was Ahmed. It would have to be, thought Helen with a sigh. He pointed out various landmarks as they travelled – including a massive statue of Ramses the Second – but mostly he let them look for themselves, and chat. He indicated that tomorrow they would begin their Egyptian education in earnest; tonight they could relax.

In the lobby of their four-star hotel, they sank into comfortable armchairs while they waited for their rooms to be allocated. One of the single men leant over to Helen, offering his hand.

'I won't pretend I don't know who you are,' he laughed. 'I'm Jonathan Seabrook. I'm in television too. Other side of the camera though – a designer.'

'Very pleased to meet you, Jonathan.'

'As we're both travelling alone, I wondered if we could have dinner together.'

She hesitated. 'I'm not very good company at the moment, and I'm tired, so I thought I'd probably have a sandwich in my room.'

'I only meant something light in the coffee shop.' He smiled at her. 'I'm pretty knackered myself.'

'I'm sorry, Jonathan. I didn't mean to sound ungracious. Let's go to the coffee shop, then. I'll meet you in an hour. Once I've had a bath, I'll be much more sociable.'

Inside her very large room, with its two double beds, she felt very lonely. She was in Sam's country but, as yet, that fact had hardly penetrated her brain. She might have been in a luxury hotel anywhere in the world. The air conditioning protected her from the outside temperature, and from her window the Nile looked much like any other significant river.

After bathing and washing her hair, her mood improved. She selected a light-weight pink dress and sandals and applied some cream blusher, a hint of lipstick and two coats of mascara and she was done. Right on cue, there was a knock on her door.

'Gin and tonic?' asked Jonathan.

'Great idea!' She beamed at him.

In his room, which was identical to her own, he broke open his bottle of duty-free gin.

'I've been here before,' he told her. 'On business though. And I found out that though the Egyptians are more relaxed about alcohol than most of the Arab world, they don't really want it to be too available, and when you find some – especially in a place like this – you have to take out a second mortgage!'

Jonathan was pleasant and uncomplicated company she decided as they wandered through to the coffee shop, ordered club sandwiches and lots of water, and chatted away. Again, Helen had the sense that she could be anywhere. Perhaps once they started viewing all the ancient monuments it would sink in that she was really here.

After they had eaten, Jonathan suggested they go to the piano bar.

The barman, called Ahmed, was charming and insisted on exercising his English. 'I went to English school,' he said. 'Many of us did before 1956. We love you!'

It felt like a good start, thought Helen as she looked out at the magnificent view of the city at night from her vantage point on the top of their very high building.

'Where do you think everyone else is?' she asked.

'Probably sleeping. They obviously don't have our stamina!'

'What do you make of them all?'

'Joanna, the girl with the floral dress works in fashion. She's some sort of PR person. The couple from Leeds, Steve and Rosie, seem fun. And the shortish, fair-haired chap is a psychiatrist. His name's Freddie Longhurst, you might have heard of him – he does quite a bit of telly and radio.'

'I suspect the family won't mix with us much. I think only the dad speaks any English. But what about the old army man and his wife?'

Jonathan pulled a wry face. 'I just hope he doesn't keep lecturing us on Cairo past and present.'

'You're a wicked boy.' She grinned.

Two exorbitantly-priced cocktails later, drunk to the accompaniment of some very accomplished piano playing, Helen was beginning to feel a bit vague, and decidedly fatigued.

'I'd better go while I can still walk in a straight line,' she told him. 'What time do we meet in the morning?'

'Eight-thirty.'

'Oh, that's not too bad. Didn't the brochure say something about some tours beginning around three?'

'Yeah. But when we get further south, you'll be amazed at how hot it can get. You couldn't cope with sightseeing in those midday temperatures. You have to get your culture fix before you pass out!'

'Thanks for taking me under your wing, Jonathan,' she said, and she meant it.

'My pleasure. See you in the morning.'

While she was in company, she felt like the Helen the public knew and expected. But back in the solitude of her room, her longing for Sam hit her like a hurricane. What on earth was she doing here without him? She sat down and blinked away the tears that threatened. Mustn't cry here, she told herself. I have to be indomitable.

The phone rang. She expected it to be Jonathan checking that she had negotiated the lift and hotel corridors without incident.

'Miss Bartlett?' asked the hotel operator.

'Yes.'

'I have a call for you.'

'Hello,' said the familiar voice.

'Sam! How did you find me?'

'Well, you let slip which travel company you were going with and I did a bit of detective work. How do you like my home country?'

'I haven't seen much of it yet – just what one could take in on the journey here from the airport.'

'Are there any nice people in your travel group?'

'Mmmn. Seem to be. One in particular. His name's Jonathan. He works in the industry too. He's a designer.'

'Oh.' Sam's voice was cold. 'I see.'

'Please stop that, Sam. You don't really think I've come here with the intention of having a holiday romance, do you?'

'No, I suppose I don't. What's he like?'

'About my age. Very dapper. Well-travelled. Almost certainly gay.'

'Oh good!'

She raised her eyes heavenward. 'Sam, you're impossible. Can I remind you that you're the one who's engaged to someone else?'

'Sorry. I know... Helen, do you remember the night we met when we both turned up at the Harrison's dinner party?'

'How could I forget?'

'I'm not totally insensitive. I wasn't, even then. I knew how upset you were, and yet you kept entertaining all the other guests and kept the dinner party going till you got tired, suddenly.'

'Or drunk, suddenly.'

'You weren't. Anyway, whatever, I was extremely impressed by your bravery.'

'That's a nice thing to say.'

'Well, let me tell you, I'm even more impressed with you now. I really don't deserve you. I know you love me, and I can't believe my luck. It's awful that I'm treating you so badly and I really wish I weren't. I love your mind. I love your body. And I love your courage.'

'Sam, listen. One of the reasons I came here was to get myself together and to get my wayward emotions under control, so please don't go on.'

'I had to tell you.'

'And I am so, so glad you did. But you do deserve me. And I just hope that somehow we can wade through all this and be together.'

'I know, darling. And I am going to do something positive to try to help.'

'Oh my God, what?'

'I'm flying to Paris at the weekend to speak to Jeremy.'

'Who's that?'

'He's my oldest friend and another surgeon – a gynaecologist actually.'

'Oh yes, you mentioned him.'

'You said I should talk to someone else, and I suddenly realised that it's the only thing you've ever asked of me. You're the one person in my life who never pressurises me – so it's the least I can do. You'll be on the boat over the weekend anyway, so I won't be able to contact you.'

'You seem to know a lot about my trip.'

'I don't mean to check up on you. I just want you to know that I am trying to do something to sort this.'

'Thank you.'

In the silence that followed, she felt a tangible link with him, as though they were holding hands across the miles. She pictured him, tall, liquid-eyed, beautiful. Her man. Eventually, she broke the spell. 'How's your day been, Sam?'

There was another pause before he answered her, and she knew that he too had been feeling their connection.

'As far as the job goes,' he said, 'very well indeed. A patient I was worried I was going to lose suddenly picked up and I think she's going to make it after all.'

'That's wonderful. Maybe other things will get better too.'

'That would be good. I love you, my dearest angel.'

'And I love you, dear boy.'

Eight in the morning came all too soon – of course it was only six in England. Reassured by her phone call with Sam of the night before, Helen had slept better than she had for weeks and though she was excited at the prospect of seeing Cairo, she longed to stay in bed.

After breakfast, Ahmed arrived, all smiles, to begin his task and to tell them that a mini-coach was waiting to convey them to the Citadel.

As their tour progressed through the ancient World Heritage site, for the first time, Helen began to appreciate, and piece together, the various periods of history in this country. It felt much more Arabic than she had expected. And when singing broke out from the minarets calling the faithful to pray, she was astonished to see masses of ordinary people – shoppers, bus drivers and market stallholders – drop to their knees quite unselfconsciously and prostrate themselves in what she presumed was the direction of Mecca.

They went next to the Cairo Museum which was so huge, Helen wondered how they could possibly cover even a fraction of it in the one and a half hours that had been allocated. She was reminded of a visit to Paris when she had been meandering around the Louvre; suddenly she had been accosted by a horde of noisy Americans – clearly a group with a tight timetable – demanding she point them in the direction of the *Mona Lisa*. They had passed her on the stairs again three minutes later, with their mission accomplished. Probably the tour bus had kept its engine running. Calm had descended on the space, leaving those taking the trip more gently to regather their rhythm and thoughts in the wake of the tornado that had threatened to flatten them.

Ahmed was a knowledgeable and quick speaker and Helen did her best to absorb all the information that was coming her way. She wished she could ask more questions and slow the process down; in her mind she could not help but think of the children she wanted to have, who would be part of this heritage, and she wanted to know so much more about it.

The highlight of the visit was the treasure of Tutankhamun. It stretched over an entire floor and Ahmed bid them take away as much of an impression of it all as they could, so that when they visited the tomb in a few days, which was apparently very small, they could compare its size with the cornucopia which it had held to itself for so many centuries before Howard Carter had disturbed it.

'It is only because he was such an inferior king that his tomb remained intact,' Ahmed pointed out. 'More prominent monarchs had their tombs plundered long before, and most of their bounty lost.'

There were two hours for lunch before they were to reconvene at their hotel, and Helen decided to break away from the group. Alone, the city felt more alien and frightening. First at the doors of the museum, she was pestered to change money.

'Dollars?' asked a succession of poor, traditionally dressed men.

'No, thank you.'

'You English.'

She nodded.

'You wish change money? Good rate here.'

She asked how much and was astounded to be offered much more favourable terms than those of the official dealers. She changed fifty pounds, aware that, perhaps, in this country where bartering was second nature, she should have pressed for more. But she was proud she had managed on her own and did not want to be greedy.

Although the hotel was nearby, it took a while to reach it, and the fumes from the traffic were oppressive in the middle-of-the-day heat. Also, Cairo appeared to be undergoing extensive modernisation, and dust from all the construction hung in the air and irritated her throat.

She had supposed that the sight of Europeans was common here, so she was surprised at the many comments during her short journey.

'You English?'

'Yes.'

'Beautiful lady, welcome.'

Little children in particular went out of their way to smile, speak English to her and generally ingratiate themselves with her. Perhaps the tourist drive was a subject on the schools' curriculum.

As she reached the hotel, it occurred to her that she had not felt at all unsafe in the city and that she had not even considered that she might be mugged. She remembered Sam having told her that theft is forbidden in Arab culture. It was gratifying that the rule was so clearly adhered to.

She had planned to explore the city further once she had had a cold drink and sat down for a while, but as soon as she returned to the sanctuary of her bedroom with its air conditioning and comfortable furniture, she decided to stay there.

She ordered a litre of mineral water and a chicken sandwich, then lay down on the bed.

Could this country ever be home to her, she asked herself. The people were friendly – but then, so far, she had encountered only the working and out-of-work classes. The hierarchy – families such as the ones Sam and Hamaida came from – might be very different.

Room Service arrived swiftly with her order, plus a bottle of champagne in a silver pail.

'That's a mistake,' she told the waiter. 'I didn't ask for that.'

'Compliments of Mr Aziz,' he replied.

So, it seemed that the man who declared he could not be with her, could not let her alone either. How was it going to be possible, even had she wished it, to put him out of her mind?

'Don't open it now, thanks. I'll never catch up with my sight-seeing party if you do!'

'Whatever you say, madam,' agreed the young man, flashing her a smile. She tipped him and noticed that the name on his badge was George. He was the first man she had met here who was not called Ahmed.

Jonathan looked relieved when she joined the others in the lobby. 'I wasn't sure I should let you go off on your own,' he said, rather seriously.

'Well, I came to find out certain things, and I can't do it surrounded by Brits.'

The afternoon mini-coach took them into Old Cairo. Here, the level of real poverty was much more apparent.

'We look after our own people,' Ahmed told them. 'In our culture, we are responsible for each other. When we have – we share.'

Helen felt the system must be breaking down; there were bedraggled and under-nourished beggars everywhere she looked.

They stopped at an old Coptic church, St Sergius, reputedly built on the site where the Holy Family found refuge on their flight into Egypt. Helen asked more questions than most. How many Coptic Christians were there? Did they live in harmony with Moslems? Was the form of their religion more like Catholic or Orthodox Christians?

'Darling,' interrupted Jonathan. 'Are you doing research for a programme?'

Helen grinned. 'Sorry. Interviewing people is a bit of a habit for me.'

She bought a couple of books, and a copper, silver and brass plate of the Holy Family, questioning herself inwardly as she did so whether she was attempting to curry favour with the Almighty, always supposing He existed.

On the way back to the hotel, the party was held up in dense traffic. Unlike in London, Paris or Rome, and despite the heat, the drivers rarely sounded their horns. They seemed to accept the situation as the norm; perhaps indeed it was. In the coach, which was not air-conditioned, they began to wilt. Only Jonathan remained lively as he determinedly made plans for the evening.

'After all,' he cajoled the rest of them, 'we surely didn't come all this way to eat club sandwiches in an international hotel. I'll ask Ahmed where one goes to get good local food.' And off he went to the front of the bus.

In his absence, the Scotsman took it upon himself to advise everyone loudly that they must not eat the salad.

Jonathan returned, all smiles. 'OK, I've got the name of a good place. So, who's coming?'

The other three single people plus the young couple all put up their hands.

'Shall we say eight in reception?' Jonathan suggested.

Helen checked her watch, hoping that the traffic would ease soon so that she could get an hour's sleep at the very least before going out again.

'Let's get dressed up.' Rosie giggled.

'I'm game,' Joanna agreed. 'Helen?'

'Why not?' Remembering Sam's present, she invited the other diners to come to her room at seven-thirty to have a glass of champagne.

In her room, she fell asleep as soon as she lay on the bed. The heat had been enervating and she was exhausted from the sights and sounds and history that they had seen.

When she woke again, she felt surprisingly lively, and quite excited at the prospect of going out on the town. She washed her hair and let it dry naturally, made up her face, and then opted to wear a colourful sequinned top, and her favourite layered taffeta skirt, which she had packed without holding out much hope that there would be an occasion to suit it.

Steve volunteered to uncork the champagne. 'This must have cost you a fortune, Helen.'

'No. It was a gift.'

'I knew it! You have an Arab lover. That's why you disappeared so mysteriously at lunchtime.' Rosie looked thrilled at the possible intrigue.

'Don't you go out with that dishy heart surgeon?' Joanna asked. 'I'm sure I've seen you together in the papers.'

'That's right.' Helen avoided the other woman's gaze.

'I suppose you're meeting his family?' Joanna pressed.

'Something like that,' Helen replied, suddenly uneasy about her plan. 'Now, let's get you all a glass.'

For a group of six individuals thrown together entirely by chance, they mixed well. Joanna was the most poised and elegant, in a little black dress with a single strand of pearls. Helen suspected that she earned a very healthy salary at the public relations company she worked for. Perhaps she owned it. Rosie was in black too. She was plumper than the other two women, but youth was on her side and her good humour was infectious. The men were more casual, dressed in linen jackets and trousers, but no ties. The quietest of them was Freddie, the psychiatrist. He did a lot of observing but said little.

Once the champagne was finished, they went downstairs where two taxis were waiting for them. Jonathan negotiated the price before they left, and soon they were driving at speed through the crowded streets.

They were, they quickly realised, distinctly overdressed for the restaurant. But nearly everyone else there appeared to be local, so that gave it a stamp of approval in Helen's eyes.

A friendly cross-eyed waiter, in a long flowing robe, hurried them into squashy, comfortable seats and produced English menus for them all, typed somewhat inexpertly.

'What shall we drink?' Steve asked. 'Can I see a wine list?'

'We have white and we have red,' said the waiter.

Jonathan smiled. He was the only one present not to be surprised by the comment. 'One of each then, I should think,' he nodded at the waiter. 'We can always order more if we want. Ooh, and we'll want a lot of mineral water.'

Several other waiters swooped on them almost immediately bringing an assortment of dips – most of which seemed to have lentils as their basic ingredient – and a large quantity of flat bread. Before long, dishes arrived of tiny chickens and pigeons that looked as though they had died of malnutrition.

'I don't think we need worry about any hidden lead shot,' Freddie remarked.

Helen laughed though inwardly she was worried that they might all end up by being seriously ill.

Another waiter brought delicious, crisp looking salad.

'Don't eat the salad!' they chorused, mimicking the old Scottish soldier.

Helen enjoyed the evening – happy to find that, just for a while, she could park her anguish over Sam and be sociable in a spontaneous and unexpected way.

The wine – which was all of one brand that none of them had heard of – was quite awful. They all agreed on that, but it did not stop them drinking it, or indeed ordering two more bottles when their initial order ran out.

'And perhaps all this alcohol will pickle everything we've eaten and stop us getting food poisoning,' Freddie reflected, and he pulled a slightly woeful face.

Back in the hotel. Jonathan was insistent that they should make a night of it in the piano bar that he and Helen had discovered the night before. The well-heeled Egyptians who were drinking there were indulgent of them despite the noise they were making. There was some surprise among the native clientele, Helen gathered, that they were English rather than American. And soon Jonathan was buying them drinks and receiving them in return. After a while, he decided to give them a turn on the piano, and the resident pianist agreed to his request good naturedly. He struggled through 'Für Elise', which – most likely, thought Helen – he had learned as a boy and not played very often since then. Next, he launched into 'As with Gladness, Men of Old'.

Helen was not sure how well a Christmas carol would go down and decided that she would leave the rest to their carousing.

Back in her room, Helen kicked off her shoes and was in the process of stepping out of her skirt when the phone rang. She toppled over onto the bed as she reached to answer it.

'You were out late.'

'Hi, Sam. Did you call before?'

'Mmmn. What have you been up to?'

She told him about her day, and the museum and traffic and then launched into an account of the evening. 'Six of us from the group went to a local restaurant, which turned out well, and then we've been in the piano bar. It's been a very enjoyable evening. I kind of surprised myself by how much I was able to relax and just have a good time.'

'Are you alone?'

'Of course I'm alone, Sam.'

'Do you miss me?'

She sighed, feeling a wave of longing sweeping over her. 'What do you think? Massively. But I have had a good day and so far your countrymen have been friendly and hospitable.'

'They'll love you,' he said. 'They'll think you're a goddess, as

I do! Wait till you get further south. They'll be offering a thousand camels for you.'

'Gosh, that's a lot.'

'You haven't seen the camels!'

Lying in bed later, Helen felt more optimistic than she had for weeks. Maybe this trip had been a good idea for a number of reasons.

'Ahmed!' shouted a commanding voice from the back of their coach. 'If you don't give us a coffee break soon, I'm going to be sick all over your bus.'

Everyone laughed. It was the first utterance of the day from Jonathan. He had been the last to join the group and had looked almost green with fatigue and nausea. It turned out that the soirée had transferred to his room after the piano bar had closed. Helen was surprised that she had slept right through it, because it seemed that quite a number of revellers had taken him up on his offer to prolong the party.

'What time did you leave his room?' she asked Freddie, who was sitting beside her.

'Around four.'

'Well you don't look bad on it.'

'Ah well, (a) I'm a hardened drinker and (b) I paced myself more than the others.'

Ahmed, clearly worried about his coach, shouted something at the driver and within minutes they had pulled off the road for refreshments. There was desert for as far as they could see, and nothing of a motorway café about the facility; it was just a stall manned by two painfully thin locals. Most of the party chose soft drinks but Helen and Jonathan pleaded for coffee. When it came, it was in small paper cups, and of the Turkish variety – strong and very sweet.

'Bloody fantastic,' Jonathan announced. 'Just what I needed. Have I time for another?'

Helen smiled and ordered two more. 'That certainly hit the spot,' she agreed.

She had been flagging after their very early start for the visit to Memphis. Afterwards, she would have been happy to turn around and go back to bed, but they were now on their way to Sakkara. This holiday was hardly a rest cure.

Back in the coach, she watched as the countryside slipped by. If Cairo seemed foreign and unfamiliar, these scenes were that and more; they were a journey back in time.

There were small farms dotted alongside the Nile and she saw emaciated oxen bearing yokes supporting buckets at each end. Later, she caught a glimpse of a donkey walking around in circles, pushing some machinery. She assumed it was something to do with irrigation.

More and more she was coming to understand the pull of this country – its history, its culture, its traditions and its poverty – on the man she loved. But, she wondered, in the event of Sam returning, would the poor ever get near him? She supposed it would be more likely that he would end up educating other surgeons even though he had talked about starting a foundation to aid people with no money. There was no doubt, though, that he could make a difference here, and she wondered again, if she could give up everything back home in order to come here and support him.

Sakkara – with its Step Pyramid – the oldest in existence and dating from around 3000 BC – was quite overwhelming. What seemed most extraordinary to Helen was that there were no turnstiles, or protective railings. Indeed, there was nothing to stop tourists walking right up to the ancient monument and touching it.

She thought suddenly of the preparations back home for tonight's programme, and of how seriously everyone would be taking it. Sometimes, getting it together felt like as important as life and death. Now, that daily routine felt remote to her – almost inconsequential – in the face of this eternal history and never-ending landscape. The desert was spell-binding and its effect on her both moving and disturbing.

Her strange mood remained with her and even when, at last, they returned to their hotel, she was unable to shake it off. She told the rest of the group that she needed an evening to herself to catch up on sleep. Many of them followed her example especially as their wake-up time for the next morning was two-thirty.

She was keen to speak to Sam to discuss her feelings about his country, but – perversely – she decided that she needed to sleep so much that it would be better if she removed the possibility of him ringing. It might hurt him, she knew. But she was hurting, and struggling to marshal all the thoughts that were pummelling her mind.

'Don't put any calls through to me tonight,' she told the operator.

Annoyingly, though, despite her exhaustion, sleep was slow to come, and when it did it failed to refresh her as she kept dreaming about a sad, quiet woman.

The purpose of her visit had been to come to speak to Hamaida, and to Sam's mother. One of them – possibly both – held the solution to her future. Which of them was exerting more pressure on Sam? She had to find out. But she would leave it till after the boat trip at the weekend.

The knock on her door telling her it was time to get up for the excursion came far too soon. Feeling like a zombie, she dragged herself into the dawn. Thank heavens, she thought, she had had the presence of mind to pack the night before. She showered swiftly, dressed and went to the lobby where she found that the staff had provided jugs of coffee. Gratefully, she sipped at the hot liquid, surprised to find herself the first of her group to emerge.

Ahmed was pacing up and down. Pleased that she was ready, he left her to gather up the others.

Most of the group looked as tired as she felt. And there was little chat among them as they handed over their luggage and boarded the bus to the airport.

They all slept on the plane to Abu Simbel, but when it touched down at Aswan, where they would be returning later, they were forced to leave their seats and go to the terminal building – which was little more than a shack – pick up a fresh boarding card and re-enter the plane that had brought them. Mysteriously, in the short time they had been away, it had filled up with about two dozen ebullient Italians. Helen saw that her seat was now occupied, so – with rather poor grace – she went looking for another and settled into the row in front of Freddie.

He leant forward. 'You don't seem quite yourself today. Is it because it's early?'

'Probably.'

'I'm a good listener if, uh, you know...'

'I don't want to be psychoanalysed thanks all the same.'

'That's a little harsh.'

She sighed impatiently. 'I'm sorry, but I can't be reasonable all the time.'

'None of us can,' he responded, quietly. 'Look, this stretch only takes about half an hour. I should close your eyes and try to sleep. You'll probably feel better if you do.'

She did not argue.

As soon as the doors opened to their destination, Helen sensed that they were in a very different region from the one they had left; the hot air hit her like the blast from an electric heater. Plainly, Jonathan had been right; the temperature here would be intolerable by midday.

Helen walked with Freddie. Most of the others were a little way behind. She could hear Jonathan's voice complaining about something.

Joanna joined in: 'God, this better be worth it. What a schedule!'

Helen turned around and grinned. Behind Joanna were Steve and his girlfriend Rosie, who was walking with her head resting on his shoulder – which looked uncomfortable for both of them. After a few minutes, they rounded a corner and everyone stopped, open-mouthed.

'It *is* worth it.' Joanna sounded deeply impressed.

The massive grandeur of the Nubian Temple of Ramses the Second, with its gigantic seated figures on guard outside – three complete and one smashed – was a stupendous sight.

They ventured inside, and from there into the smaller temple dedicated to Hathor, the Goddess of Love. However, wonderful though their treasures were within, nothing compared with the initial breathtaking spectacle of the exterior.

They listened while a guide with an obvious love of his subject told them about the original history. He then described how, in the 1960s when the rising waters of Lake Nassar threatened the entire edifice during the construction of the Aswan Dam, the world's leading engineers had collaborated to find a way in which the whole site could be moved.

The guide explained how all the sandstone had been injected with synthetic resin and cut by hand into over a thousand huge blocks before being shifted to a new location up and away from the waters that would have submerged them.

Everything about the place – including its reincarnation – was awe-inspiring and haunting, Helen thought, and she longed to discuss it with Sam.

It was a much happier group who took the flight back the short distance to Aswan and then onto the hotel. For a couple of days, there were few commitments, and before long, they were all lying under colourful parasols by the side of the pool, sipping cold drinks and behaving as tourists do in sunny climes.

Most of them had lunch by the pool and fell asleep afterwards. And it was only later, when Jonathan persuaded them into sampling the local cuisine and breaking out of the confines of the luxury hotel, that they gathered themselves together to visit the centre of Aswan.

The streets were dusty, and where the restaurant they had visited in Cairo might have qualified for three stars, this one would not have made the cut in any tourist guide. There were no menus to be had, and the interior looked to be in urgent need of a spring clean.

Jonathan was not put off. He commandeered a waiter and asked for two bottles each of the house red and white wine.

'So sorry,' came the response, 'soft drinks only.'

'Soft drinks only!' Freddie was incredulous. 'My God, can anyone think of three more chilling words in the English language? Anyone got a hip flask?'

The food was not unlike that of the Cairo restaurant. Again, they all avoided the salad, and this time Helen waived the dubious pleasure of the ubiquitous meatballs, which were a rather odd shape and adorned with deep fingernail imprints.

The next day, the streets were a world away from the quiet shadowy walkways of the night before, and were bustling with people, colour, noise and market stalls. The further they walked, the fewer tourists they saw. This was obviously the real Aswan and they felt – perhaps for the first time – that they were encountering something of workaday Egyptian life.

Ahmed encouraged them to shop but advised them to barter. Suddenly they looked very English, and unsure of how to go about making bargains with people who were so obviously poorer than they were. Rosie, apart from the children of the Brazilian family, was the youngest of the group but it was she who took most easily to this form of shopping.

'God, I love this,' she shouted across at Helen, as she secured yet another cut price item. Before long, she had haggled her way to half the original cost of several metres of colourful Egyptian cotton cloth.

Helen settled quickly on a price for some musky essential oils and henna. Ahmed was quick to tell her that she had paid well over the odds, but she just smiled. Really, she had no enthusiasm for beating prices down, and she was pleased with what she had and felt sure that they would have cost a whole lot more in one of the international hotels that the tour specialised in.

Soon, to Helen's great relief, Ahmed decided it was too hot to continue shopping, so they were taken back to the hotel where they spent the rest of the day by the pool, eating club sandwiches and sipping mineral water. With the difficulty of obtaining alcohol, and the ruinous price of it if you could find any, it seemed to Helen that a holiday here might be as effective for problem drinkers as joining Alcoholics Anonymous.

'Darling, I had no idea you had such well-developed biceps!' Jonathan's voice made her look up from her task. She smiled at him and carried on.

Having settled on the river boat – which would be their home for the next few days – and unpacked their luggage, the group were reconvened and taken in traditional yachts called feluccas for an outing on the Nile.

They had visited Kitchener Island, an abundance of greenery and exotica, and were now on their way back to their base. And as the sun set all around them, the views were stunning. The felucca had been making very slow progress by sail, and eventually the boat owner, who looked all of ten years old, decided to use the oars.

It was an arduous task for this very slight gentleman and Helen had felt bad that she and four of the others – all much fatter than him – were reclining in his boat while he did all the work.

'Would you like someone to help you?' she had asked.

'Most kind, madam,' he had replied swiftly, so she had joined him at the business-end of the boat and taken charge of one of the oars. As it happened, she liked rowing – not the sort you do in gyms, but on the open water. Her father had taught her on her childhood holidays in the Lake District.

'You want Egyptian husband?' her fellow oarsman suddenly asked.

Helen started at his question then recovered herself, realising that he was talking about himself. She noticed Freddie watching her closely and felt uncomfortably exposed.

'We run business together,' the man persisted.

'No,' she managed. 'I couldn't do that, not really.' And she smiled.

'Darling,' Jonathan called to her, 'I would help out with the rowing you know, but it's my back. I'm a slave to it.'

Freddie said nothing, but after a while Steve insisted on taking over from her and soon *Osiris*, the splendid vessel that was their temporary home, was there, welcoming and solid, when they rounded the next bend.

The next four days were a mix of concentrated culture and leisurely afternoons spent lying on the upper deck, protected by parasols, watching the silent Nile glide by.

Each day, they left the boat in the cool of the early morning, and by the time they returned, stimulated by another history lesson, the sun's warmth was punishing.

It was strange, Helen mused, as they assessed the various periods, how the finest art seemed to be the earliest. She was appalled that so many beautiful carvings had been violated by the early Christians; the faces and feet of all the figures of the gods had been rubbed away in an attempt to render them impotent. Why was there always fear of a different culture or religion? And why did that fear so often erupt in force? Helen remembered suddenly the ugly destruction that she had been caught up in on Regent Street. Would the world ever change? Could it?

On their last night on board, moored at Luxor, Rosie insisted that they should all go shopping one last time.

'Surely, it's too late?' Helen queried. Dusk was falling and she was less than enthusiastic about such an excursion.

'No, I checked,' Rosie replied.

So, the six of them who had become such good travel companions, left the boat to exercise their bartering skills once more.

'I don't think I'll ever get used to all this haggling,' Helen remarked to Freddie. 'It's not really in my nature.'

'That may change if you end up living here,' he said.

Helen was unsure what to say in reply, so she said nothing – but that did not stop her wondering how much Freddie knew of her circumstances, or what he thought of them.

Jonathan was busy negotiating a purchase of a large quantity of rugs and leather goods and Rosie was buying up everything that took her fancy while Steve looked on indulgently.

While they were all busy, Helen decided to slip away and go back to the boat to lie down. She wanted to think about Sam. This period where she had been completely out of contact with him was painful and she had to keep fighting the thoughts that her future with him was hopeless. If she had given into them, she would never have left her cabin.

She felt as though depression, if not insanity, was waiting to claim her. As if it might be thrown over her, like a giant blanket, at any moment – and if that happened she would surely sink into madness or oblivion.

Dinner on-board that night was a superb buffet, and the best meal of the holiday so far. Afterwards, Ahmed suggested that they should all go for a drink at The Old Winter Palace Hotel. They hired two horse-drawn carriages, and Ahmed persuaded the drivers to agree to a ridiculously cheap rate for the return journey.

Clearly, the hotel had been immensely grand in its day, and Helen could imagine European dowagers there, in the twenties and thirties, whiling away their winters. It was a cross between a tribute to the British Raj and one of those old, solid, peeling hotels in British coastal resorts like Eastbourne or Broadstairs.

Jonathan was bursting with enthusiasm about his earlier purchases and said that the hotel had given him extra inspiration about what do with them all. He would, he told them, have everything shipped back as soon as possible and then create an Egyptian room in his flat.

'It'll be absolutely wonderful!' he declared, and with that, he went off to the bar to buy another round of drinks.

Ahmed bought the next round, much to Helen's surprise. She wondered at his presence, when he could so easily be off duty. But then she realised that he was particularly attentive to Joanna. Now she thought back, the two of them had been seen together often during the past couple of days. Maybe he, a strict Moslem, was enjoying a bit of extra-curricular western-styled freedom. Certainly, he was drinking tonight, which he did not do as a rule. Joanna had told the group that she had an elderly husband at home. Maybe they had an arrangement that she would holiday alone and spice up the vacations with younger men so long as she was discreet. Maybe she even entertained her husband with tales of her exploits, or was that too far-fetched? People and their private habits were quite a mystery. She herself, after all, had suggested to Sam that she would be prepared to be a mistress in the background. That was no way for a modern woman to behave, but she was in little doubt that she would settle for it.

When they returned to the boat, Helen decided to go straight to bed. Unusually, Freddie suggested seeing her to her cabin. At her door, he leant over and kissed her on the cheek. She knew she looked surprised, perhaps even irritated, as she let herself into her room without saying 'goodnight'.

The next morning, they visited the Valley of the Kings. They had been promised it would be the high spot of their tour, and so it proved to be. And when finally they came to the tomb of Tutankhamun, they marvelled at how all the treasures they had seen in the Cairo Museum could have been housed within. They also found themselves astounded by the vibrant colours of the carvings. Someone asked the guide if he was sure that no one crept in here at night and touched it all up with a paintbrush. The others laughed.

Emerging, blinking against the sun, a voice called out, 'Helen Bartlett! Fancy you being here. We watch you every night!'

The couple came from Edgeware and were keen to chat. After a few minutes, Freddie appeared at her elbow and steered her away, engaging her in conversation about another tomb she must see.

'Thanks,' she smiled at him.

'That sort of thing happens a lot does it?'

She grinned at him. 'Well, it was the first time in Egypt.'

'I imagine it goes on all the time back home. Perhaps not easy for partners...'

She looked at him quizzically before answering brusquely. 'Goes with the job, Freddie, which I'm very lucky to have.'

It was an anticlimactic party that sat in the dusty transit lounge at Luxor airport later that afternoon. The four days on the boat had been packed with truly amazing visions and wonderful experiences. It had been a lot to process.

'I wish,' Jonathan said, 'that we were flying home now. I don't feel I have the energy to travel back to Cairo and then out to Giza.'

The others nodded, including Helen, but inwardly she knew that she had to go back because of what she yet had to do.

Once settled in the hotel in Giza, Helen decided that she needed some space to herself and opted to spend the evening alone. She could see one of the pyramids from her window. It drew her eye again and again, so much so, that she felt almost as if she were being hypnotised. When, she wondered, would she would return to this curious country and continue her love affair with its history and idiosyncrasies?

She turned from the window and noticed, for the first time, the large arrangement of tropical flowers which dominated a table they had been placed upon. This was certainly a very upmarket hotel, she thought. Perhaps she would eat in her room. She reached for a menu, which was in a box behind the flowers, and decided that she could risk eating salad here.

228

Her meal came quickly; spicy chicken, salad, olives, bread and a half bottle of wine. It looked very appetising and she was just about to start eating when the phone rang.

Her heart leapt and yet could he have found her here?

'Darling!'

Gladness flooded her body.

'Are you all right? How has the trip been? Did you get my flowers?'

'Oh, Sam,' she began. She paused needing to control her breathing and her mood. 'There's so much to tell you.'

She looked across at the flowers. There was no card with them, but of course they were from him. 'And thank you. The bouquet you sent is spectacular. Lots of tropical plants in it. It's exquisite. It's a pity I can't bring it back to London.'

'Just bring yourself back, that's all I ask.'

'How are you, Sam?'

'Much better! I've been longing to talk to you. I went to Paris at the weekend and had a great time with Jeremy. Not sure he did, he's really going through it. His wife walked out recently and went off with another surgeon – one of his friends. Very messy and upsetting. But he was really helpful to me. I told him everything, well almost, and he put a different perspective on it all. I've written to Hamaida to see if she might agree to accept some sort of financial compensation in lieu of marriage. I still don't know whether I should plan to work at least part of the year in Egypt, but I'll settle one thing at a time.'

Helen's pulse quickened. Dare she hope that they might have a future after all? She felt deliriously happy but quickly cautioned herself against expecting too much.

'How do you like Egypt?' he asked her.

'I love it.'

'It can be very exasperating though, can't it?' He laughed.

'Well… on occasions, I suppose. But it's fascinating, and the trip on the Nile and all the places we saw, and the treasures and the statues and the buildings, it's just beyond amazing.'

'I'm glad you feel that way… Helen, you know I love you desperately.'

'And you know I feel the same way,' she replied almost in a whisper.

'Will you bear with me a bit longer?'

'Of course. Anything. I'll do anything.'

'Well, I feel, while I sort this out, it might be better if we didn't meet for a while.'

'What!'

'It might be for the best.'

What fresh hell is this, she wondered. One minute she seemed to be riding around on her joyful carousel, and the next flung off it, with nothing left to her except to watch it continue carrying everyone else as it revolved.

'Whatever you think, Sam,' she answered wearily. And without saying 'goodbye' she put the phone down and turned back to her supper, which no longer held much appeal.

The next morning, the group visited the pyramids and Sphinx. They had to queue for ages for admittance to the Great Pyramid, but once inside on the tiny, cramped stairway with the pushing and pulling of people from a variety of nations, Helen felt unbearably claustrophobic and left the rest of her party to battle her way back outside.

But as soon as she was in the open air, she was surrounded by salesmen wearing turbans, sandals and flapping gowns and offering her a wide range of goods.

'No thank you,' she kept saying, politely. Clearly it was a mistake to speak at all. They seemed to be encouraged because she had opened her mouth, and evidently thought they could win her over.

'You wish Egyptian husband? I give one thousand camels for you.'

She almost laughed, remembering Sam's prediction.

'No, leave me alone.'

They stayed, waving their wares at her. She was not frightened of being robbed but she did feel threatened by their invasion of her space and privacy.

'Go away!' She was shouting now.

None of them moved.

'OK,' she cried angrily. 'I'll go.'

'Where you go?' demanded the man who had offered the camels.

'Back to my hotel.'

'I walk with you.'

'No!' she screamed. 'I was really enjoying being here, but you've totally ruined it. All I wanted was to be left alone.'

They looked at her, uncomprehendingly. She pushed through them and marched away, but it was not until she was halfway down the hill that the last of the vendors gave up on her.

Back in her room, she wept with frustration, and must then have fallen asleep because, when it came, the knock on her door woke her up.

'It's Freddie.' She heard him call. 'Come on, we need to get going.'

She fumbled with the catch and peered round the door at him.

'We're off to the Papyrus Institute now. What are you doing back here?'

'I had a bad scene up there. I got surrounded by a bunch of salesmen and they wouldn't leave me alone. It was horrible.'

'Well come on, that's all over now.'

'I don't care. I'm not going anywhere else.'

'Oh yes you are,' he contradicted her. 'You're going to get your ten out of ten and a gold star like the rest of us. But you had better wash your face first.'

His tone was uncompromising and devoid of any sympathy. But it did the trick because, meekly, Helen did what she was told.

As it happened, the Institute was fascinating. The whole process was explained, and they watched the reeds being laid, criss-crossed and then rolled to mesh the layers together.

231

'Papyrus, *real* papyrus, not the banana-skin imitations you see everywhere, lasts three thousand years,' explained the young salesman as he encouraged them to walk around and select samples to take home.

'You can write your essay now,' whispered Freddie and – forgetting her earlier trauma – she smiled at him.

'We have the afternoon "at leisure" as they say in the trade. Come back and we'll have a drink and some lunch at the hotel. Just the two of us.'

He took her hand, which was as surprising as last night's kiss had been.

They sat in the lounge of the hotel, and Freddie ordered Campari and soda for them both. Feeling unsettled by his sudden attention, she plied him with questions. And, as she did so, she looked at him more intently than she had done before – taking in his baggy linen suit with the sleeves fashionably rolled up. He was a little too short, portly and old to look trendy, but he was smart and attractive in his own way.

'Are you married?' she asked after she had posed several less personal questions.

'Getting out of it, actually.'

'Oh.'

'It's OK. I can talk about it. My wife Sally left the proverbial note behind the clock and disappeared from our Suffolk cottage, taking my Labrador dog with her. I probably deserved it. Later, she sent for all the furniture.'

'That wasn't very nice.'

'No, it wasn't. But I don't think I was the best of husbands.'

'Is there a chance you could get back together?'

'Doubt it. So, that's why I'm running away for a bit. Why are you?'

'I'm not running away.'

'Oh yes you are. People who come on this kind of holiday alone fall into certain categories.'

232

'OK. If you're so clever, what are they?'

'They have to be quite well off for a start.'

She grinned. 'That's certainly true.'

'Secondly, they're either here because they've accepted their solo state and are quite happy with it, or they're like you and me, trying to prove they can function on their own and appear confident and fun to the rest of the world. Trouble is, we're constantly pulled back to the realities of what we've left behind. So, if this thing with your bloke doesn't work out...'

'I don't know what you're talking about.'

'Yes, you do. I've watched you. You're an attractive and capable lady. You're also very sad.'

Helen's eyes filled with tears.

He reached for her hand. 'Sorry – I didn't mean to upset you. My wife always said I was too blunt.'

'It's OK.'

He signalled to the waiter to bring each of them another drink. 'Maybe I could call you when we get back.'

'Surely that wouldn't solve anything? Don't people have to put everything properly behind them before grabbing the first bit of driftwood that floats by?'

'I've been called a lot of things...'

'You know what I mean. You're a psychiatrist, after all.'

'Not sure it helps in one's own case! Let's just have an uncomplicated meal together some time.'

'I need to think about it.'

'You have to eat. Anyway,' he went on, 'whatever your problem – and I suppose it's something to do with his family not approving of you or the other way around – I'm sure he'll get it right. He'd be mad to let a woman like you go.'

Helen raised an eyebrow and then sighed. 'Do you mind if I don't stay and have the lunch,' she asked. 'I don't feel very sociable and I could do with a nap.'

She left then, without waiting for an answer.

Back in her room, she packed hurriedly. In truth, she was too nervy to sleep and before long she plucked up the courage she had lacked hitherto to pick up the phone.

When she got through, a voice said something in a language she did not speak.

'Sorry,' she said. 'Do you speak English? I wish to speak to Madame Aziz.'

'Ah.' The woman understood. 'Yes, Madame. I go see. You wait.'

'Hello,' said a voice that Helen recognised.

'Hello, Madame Aziz. It's Helen Bartlett here.'

'Helen.' Sam's mother did not sound very surprised. But she did not sound very welcoming either. 'How are you?'

'I'm fine. Look, it's a lot to ask, but I wonder if I could come and see you?'

'Where on earth are you?'

'In Giza.'

'My dear. Have you come specially to see me?'

'In a way, yes.'

'When would you like to come?'

Helen took a deep breath. 'Could I come now?'

There was a long pause. 'All right, Helen,' the older woman said with a hint of resignation in her voice. 'I'll see you when you get here. It'll take you about fifteen minutes by taxi.'

In the cab, Helen forced herself to focus on the passing streets as she rode towards one of the most crucial meetings of her life. To some extent, the drive reminded her of the taxi ride the night of the Harrisons' dinner party when she had encountered Sam. Then too, she had travelled from a fairly run-down area to a more select one.

They were soon in a suburb that reminded Helen more of a tour of the movie stars' residences in Beverley Hills than the gentility of St John's Wood. The driver drew up in front of a mansion that was little short of a palace.

'Please wait for me,' she told the driver, praying that his English was good enough to understand her.

'OK, princess.' He flashed a toothy smile at her.

The house was Moorish on the outside, but the interior was more European. Certainly, the drapes and pictures looked to be French.

It was a vastly impressive house and Helen felt quite overawed by it. Her high heels tapped loudly on the white tiled floor.

Madame Aziz was waiting for her, seated on an elegant antique sofa. She rose to meet her, offering one cheek then the other to be kissed.

'A little mint tea, Helen?'

'That would be wonderful,' Helen replied.

She sipped the unfamiliar brew gratefully, feeling hot despite the fact that the air conditioning was very efficient. This is Sam's home, she thought. And it's like another world. Her mind traversed the miles between them to her own flat in Holland Park. She had always thought it quite smart, but how ordinary it must have seemed to him.

'And what brings you to Egypt, Helen?'

She looked at the older woman. She could dissemble and talk round the subject in the hope of finally weaving her way into the important topics without seeming too crass or impatient. On the other hand, she could offer herself and the truth of her love in the hope of being understood and perhaps winning the tussle between the traditional and modern worlds. Honest and direct by nature, she had no real option.

'I came,' she began. Then she coughed and had to start again. 'Sorry, I came to get away and have a holiday. But my main reason for selecting your country was to talk to you.'

'Go on.' Sam's mother's expression gave nothing away.

'You once spoke very candidly to me,' Helen ventured. 'And I want to do the same with you. By the way, Sam doesn't know that I'm here. And I'd prefer it if you didn't tell him. I just want

235

you to know that he means the whole world to me. I love him. I need him. And I promise I would look after him and cherish him through our lives together if you were ever able to accept me as his wife.'

'Have one of these sweetmeats,' Madame Aziz held out a wafer-thin china plate with the delicacies neatly arranged upon it.

Helen sighed, but took one nonetheless.

'I appreciate your openness,' said Sam's mother. 'And actually, I like you very much, but what you ask is not possible. You're not one of us. Ahmed is promised to another. His place is here. He should work in his own country and he should marry.'

'He can't give you grandchildren if he marries Hamaida.'

'Ah,' Madame Aziz raised her eyebrows, 'you know more than I thought, but it doesn't matter. My husband wanted this match. Sam, as you call him, has ruined Hamaida's life.'

Did the older lady know that Sam had taken Hamaida's virginity, she wondered.

'She has waited for him more years than I care to remember.'

'Well,' Helen interrupted. 'He proposed once.'

'I don't want to discuss this.'

Helen had never been faced with such total intransigence.

'She is a well-connected, dutiful, lovely woman.'

Helen retorted. 'I'm sure she is, but I doubt very much if she loves him like I do. I want to meet her. I think we should speak.'

'As it happens, she takes tea with me most afternoons. She'll be here any moment. You can choose whether you stay or go.'

Helen felt suddenly as though she had strayed into a Hollywood film. She longed to run away, but curiosity got the better of her. This was, after all, why she was here.

'Very well, stay, but I must ask you not to give any indication to her of the intimate nature of your relationship with my son. She's not been well. I don't want her upset.'

Helen bit her lip to stop her from shrieking at Sam's mother about the injustice of the whole situation, and the two women sat in silence till Madame Aziz put down her cup and saucer and jumped to her feet, smiling broadly.

She said something in Arabic but then continued, 'We will speak English in honour of our British visitor. A regal arm indicated Helen to the newcomer. 'I met Helen when I visited Ahmed. She works in television.'

Helen gazed at her rival. She was petite and very dark haired with olive skin. Her hair was immaculate, her nails professionally manicured and painted. Her smile sweet if not overwhelmingly happy; her eyes round and slightly sad.

'I'm pleased to meet you, Helen.' Hamaida's English was heavily accented. 'I've never been to your country, but I hope to visit soon. Do you know my fiancé?'

'A little,' Helen croaked. There was such a lump in her throat that she could barely speak. She looked towards Sam's mother for comfort. The woman with her lover's eyes nodded almost imperceptibly. 'Um, Madame Aziz says you've been ill. I'm very sorry.'

'I have. But I am better now. And I look forward to my wedding. It will be a new start. I shall grow strong planning our house and our future.'

Helen felt light-headed and breathless. Was Sam this woman's whole reason for living? Did she not *do* anything? She wanted to scream at Hamaida that Sam was everything to *her*. He was her soulmate. Her other half. Her great and passionate love. But she knew it was out of the question. Furthermore, she knew in that moment that she could not ask this frail, traditional heroine to give up her dream. She, who everyone perceived as being eminently capable and fortunate, had no right to deny this gentle, dull girl her only ambition in life.

She thought suddenly of the letter Sam planned to write to Hamaida offering her a financial settlement. It could not possibly work. And it was going to cause the woman untold pain. She had wanted to find out if she could have a future with the man she adored, and she had.

Looking across at Madame Aziz, she felt her eyes fill with tears and searched for sympathy in the expression of the older woman. But Sam's mother carefully avoided her gaze, and that obdurate refusal to compromise felt like the final stab to her heart. She was the outsider; she could never belong.

With difficulty, she found her voice. 'I wish you happiness. Forgive me. I must go.'

Somebody must have shown her out and put her in the taxi. Had she paid the driver? It was a blur.

She was sitting in her hotel room. It was dark outside. Her chest was locked in a vice. She could not move. The phone rang. Had that just begun or had it rung before? Eventually, it stopped. Now there was banging on the door. Well that would go away too if she ignored it. Was it tomorrow? Was she late for the plane? No, it was still tonight.

Someone was shouting. 'Helen! Helen! For God's sake, come and open the door.'

Almost in a trance, she felt compelled to do what the voice asked. Freddie stood in the corridor.

'What the hell is wrong with you? Have you been drinking?'

She shook her head, then replied, 'Actually, I have. I had mint tea. Lots of mint tea.'

Suddenly, that struck her as funny and she began to laugh.

'Helen, stop it.'

'Sorry, but it was very good mint tea. Awfully elegant, don't you think?' Mid laughter, her mouth wide open, something caught in her chest and all at once tears coursed down her cheeks. She sobbed and gasped for breath.

Freddie held her and she felt him rocking her back and forwards as though she were a baby.

'Oh, Sam,' she murmured.

'It isn't Sam,' he said crossly. Then he pushed her on to the bed.

He picked up the phone. She knew what was happening and yet it all seemed confusing and a long way away.

'You'll have to go on,' he was saying. 'Don't argue, Jonathan. Helen's not well. I'll bring her along shortly.'

'I'm not sure I'm going anywhere. Why are we going out? You go. Leave me alone.'

'Helen!' Freddie pulled her into a sitting position and grabbed her by the shoulders.

'You're hurting me.'

'Sorry, but you have to get a grip.'

'I just don't really know what you're talking about, that's all.'

'We were all supposed to be going out for our last night, do you remember?'

'If I ever did know, I'd forgotten,' she admitted.

'I'm sure it would do you good. God, you look awful though.'

'Thanks for that.'

'Look, Helen, I know you're suffering. But... you're not on anything are you?'

'What do you mean?'

'Drugs.'

'Don't be ridiculous.'

'Sorry. Wait here.'

Minutes later, he was back with a glass of water and two small white pills.

'I don't take tablets. Especially stuff I don't know anything about.'

'Well you do now,' Freddie insisted. 'You're going to have to trust me on this one. I think we need to get out, and we need to get you on that plane tomorrow. And this will calm you down and enable you to function. OK?'

She shrugged helplessly.

'Now, for the second time today, I advise you to go and wash your face, and then we'll get going.'

'I ought to change.'

'Yes, well, carry on.'

'Go away then.'

'Helen, I'm a doctor, just get on with it.'

She slipped out of her sundress, and stood, swaying slightly, wearing only a bra and knickers. 'What should I put on, I wonder?' she said vaguely.

Impatiently, Freddie rummaged in her stuffed suitcase and pulled from it a cotton two-piece garment. 'This'll do.'

In the bathroom, she cleaned up the streaks of make-up on her face, then applied a new base and lipstick and mascara. Her hand wobbled when she painted on the liquid eyeliner, but she hoped she had got away with it. Who cared, anyway.

'Good girl,' Freddie said when she returned. 'Those pills will calm you down. Just don't drink too much, OK?'

She nodded and allowed him to propel her out of the room and down the stairs and through the front door. As soon as she reached the restaurant, she snapped back into her public persona.

'You all right, Helen?' the others chorused.

'I'm fine. Just got a bit too much sun, I think.'

The rest of them were in festive mood and sinking generous quantities of the local wine, while vowing never again to touch the stuff. Mindful of Freddie's warning, she sipped very slowly. She did not eat much either.

The six of them, who had shared the holiday in each other's company, exchanged phone numbers and addresses. The scene reminded Helen of the closing night of a production in the theatre, when actors promise eternal friendship to their fellow thespians, only to come across a scrap of paper in a pocket some weeks later and have to search the memory for a face that fitted the details.

Back in the hotel, Freddie accompanied Helen to her room. He gestured towards the flowers.

'From the man, I suppose.'

Helen nodded.

Freddie grunted before saying, 'I was proud of you tonight.'

'You were very kind to me earlier, Freddie. I appreciate it.'

'Do you want to tell me what happened?'

'No thank you. I just did something that… that I knew was a recipe for disaster, but it was no help at all to discover I was right.'

'I'll go.' He stood up. 'You need to sleep.'

Helen rose, weakly.

'He's a lucky fellow, your man. We must keep in touch though.'

'I think I'm far too emotional here to make any plans for the future,' she said as steadily as she could.

'What a mixture; a lovely *and* level-headed woman. Very rare.' He grinned. 'Your man will move heaven and earth for you if he's got any sense.'

Strange. Perhaps it no longer mattered what Sam felt. How could he ever stand up to all the culture and tradition that was stacked against him?

She spoke slowly. 'It's over, Freddie. It really is over.'

'I wonder,' he murmured as he walked to the door. Then he turned. 'I bet you anything you like that he'll be waiting at the airport when we land.'

Chapter Twelve

'Told you!' Freddie said.

Despite protesting to him that Sam would not meet her, Helen was so very, very glad to be proved wrong.

She had sat with Freddie on the plane and he was right behind her as they emerged from Customs and spotted Sam's waving figure even before she did.

Turning to Freddie, she took his hand and thanked him.

'Don't thank me,' he said brusquely. 'I'll be in touch.'

Helen held herself back slightly as Sam embraced her though she had longed for this renewed closeness. Her mind was full of his mother's righteous and implacable expression and the dark, sad eyes of his fiancée.

'Aren't you glad to see me?' he demanded, his face contorted with anguish.

This was a boy who had never been loved properly by any female other than her, she thought. And it showed.

'Glad? Sam, I'm overjoyed.' And as she spoke, happiness released itself into every cell and tissue of her body. She felt like one of his patients when the blood supply is connected to a new heart; her blue coldness replaced suddenly with pink warmth.

'Who was that guy?' Sam asked as soon as she was stowed in his Mercedes. 'Was it Jonathan?'

She smiled at him. 'You've got a good memory. But no, it was actually Freddie.'

'What does he do?'

'He's a sort of media psychiatrist.'

'Hmmn, pretty high-flown sort of trip then with three of you working in the television industry.'

'It was great,' she responded, deliberately ignoring Sam's petulant tone. 'Wonderful country, good company and plenty to see.'

Should she now admit to everything that had transpired yesterday? She wanted to, because she was not good with secrets, but she knew that her actions would be construed as interference.

He drove her back to his house and only then did she dare ask what had happened to his decision that they should not meet for a while.

'I had second thoughts,' he smiled, looking much brighter suddenly and endearingly boyish. 'I'm doing all I can, Helen, I promise you. And I so badly needed to see you. I hoped you would feel the same. In fact, I was wondering if you would stay here over the weekend... as my friend?'

Helen, back in the role she despised of being a woman who would accept crumbs of comfort whenever they were offered, could not help but accept. The alternative was an empty and lonely flat and no work to occupy her till Monday.

'I'll try if you'll try,' she answered quietly.

It was a strange two days, for though their desire for each other was as intense as ever, and his, at least, quite physically obvious on several occasions, they did not consummate their passion.

In the office on Monday, Laura burst in on Helen, a few minutes after her arrival.

'I've got something to tell you,' she gasped.

'You got married!'

'How did you guess?'

'I didn't. I was just being funny. But then, maybe, I don't know. Maybe there's something about you that gave it away. Congratulations! When did this happen?'

'Saturday.'

'Oh, you rotter, that was the day I got back, I could have come.'

'We didn't invite anyone. Right up till the last moment, I think we both thought one of us would call it off!'

'Are you happy?'

'Blissfully. Boringly, perhaps.'

'Well, I'm delighted. Thrilled, in fact,' Helen said, though she could not help feel a pang of envy.

'So, what happened in Egypt?'

Helen looked at her watch. 'I haven't got time to go into it now. But can you stay and have a drink after the programme, or is that no longer allowed now you're legally attached?'

'Don't be ridiculous. Nothing's changed. Anyway, he's gone filming.'

'Did you meet anyone?' Laura asked later when they were settled in the club with a gin and tonic apiece.

'Lots of people.'

'You know what I mean.'

'Well, there was Jonathan. Great fun. But gay and probably one of those people who keeps possible partners at arm's length. I got the feeling he isn't looking for company or commitment. Then there was Freddie...'

'Let's concentrate on him.'

'Well, he's not very tall, fair, slightly plump, about forty, a psychiatrist who does quite a lot of radio and telly, and in the process of getting divorced.'

'And...'

'Towards the end of the holiday, he was very kind to me.'

'Good. Did you go to bed with him?'

'No!'

'Why not? You're not a born-again virgin, are you?'

'I just happen to be madly in love with Sam Aziz, or had you forgotten?'

'So what's happening with him?'

Helen sighed. 'Having rung me in Egypt all the time, he then went to see a friend in Paris and talked to him. He told me it had been a big help. But then he announced on the phone that he thought it would be a good idea for us not to see each other for a while. However, having said that, he was at the airport to meet me, and he drove me to his home and we spent the weekend together, with a bit of kissing and cuddling but absolutely no real sex.'

'Is this man normal?' Laura sounded impatient and cross on her friend's behalf.

'Oh yes, he's normal all right.'

'But this is weird behaviour and there certainly seems to be far more grief in your relationship than there is joy. For you, anyway.'

Helen nodded. 'But I'm beginning to see what his background is all about and how that is influencing what he does now.' She paused and thought carefully about discussing what had happened at the curious tea party on her last day but decided against it.

Laura looked at her quizzically. 'And are you seeing him tonight?'

'No,' Helen replied sadly. 'I told him I need some time alone.'

'And do you want to be alone?'

'Not really.'

'Me neither. Let's go and get a curry.'

Lying in her bath later, Helen reviewed the advice that Laura had given her. It was almost, she thought, that now Laura had married, she had attained a special status and was more confident about giving relationship guidance.

'Don't be too available,' Laura had said. 'If you look at what happens every time you go away or make some sort of stand, he always comes running. If you still want him, make sure he has to work at it.'

Helen tried to sound off-hand when Sam called. She watched herself in the mirror as they spoke and saw how she flushed with pleasure when he told her how much he loved her, before manoeuvring her face into a stern expression before replying.

He noticed, of course, immediately. 'Why am I getting the cold shoulder?'

'Because we're in a state of limbo. You keep telling me you're sorting everything. I know that you're trying. But I also know that you're keeping a very significant part of you from me. I'm simply responding to that by staying away until things are resolved. You partly want to see me, but partly you don't, and you certainly aren't prepared to make love. So, why don't we do our own thing and not meet till the weekend?'

'What does that mean – "do our own thing". What are you going to do?'

'What are *you* going to do?'

'For God's sake. Work, I suppose. I don't know.'

'Well, I don't know either. But I'm not about to jump into bed with anyone else if that's what you're worried about.'

'Helen, you're distancing yourself from me.'

'I am.' Her voice wobbled and tears pricked at the back of her eyes. 'But it's my only protection.'

'Will you promise to meet me on Friday then? Jeremy's coming over.'

'But wouldn't it be better if you had some time alone with him?'

'Helen, enough is enough. Please stop punishing me. I want you to be there. I want him to see how special you are. I want to show you off.'

Did he mean to sound that proprietorial? Probably not. In any case, she could hardly challenge him about it when she felt annoyingly proud that he felt that way.

'OK, Sam. Pick me up after the programme?'

'Yes. Helen. I love you. I care for you. I need you.'

Drawing herself up to her full height, she replied: 'I'm glad' and then she had to swallow hard to prevent the words she longed to say from spilling out of her lips.

Putting down the phone, she spoke them to the empty room. 'I love you, Sam. Desperately. Today and forever.'

The next day, Helen was due to record her fortnightly medical feature. The resident doctor, Ken Murdoch, turned up as usual, for lunch.

'I did what you asked,' she said to him conspiratorially.

'Excellent. Good production values, eh?' Dr Murdoch was proud of his command of television terms.

'Derek won't like it though.' Helen winced slightly.

'Probably not. But it does illustrate a point.'

'True, and he's always saying to me that I might as well work in radio if I don't provide good visuals.'

They laughed, enjoyed a quick meal of baked potatoes in the canteen and then made their way to the studio, where the crew were already rehearsing their shots for the recording.

Almost as soon as they arrived, the floor manager asked Helen to pick up the phone on the news desk.

'Helen, it's Derek. What *is* that?'

'What's what?'

'You know exactly what I'm talking about. That... thing in the glass bowl.'

'It's a placenta, fresh from the hospital. I had the baby born specially this morning.'

'You can't use it. It's gruesome.'

'Oh, Derek, don't be so... male. It's good television, as you would say.'

'Well, what's the point of it?'

'Today's subject, as you know, is postnatal depression. The placenta is loaded with progesterone. The woman carries it for nine months and suddenly it's gone, so to speak. Many experts believe the condition is caused by the sudden hormone change.'

'Why doesn't every woman get depressed then?'

'See – you're getting interested now! That's what I'm hoping to establish.'

He sighed. 'Well, all right then, if you must. But absolutely *no* close-ups. I'm going to tell the director that too. Really, Helen, you and your ideas will be the death of me.'

The floor manager started the clock and as it reached zero, cued Helen with a wave.

'Animals don't get postnatal depression, as far as we know,' she began. 'Could that be because they eat their afterbirths?'

Ken beamed at her and then into camera. Helen smiled. His energy and enthusiasm poured out of him which was why he had turned out to be such a good media doctor.

'Well,' he answered, 'I don't wish to put people off their tea but, as you can see, this is a placenta. It's packed full of really good stuff – so much so that placentas often find their way into cosmetics because of their beneficial hormonal content. So once the woman has given birth, she loses all this very suddenly, right after the baby is born, and some women react very badly. Maybe you're right about eating it. I did hear of a woman in Hampstead who fried hers up with some onions, but that's by the by! Now, why do some women get depressed and others not? There does seem to be a correlation here between those who do and women who suffer from PMT...'

Ken expounded the latest theory and Helen finished by giving the name of a useful support group.

'I think you went too far,' Derek called out to her as soon as she reappeared in the newsroom.

'We'll see,' she answered. 'If we do get any complaining phone calls, I bet they'll all be from men! We're giving useful information that women need.'

'I know you mean well, Helen, and that the viewers tend to love what you do. I'm just saying you might have gone a bit over the top. But we'll see when it goes out later.'

After the programme, she left the building for home. For a heavenly moment, she thought she saw Sam's car waiting for her outside. But she was mistaken.

Back in her flat, she kept busy. She phoned her mother. She rang her old friend Deirdre to fix up a tennis game for the following evening. She longed to call Sam but managed not to. Instead, she poured herself a generous drink. Before long, she poured another. She recognised that this could be a very slippery slope, but she felt she needed the alcohol to blur the edges of her uncertainty and pain. When the phone rang, she ran to it with indecent haste.

Sam too was drinking alone. She longed to ask him why they were putting themselves through so much torment, but she restrained herself. He volunteered that he was torn in two. He sounded terrible.

Freddie phoned to invite her to dinner. She declined.

The next day dragged. She focused on her job. She played tennis. And she berated herself for being pathetic as she ticked off the hours till she could be with Sam.

Then, just when she was about to go to bed, Laura turned up at her flat.

Distraught, she told Helen, 'I knew we shouldn't have got married. We've just had the most awful row. I knew this would happen.'

'You've had rows before. Why is this so terrible?'

'Because we're married,' Laura wailed.

'That's ridiculous. You're the same people. It's only a worse row than usual if it really *is* a worse row than usual – not because it's a pretty typical one that you just feel is worse because you've tied the knot. What happened anyway?'

'I went to the club hoping to meet you and had rather too many drinks before going home.'

'I didn't think you'd be there, so I went off to play tennis.'

'Ian was supposed to be out. But he got back early, and I was a bit tipsy when he arrived and somehow we both got cross and

I threw a dinner plate at him and he threw a jar of marmalade at the wall. It was a hell of a mess.'

Helen giggled. Laura shot her a furious look.

'I'm sorry, Laura,' she said, 'it just sounds so awfully Tennessee Williams.'

'We often throw things.' She smiled suddenly. 'I suppose you're right. It's no worse than usual. But do you think that Ian thinks we shouldn't row now we're married?'

'Why don't we ask him?'

'We're not ringing him.'

'I think we should. Quite apart from anything else, he's probably worried sick about where you are.'

'I doubt that very much,' Laura said firmly, though she did not try to prevent Helen from picking up her phone.

'Hi, Ian. It's Helen. I've got Laura here.' She held out the receiver to her friend before walking out of the sitting room to the kitchen.

Two minutes later, Laura rushed in, her eyes shining.

'Thanks, Helen. I'm off home.'

'Good. Off you go.'

'At least we've got our first married quarrel out of the way.'

Helen smiled. 'Go straight to bed. I'm sure you will. Enjoy it.'

'I'm sorry, Helen. It's awful for you having to be here alone. Are you OK?'

'I'm surviving. But around this time of night, quite apart from loving him to pieces and longing for him to solve everything so that we can be together, I just want to curl up in bed with him and basically, well, you know, fuck each other's brains out. Not to put too fine a point on it!'

On Friday, it was very difficult to focus on the work before her. She was anxious about meeting Jeremy, afraid that he might not like her, and might therefore cast his vote in favour of Egypt. More and more, she wanted a future with Sam and was prepared to go to any length to secure it. But at the same time, increasingly, she was unsure what that might entail.

She felt that the programme went well, which was gratifying as she was sure that Sam would have encouraged Jeremy to watch it. Afterwards, she and Laura went to the club to wait for them.

'Hey, the friend's terrific looking,' Laura was facing the door as the two men came in. Helen stood and turned. Jeremy was slightly taller than Sam with steely grey hair and startlingly blue eyes, she noticed, as they shook hands. His were soft but his grip was firm. Unusually, Sam kissed her full on the lips; he generally behaved more discreetly on her territory. She felt as though he was staking his claim. Part of her thought that was unfair since it seemed likely that he was not going to be able to honour it, but she was filled with a mad kind of joy nonetheless.

Helen signed the guests in and bought everyone a drink. Ian appeared suddenly, and she was amused to see that Laura blushed slightly. Her friend's eyes danced with delight, and she had never looked more beautiful. Clearly, she was deliriously in love no matter how much she tried to deny it. Had Sam noticed the change in Laura? And would this example of marital bliss create in him the longing it had in her?

Later, in one of their favourite restaurants by the river, it seemed to Helen that Jeremy's presence was acting as a catalyst that was transporting Sam and herself back to the uncomplicated relationship they had enjoyed in their early days. He stroked her arms and kept pulling her to him and kissing her in a very romantic way. Was this because he felt more confident about their future? Or was it an act for his friend? Was he assuming some kind of role in an attempt to persuade Jeremy that his troubles were not too great, or to prevent any in-depth discussion? Was he trying, in his own way, not to lose face? Had he really told the whole story?

The confirmation that the two men had talked extensively was given by Jeremy when she and he were left alone at one point.

With a quick look at Sam's retreating back, Jeremy leant across the table and took her hand.

'Helen, I am so pleased to meet you. Sam made me watch your programme and I'm so glad I did. You're terrific – on and off screen. In fact, everything he's told me about you is obviously true. I know you've been through hell with him, and he knows it too, but please stick it out. I've never seen him like this. He's so much in love with you, I think he'd die if you gave up on him.'

Helen smiled at this stranger. In some ways, he was not unlike Sam. Maybe that's why she felt so much at ease with him. They both had soft hands with perfect nails and both were immaculately and expensively dressed. The only differences were in their skin tones.

Sam returned, followed by a waiter bearing a bottle of Bollinger.

'Helen,' he said softly as the waiter retreated, 'I've put you through so much and I hate myself for it. My only excuse is that I haven't been able to help it.'

'Right, you two,' Jeremy interrupted, raising his champagne glass, 'a toast to your happiness. I'm not going to let you get this wrong. You're totally in love and you're made for each other – it's as simple as that.'

'It isn't at all!' Helen sprang to her man's defence. 'You know the story, and you know about Hamaida, and you probably know Sam's mother.'

'I don't know her, but we have met,' he admitted. 'But Sam old boy, you absolutely cannot let all that stuff stand in your way. Why don't you two just get married and sort it out afterwards? Just get it done!'

'Helen would never agree to that.'

Jeremy sighed as he focused on her. 'Dear God, you're as bad as he is.'

'If this is going to be forever,' she responded, 'we have to get it right.'

'You're a remarkable lady,' Jeremy said, 'which is another very good reason why Sam should hold onto you. Listen, I'm

253

talking from experience. I've been a louse and a cad, which I regret, but it's too late now. My wife is French, and I was under the impression that French wives understood men and tolerated their little flings and affairs. Well, Lucile understood all right. But she decided that she was no longer going to tolerate them. Then I realised that none of the others had meant anything to me. Not really. And that she was a fabulous and sexy woman, and I should have treated her like a queen, not like dirt. I have to live with that. So, what I'm saying is that when you have something special, you must nurture it. Not let it go. If you do, you'll regret it for ever.'

Helen turned to Sam. 'Does Jeremy know the whole story about Hamaida?'

'If you mean, do I know about him "robbing her of her virginity" or whatever nonsensical phrase he used, yes I do. Now, I understand that all this means a great deal more in your culture, Sam, but are you really going to let a small mistake like this ruin your entire life? It seems to me she's a conniving little minx and you shouldn't give in to her.'

Helen was shocked by Jeremy's candour and braced herself for an outburst from Sam, but it never came. However, the two men wound up the evening fairly swiftly afterwards and ordered a taxi to Chiswick. Helen noticed that she was not asked if she was happy to come back to Sam's home, but said nothing.

Inside, Jeremy – who was obviously a man of considerable tact – declared himself to be 'absolutely knackered' and made for the spare room.

'Well, how do you feel after Jeremy's lecture in the restaurant?' Helen asked, putting an arm around Sam's shoulders.

'The English side – the boy who went to school with him – agrees totally. It's just…'

'I know, Sam. It's hard. Perhaps we've talked enough for one night.'

'Come to bed,' he murmured.

Once there, she offered no resistance when he began to make love to her. Fleetingly, she wondered if he would regret it afterwards, but her mind and her body were locked into their mutual passion and she could not have stopped him even had she wanted to.

It was as powerful as it had ever been – better, perhaps because of their recent abstinence. Neither of them slept much as they clung to each other through the night, and their need for each other surfaced again and again, and was satisfied.

Jeremy left them alone till the evening when they all had dinner together and Helen found herself telling the two doctors about her medical slot of the other day and the fight over the placenta. To her amazement, both of them sided with Derek, her editor. 'Too gross,' Jeremy said.

'But you're a gynaecologist,' she protested. 'If you can't stomach it, what hope is there? This sums up exactly what makes life so difficult for lots of women. No one talks about hormones and the scientific reasons why lots of ladies have a really miserable time after giving birth. Really, you're impossible.'

The two men looked taken aback at her outburst and Jeremy apologised for his remark. Sam looked almost frightened. 'You're not really angry, are you?' he asked her.

She gazed at him for a moment, before letting her shoulders drop and smiling. 'I was, but it's over now.'

The next morning, Jeremy brought tea in bed to the lovers. Helen was astonished at the gesture – kind though it was – because she was sitting up in bed with nothing on.

Jeremy appeared not to notice, but Sam hurriedly threw her a bathrobe, indicating with his eyes that he would like her to cover herself.

'Now,' Jeremy asked, 'what are we going to do today? I'm having the best weekend with you two and I want to make the most of it.'

'Well, you and Helen can plan it. I've got to go and see a couple of patients in the clinic, but I'll be back mid-morning. Perhaps we should drive out and have lunch in the country.'

'What I'd really like to do is to visit Brighton,' Jeremy responded. 'I haven't been there since I was a boy.'

'Not a bad idea,' Sam smiled. 'Can you get some coffee on while I take a shower?'

Helen stayed in bed till Sam had left and then, still wrapped in his dressing gown, sprinted downstairs to the kitchen. Jeremy was dressed now in the slightly old-fashioned garb beloved of well-heeled Englishmen of a certain vintage. His mustard coloured Norfolk jacket was beautifully cut, and he was wearing cavalry twill trousers. Helen was pleased he had put on a tweedy-looking tie. If he had been sporting a cravat he would have reminded her rather too closely of her first boyfriend in Bournemouth.

She offered him a mug of coffee, which he accepted, then he said, 'I meant what I said the other day. You're a remarkable girl, Helen. Sam's very lucky. He won't let you down in the end. He's very stubborn, you know. And he always gets what he wants in the long run. And he certainly wants you. You obviously have the most tremendous time in the sack!'

Helen felt herself blushing. 'How do you know? Has he told you?'

'My dear lady, I have been sleeping in the next room to the two of you over the past couple of nights – feeling, I may add, more and more randy by the moment!'

'Oh.' She busied herself with some washing-up in the sink and refused to meet his gaze.

'What an English rose you are,' he said after a moment. 'Come here.'

She walked towards him and he gave her a very tight hug.

'To tell you the truth, I think it's possible that things will get worse before they get better,' he warned her, 'but hang on in there. You two are meant to be together. In the meantime, I'm going to give you my phone number, just in case you need someone to

256

talk to. And I'd like yours if that's possible as I may need a listening ear too.'

'Sorry. I keep forgetting that you're having a dreadful time too.'

'Mine's of my own making though so don't feel sorry for me. But being here this weekend has made me think about my future and I'm beginning to think I might come back and settle and work here again.'

'In a way then, you're acting rather like Sam. There's something about a crisis that seems to send people scurrying for their roots.'

'It's totally different.'

'I'm not so sure. Are you getting divorced?'

'No, Lucile's a Catholic and doesn't believe in it. And neither of us want our two sons to finish their upbringing in a broken home.'

'But what about you living here?'

'Paris is a short hop, Helen!' He smiled at her. 'Anyway, they're at boarding school here, so it might work out quite well. And, if I get very, very lucky, I suppose it's just possible that after a while Lucile might miss me and want me back. Not holding my breath though.'

In Brighton, they behaved like a trio of teenagers. They ate fish and chips in a café, played the machines on the Palace Pier and walked around the Regency Pavilion, which all of them recalled having visited last on school trips. They were in light-hearted mood and Helen said suddenly that she wished she had had a brother like Jeremy.

'You'd have been the perfect sibling,' she announced.

Sam roared with laughter. 'I'm not sure he views you as a sister.'

'Shut up,' said Jeremy, though he laughed too.

The next morning they had to go their separate ways. Sam left for the operating theatre early. Jeremy was catching a mid-morning flight, so he saw Helen out to the cab she had summoned, before leaving Chiswick himself.

'Don't worry,' he said.

'I'm not. Well, not at the moment anyway. I feel on Cloud Nine actually. You've been such a help.'

He kissed her on both cheeks, before opening the taxi door for her. She smiled at him then jumped in and waved as the vehicle moved off.

In the newsroom, Laura sought her out almost immediately.

'Gosh, you look better,' she said.

'I am. We've just had the most brilliant weekend. Sam and I are totally back to normal. Jeremy seems to have worked some sort of magic there. It's such a relief. Laura, I am so, so, so in love with Sam, I honestly can't think straight. After the meeting, I'm going to pop out and buy myself something to wear tonight to celebrate. We're going to that visiting ballet company at the Coliseum and then having dinner at the Pelican – and after that, who knows?'

After the programme, Helen modified her television make-up and slipped on her new purchase – a Caroline Charles drop-waisted heavy silk lavender dress. Glancing at herself in the full-length mirror in her dressing room she could see that she looked good, and she felt good too.

She ran downstairs to where she knew Sam would be waiting, her high heels announcing her arrival as she came into view.

Something about his demeanour halted her in her tracks. He was not the same man who had waved farewell so breezily this morning. Perhaps he had lost a patient; that always depressed him.

He did not kiss her. 'Do you mind if we forget the ballet and drive straight home?' he asked quietly.

'No,' she said, suppressing very real disappointment. 'What's wrong?'

'I'll tell you later,' he answered.

He said nothing more till they were in his sitting room. He walked straight to his drinks table and poured two very large brandies and held one out to her. She perched, nervously, on the

258

edge of a sofa while he strode away and stood with his back to the fireplace. His face was drained of all colour.

'There's no easy way to tell you what I have to say – not for you and not for me, so please just listen. When I finished operating today, two men were waiting to see me. Those two men were Hamaida's older brothers. I had written to her, as I had said I would, and when she got that letter, apparently she summoned her family and told them – for the first time – what had transpired between her and me all those years ago. Obviously, she was perfectly entitled to do that. She was upset, and felt rejected I suppose, but I had not foreseen this would happen. The brothers were as angry as if I had raped her. Maybe they believe I did. They told me I had insulted their sister, their family and their father's memory. In days gone by, I suspect our tribes would have gone to war over it. But in 1985, there's a different option.' His voice was as unemotional as if he were delivering an academic paper. 'So, before I left the hospital I gave in my notice. I'm returning to Egypt on October the third, and on October the tenth, I shall do my duty and repair the damage between our two families by marrying Hamaida.'

Chapter Thirteen

Making a kind of 'errgh' sound that, even in her drunken state she recognised as being most unattractive, Helen stood in front of her bathroom mirror, poking out a furred tongue at her image. It was three o'clock in the morning.

'When are you going to stop playing Russian roulette with your life?' she demanded. She pinched the skin round her jawline, which seemed looser than it had just a few weeks ago, making her look like a pale, puffy downtrodden wife who drinks away the hours till her negligent husband deigns to put in an appearance and brighten her day.

'The only difference,' she sneered at herself, 'is that no man comes home to you – ever.'

She padded through to the kitchen and poured herself a large glass of iced orange juice. She felt queasy but downed it in one breath like a traveller in the desert who has been starved of liquid for days. She was still thirsty, so she drank a tumbler full of Perrier. And then another, before staggering back to bed.

Lying there, with the room swimming before her, she groaned, 'Oh God,' into the stillness. But God did not enter into it. There could be no God, or if there was one she hated him. And she hated Freddie with whom she had spent the evening, because he was not Sam. She hated Jeremy too, because her fall had been all the more humiliating so soon after his unshakeably confident predictions that she would win in the end. Most of all, she hated herself.

The previous few weeks were the longest she had ever known. She had struggled through each day, hoping that she was managing to deliver what the company expected of her. But once the programme was over every night, she had dedicated herself to drinking to oblivion. She had accepted every invitation going – as long as it involved alcohol – but when there was none, she went to the social club and stayed till closing time. She was becoming a drunken bore, and she knew it. At last, as the birds began singing, she fell asleep again and slumbered fitfully till it was time to get up and begin the whole sorry routine again.

The telephone rang. She reached for the receiver on her bedside table and barked 'Yes' into the mouthpiece.

'Miss Bartlett?'

'Yes,' she said again.

'It's Mildred Smorthwaite.'

'Oh!' That was a surprise. 'How are you?' She tried to sound as if she cared.

'I'm fine. How are you?'

'Pass,' said Helen, knowing she should make more of an effort but failing to find the energy to do so.

'I'm ringing about my boss. He's gone into theatre early so I know I won't be interrupted by him.'

'OK,' Helen said, completely bewildered by the call.

The older woman sighed audibly. 'Look, Miss Bartlett, you're my last resort. Can you do anything?'

'About what?'

'About him?'

'Why?'

'I think he must be ill. He's forgetting appointments. He's making mistakes. He's… just not the man he was.'

'I shouldn't worry. You'll have a new boss soon, won't you? He's resigned.'

'I have no idea if he'll be replaced or not. The whole transplant programme is going to be reviewed. There's not enough money for it. And, as you probably know, he never drew an NHS salary, he only profited from his private clinic.'

'I *didn't* know that.'

'If he goes, people will die. To be honest, I'm not sure that the hospital will fund the programme without him, and so, a lot of us who are really dedicated to what we achieve here, will have to look for new jobs.'

'That's terrible.' Helen was shocked. 'But what on earth can I do?'

Miss Smorthwaite paused, then spoke in a confidential tone. 'I understand that the two of you are no longer together. But please, please think of what you're doing to him. I'm sure you have your reasons, but you can't begin to imagine how lost he is without you.'

'I don't think you understand, Miss Smorthwaite. I haven't given him up, he finished with me. He's going back to Egypt. That's what he wants.'

'He's got a very funny way of showing it then. Please talk to him.'

'I'd like to help. Believe me. But we're no longer in communication.'

'Well, at the risk of even more trouble, I'm going to tell him about this conversation. And I'm going to tell him that you sound absolutely dreadful. In fact, you sound pretty much like he looks.'

'Sorry… but please don't say anything to him. It won't help.'

'Helen, may I call you that? I don't know what the problems are, but surely they can be resolved? He was so happy with you. He's a broken man.'

Helen burst into tears. 'For God's sake, this is all in his hands, not mine. Every day is a complete nightmare. But there's nothing I can do. He'll never change his mind. Goodbye.'

Laura came looking for her soon after she arrived in the newsroom but – as she tended to do most days – Helen said she was too busy to stop and have coffee. She hated herself all over again when Laura withdrew, looking hurt, but she could not help the fact that her friend's stable situation only served to aggravate her own misery.

Sue put her head round Helen's office door. 'Do you want to do some letters?'

'No,' Helen answered, 'but I will. I'll draft out what I want to say in longhand and bring them through.'

It was a less-efficient way of doing things, but she did not want to have to converse or be polite to anyone else. And she wanted, as much as possible, to avoid any concerned, compassionate or prying eyes. She was better on her own.

As Sue left, Helen thought she heard her say: 'She's definitely getting worse.'

Of course, she could have been talking about someone else, but it did not seem likely.

After the programme, she went to the social club, intending to drink there all evening. However, as she embarked on her third drink, the club steward interrupted her to say there was a phone call for her.

'Who is it?' she asked, crossly.

'He wouldn't say.'

'God help us, can't I get a bit of peace and quiet after a busy day?' she snapped, though she stood up and followed him to the phone nonetheless.

'Helen, it's me.'

'Sam! Why are you calling me here? It's not fair of you.'

'I need to speak to you. I'm coming over.'

'No! I can't have people here knowing any more of my business. Don't you dare come.'

'OK. Come here, then.'

'No.'

'Please.'

'What good would it do?' she asked, her weary voice warbling with emotions that she was unable to control.

'Helen, I beg you…'

'All right. I'll get a taxi. I've drunk too much to drive.'

Three quarters of an hour later, he opened the door to her. Helen stared at him – this man who was responsible for the best and the worst feelings of her life. He took a step towards her and suddenly they were in each other's arms, clinging together as though they were the only couple left after World War Three.

When they woke the following morning, they were curled round each other like two puppies in a basket.

The night before, they had talked till their combined exhaustion had allowed them to sleep. Now, though it was Saturday, he told her he had to go to the clinic. She lay in bed, remembering happier times, while he went to take his bath. After a few minutes, she wandered into the bathroom after him and perched on the edge of the tub, like she loved to do, and talked to him while he soaped himself and shaved. What a marvellous thing of beauty he was, she thought.

A tear trickled slowly down her cheek. He leant over and kissed it away, then jumped out of the bath, wrapped himself in a large towel and picked her up before carrying her back to the bedroom.

'You still don't understand,' he said.

She never responded to this phrase which he used so often. What was there to say, after all?

'Do you?' he persisted, as he put her down by the bed, unwound the towel from his body and laid it on the bed before the two of them fell on to it.

'I think I understand only too well.'

'You haven't accepted it though.'

'I have. I have,' she said, sniffing away the threatening tears. 'I didn't call you last night, remember. You phoned me. I was getting on with things… things as they are. I have accepted our situation. If I thought there was any hope for us, I wouldn't feel so devastated.'

'I want you to be happy, Helen.'

'That's a ridiculous thing to say. Are you happy?'

'That's not the point.'

'It is. It absolutely is. I can't possibly be happy. I love you. I want to be with you for the rest of my life. I want to be the mother of your children. It's natural to be overwhelmingly sad and to grieve at the end of an affair.'

He winced slightly. Perhaps the word 'affair' offended him. 'Helen – you know I care, don't you?'

There was silence.

'Don't you?'

'I don't know what I know.'

His mouth pressed onto hers; it took her breath away. Eventually, he pulled back to say, 'I spend every waking hour thinking of you. Don't you know the regrets I have? Haven't I shown you in every conceivable way how much I care for you?'

His tongue began circling her ear. Then he sought her lips again and attempted to part them. She kept them closed. She knew she must reject him now, to save their sanity. If she capitulated, they would be more crazily enmeshed than ever.

He drew back, his eyes dark and liquid and troubled. 'I want you, Helen. More and more. I fancied you so much the day we met. I promise you I did. It was a kind of madness, how much I desired you. And then we got together, and it was sensational. But I truly love you now. It's not just physical attraction. I adore every part of you. I long for your company. Your mind. Your beauty.'

He kissed her again and this time she allowed his tongue to push between her lips and did not try to stop him as he caressed her breasts and then moved his hand lower till it took control of the very centre of her need and where she most longed to be touched. She surrendered herself to the sensations building between them. His breathing was fast now and his movements on her more insistent. She reached down with her hand, and stroked him, feeling his arousal growing. Then suddenly he was inside her. Why did it have to feel so good? Effortlessly, he seemed to fill every part of her being and slowly and deliberately he thrust into her, again and again.

Together, they rode to the inevitable outcome and he held her tightly as her body began pulsing around him. Their cries of joyful relief sounded together and they lay, joined in every way, passion spent but their love re-energised and overwhelming.

'Well, I guess all the neighbours are awake now,' he said at last. And they laughed as if there were no cares, no obstacles, just a perfect relationship that would sustain them through life.

Abruptly, the mood changed. His facial expression grew grim and he said, 'I want you to get out and about. You need to forget me.'

How quickly the pleasure was replaced by pain.

'I'm doing my best,' she retorted. 'I've had dinner with several different men over the past fortnight.'

'Have you slept with anyone?'

'Why are you being so awful? Do you honestly think it would solve anything if I had a quick screw with Tom, Dick or Harry?'

'I don't know.' His face took on a look of abject despair. 'The truth is, I don't know anything.'

'Neither,' she responded as she took his hand and stroked it, 'do I.'

'We'll talk about it when I get back,' he said.

Helen sighed. Surely there was nothing left to talk about.

Once he had gone, she wandered around the little house that had been their haven. Now it seemed as though it was taunting her and saying that she no longer belonged. They had never discussed where they might live after their marriage, but she had imagined it would be here. She stood in front of the Tom Merrifield sculpture, hoping it would weave its usual magic for her, but instead, it made her cry. She must pull herself together. What was the point of hanging around Sam all weekend when, even though he had been so desperate for her company and her body he had not, for one second, hinted that he could alter his long-term plans?

She ran a bath and lay in it till the persistent ringing of the phone forced her to leave it.

'Darling, it's me.'

'Have you seen your patient?'

'Not yet. I thought I'd ring you first to check you're OK.'

'I'm all right, but I think I'm going to leave in a moment.'

'Where are you going?'

'Um,' she searched her mind for inspiration. 'Norfolk,' she said, triumphantly.

'Why there?'

'Because I had a lovely holiday there once when I was small.'

'Helen, please. Don't do this. At least wait till I get back.'

'I can't promise that, Sam,' she said, putting the phone down.

She dressed in yesterday's clothes and sat trying to make sense of everything. She picked up a novel from his bookshelves but could not focus. She twiddled with the radio but failed to find a station she wanted to listen to. Time passed. She should go. What was the point in waiting?

'Don't leave me,' he cried as he hurtled through the front door.

'Sam, I'm sorry but I have to go. I can't be here, in this house. It's too painful. Everything was so special here. Now, it's a nightmare. Maybe tomorrow will be better,' she finished, bleakly.

He poured out two brandies and handed one to her. 'What have I done to you, Helen?' he asked softly.

She studied him, but her mouth would not connect with her thoughts and no answer came. She sipped from her drink. It slipped down too easily. He moved towards her, intent on refilling it, but she stopped him, knowing that if he succeeded in getting her to drink more, he would be in a stronger position to insist that she did not drive anywhere.

'Will you come and see me tomorrow?'

He sounded like a little boy who was being left at a boarding school for the first time. Was that what he was remembering?

'Perhaps,' she managed.

'Let me drive you home.'

'No, thank you. I'm going to walk for a while. Quite a long while, I suspect. And when I get tired of that, I'll take a taxi. I love you, Sam, probably more than you'll ever know, but I have to go now.'

She walked by the river, stopping every now and again to look into space. Eventually, she hailed a cab. Back in her own flat she washed and dried her hair. Viewing herself in the mirror, she looked as if she drank too much and slept too little. 'What a mess I am,' she whispered.

In her bedroom, she slid open the doors to her built-in wardrobes and saw immediately, the Caroline Charles lavender dress. It lay, where she had dropped it weeks ago, in a crumpled heap; a symbol of her bitterly crushed hopes.

She found some casual clothes that would do, then listlessly mooched around her apartment. Nothing made sense. Her flat, her job, her life – what were they without him? She wandered over to her bedside table and opened its drawer. Inside, she found some blue pills, though she had no clue what they were. There was a bottle of paracetamol tablets too. She shook them out into her hand, before arranging them along with the blue pills, in a neat pattern. Would they be enough to do the job?

The sun was shining through the windows. She pictured the headlines: 'TV star in suicide drama.'

She should call someone for help. But there was no help for her. Probably the world would be better off without her in it. She was complicating Sam's life and being a complete drain on her friends. There was no fight left in her, just a hideously bleak calm. I don't exactly want to die, she thought, but I do want it all to stop. All of it. Mechanically, she gathered the pills together, and put them into her handbag. Then she threw a change of top and some toiletries into an overnight bag and left.

Through the car windows, she could see that life for most people was continuing much as normal, but she was cocooned in her own bubble away from the teeming pace of Ladbroke Grove and the districts that followed. A red light on her dashboard flashed. She was almost out of petrol. How exasperating. She would have to stop at the next garage.

Even before he saw her name on the credit card, the cashier was eying Helen with more than the usual interest he reserved for solo, attractive women in smart cars.

'It is, isn't it?'

She nodded.

'You get up to some crazy things, don't you? What about that knife-thrower, and the day you went into the lions' cage? Sooner you than me. Still, I 'spect you make a lot of money.'

'It's a myth that we're paid a fortune,' she replied.

'Is that a fact?' His tone was unconvinced.

She forced a smile, signed the grubby scrap of paper he thrust in front of her, collected her receipt and escaped.

Somehow, she was following the right route, without too many mistakes.

'There we are,' she said aloud, 'you're getting there; you must be OK.'

The next time she looked at her watch, she was in the curiously flat landscape, dominated by sky and dotted with pink cottages, of East Anglia. And, at last, she came upon the unpretentious little town of Cromer and instinctively made her way to the once grand hotel where she had stayed as a girl.

Heads turned.

'Oh, I just felt like an afternoon out of London,' she announced breezily to the young receptionist. 'Do you have any vacancies?'

'Certainly, Miss Bartlett,' said the young woman who was obviously in some hurry to get rid of her so she could tell other people that they had had a celebrity staying.

In the quiet of her room, Helen tried to process her morning. She was in Cromer, though she was unsure why. I suppose I didn't run over anyone on the way, she thought as she got all her pills out of her handbag and lined them up on the dressing table.

Not sure what to do, she went out for some sea air. Wearing dark glasses, she was able to wend her way through the bunched groups of families and friends without being stopped. As she surveyed the sandy beach, she saw various children running in and out of the waves, shrieking with excitement and laughing in that completely uninhibited way that infants have. She felt a stab of envy for their innocence and peace of mind as they browned their sea-sprayed bodies in the sun. Family dogs were running around in circles – trying to join in with the children but then opting to run far into the distance. How absurdly and easily pleased dogs are, she thought.

Gradually, as she watched the people all around her, she began to feel more of a connection with them and with the world in general.

'I think you're all right after all,' she reassured herself.

Her eye was taken suddenly by a youngish man in a Fair Isle sweater who had covered his head with a handkerchief, knotted at four corners. His wife was unfashionably dressed too, and they were helping their daughter to build a sandcastle. It was like a film clip of her own childhood in the fifties. She felt nostalgic for a moment, but then realised that her longing was not for times past, but for the future she had hoped to have, which now seemed less and less likely.

There would be no husband for her. No children. No family scenes with a pet dog. The appalling sense of loss of what would never be, kicked her in the stomach and she nearly fell over with the strength of it.

She continued to dwell on her childless state. That would never alter now. There could never be another Sam and she was running out of time to make babies with anyone else, even had she wanted to.

A thought niggled at the back of her mind. It was vague and inchoate. She tried to reach for it in her fevered brain and to give it an identity.

When had she last had a period? That was it. When had that been? Definitely not since the wonderful weekend when she and Sam had abandoned themselves to each other while Jeremy lay wakeful in the spare room.

So, when? She remembered a programme before that happy two days, when she had interviewed a particularly slippery politician and had had to dose herself with the anti-rheumatic pills she resorted to when she had severe menstrual cramp. She hated taking them because they made her feel drowsy, but the pain had been so bad she had had no alternative. When had that been? It had been tied to a by-election. Counting back on her fingers, she realised that it must be about six weeks ago. How had she not noticed? So much had been going on, she supposed. So much stress... distress...

I couldn't possibly be pregnant though, she decided. And with that certainty came a wave of grief.

'Keep normal,' she hissed at herself. 'Go and eat something. Get a grip.'

She saw a passer-by react to her talking to herself but dropped her gaze and hurried back to the hotel where she ordered a tray of tea and a chicken sandwich.

In the bedroom, which was pretty in its sedate way, the incongruity of her situation hit her. Perhaps she would end up not only without Sam, but lonely, old, eccentric, and maybe even living in a once-grand hotel by the sea. She had a vision of herself, aged seventy-five or so, with a walking frame and egg stains on her jumper. Might she bore people about her days in television in exchange for a gin and tonic? Would they humour her as she talked about when she had been little more than 'a gel'?

Her meal arrived. She tipped the porter, who might have preferred to wait and chat had she given him the chance. The sandwiches were nestling in a crisp white doily. She selected one and found that she was hungry. It dawned on her that she had eaten nothing since a bag of crisps with her first drink in the club the previous evening.

She remembered her medicinal brandy with Sam this morning. Dismissing the memory, she resolved to be more sensible, to eat properly, to stop drinking like an alcoholic and to decline cigarettes from smokers in the club who could see she needed as many comforts as they could provide.

If I were to be pregnant, she thought, I haven't exactly given the poor little bugger a good start, have I? She sighed loudly. Something else I've done wrong.

I've got to find my sense of purpose again, and seize everything that's good in life, she told herself. Then, feeing hot and tired with that responsibility, she stripped off and discarded her clothes on a nearby chair, stretched out on the counterpane of her single bed, and closed her eyes.

The flapping of the curtains at the little open window woke her. She was slightly chilled now that the afternoon sun had gone and been replaced by an evening breeze.

She had, she realised, a side view of the sea, overlooking a patchwork of roofs with pantiles, broken tiles and no tiles at all. The beach was quieter now. She supposed people had left for the day or gone back to eat in their lodgings. The next few hours stretched uninvitingly before her, so she decided to go out. It was strange to be so directionless.

Walking down the steep path from the hotel to the promenade, she was jostled by families, eating soggy, flaccid chips out of trays. She thought she heard someone say, 'Looks like that woman off the telly.' Her pace quickened, and she studied her feet as she strode on.

Then she saw a poster, advertising 'Seaside Special – The Last Authentic End-of-the-Pier Show'. It was due to start at 8.15. It was 8.10 and she had found a schedule for her evening.

Someone had had a great marketing idea that this was a show, or maybe even an institution, with a preservation order stuck on it. The auditorium was surprisingly full, and she recalled reading a review of a documentary that she had failed to see, about traditional summer shows. She fancied it had featured Cromer.

It was good entertainment, she discovered, of the type she might have enjoyed with her parents as a child – though it seemed to her that the glittering leotards of the dancing girls were cut higher on the leg than in days gone by.

'I love a lassie,' she sang along with the rest of the audience. The singer had built his act on the theme 'Around the Country in Song' and soon the Scottish melody was replaced by the Welsh 'There'll be a welcome in the hillsides'.

'Anyone from Wales in tonight?' bellowed the singer over the final chorus. There was a cheer from the back of the auditorium. Soon they were on to 'When Irish Eyes are Smiling', though halfway through it, she found herself unable to continue singing because she was weeping. Why? She had never even been to Ireland, even though she had had an Irish grandfather.

Where on earth was the Helen Bartlett that the world knew? On the end of a pier in Cromer, seriously questioning her sanity.

After the show, she walked swiftly through the busy, brightly-lit bar. Her mascara had probably run down her face and she most certainly did not want to be recognised. Outside, she stood for a while, watching the tumbling waves that were edged in the reflected coloured lights on the pier. The tide would come in and go out again, no matter what. No man is an atheist when confronted by the ocean, she mused. She was sure somebody significant had said that at some time.

The movement of the sea was hypnotic, and it looked like rich, black, icy velvet. Velvet was a word normally associated with comfort and warmth, but not here. For a second, she wondered what it would be like to walk off the pier, down to the beach and into the waves until their coldness consumed her.

'Oh God,' she whispered into the blackness, 'forgive me. I know I'm being despicable and sorry for myself.' And she turned and walked back along the length of the pier and up to the hotel.

Once there, she asked for a glass of warm milk. It appeared that there was only one ancient retainer on duty – a polite bald-headed gentleman in a faded maroon jacket. She thought it unfair to make him trudge up to her room, so she waited in the lounge. Again, she felt as if she was being propelled back in time. When had she last drunk hot milk at bedtime? It was something her mother had insisted upon till she was about fifteen and finally allowed to decide what, if anything, she would like last thing.

The porter returned with a tray bearing a silver coffee jug full of milk, a tall glass, and a spoon.

'Put the spoon in the glass before you pour the milk, madam,' he advised. 'That way, the glass won't crack.'

It was all so wonderfully old-world. She smiled at him, nodded and bade him goodnight.

In her room, she debated whether or not to call Sam. At the moment he did not loom too large here, but if she spoke to him, that would change. She found herself worrying about how anxious he must be, but perhaps that might jolt him into sorting his priorities in a way that was appropriate to the time they lived in.

She sighed. How very western her thinking was, she acknowledged. The truth was that he *had* sorted his priorities, and for him the call from the east was stronger than the one from her world.

She looked across the room to where her pills lay, in a row, ready for her to take them and finish the pain. It felt like far, far too much effort to walk across and pick them up. They would be there still in the morning.

Helen woke to a sunny Sunday. She lay still, hardly daring to breathe, waiting for the customary onslaught of misery and anguish to hijack her, but nothing happened. Gingerly, she sat up. Everything seemed real and normal. She put a foot on the floor. It felt solid. There was, at the back of her head somewhere, a perception of pain, but it was dull, like a receding migraine.

She pushed open the windows as far as they would go and breathed in the air, which was invigorating. She was hungry, she realised, so after a quick shower, and putting on her clothes and enough make-up to pass muster, she made for the dining room where she ordered poached eggs and grilled tomatoes on brown toast and a jug of coffee.

There are so many simple pleasures in life, she reminded herself. This is what she must do. Take everything a step at a time. Enjoy basic things.

After breakfast, she considered staying in Cromer, but she felt it had worked its magic and that she was ready to return to London, to do her job, and even to see Sam.

He was overjoyed when she arrived, but clearly put out by her disappearance of the day before. Saying nothing, she listened as his recriminations mounted. She should have phoned. She should have realised how desolate he would feel not to have contact. She should have been aware that he would be worried sick that she might have crashed her car because she was in such a state.

She smiled at him, a warm generous smile which stopped his tirade.

'Well, I'm here now. And I want you to know that I'm OK and that I think I've come to a point where we can be platonic friends. I know that's what you want. And I'm going to have a real go at doing just that.'

'Let's go to the pub,' he said. 'If we hurry, they'll still just about be serving lunch.'

'All right. But I'm going to get fat. I had a big breakfast.'

'Sweetheart,' he responded drily, 'there's more fat on a French fry!'

Back in his house after lunch, they read the Sunday papers and then the restlessness began. The restlessness they had submerged in order to be civilised, and friendly. The restlessness that cannot be denied when two lovers are unable to keep their hands from reaching out and touching. She moved first, to stand behind the armchair in which he was seated. Unable to help herself, she kissed the back of his neck and he grasped her left hand and held it to his cheek. Waves of comfort and love filled her being and she felt them oscillate between the two of them.

'Come to bed.' His voice was soft but urgent with desire.

She walked round to the front of his chair and pulled him into a standing position, then led him by the hand to his bedroom.

They lay together, hardly daring to move. A ring from the phone on his bedside table made them both jump.

'You had better answer it,' she urged him.

He shook his head.

'It may be someone in Egypt.'

'It may,' he agreed.

'I'll go off to the bathroom and you can take it.'

'No!' He grabbed her arm and restrained her. 'Whoever it is will ring again later.'

'You should get one of those new answer machines.'

'I've got one. But I haven't got round to setting it up yet.'

The ringing went on.

'Sam, you need to answer it. Suppose it's something serious at the hospital or the clinic?'

'It'll stop in a moment. I will not answer it. Don't ask me.'

She never argued with him when he was that vehement and allowed herself to be held tightly while they waited for the ringing to stop. But the mood was different now, and she found herself shedding yet more tears.

He kissed her and pleaded, 'Don't cry, my angel. I can't bear it. Please don't. You know how much I love you.'

'Yes, I do.' Her voice was a whisper.

'Helen,' he said, firmly, 'whatever happens, I want you to live out your life in the certain knowledge that no matter who has loved you in the past – your parents, your husband, other lovers, whatever… and whoever loves you in the future, I love you more than the sum total of them all.'

She closed her eyes and sighed.

'Say something,' he said.

'I can't, Sam. Don't ask. I just can't.'

She felt him turn away from her, and for a moment she thought they might both sleep but then she sensed his hand reaching out behind him to fondle her. It was as if his face was turned to his future, but that his body could not help but respond to what he knew and loved here and now. He turned and grasped her in his arms and kissed her passionately, then he turned her so that her back was towards him and swiftly entered her, reaching around to caress her as he began to get into the rhythm which they both knew would take them to the delight they desired.

She felt as if she was on a swingboat at one of the funfairs of her youth. Any moment now, she would feel the rapid sensation of little pulses, like smiles, deep inside her. The warm, prickly sensation began to spread upwards from the soles of her feet.

'Sam, what the hell are you doing?' she cried, because at the very second she was going to abandon herself to the warm pleasure of their mutual climax, he pulled away, roughly.

Nothing that had gone before in all the months of turmoil compared with this moment of degradation. She felt like a prostitute whose client withdraws in shame and moral repugnance. Refusing to look at him, she swung herself off his bed, and quickly gathered her clothes and made for the bathroom.

Inside, she filled the tub with water as hot as she could bear it and lay in it, trying to erase from her mind what had happened in the bedroom. Eventually, she got out and dried herself then pulled on her trousers and top and stepped into her shoes.

He was standing outside the door when she emerged.

'I don't suppose there's any point in my saying that I'm sorry. But I am. Desperately.'

'No, there's no point, Sam. And there's nothing more to be said.'

Driving through the sunny evening streets to her flat, she contemplated what death must feel like. Surely it could not be much different from this; the end of everything. She considered driving on and on, perhaps to the south coast, onto a ferry, disappearing. No one would find her. Or maybe it would be simpler to crash into a wall and wake from this nightmare for one searing second before she died.

Some time later, she realised that she had no concept of where in London she was. She stopped the car, shaking all over and feeling as though she had stumbled into an alien land. Her mind was no longer functioning normally. Her Greater London atlas that was dusty through lack of use lay on the back seat. Gradually, by driving till she found a street name, she pieced together where she was and forced herself to focus on the maps in front of her, till she had planned a route that would take her home.

She went straight to bed and must have slept because a persistent buzzer woke her. Grabbing at her dressing gown, she lurched to the door and picked up the entry phone. Perhaps all the suffering was worth it. Perhaps finally Sam had come to his senses.

'Hello.'

'Helen, it's Freddie.'

'What do you want?'

'That's not very friendly.'

'I don't feel friendly.'

'Never mind, just let me in.'

She pressed the button that would open the big heavy door in the hall and waited for Freddie's steps outside her own apartment. He took one look at her.

'You need a drink,' he said.

'I've decided to give up booze.'

'Today is not the day,' he said. 'Where do you keep it?'

She led him into her sitting room and he helped himself to a Scotch from her drinks trolley then waved the bottle in her direction. She shook her head. He picked up the bottle of brandy beside it and poured out a large measure.

As he sat down beside her on the sofa, he handed her the drink and said, 'If you're not careful, you're going to make yourself very ill.'

When she said nothing, he took her free hand and stroked it. It felt too personal.

'What the hell do you think you're doing?'

'Ah,' he smiled. 'A reaction.'

'Get out. Go away. Leave me alone.'

'Helen, I'm sorry. I thought I was helping.'

'Well you're not.'

He backed off the sofa. 'OK, Helen. Calm down. I'm going.'

She did not see him to the door. Instead, she took a long look at the half-filled brandy glass before her and – with great deliberation – walked slowly into the kitchen and poured it down the sink.

She took another bath and then, before retreating to her bed for the night, she looked out the Jane Fonda workout tape and left it by the video machine. Tomorrow, she would begin her campaign. She would transform herself into super-woman – and be super-cool, super-efficient and super-self-sufficient. It was her only option.

'Something completely different for you today, Helen,' Derek said at the next morning's meeting. 'Don't say I never give you the good jobs!' He roared with laughter.

'Oh yeah?'

'Mr Danger from Denmark.'

'Enlighten me!'

'He's touring the country – not big theatres but moderate size ones – and doing his act, but the news angle is that people are fainting or walking out or being sick!'

'Oh my God, what does he do then?'

'Basically, he sticks daggers into himself accompanied by a recording of "The Ride of the Valkyries".'

'Oh fine. So, at the moment, he's upsetting dozens of people at a time, but we're going to ensure that he distresses the whole country. Nice one, Derek.'

'It'll make terrific television.'

'Oh heavens. Where have I heard that before? Well, you're the boss of course, but I'd like to put on record the fact that I think this is bloody irresponsible.' And with that, she swept up her papers and left his office.

To facilitate Mr Danger reaching his next venue by the evening, they had to record the interview at 11.30, so she made her way to the make-up room. On her way, she walked through reception.

'There are flowers for you,' said one of the security men. 'Just arrived. I put them in your dressing room.'

'That's very kind,' and she made a swift detour to see who they were from. Though she was adamant that she wanted no more contact from Sam, she was shaking in anticipation that they might be from him.

She looked at the card, which read: 'You're terrifying when you're angry! Love, Freddie.'

In the make-up room, she did her best with a face that reflected all too clearly what she had been going through. Her skin was blotchy from weeks of heavy drinking and frequent weeping. She was just applying a second layer of foundation when the phone rang.

With no one else to answer it, she jumped up and lifted the receiver.

'There are flowers for you,' said another security man.

'Yeah, I know. I've got them. Your mate put them in my dressing room.'

'No, not those. Another bouquet. Is it your birthday or something?'

'No.'

'What it is to be popular,' he laughed. 'I'll pop them in your dressing room with the others.'

Her hands shook as she lined her eyes and applied rather too much blusher. Freddie must be fond of her, she supposed. But this was a bit over the top. She removed her heated rollers and brushed out her hair. At least that looked normal. Then she went to change.

The second lot of flowers were considerably more splendid than the first and her fingers trembled as she unpinned the attached envelope and read the message inside.

'A million apologies to the only love of my life. Yours forever xxx.'

Unable to help herself, she pressed the card first to her lips, and then to her chest. How was it possible that their amazing relationship had gone so very, very wrong?

Mr Danger from Denmark was waiting in the studio when she arrived. He was about six feet six inches tall, heavily built and dressed like Tarzan in the movies. She wondered, as she looked at him, how good he was at his act because his body was a mass of unsightly scars. She offered her hand which was lost in the giant paw held out to her.

'I've heard what you do,' she told him. 'It sounds horrendous. But anyway, what will happen is that we will take a shot of you handling the tools of your trade' – she viewed the assembly of knives and enormous hatpins he had brought with him, feeling more queasy by the second – 'and then I'll walk in and join you. We'll talk for about two minutes, then we'll increase the volume of your music and you can do the shortened version of your act that you discussed with my researcher. Is that OK?'

He nodded. She supposed he spoke English.

'Let's just rehearse your act. You don't have to pierce yourself or anything, just mime what you're going to do to the music, so the cameramen can plot their positions with the director.'

He nodded again and picked up a couple of sharp objects and started pretending to dig them into himself.

'Excuse me,' the strangulated cry came from a very pale-looking cameraman who rushed from the studio. There was a hiatus during which Helen grew confident that they were going to call the whole thing off. Not so. Another cameraman appeared, listened to his instructions from the director's box and made a few notes.

'OK, let's get on with this,' said the floor manager.

He turned to Mr Danger. 'You'll have ten seconds before Helen walks in, so either look at your daggers or something, or if you want to do something a bit more dramatic, that's fine with us. Putting a clock on it now. In thirty seconds... fifteen... three, two, one and cue...'

The picture came up on the monitors just as Mr Danger gave a blood-curdling cry, plunged a dagger into his left arm and proceeded to wiggle it backwards and forwards till it went right in.

Helen walked in, trying not to look. 'I understand that people are very frightened and horrified by your act. And I think I can see why.'

'I'm unique,' he declared.

'I wouldn't doubt that for a minute,' she responded. 'Um, do you always plunge the daggers into the same holes?'

'Oh no,' he answered and with that, he selected a long, thin pin and pierced through one cheek, through his open mouth and out of the other.

Helen began to sway. She breathed deeply. Without realising it, she covered her face with her hands and though there was still a minute left for the interview, she wound it up by saying, 'I think we'll bring up the music now, and allow you to do the rest of your act. Thanks for coming in.'

She walked out of shot, up to the far end of the studio where she downed two glasses of water. Wagner, she decided, must be turning in his grave.

Keeping her eyes averted from the guest, she gazed at one of the soundmen, who shook his head very slowly at her. At last, it was over.

'Just wait for a clear,' said the floor manager in an unusually subdued voice.

'Well, I'll tell you something,' Helen piped up. 'If there's anything wrong with that take, there's no way I'm doing another one.'

'Quite right,' shouted one of the cameramen.

'We're clear anyway,' the floor manager told them.

Helen noticed that Mr Danger had threads of blood oozing from the areas he had pierced, then she looked away again, as he withdrew the daggers and pins, one by one.

When he had finished, determined to be sociable, she offered him a drink.

'That would be most kind,' he said in his heavy Scandinavian accent.

They went to the green room and were just beginning to chat when two gin and tonics arrived. Helen began to giggle as, surveying his face, she realised that the dimples in Mr Danger's cheeks were actually holes. She tried to stop her mirth, anxious that her guest would be offended, but the more she tried to suppress her laughter, the more it burst out. She could not wait for him to take a sip of his drink, believing that at any moment, it would come spraying out of both his cheeks, like a trick performed by a clown.

Nothing of the sort happened, which was not a little disappointing.

'What else do you do in your act?' she asked him.

He put his glass down and stared into her eyes. 'I hypnotise women. I *love* beautiful women.'

Helen felt slightly strange. For a second, she hovered between what felt like a dream and normality. His eyes were so fixed on hers that she felt he could see into her soul. She shook her head vigorously. 'I didn't ask for an encore,' she rebuked him. 'Thanks for coming in. I need to get back to my office now. I'll send someone to see you out.'

In the newsroom, Derek was waiting. 'Wonderful stuff. Wonderful! The best television I've ever seen. You were great. You looked absolutely horrified.'

'I wasn't acting,' she murmured.

'Quite. Yes, well anyway, terrific but, look don't be annoyed, but it was actually much more graphic than I'd imagined. It's far too horrific to transmit at six. It'll never go out, I'm afraid.'

'And when Derek, that's my boss, said "It'll never go out, I'm afraid", I thought I might kill him.'

Jeremy roared with laughter from his end of the line in Paris. 'What a frightful experience,' he said. 'Anyway, the reason I'm phoning is to find out what on earth is happening with Sam. When I left the two of you, everything seemed set fair. But obviously it's not now. I don't mean to upset you, but what the hell is it? I keep phoning him at work. I get the dragon, Miss Smorthwaite, who gives nothing away. So tonight, I waited till ten o'clock and rang Sam at home. He was polite, but very, very distant.'

'But how was he, do you think?'

'I haven't a clue. But I rather hoped you would throw some light on it.'

'I can't, I'm afraid, except to say that our relationship has completely disintegrated. I don't know how much I should say, but, well, do you remember that Monday when you went back?'

'Of course. I had high hopes of the two of you. Also, I thought I got you to promise that if anything went wrong you'd call me.'

'Did I agree to that? I'm sorry.'

'Never mind. Look, Helen, what's going on?'

'That very day, Hamaida's two brothers turned up at Sam's clinic. He told me later that he'd not only agreed to marry Hamaida on the tenth of October – "do his duty" was how he put it – but that he was going back to Egypt for good on the third, and that he'd resigned.'

'Oh my God. I can't believe this. I wish you'd contacted me.'

She sighed. 'Well, instead of doing something sensible like that, I'm afraid I went on a total bender. I was in such a state I couldn't really speak to anyone. I got very drunk, every night for three weeks. Then last weekend, at Sam's instigation, we met up. I don't feel I can explain what happened, but it was absolutely the worst you can possibly imagine. The only tiny ray of sunshine in this bleak tale is that somehow this week I've taken stock and have followed a very boring routine of going home early after the programme and not drinking any booze. I'm trying to be super-woman which isn't working but perhaps, just perhaps, I have stopped being a total wimp.'

'Helen, you're not a wimp. I think you're a very brave lady. Look, I'll come over next weekend.'

'I shouldn't. I'm fine.'

'Helen, you should stick in there. He may not go home after all, or even if he does, he'll soon realise it's never going to work. He'll be back.'

'Stop it, Jeremy. I've been over and over this scenario a million times. I cannot have hope. I have to accept it's over. Anything else is going to lead to a complete breakdown in my ability to function.'

'OK,' he said, softly.

'How are you, by the way?' she asked him.

'Coming on, I suppose. I'll tell you when I see you next weekend. I'll ring you when I get in.'

'All right. I must admit it will be good to see you... Can I ask you something by the way? Kind of related to your job?'

'Fire away.'

'Is it possible to get pregnant less than a month after you stop taking the contraceptive pill?'

'It's possible, but unlikely. Usually, people have to try for a quite a while.'

'That's what I thought.'

'Why are you asking?'

'Oh, um I've got a friend who's in that position. She was wondering about doing a pregnancy test. Perhaps she should.'

'Mmmn. Wouldn't do any harm. See you soon then.'

The phone rang again almost immediately.

'You've been on the phone for ages,' Sam said accusingly.

'I suppose I have. It was Jeremy.'

'Did you tell him everything?'

'Well, not the lurid and insulting details of last Sunday afternoon if that's what you're asking.'

He was silent for a moment. 'Jeremy rang me too.'

'He told me. He's worried about you.'

'He doesn't need to be.'

'That's good then.' Her tone was brisk.

'I was just thinking, about the weekend that Jeremy was with us, and how great it was.'

'Yes, great,' she agreed.

'Helen!'

She heard him take a deep breath.

'Helen,' he began again, 'please let me make love to you – just one last time. Last weekend was so terrible. I won't go on about it, but I'm deeply ashamed. I'm also lying here with the most massive erection. Please come over here. Let's make love properly. Make it the best it's ever been.'

She bit her lip. 'No, Sam. I'm sorry.'

'Listen, Helen. It's Friday the ninth of August. Two months tomorrow, I'm due to marry somebody else. Someone I don't love. And it means I have to leave you, the person who means more to me than anyone ever has or could do. It'll be forever, Helen, so please come. Honestly,' his voice became boyish with pride, 'if you could see me now, you probably couldn't resist.'

Hating herself, she heard herself say, 'All right.'

At least, because of her ban on alcohol, she was fit to drive, even though it was gone midnight. But was she wise? If it was wonderful tonight, it would simply reopen all her unhealed bloody wounds and if it were awful, she was not sure that this time she could survive.

'Turn the car around, and be sensible,' she shouted at herself. But, as she had known she would, she continued in the direction of Chiswick.

He opened the door, dressed in a bath robe, before she had a chance to ring the bell. He pulled her into the house and embraced her passionately, then started caressing her body through her hastily donned tracksuit, then leant over to kiss her breasts.

He pulled her towards the stairs and up into the bedroom where he removed her clothes in a frenzy as she reached for his body and tried to free it from the dressing gown.

'Damn,' he cried, 'damn, damn, damn. I was so ready for you before you arrived, now look at it.'

'Darling, don't get upset, it doesn't matter. Lie back, let me help you. It'll be all right, you'll see. There's no hurry.'

Her fingers coaxed him gently, but nothing stirred.

'This is the most demoralising moment of my life,' he said. 'I wanted so badly to make love to you, Helen. Like the best of times.' He burst into tears. 'I am so, so sorry, Helen. So very sorry.'

'It doesn't matter,' she said in a calm voice she barely recognised as her own. 'It's nobody's fault.'

In a repeat performance of the previous Sunday's sexual disaster, she gathered her discarded clothing, dressed hurriedly in his bathroom and left the house.

'It doesn't matter,' she said again into the darkness as she jumped into her car and drove off at speed without checking that it was safe to do so.

'Nothing matters. Absolutely nothing at all.'

Chapter Fourteen

The pain felt as though a sledgehammer had buried itself into her abdomen. How had it got there? She would ignore it. It must be something to do with a dream, or maybe she had been lying in an awkward position. Or there was always the possibility that she had strained something while exercising. Breathing deeply, she waited for the discomfort to ease and tried to focus on all the non-hurting bits of her.

Did she feel ill? Not really. It must be muscular then. She was pleased with the diagnosis; she did not present and produce the medical slot for nothing.

It was still early. She could lie in bed for a while yet.

It had been an odd week. Was it really only seven days since she had last seen Sam? It seemed much longer. Mind you, he had been on the phone every day – twice a day sometimes. But despite him, she had thrown herself into a strenuous fitness regime. She performed to the Jane Fonda workout tape morning and evening and she had joined a health club so that she could go there any lunchtime when she was not overburdened with preparation for the programme or a recording. She filled every hour she could with work and had delighted the public relations department by agreeing to go, on their behalf, to a large number of 'fayres' and charity events over the next six months.

She was being positive and as cheerful as she could manage. It was nobody's business that she wept when she was alone. No one knew about that. Not even Sam.

Freddie was the only one who tried to probe her real feelings. She had been surprised that he had followed up his flowers with invitations to meet. There was no place for him in her life; a fact she told him often. So she was efficiently bright and breezy with him whenever he tracked her down.

'I like you better when you're more real and show your emotions,' he had said angrily the last time he had telephoned. For a second her resolve to remain distant had wavered, but she stamped on the feeling. She would not let him near. She would let nobody near. In that way, she would render herself impervious to any further hurt. She might never, she reasoned, ever be happy again. But she would not let the world witness her weakness.

She suddenly realised that the spasm in her abdomen was not easing off. If anything, it was getting worse. It was eight-thirty, so she reached for the phone by her bed and called the newsroom.

Derek's secretary answered.

'Maggie, is he in yet?' Helen asked.

'Yes, but he's on the phone to one of the units. There's been a major pile-up on a contraflow system on the M1.'

'Not again! Well, don't disturb him then. But when he's free can you tell him I'm not feeling well. I'm going to the doctor, but I hope to be in later. I'm sure it's nothing.'

'That's not like you.'

'No.' For the first time, Helen felt slightly anxious. 'No, it's not. But I bet it'll be fine.'

After she put the phone down, she considered her next move. Really, this was the most ridiculous predicament. Bracing herself against the pain, she swung her legs over the side of the bed. Instinctively, she wrapped her hands round her waist, then allowed them to move down towards her groin. Her body felt rigid to the touch. She took a deep breath and tried to stand, but the stabbing sensation was too intense, and the room began to swim before her eyes. Putting her hand to her head, she realised she was perspiring, and yet she was suddenly icy cold. Surely this would pass? In a moment she would be back to normal.

That moment came and went. There was no relief

The phone rang.

'Darling heart.' It was Sam.

'Hello.'

'Sweetheart, what's wrong?'

The concern in his voice caught her off-guard. 'I can't, well, I can't actually move or stand. I seem to have twisted something in my tummy.'

'Oh God.'

'Keep calm,' she said.

'I should be saying that to you.'

She laughed. 'Oooh that really hurt.'

'I'll come over.'

'I don't suppose you can,' she said wistfully.

There was a sharp intake of breath at the other end of the line. 'You're right, I'm just about to scrub up. I'll ring your doctor. Who is it?'

'Sam, it's OK. You go and work. Save a life. I'll be fine. I'll call him myself.'

She put the phone down quickly to prevent further argument and to stop herself from saying: 'Yes, please do come. As soon as you can. I need you.'

The surgery was engaged when she called. She dialled the number again. And again. At last, she got through.

'Sorry to bother you. It's Helen Bartlett here.'

'Oh, Miss Bartlett, how are you?'

She bit back an irritated response and said, 'Well, actually, I can't move. I've got severe pain in my abdomen and when I try and stand up I feel faint.'

291

'That doesn't sound very good. I think you better get yourself down here right away.'

It was on the tip of her tongue to say that she was in no fit state to go anywhere, but she found herself replying that she would do her best. After all, it might be ages before a doctor could come out to her, and it seemed rather melodramatic to call an ambulance.

She booked a taxi and, fighting waves of nausea, forced herself into a tracksuit and slipped her feet into a pair of sandals. Trainers would be more comfortable, but she couldn't see how she might tie the laces without causing herself an increase in the already considerable discomfort. On her hands and knees, gradually she negotiated her journey to the front door of her own flat and pulled herself up to a standing position by using the doorknob. Slowly and painfully, she manoeuvred herself out of the apartment, then returning to all-fours, she crawled towards the stairs. It would be dangerous, she imagined, to continue head first down the twenty steps ahead of her, so she swivelled around and sat on the edge of the first one before tentatively lowering herself onto the one below. She thought she was going to be sick, but she breathed deeply and eventually reached ground level. She sat for a while to regain some strength then edged herself, on her bottom, along the communal hall. She was weak now, but by grasping the big table where the residents' post was laid out every day, she managed to get back to her feet and lurched for the front door.

The taxi driver was coming up the path as she stood swaying in the entrance.

'God Almighty,' he said as he took in her appearance. 'Miss Bartlett, you look all in. Are you going to be able to walk to the taxi?'

She grasped his arm and leant heavily on him while she contrived to nod her head.

Later, she had no memory of the short journey to the surgery. Perhaps she had slept. On arrival, she was embarrassed to discover that she had no money.

'Don't worry about that,' said the driver and he hauled her out of the cab and half carried her into the health centre.

Someone must have put her in a chair because that's where she waited while a little boy played at being an ambulance – running around and making high-pitched siren noises.

I don't think I can stand this, she thought and then she mentally castigated herself about how her life had become one drama after another and how it had to stop and how she was OK and had to wait her turn like everyone else.

The receptionist assembled a somewhat concerned expression as she put her head near to Helen's face and said the doctor would see her now.

'Can you stand?' she asked.

Helen nodded, and grasped at the woman's shoulder before the room went dark.

When she came round, she was lying on a couch with a nurse pulling as gently as she could on Helen's elasticated trousers. When they were at her knees, the doctor moved in and put a gloved finger inside her and probed around. It hurt. She closed her eyes before feeling something heavy on her abdomen. He seemed to be leaning all his weight into his hands which were pushing into her. Then, he pulled away suddenly and Helen screamed as her body went into a series of painful quivering movements that went on for several seconds.

'Sorry, my dear,' said the GP. 'Now, presumably your company has a private health scheme?'

'Yes,' she whispered.

'And do you have regular check-ups with a gynaecologist as part of that scheme?'

She breathed deeply. 'Mmmn. Sebastian Turnbell at a clinic in Harley Street.' She gave the telephone number, knowing it by heart, as Sam used the same building for his private work.

'We'll ring him and get you there by ambulance shortly.'

'Surely that's not necessary.' Now that someone was taking her

293

predicament seriously, she felt like a fraud. Perhaps if she tried hard, she could get off this couch and take charge of the situation. She attempted to sit up, but the doctor gently stopped her and laid her down again on her back.

'I don't think you'll be going anywhere under your own steam, I'm sorry to say. Just stay and rest, I'll be back to you in a minute.'

Alone, she gave into her distress and began to whimper with pain. Where had all this come from? She was never ill.

The GP returned to her side. 'Forgive my asking but do you think you could be pregnant?'

'I don't think so.'

'But is it possible?'

She nodded.

'Well, I'm sorry to tell you that you may have an ectopic pregnancy. Do you know what that is?'

'Something to do with the foetus growing in the fallopian tube, isn't it?'

'Exactly.'

'Does that mean that Mr Turnbell would have to operate?'

'Oh yes, but let's leave the rest of the questions for him, shall we?'

After that everything in the weird dream that had taken over her morning began to happen very quickly. She was carried out on a stretcher to the waiting ambulance and the next thing she knew, she was being wheeled into a room and slid onto a bed. Someone punctured her left arm and set up a drip. This is very bizarre, she thought. It seemed to be happening to someone else.

Sebastian Turnbell, a clean-faced man with greying hair and dressed in a well-cut suit, loomed up before her.

'Well, well, Helen,' he said and he squeezed her shoulder. 'Sorry about this.'

She felt reassured by his presence. Not only had she seen him several times for a gynaecological MOT but he had been at one or two of the functions at the clinic that she had attended with Sam.

He drew up a chair and sat down beside her. 'OK,' he said quietly, 'now when did you have your last period?'

Having calculated it on her day out in Cromer, she added on the time that had elapsed since. 'Um, about two months ago, I think.'

'Have you had a pregnancy test?'

'No. I'd stopped taking the Pill actually, for reasons I won't go into. And when my period never came, I assumed, well, to tell you the truth, there's been, uh, a lot of emotional upset. I didn't think...'

'Well, it might be an ovarian cyst, but my gut feeling is an ectopic.'

'Does it mean I'll lose the baby, if there is one?'

'Oh yes, afraid so. You're going to have to sign a form, Helen, because until I get you on the table I'm not going to know anything for certain. Who's your next of kin?'

She burst into tears. 'Oh, I don't really know. I thought it was... oh. This is so awful. Put the company down. I can't bear to involve my parents.'

He took her hand. 'Helen, does Sam know you're here?'

'No, but he rang this morning and I did say I wasn't well. But you mustn't tell him anything. He's got enough to cope with and anyway, we're no longer together.'

'I'm sorry to hear that. I heard he'd resigned. He hasn't been himself lately. Not at all. Still, we'll talk about that later. Sorry this is a sensitive subject, but is he likely to be the father?'

'Of course!' For the first time her voice was loud and firm. 'But I meant what I said. It won't help to discuss this with him. Please don't.'

'Well, that's up to you,' Mr Turnbell said, somewhat sadly as he stood up and turned to go.

'Please,' she cried, 'please if there is a baby, please do you all you can to save it.'

She was deeply upset now and did not bother to try to hide it.

'Helen, if there is a baby, there's no way it'll survive. I'm sorry. Now, I'm going to give you an injection. It'll make you extremely drowsy. Things won't seem so bad then.'

Helen flinched as the needle went in and shortly afterwards, for the second time that day, blackness enfolded her.

She knew that she was thrashing about on the bed, but why? There was a warm stickiness beneath her, her throat felt as if it were packed with crushed glass, and there was a smouldering pain somewhere below her waist.

Blurred images hovered. She could hear them but not make out who they were. Her lips would not form words, so she tried to indicate that she needed a drink, but they took no notice. To gain their attention, she started shaking her head from side to side.

'People don't usually come round this quickly,' someone said.

'She seems very restless and distressed. I'll give her something.'

Helen felt like a trussed and tranquillised tiger on a veterinary operating bench as she was rolled over and felt a sharp needle plunged into a buttock. A feeling like reaching the summit of a roller coaster began in her toes and swept in a curve through her body, engulfing her brain. Everything stopped.

The next time she was aware of anything, the room around her seemed more real and someone was holding her hand. 'I... need a drink.' Her voice cracked.

'OK, Helen.' The voice attached to the hand answered her.

'Sam...'

'He'll be here soon. It's Jeremy.' He bent over her offering a beaker of water in which there was a bent drinking straw. Gratefully, she gulped at it, but he steadied her. 'Take it easy. Just little sips or you're going to be sick.'

She continued to drink deeply. 'My mouth tastes like the inside of a vacuum cleaner.' Her voice came out more strongly now.

'Good description! It's the anaesthetic. Horrid, I know, but just take one more sip. You can have another drink soon.'

She closed her eyes then heard the door open and was immediately awake. But it was Sebastian Turnbell who had entered the room.

Jeremy leant over and kissed her cheek. 'I'll leave you now, but I'll be back tomorrow.'

Sebastian sat himself in the chair Jeremy had just vacated. 'Who was that?'

'Jeremy Woollard. He's a friend of Sam's.'

'Oh yes. Practises in Paris, doesn't he? He's written some very good papers.'

'I didn't know that,' she said. Then she looked straight at the surgeon. 'I expect you're here to explain what you did to me. So, fire away.'

'It was exactly as we thought. I had to remove your right fallopian tube and I also decided to take away your right ovary which wasn't in great shape.'

'Was that entirely necessary?'

'In my judgement, yes it was. I'm not sure you understand this, Helen, but if I hadn't operated, you would have died.'

'So, my baby?'

He patted her hand. 'You're not too old to have another. And your left side is functioning OK. It'll be more difficult to get pregnant, but not impossible. And of course these days you've got the IVF option. I could refer you to Patrick Steptoe at Bourn Hall…'

'I forgot for a moment, but actually, none of that matters now.' Her voice was weary.

'Helen, you're very upset, and you've been through a lot and you seem to me to be totally physically and mentally exhausted. I'm going to give you something to make you sleep. You need it.'

She shrugged. 'Why not?'

Some time later, her hand made contact with blood beneath the sheets. Feeling very vague, she tried to work out whether it was seeping through the surgical dressing covering her wound or flooding from her vagina. It was hard to tell. She pressed the bell that was attached by a safety pin to her pillow.

Two nurses appeared, followed by a very young doctor. They pulled back the bedclothes and looked carefully, whispering. Did one of them mention surgery, she wondered. But she fell asleep again before she could establish what was happening.

'She's quite poorly,' a nurse was explaining in her doorway. 'We've given her two pints of blood and are just monitoring her now.'

'I must see her.'

Helen's heart began to beat faster at the sound of the familiar voice.

It was dark outside. Helen supposed it must be quite late. Sam stood beside her, haggard and pale.

'Darling, I'm never here for you when it counts. I'm so, so sorry but I've been in theatre since shortly after I spoke to you this morning. I knew you were here though, because Turnbell got a message to me.'

'What time is it?'

'Ten-thirty.'

'You must be awfully tired,' she smiled at him.

'Darling, what happened? Turnbell wouldn't say anything. Said you'd told him not to. I've spoken to Jeremy, but he didn't seem to know what the score was, or if he did, he wasn't saying.'

'I had an ovary removed,' she said, and she turned her head away so that she could avoid the concern in his eyes. 'Some sort of cyst, I believe.'

'Really?'

Though she was in a haze of drugs and pain and fatigue she suspected that he knew she was lying.

'I'll go and let you sleep. Thank God Jeremy's here.'

'Go carefully, my love,' she murmured.

Suddenly, his face was close to hers, and he gave her the lightest and most tender of kisses. She thought he was crying, but perhaps the tears she could feel were her own. Stay with me, Sam. Be with me. Love me forever. Her thoughts remained unspoken. They had not prevailed before and were equally useless now.

Mr Turnbell visited her early the next morning, despite it being Saturday. That's what being a private patient gets you, she thought, feeling grateful but guilty all at the same time.

'When can I go back to work?' she asked.

'Oh heavens. Somebody warned me you were a workaholic!' He beamed at her. 'Not for a while, I'm afraid. You're not well. Don't you realise how serious this is?'

'Oh, I realise,' she answered quietly.

'You're going to be here at least a week,' he told her.

'Oh my God, I can't bear it.'

'Well, I'm afraid you're going to have to. Sorry.' And he left before she could argue further.

Her room began to fill with flowers – from Sam, from Jeremy, from Derek, from the company's HR department, from the girls in the newsroom and from Laura. By lunchtime, it was embarrassing.

A nurse appeared and asked her if she wanted to take a call from Laura and when she agreed, plugged a phone in on her bedside table.

'You gave us all a scare,' said her friend. 'I'm so sorry you were taken ill. What happened exactly?'

Helen deliberated before murmuring, 'The official version is that I had an ovarian cyst.'

'And the unofficial version?'

'I will tell you, but can we leave it for a while. I, uh, I don't feel very well actually.'

She felt worse after Laura had rung off. In a way, she wanted to talk to someone but how would she ever find the right words to discuss something of this magnitude? Seeking distraction, she reached for the remote-control on her locker and switched on the television set.

The news was just starting.

'There is still no trace of four-year-old Cindy Patterson, who disappeared while playing outside her home in Notting Hill Gate at around eleven yesterday morning.'

The picture of a smiling toddler flashed onto the screen. 'Fears are growing for her safety,' continued the newsreader, out of vision, while the image dissolved into a short clip of the distraught mother pleading for her daughter's return.

Helen's heart went out to the woman. How strange that at the very time she had had her baby cut from her, this other mother should have lost her viable and energetic child.

The world seemed such a grim place that she hardly recognised it as she began to ponder on the infant who had died in her arms in the Regent Street bombing, her own embryo and now this little girl. Oh God, she cried inwardly, why are you doing this? Why are you so cruel?

Later, Sam came to see her, but she was too upset to talk. Jeremy arrived soon afterwards, but she turned her back on him and pretended to sleep.

Mr Turnbell appeared and told her that he was writing her up for a different sedative. 'I hope this will help you,' he said. 'I understand that you're distressed and grieving for your lost pregnancy, but I'm worried that if you don't rest properly you're going to impede your recovery.'

'OK,' she answered, quite beyond caring.

'And I'm afraid I'm putting a ban on all visitors.'

'Good,' she said.

Saturday passed, and most of Sunday. She was lying with the television on, but the sound muted, a couple of unopened newspapers on the bed, and an untouched supper tray on the nearby table, when Jeremy crept in.

'I've had to jump through hoops with Turnbell,' he whispered, 'but I'm flying back to Paris first thing tomorrow and I wanted to see you.'

She gazed at him with eyes as heavy as her heart.

'You had an ectopic pregnancy, didn't you?' he asked softly.

'No, it was an ovarian cyst.'

'Helen,' he took her hand, which remained rigid within his, 'Trust me, I think I know the difference by now. Listen, have you ever asked – begged – Sam not to go home but to stay?'

'Probably not in so many words,' she replied.

'I think you should. That man is devastated. He adores you. He's dreading going back. You must tell him about the baby and you must ask him to stay.'

'I won't grovel.'

'That's not grovelling. He needs to be saved from a terrible fate. Please try.'

'I really don't feel well, Jeremy. Sorry. Do you mind going?'

He stood up. 'All right, but I'll ring you and I'll be back as soon as I can. Oh, Helen...' he began again.

'Goodbye, Jeremy,' she said, closing her eyes.

The days in the clinic passed gradually. Helen did what she was told. She took a bath when she was encouraged to do so. She submitted to Mr Turnbell's physical examinations. She attempted to eat. The only real commitment she made for herself was to watch several news bulletins a day. There was still no sign of the missing Cindy. Surely, she must be found soon?

Sam visited every day. He held her hand but neither of them said much.

A week after her operation when Mr Turnbell came to see her, he said, suddenly, 'Helen, do you want to tell me what's going on?'

'I don't know what you mean.'

'I'm aware that you've been through a lot recently, including being caught up in the Regent Street bombing, so it's not surprising that you're...' He looked embarrassed. 'What I'm working round to is I wonder if you would agree to see a psychiatrist? You see, you're almost physically fit enough now to go home, but I'm worried about your state of mind.'

'When can I go?'

'Sunday, I should think.'

'Good.'

'And are you going to answer my question?'

She shook her head.

'Well, the thing is that I don't think you should be on your own at home.'

'Don't you? Well, I really, really want some time to myself. But, as it happens, I know a psychiatrist, Freddie Longhurst. I can always call him if I need to.'

'But will you know?' Mr Turnbell asked before shrugging his shoulders and leaving the room.

When Sam came in later, she told him she was going home on Sunday. He offered to drive her back to her flat.

'Thanks,' she said, and that was all.

Refusing a wheelchair, she walked out of the clinic on his arm. It was further than she had thought, and the surprisingly cool breeze outside seemed to go right through her. She faltered, just slightly, on the steps, but Sam supported her, and she made it to his car, despite the trembling and weakness in her legs.

'You're doing so well,' he assured her as he put the seat belt around her.

He continued to be heart-achingly solicitous and kind as he drove carefully to Holland Park, guided her up the steps to the apartment building – which presented another challenge to her – and sat her down in the main hall so that she could regain her breath and strength.

'Darling, are you OK?'

Unconsciously, she gave a little shake of her head, though she smiled into his concerned face.

Upstairs, she leant on her front door while Sam unlocked it. His strong arm supported her as they entered.

'All right, so far?' he asked.

She nodded, and together they walked the last few paces to her sitting room. She jerked upright with surprise at the sight that met her; her furniture had been rearranged, and by the window, all gleaming and shiny black, stood a baby grand piano.

He clasped her tighter to him. 'A welcome home present,' he whispered into her ear. 'Do you want to try it?'

She kissed his cheek, feeling instantly more energised, and she walked over to the piano unaided and sat down. At first, she simply admired the black lacquered beauty before her, then she placed her hands on the keys and played an arpeggio. Its sound had a magnificent depth to it. She played some of the low notes and marvelled at the richness of the tone below Middle C.

She turned to Sam. 'It's too much,' she whispered.

'On the contrary,' he replied with the most miserable looking smile she had ever seen. 'It's not nearly enough.'

There was silence in the room. Gladdened and saddened by his kindness and generosity, she remembered Jeremy's advice to her.

'Sam, thank you. Thank you very, very much. Can I ask you something?'

He took her hand.

'If I pleaded with you now to stay with me, and to give up all idea of returning to Egypt, could you do it? I need and love you so, so much.' Her voice broke.

His stricken expression answered for him.

'I thought as much,' she murmured. 'Shall we have a cup of tea?'

'I asked him,' she told Jeremy when he phoned her six days later.

'Can I come over and visit you tomorrow?'

'Yes, but don't tell Sam. I don't want to see him.'

'When did you have that conversation?' Jeremy asked.

'Right after he brought me home from the clinic. But, in truth, it didn't amount to much. I asked the question. He looked ashen faced. We didn't mention it again.'

'So, have the two of you not met since then?'

'No.'

'He's very distressed.'

She breathed out sharply. 'There's nothing I can do about it. Do you know, Jeremy, they still haven't found that little girl? But she must be alive. Nothing else makes any sense at all.'

'Helen, sorry, I don't know what you're talking about. What little girl?'

'You must know.' She had not meant to sound irritated, but she knew she had. 'Doesn't matter. I'll see you tomorrow. I have to ring off now. I need to go to bed.'

The next day while she was waiting for Jeremy, the phone rang twice. She ignored it. In a way, she was touched by the concern her various friends were showing, but mostly she felt quite removed from them, their thoughts, their lives. But the good thing was that she was entirely tranquil. It was a welcome relief. She had no desires. No hopes. No plans.

She supposed, in an idle way that when she returned to work in a few days, she might be rather more involved with life. She assumed she would still be able to function, as she always had, for the cameras. But the making of television right now seemed as unreal and unfamiliar to her as it must to the average viewer.

The only time she felt connected with reality was when she thought about Cindy Patterson. She was absolutely desperate for her to be found alive. She watched endless bulletins for any developments and scoured the newspapers for information that might be cause for optimism.

The phone rang again. This time, she reached out a hand and picked up the receiver.

'Helen,' said Laura, 'I know you're ill, but I want to see you. I'm sure you're in your flat all – or most – of the time. I keep ringing you. You just don't pick up, do you? I don't understand what's going on.'

She had to face up to this at some point. 'Well, come over and I'll try and explain. Not today though.'

'Tomorrow?'

'All right.'

Before long the telephone rang again.

'If you must hide away in your flat,' Freddie said as soon as she answered it, 'why don't you invest in an answer machine. At least then people could leave messages. And you'd know who actually cares about you.'

'I know who cares about me. Anyway, they're expensive, and probably I wouldn't know how to work it. And what happens when the tape gets filled up with people. Honestly, I don't think I could stand it.'

It was only the second time since her operation that she had spoken to Freddie. On the first occasion he had seemed very put out that she had not let him know that she was ill. He did not seem much happier now.

'Why won't you let me see you?'

'Because I'm supposed to be resting.'

'Ridiculous.'

'I've been poorly you know.'

'Sorry,' he said, 'but surely you're up to a ten-minute visit now?'

'Uh, OK. It's going to be like Clapham Junction around here soon. I've already agreed to see my friend Laura tomorrow. Could you make Tuesday evening?'

'Certainly, I'll be with you about six.'

'Fine,' she said, though nothing was.

Jeremy arrived. 'What little girl?' he asked as soon as he had sat down.

'Cindy Patterson, the four-year-old who disappeared, just up the road from here, on the day of my operation.'

'Oh yes. I think I saw something in one of the newspapers.'

'Something!' she said, witheringly.

'Sorry.' He looked bewildered, then his gaze on her became more searching. 'How are you, Helen?'

'Rested,' she answered quickly.

They talked for a while, but Helen felt as though she were encased in glass. It was of little consequence. Perhaps, it was desirable.

'I'm worried about you,' he said at last.

'You don't need to be.'

He began to talk more loudly. She could see he was getting exasperated, but she had no clue how to stop that. Suddenly, he reached over and grasped her hands and then pulled her to him and kissed her on the lips.

She pulled back, appalled. 'I don't think that's very respectful to Sam,' she remarked coldly. 'He's your best friend, isn't he?'

Jeremy sighed. 'I've done all I can to keep you two together. I could shake you both. But even I can see it's not working now. I know you're still massively in love with him. And there's no question the same applies to him. But if he does insist on making this ridiculous and archaic gesture, I won't keep silent about my feelings for you. I think about you a lot. Sam knows as much. He partly hates it, but partly he wants someone to be there for you when he's gone.'

'I'm not a commodity to be passed on to some sort of "reserve".' She was furious now.

'Don't be cross. You've really got under my skin. I think you're a wonderful girl.'

Helen looked at him blankly. How could anyone like, let alone fancy, her as she had become?

'I shouldn't have spoken up, Helen,' Jeremy murmured. 'It's far too soon. And Sam may yet come to his senses. Also, you're still not well and you're quite shocked.'

'Am I? Is that what is happening to me?' Her voice cracked.

'I think so.'

'You're very kind, Jeremy. But you're grieving too. For your wife. I think you'll find that's what all this is about. I just happen to be someone to focus on while you're lonely. It's not real. She's the one you want.'

'Sam's a very fortunate man.'

'I don't think so. He's going through absolute hell.'

'He is, but I don't see how he can turn his back on you. He may walk through the departures gate, he may get on a plane, but for the life of me I cannot imagine that he won't somehow extricate himself and come back to you. You're his world. I'll ring you from time to time, but I won't be back. Not till we see what happens.'

'We know what's going to happen.'

'Do we?' He kissed the top of her head and indicated that he would let himself out.

Helen had intended to tell Laura everything, but that changed once her friend turned up.

'You look wonderful,' Helen said, and she realised that she meant it and that she could actually feel some joy in the well-being and palpable happiness of her friend.

'Thanks, Helen. I *feel* wonderful. You'll never guess what.'

She thought that, probably, she could guess, but said that she could not.

'Well,' Laura paused dramatically. 'I'm pregnant.'

It was as she thought, but she was unprepared for the real searing pain that felt as if it was tearing her in two.

'Are you pleased?'

'Beyond pleased,' Helen forced her face and voice into a smile of gladness. 'Absolutely more than I can say. And how do you feel?'

'So thrilled I can't even sleep at night.'

'How marvellous,' Helen said, and she distracted herself by pottering out to the kitchen and pouring boiling water into the teapot. She returned shortly.

'I'm not drinking at the moment, but let's toast your news with some decent tea – and these biscuits are rather special. Some visitor or other brought them – from Fortnum and Mason!'

Laura chuckled, accepted a mug of tea and sat down again on the sofa, tucking her legs under her.

'Now, enough of all of that. You promised to tell me everything. So, what exactly was wrong with you?'

'I had an ovarian cyst.'

'Didn't you say that was the official version?'

'Did I? Don't remember. I suppose what I meant was that it wasn't the whole story. That ovary was in a hell of a mess, and Sebastian Turnbell took out my right fallopian tube too. I think he thought both the ovary and the tube might flare up again, or something.'

'That sounds quite serious.'

'I suppose it's not that common. Or maybe people just don't talk about it.'

'You've obviously been very ill though.'

'I think the general consensus was that I had been overdoing it. And should have perhaps taken time off after the Regent Street bomb. But we keep going, don't we? It's what we do.'

'That's true.'

They chatted for a while but when the tea ran out Helen did not offer to make more, and eventually Laura said, 'I expect you need a rest. Would you like me to go?'

'Good idea.' Helen realised she had sounded too enthusiastic but was desperate to be alone again.

There was no news for the rest of the day about Cindy Patterson. It seemed to Helen that she had slipped so far down the bulletins' running order that she was being forgotten. Once she got back to work and into the newsroom she was going to make sure that on her station, if nowhere else, they kept reporting on the missing child.

There was no news the next day either. Hours passed. Nothing happened. She had forgotten that Freddie was coming and when he turned up she realised she should have made more of an effort for his visit. His look as he surveyed the state of her flat made her see it with fresh eyes – there were discarded newspapers every-where, and in the kitchen the sink was full of dirty teacups and empty mineral water bottles.

'Don't you have a cleaning lady?' Freddie asked as he cleared himself a space on the sofa and sat down.

'I gave her a holiday. I didn't really want her fussing around me while I was at home all day.'

'Are you eating properly?'

'Of course.' Her reply was automatic.

Freddie stood up and walked over to her drinks trolley and poured two glasses of brandy.

'I no longer drink,' she said.

'For God's sake, Helen. One drink won't hurt you and may well do you some good. You're not an alcoholic.'

'How do you know?'

'Because I treat them, you idiot. It's part of what I do. You do have a dependency problem though.'

'Oh, please enlighten me,' she said sarcastically.

'After your marriage it was the job, then it was Sam, then it was the job, then it was drink, then it was the job again, coupled with the keep-fit regime. You like intense focus. But then, it's probably got you a long way! Anyway, we'll have a drink, but we'll leave it at one, and then we'll go out and get something to eat.'

She took the glass and sipped from it. 'I don't want to go out,' she said.

'Have you been beyond the front door since you came home?'

She shook her head.

'Helen, listen to me. You're not well. I can't treat you because, well, I feel emotionally involved with you, but would you see a friend of mine?'

'I'm OK, Freddie.'

'You're not OK.'

'Well, I'm improving. I'm doing much better. I'm just tired. I lost a lot of blood. Anyone would take a while to recover from that. You don't need to worry. I just want to sleep. Let's do this another time, do you mind? I want to get my head down.'

The police issued an identikit picture of a relative of Cindy Patterson's. They said they wanted to eliminate him from their enquiries. There was growing concern that she was dead. In fact, everyone seemed to believe that she was – apart from Helen, and the child's mother.

She took to playing her new and very beautiful piano. Having found some sheet music in a drawer that she must have kept for a time when she would be able to play again, she picked the Mozart A minor sonata and started to learn it. The plaintive theme of the first movement unlocked her coldness and the odd hot tear escaped from the prison in her head to roll to freedom down her cheeks and on to the black and white keys.

Sam rang. Her mother rang. Sebastian Turnbell rang. Derek rang. Jeremy rang. Freddie rang. Laura rang. Sometimes it seemed there were endless bells in her head.

'I'm going back to work on Monday,' she told each of them in turn, and was then, predictably, asked: 'Are you sure you're fit?'

She was sure. However, when Monday came, so did a wave of uncertainty. She also felt surprisingly unsteady on her feet, and as she put make-up on for the first time in weeks, she noticed how thin her face had become. It looked older too.

In the office, there were vast quantities of mail to be dealt with, so she spent the day tackling it, quietly and mostly alone, in her office. Luckily there were no afternoon recordings to be done so, having made a tiny dent in the correspondence, she spent time going over and over her into-camera links for the programme, as well as the research for the live interview she was scheduled to do. Probably, she thought, she had never been this nervous – not even the first time she had presented the programme. She had been more excited then. More determined. Less aware, in a way, of what the job entailed. Now she knew, and it was terrifying.

310

The gods were with her it seemed. There were no technical hitches, she did not stumble over her words, she even looked quite reasonable on the monitors. It was a routine programme. Maybe even a touch dull with no important breaking story. But she was grateful for that.

They were into the last item of the show – a pre-packaged piece about the diminishing number of hedgehogs – and she quickly scanned the final link and checked how long she would have to wind up the programme and say 'goodnight'.

Suddenly, Derek spoke in her earpiece. 'Newsflash,' he said. 'Read what's on the bit of paper I've just sent down. Forget the closing link. I'll try and grab an extra ten seconds from presentation. Just watch the count and do your best.'

She nodded as she was handed a short script, speedily typed – judging by a couple of spelling errors – and the picture mixed through to her.

'We end with news that's just come in,' she read. 'A young child's body has been found in a ditch in a remote part of the Cotswolds. It's believed to have lain there for several weeks. Police say it is too early to positively identify the victim, but there is speculation that it might be the London four-year-old Cindy Patterson.'

Helen looked up from the paper and gazed directly into camera as she said, 'A very sad note on which to end. See you tomorrow. Goodnight.'

After the programme, she left immediately and took a taxi home. Inside her flat, she threw her coat one way and her bags another and sat down at Sam's piano and played through everything she knew. And when she had done that she began again. And again. She might have played all night had it not been for the disturbance from her entry phone. It kept buzzing. She wished everyone would leave her alone.

Eventually, she looked at her watch. Somehow it was nine o'clock. Sighing, she walked to her front door and picked up the entry phone.

'Helen, it's Sam.'

She pressed the button that would allow him to enter the main entrance and waited by her open door till he appeared.

They stared at each other for a moment then she launched herself into his arms and wept.

'It's so awful, Sam,' she gasped. 'Our baby. Our baby.'

She felt him tighten his grasp on her and heard him muttering soothing noises into her ear. At last she was quieter, and he led her into her sitting room and guided her to the sofa.

'Jeremy told me how upset you were about the missing child,' he said as he sat down beside her. 'But it's really unlike you to get so distressed about a news item.'

'She had to be alive. I was so sure she must be,' Helen said slowly as if she was explaining a difficult concept to someone with limited understanding. 'You see, that would have made some sense, and been some small recompense for the child who died in my arms in Regent Street and for the death of our baby. Surely you can see that?'

'Helen, darling,' he leant over and kissed her teary cheek, 'I don't honestly know what you're talking about.'

She studied her hands as if there were answers to be found there, before saying, 'It wasn't an ovarian cyst.'

He sighed. 'I'm not sure I ever believed that it was,' he admitted, 'but I pushed the other possibilities out of my mind.'

'It was an ectopic pregnancy.'

His eyes pooled with tears. 'Oh God, Helen. I wish it could have lived, and that you could have had some tangible evidence of our love and our time together. At the same time I wonder how on earth you would have coped? Or how I would – knowing that I was absent from the upbringing of my own flesh and blood.'

She took his hand and stroked it. 'I didn't get pregnant deliberately. But I had stopped taking my Pill because we were no longer making love. And then the weekend Jeremy came, it was as if everything was fine. I never thought of the consequences, to

312

be honest. And it never occurred to me that I could be pregnant. And then I was so, so distraught about losing you that I smoked and drank it to death. I've murdered my own child. I was given the chance to keep a piece of you, and I destroyed it.'

'That's not true,' he assured her.

She looked at him bleakly. 'It is true. And I will always know it to be the case.'

'Helen, listen to me, you didn't harm our child, it was an accident of nature. It was just in the wrong place.'

'Yes, the wrong place and the wrong time.'

'Helen, my angel, I can't bear to see you like this. Let's always be friends.'

She looked him straight in the eye. 'We both know that's not possible,' she said coolly. 'For a start I don't need you as a friend. I've *got* friends. I needed you as my lover, my spouse, the other side of me, my companion and my soulmate. You can't be those things. And can you imagine us trying to be platonically fond of each other? Me ringing you up and saying "How's the wife, Sam?" That's never, ever going to happen.'

He pressed his lips hungrily to hers. She fought to keep control of herself but responded with equal passion. Then, when they drew apart to breathe, he hugged her to him and moaned into her hair, 'Helen, Helen, Helen...'

Pulling herself away, she forced a smile. 'One month from tomorrow, you're going to marry someone else. I'm so glad that you came here today, and I will always, always love you. But, I can never see you again, Sam. So please stay away from now on.'

'Helen.' He grabbed both of her arms so fiercely that it hurt her.

She extricated herself immediately and walked over to the piano he had given her.

'I'm going to play some music, and then I want you to go.'

She sat at the keyboard and launched into a piece that she had been working on.

'That was beautiful,' he whispered. 'What was it?'

She stood up, walked over and took his arm, then urged him to her front door, and opened it.

'It's one of the Bach two-part inventions.'

'I don't really understand what that is.'

'It's a short piece of counterpoint for two hands.'

'Or two players, I suppose,' he responded.

She nodded. He held her gaze in the doorway, and she could feel waves of love and despair flowing between them.

'Always remember that I adore you,' he said at last, then he turned and walked away.

Chapter Fifteen

A bee was buzzing around a colourful flower bed. It was an idyllic scene. She was reluctant to leave it, reluctant to be awakened, reluctant to deal with the insistent noise emanating from her entry phone.

She dragged herself from bed, on this most dreaded of days when Sam was going to leave the country.

'Yes,' she said into the handset.

'Streamline Taxis here. I've got something for you, Miss Bartlett.'

She left her door on the latch and ran down the stairs to the front door of the building.

'I was told you shouldn't lift it,' the driver warned, as he indicated the tea chest beside him. 'The gentleman tipped me very well and asked me to take it up to your flat.'

Once the cabbie had gone, Helen stared at the box and tried to guess what it might contain.

Surely the 'gentleman' could only be Sam. She emptied out armfuls of polystyrene squiggles and found a substantial object wrapped in layers of newspaper.

It was the Tom Merrifield sculpture of the ballet dancer that she had loved ever since seeing it for the first time almost a year ago. Attached to the figure was a tiny card on a string.

'Love you forever,' it read.

Suddenly, the anguish was back; the feelings she had fought against and had tried to convince herself were in the past.

She sprinted to her telephone and picked it up, instinctively longing to thank him and hear his voice. The dialling tone sounded loud in her ear. It mesmerised her. Slowly, she forced herself to replace the receiver.

I am so sad, she thought. The word 'ineffable' came into her mind. She tried it out for size, murmuring into the empty room; 'I am filled with ineffable sadness.' Yes, that was it exactly, she decided. And how on earth could she live with it?

She would have to.

Looking back, she could see that when everyone had been so worried about her, her thoughts and actions had not been entirely normal. But she was better now. More in command. She had done all she could. It had made no difference. She was now a woman who must walk alone.

As soon as she appeared in the newsroom, Laura turned up bearing two cups of coffee.

'I thought you might find today rather difficult,' she said.

It was kind of her friend to remember. 'Probably after today things will get better.'

'Well,' Laura replied, 'I hope so. But you're already much more together than you were a couple of weeks ago. I don't mind telling you now that I thought you were heading for a complete breakdown.'

'That makes two of us,' Helen responded softly.

'Maybe he'll come back.'

'Maybe he will. His friend Jeremy thinks so. But for my sanity, I have to convince myself that he won't.'

'You don't think he's just one of those men who can't commit?'

'Laura, please don't ever suggest that again. I can't bear it. I have to believe that he truly loved me and intended to make me his life-partner. And that he wanted our future as much as I did. If I don't have that, then it's as if the whole of the last year has been a lie. So, I need to remain convinced that had he not had a real sense of honour about what his father and family expected, then we would have been together. Perhaps I'm deluded, but I have to hold onto it. It's all I have.' There was a tremor in her voice as she finished.

Laura reached out and stroked her hand, before they picked up their coffee cups and sipped in silence. After a while, Helen decided to mention the Tom Merrifield sculpture.

'That was nice,' Laura said. 'Was there any message with it?'

Helen nodded. 'Just, you know, that he loves me.'

'Then I'm sure he does. But I could murder his fucking mother. If she hadn't come here, I bet everything would have been all right.'

'You can't blame her, Laura,' Helen murmured. 'I've thought about it a lot. And I realise it's rather presumptuous of us to believe that our view of things is not just modern but correct. After all, Madame Aziz has her reasons for thinking as she does. She's thirty-five years older than me for a start. Does that make her wiser? I don't know. But I realise that one can't fly in the face of long-held cultural traditions. And maybe one never should.'

'You're taking this very well.'

'Not really. I'm screaming inside. I feel that the very moment I finally relinquished my future to him, he began to prise my fingers from the certainty of him, one by one, even while he was reassuring me that what we had would last forever. I won't ever get over it. But I suppose, eventually, I will find a way of living with it.'

Around one o'clock, Derek came looking for her.

'I want you to interview Arnie Franks,' he said.

'Fine. Who's he?'

'Your mother would remember!'

'Well that doesn't help me.'

'He was a very famous crooner in his day. Came from Barnsley but made it big in the States. He's passing through London on his way up north to do a farewell tour.'

317

'What's the point if no one remembers who he is?'

'Some will, even if he must be older than God by now. But we've got to do him. The programme's packed with politics and trouble. I need something light-hearted to end with.'

'OK. When have you booked him into the studio?'

'Oh, he's not coming here. He hasn't got time. You're to meet him at the Pan-Am Clipper Club lounge in Terminal Three at Heathrow, at two-fifteen. So that means you've got to get through Departures to airside. Maggie's got your clearance. Get it from her and go. There's bound to be a lot of traffic. The crew will meet you there.'

Helen panicked. 'Oh no, Derek, I can't go… I'm too busy, I…'

Unusually, Derek was on a very short fuse. 'Look, it's a bugger of a day. Just go. I haven't got time to argue.'

So, she thought, as she motored out of the company car park, fate had not finished with her yet. She had never before interviewed anyone at Heathrow. So why, in God's name, did she have to do so today?

Deliberately, she had not asked Sam what time he was flying out, indeed, over the past few weeks, she had done everything she could to keep him out of her mind. She had had dinner with Freddie a couple of times and spoken to Jeremy on the phone, and to some extent that contact had been useful in distracting her. Other than that, she had focused on getting through one hour, then one day at a time, and refusing to allow space in her mind for that small voice which insisted she could not and should not go on – and that from now on, life was not worth living.

It was a breezy day and a flurry of autumn leaves whirled into the air from the gutter as she drove by. Immediately, her mind transported her back a year to the dinner party and Sam driving her home afterwards. She recalled how she had almost slipped on some wet leaves as she had made her way, unsteadily, from his car to her front door.

Then she remembered a recent interview with a nutritionist who had said: 'Often we have to avoid our favourite foods, because the very items we're addicted to, are those to which we're allergic.'

Was Sam an allergy as well as her addiction? It was difficult to say, but she acknowledged – though she was loath to do so – how detrimental to her health this past year had been despite the fact that she longed to relive it, over and over again.

'Oh, Sam,' she cried, 'how can you leave me when we love each other so much? How *can* you go?'

The crew were waiting for her by a newsagent, near the Clipper Club lounge.

'Have you met the singer?' she asked Mike, a cameraman she liked and often worked with.

'Yeah – and Jerry, his objectionable PR man. You'd think we'd got Frank Sinatra or Tony Bennett here the way he's carrying on.'

Her heart sank. Hype on the one hand, and disgruntled colleagues on the other were not the ideal ingredients for a successful interview.

She followed the cameraman into the lounge, which was full of passengers sporting that peculiar pallor that accompanies jet lag and the surrender of their being and luggage to forces beyond their control. The television was blaring away at the far end and Arnie Franks stood in front of it, clearly restless and out of sorts.

Before she made herself known to him, she studied him for a moment. His hair looked too bouffant to be real, and it was a most unlikely colour. He was tanned. His teeth were expensively capped, and he was wearing far too many chunky gold rings.

'Mr Franks,' she greeted him over-enthusiastically, 'I'm Helen Bartlett, and I'm doing the interview with you, but I'd like to suggest we do it outside of the lounge. It'll give more of a sense of urgency with people milling around, and you rushing off to get your plane, that kind of thing. And this,' she gestured at the assortment of untidy bodies and used coffee cups, 'is not ideal.'

'OK, lady,' he agreed.

She left him for a moment to agree a location with Mike.

'Thank God you're always so decisive, Helen,' he said.

She was taken aback by the compliment.

'Oh, thanks. I try.'

'Well, you're bloody good,' he responded. 'Not like some I could mention.'

She grinned and thought for a moment how lucky she was. At least she had her job, and that part of her life was fine. She went back into the lounge and talked to Arnie until Jerry, his PR man, disturbed them to ask how long the interview would take.

'Not too long,' she replied sweetly. 'But are you sure you have the time? I gather you have to catch a flight to Manchester.'

'How many viewers do you have?' Jerry queried.

'It averages around fifteen million.'

'Hey, we definitely have the time!' The singer spoke before the PR man could answer for him.

As they positioned themselves, Helen glanced up at the monitor above them and felt her heart lurch as she saw the flashing 'last call' symbol beside flight MS 778 to Cairo.

Beyond them, some ten yards away, were jostling crowds exiting through the departure gates. Her pulse was pounding in her ears. She was desperate to see Sam, one last time, but equally, praying that she would not.

'Shall we do this thing?' Arnie drawled.

'Yes, let's. Sorry.'

The electrician switched on a couple of lamps. Helen was so used to them that she was almost oblivious to their brightness, but passers-by were drawn by the illumination and stopped to watch.

Helen launched into her questions. At the same time, her mind went into overdrive about Sam and his arrangements. Even if he had not left, he could not know that she was at Heathrow, so would not be looking out for her.

'How long is it since you were in England, Mr Franks?' she heard herself say.

'Well, let me see now, I guess it's all of twenty years.'

'Really, and where will you be performing?'

'Manchester, Leeds, Newcastle...' The list went on and Helen struggled to keep her focus on the job.

'And what would you say was the song that you were most famous for?'

'Oh, shucks, there were so many. But on my tour, I'll have something for absolutely everybody.'

Suddenly, she saw him. Other passengers and the assembled onlookers kept moving and impeding her view. But peering between them, she watched as he put down his briefcase and searched for something in his breast pocket. Then she registered the moment when he became aware of the television lights. He picked up his case, turned and stared straight at her. Someone walked in front of him. Then he reappeared.

'Helen!' She saw him say her name, though the noise all around prevented her from hearing it. He took a few paces towards her.

'Excuse me,' she said and pushed her way through the throng that surrounded them.

She saw him mouth her name again, and this time he stretched out his free hand in her direction. She walked towards him, then stopped. He was being buffeted by travellers intent on reaching their planes. She willed him to come to her. He could. He could move through the madding crowd and take her in his arms and make the decision to stay. She closed her eyes for a second and when she opened them, there was an even greater sea of faces between them. He gazed at her.

Don't give up on me, Sam, she pleaded silently.

He stood motionless as the signals flashed back and forth between their anxious eyes.

'For God's sake,' she muttered, 'Sam, please move. I'm here for you.'

He stood, fixed to the spot. She turned from him but regretted it instantly and looked back to give him one last chance.

Slowly, he shook his head, mouthed, 'I love you, massively,' and began to walk away. After a few steps, he looked behind him, with the haunted look of a prisoner mounting the scaffold. 'I love you,' he shouted. But, maintaining eye contact for a moment, he seemed to stand taller, then he turned away and walked purposefully through the gate and disappeared.

'We really must get on.' The PR man was tugging at her elbow.

'I'm sorry,' she murmured as she rejoined the group. 'Just someone I... thought I knew. Mike, can you pan off a passenger or something to give me a cutting point and let's get rolling.'

He did as she asked. 'Running,' he said.

'Well, Mr Franks, many of your fans will catch up with you on tour, but for those who won't, how about a quick burst of song?'

'Sure,' Arnie smiled directly at the camera. He was centre-stage and loving it. He reached for Helen's hand and stared deep into her eyes. 'But I miss you,' he warbled in his husky, over-generous vibrato, 'most of all, my darling, when autumn leaves start to fall.'

There was a pause. Helen edged herself back out of the shot. She saw Mike tighten to a close-up of the singer. Catching his eye, she slowly raised her head, then nodded.

'OK,' she whispered. 'Cut!'

About Christine Webber

Christine Webber originally trained as an opera singer but had to rethink her career plans when her voice professor told her: 'Your voice is OK, but your legs are very much better!'

Musical theatre beckoned. There was some success. But not much.

In 1979, she became a news presenter for Anglia TV. At last she had found something she enjoyed that other people thought she was good at. It was such a happy relief that she stayed for twelve years.

After leaving Anglia Television, she became an agony aunt for various publications including *TV Times*, *Best*, *Dare* and *BBC Parenting*. And she wrote a relationship advice column for *The Scotsman* and one for *Woman*, called Sexplanations. She also regularly broadcast advice on *Trisha*, *The Good Sex Guide... Late* and from the sofa on *BBC Breakfast*. Much of her work was in collaboration with her late husband, media doctor David Delvin. Together, and for sixteen years, they wrote the sex/relationships content on www.netdoctor.co.uk. They also penned a joint column for the health section of *The Spectator* and co-authored *The Big O* as well as numerous other smaller publications.

In 1995, Christine decided to train as a psychotherapist. This led to her having a practice in Harley Street for twenty years.

Now, her focus is on writing fiction full-time and she is planning another novel on the unexpected turbulence and contrasting humour of mid-life.

If you enjoyed *In Honour Bound*, you might like to explore other books by the same author.

Fiction

Who'd Have Thought It?
It's Who We Are

Non-fiction

Get the Happiness Habit
Get the Self-Esteem Habit
How to Mend a Broken Heart
Too Young to Get Old